THE MONSTERS WE FORGOT

VOLUME 3

DAN ALLEN   NEALA AMES   R. C. BOWMAN

MANDY BURKHEAD   K. M. CAMPBELL   C. E. CLAYTON

CRAIG CRAWFORD   GARY S. CRAWFORD   ALISON CYBE

G. R. DAUVOIS   ELIZABETH DAVIS   EVELYN DESHANE

CHRISTINE DRUGA   STEPHANIE ELLIS   JO FAIRCLOUGH

ANGELIQUE FAWNS   ZACHARY FINN

RHONNIE FORDHAM   MELODY GRACE   B. R. GROVE

MASON HAWTHORNE   C. S. HELLSTROM

JOHN HIGGINS   ARSENI JIGATOV   CECILIA KENNEDY

MOHAMMED KHAN   A. L. KING   LINDSAY KING-MILLER

DMITRY KOSTYUKEVICH   RAE MCKINLAY

STEPH MINNS   NICK MOORE   WATT MORGAN

PETER NINNES   ERIC NIRSCHEL   M. BRANDON ROBBINS

MARCIA SHERMAN   PHILLIP T. STEPHENS   A. E. STUEVE

J. B. TONER   ETHAN VINCENT   SHELDON WOODBURY

TREVOR JAMES ZAPLE

Edited by
GABRIEL GROBLER & R. C. BOWMAN

SOTEIRA
PRESS

CONTENTS

THE MONSTERS WE FORGOT

VOLUME 3

DARLIN', YOU'RE MY WORLD

MASON HAWTHORNE

The road is smooth and unfurls through the dusty fields in a dead straight line. The moon is yellow as a toenail and the stars flash like chips of glass in the bruised sky. Crackling and fading, the radio keeps on playing, pub rock classics interspersed with a strident, nasal disk jockey who keeps using words like *hip* and *stylin'* and trying to flirt with the folks who call in on the requests line.

One blunt, square hand rests on top of the steering wheel, thick fingers drumming along to an independent rhythm. The driver bobs his head along to his own tune, and he hums off-key, eyes staring into the middle distance out over the endless black of the road and the night sky, fixed on the point ahead where the headlights peter out. Now and then he cuts his eyes across to the passenger seat.

"You're my world, darlin'," he croons, bobbing his head along, "You're my woooorld, daaarlin'."

In the passenger seat, Darling is as insubstantial as a bundle of sticks; her dark, glossy head lolls against the window and in the moonlight her eyes are pits in her skull, her cheekbones stand out sharp as knives and every slight bump in the road jostles her. Even with a towel carefully tucked around her shoulders she knocks against the window with each pothole, the rumble-thump of the wheels barreling over, followed by the sharp crack of her head against the glass.

"You're my world," he repeats with a terse finality, and then subsides again to the driver's view, eyes watery. His left hand is in his lap and he rubs his thumb over his fingertips, feeling the last greasy trace of yesterday's dinner there still. In his head he's calculating how far there is to go yet, how long the tank is going to last, calling up memories of the terrain to figure where the next service station is, and whether he can risk pulling into it, or if he should wait a while longer, let the road spool out behind them a little while more.

On either side the dusty fields rustle with dry grasses. Rusty barbed wire fences tangled round with dead weeds blur into near-indistinguishable lines in the dark. Now and then he spots the hunched figures of 'roos bounding along the fence lines, and he whistles and crosses his fingers. Hoping that they don't turn out in front of him, he puts his foot down in the hopes he can outrun them, outrun their suicidal, animal panic so that by the time they realize they're spooked he's already shot past, disappeared into the night.

Lights ahead.

A moment's hesitation and then he slams on the brakes. The tires squeal and the car fishtails, judders and slips to a halt, the engine whining with the strain.

"Okay," he says, "okay, Darlin', alright." He shifts the gears back, crunching and clunking until he finds the right one, and hauls the wheel to turn them off. The servo is so bright against everything else, stark white and chrome. The flashing red of the ICE sign catches his eye, and he finds himself blinking back tears, the light too much after having only the moon for so long. For so long, his stomach's growling. He glances over at her. Guilt wells up in his gut and he feels a whine in the back of his throat—he wasn't thinking, was he, he just drove and drove.

There's a semi-trailer filling up on one side, and he pulls into the petrol pump and pops the tank cover. Whoever owned this car before kept it shiny clean and full. Now the paintwork is dusty and the wipers are clogged with red mud. The neat rolls of coins that were in the ashtray were all used up on meat pies and cans for the road. He hops out, leaning down to look at her one last time before he starts the petrol pumping.

The truckie comes out, tucking his wallet away in his pocket. His eyes slide over the driver at the pump, over the dusty car, and then his step falters. He turns mid-stride and almost stumbles, walking toward the car like he's not sure exactly why. He gets to the passenger side and his mouth hangs open. A runner of spittle falls down his chin and stains the front of his navy singlet. He looks up to the driver who just stares and stares. The petrol pump clicks.

Carefully, the truckie opens the passenger side door and crouches down. He leans into Darling and there's a wet smack and a groan. The driver scuffs his foot against the ground. He finds the squeegee and cleans the windscreen, and then the back window. It won't last an hour once they start again, but it's something to keep him busy. The truckie collapses on the concrete beside the car. The driver hurries around to the passenger door, unclips the seat belt and picks her up, settling her on his hip the way he'd carry a small child. Her head is heavy and it falls against his shoulder. He moves her arm around his own neck, and the thought of her holding him fills his heart to bursting with love.

The inside of the servo is white, burning light. His eyes smart and water and he resists the urge to shield her milky eyes. Fluorescents don't worry her and he knows it, but he can't help fussing. At the counter he sees the kid in his crumpled uniform take a look, and then a double take. There's a moment of panic; his hand shakes as he reaches for something under the counter—emergency button, maybe—and then he freezes, trembling like a moth's wing. His jaw goes slack, and he watches her. He only has eyes for her.

It's almost enough to make the driver puff up with pride. He's the one who's taking her, driving her across the vast wasteland of the country and making sure she has everything she needs.

"She's my world, my whole world," he says, and he doesn't know if the kid hears him but it doesn't matter. He puts her up on the counter. Her arms stretch out, her head drooping like a late season bloom. The kid bends down to her, and then he's choking on something, and his tanned fingers look so dark against the chalky white of her skin. The driver can't take his eyes off them, but he leans over the counter and punches the right button so the cash drawer pops open.

Lucky, lucky, it's late and the drawer is bursting with fifties. He grabs handfuls of them and stuffs them in his pocket, and he takes a minute to grab up food. More pies, and sauce packets, and a few bottles of soft drink. Chips and a mess of other stuff. He shoves it in a bag with a chain logo printed on the side and gathers her back from the countertop. The kid is lying there, his hands reaching out over the plastic, a stupid look on his face: mouth wide, eyes bulging. The driver hitches her on his hip and heads back to the car.

Tenderly he sets her in the passenger seat, arranges the towels around her frail shoulders, wads one up to try and protect her head. When there's no more he can do, he closes the door and goes around to settle back into the driver's seat. He takes a minute to peel open a pie wrapper and eats while he starts the car. The engine grumbles to life and he rolls forward. There's a bump as the back wheel goes over one of the truckie's limbs and then they're peeling back out onto the road.

Setting, the moon looks fatter than ever. The sky is beginning to turn grey in the east and the driver keeps a watch out for a motor inn, for a hotel, a pub with rooms to rent. Worst comes to worst, he'll pull over and crawl into the boot with her. It'll be cooking in the midday sun, but that's still better than the alternative…

As the light grows, he can see her better: the dark fall of her hair, razor angles of her features, her fine bird-boned body. Her milky eyes roll, and he burns knowing she's looking back at him. His heart skips a beat and he holds his breath. Her head shifts a little, tilting to the side, and her tongue hangs out, fat and red as a cabochon ruby. Bloody drool runs down her chin and falls, drip, drip, drip across her lap.

The driver puts his foot down, roaring up the road, racing the sun and he hums to himself, and mumbles, *darlin', oh darlin', my world, my world.*

The End

ANGELYSTOR

STEPHANIE ELLIS

Always under that tree, they told me whenever we walked past its gnarled and ancient form. *He's always there, every Halloween and every 31ˢᵗ July, reading the names of those who will die.*

My cousins loved to scare me when I was small, telling me tales to keep me awake all night. "Have *you* seen him?" I'd asked, or more pointedly, "Have *you* heard him?"

They'd never answered directly. They simply said, "Well, we're still here, aren't we?" and changed the subject.

As I moved into my teens, I saw them less and less, until the year I turned sixteen. Then my mum told me Uncle Llew had died, November 1ˢᵗ to be exact, and we would be going back to Llangernyw for the funeral.

My cousins were young men by then, had even less time for me than when I was a child. As Mum made the rounds of relatives, I was dragged along for everyone to exclaim over how I had grown and then, in hushed tones, they would start discussing Uncle Llew.

"Heard his name, didn't he," said Auntie Cerys. "Went past the old yew tree on the green and heard the Angelystor. He said the man spoke his name as clear as a bell. Right shook up he was. I told him he was a daft old sod, too much booze."

She fell silent after that. Mum hugged her and they all sat quietly for a while.

"The Angelystor isn't real," said Mum. "You know that. It's just a stupid story folks have got themselves worked up about. Llew had been warned about his drinking, hadn't he? You told me what the doctor said about his liver. Coincidence."

The other women nodded in agreement and their chatter ceased yet again as they contemplated recent events, apart from Cerys who sniffled loudly into her hankie. I went out the back and found my cousins on an old bench, smoking.

"Talking about Dad, were they?" asked Dai. "Said he heard his name, did they?"

"Yeah."

"You know that's superstitious claptrap," said Twm, angrily, forgetting the stories they had once delighted in telling me. "Doctor told him ages ago if he didn't stop drinking, he'd be dead before the end of the year. It was his own bloody fault."

They didn't want to talk anymore and I had nothing to say, so I left them.

The funeral itself was a bleak affair. The sky was grey, and the small group of mourners struggled to stay upright against the buffeting of the wind in the exposed cemetery. The graveyard was on an incline and as I turned around, I could see the village below me—the green, the yew tree, a black figure—

No.

It couldn't be. I blinked and the shape vanished. I was simply seeing things.

We stayed for one more day, where I had to endure another round of "*My, hasn't he grown,*" sessions and being compared to all and sundry—although most, unnervingly, said I shared the greatest likeness with my late uncle. Spitting image, apparently—it wasn't a cheerful idea.

Another five years passed, during which I saw seen even less of my family than before due to my gravitating towards the south of England, rather than the north of Wales. Mum would keep me informed of their doings, but most of it went over my head until she rang to say cousin Twm had died. When I asked how—he was, after all, only twenty-nine—she said the coroner couldn't explain; there seemed to be nothing wrong with him.

We went back to Llangernyw for the funeral. Visited relatives as before, spent time with Auntie Cerys and Dai, who had travelled over from Chester.

Once again, the women sat in the front room dissecting recent events whilst Dai sat alone out the back, only this time he wasn't smoking.

I joined him, wondering what I could say, when he suddenly started to talk.

"As bad as Dad, Twm was. Listened to the stories. Wanted to know. Well, he bloody well found out, didn't he? Stupid fool."

"What…?"

Dai ignored me and continued. "Got a bee in his bonnet about the Angelystor. The past two years on July 31st and on Halloween, he'd go and stand near that bloody tree and wait. Saw nothing the first July, but came back all shook-up last Halloween. Said he'd seen the Angelystor. I didn't believe him. Put it down to drink. But he wouldn't change his story. Said he'd seen him *and* heard him, but that he was safe for the moment because he hadn't heard his name being read. I told him he was an idiot and I didn't want to hear any more. Then he went back this last July. Couldn't keep away, could he? Like a bloody addict, he wanted to know. He didn't hear his name, and he was happy for a while but then the doubt crept in so back he went at Halloween. This time… well, Mum said he came home, all upset, and went straight to his room. She found him dead in his bed the next morning."

"I'm sorry," I said. Empty words, but I could think of nothing else.

"He sent me a text that night. Said he'd heard my name as well."

"Well that proves it's just a myth," I said. "*You're* still alive."

"Ay," sighed Dai.

He offered no further comment after that so I left him and returned to the women.

We buried Twm next to Llew and I went back to London. I tried not to think about them, but Mum rang me a fortnight later. Dai was dead.

"How…?"

"That's it. We don't know. He'd returned home for the weekend, went to bed and Cerys found him dead in the morning. She's in bits. That's three she's buried now."

Back to Llangernyw we went. This time, though, it was only me on the bench gazing up at the cemetery on the hill, thinking things over. Two had insisted they'd heard the Angelystor say their names, whilst Twm had also claimed to hear Dai's.

When I went to the pub for a drink later on, the regulars wanted to talk of nothing else. They also told me of a few more "unexplained" deaths.

The landlord was dismissive of these, however. "Nothing unexplained about them," he said. "Old age was one, and not looking where he was bloody well going was the other."

By now though, I was curious. I wanted to *know*. I said nothing to Mum, or to Auntie Cerys, but I resolved to return at the appointed time and find out the truth of the matter.

I drove up from London on July 30th and booked in at a bed and breakfast some miles from the village. I had no intention of letting anyone know what I was doing.

On July 31st, I drove to the outskirts of Llangernyw and parked my car where no one could see it. Then I crept down a rarely-used track along some outlying smallholdings to a row of trees just across from the yew beneath which the Angelystor was reported to stand. The undergrowth was thick enough, and dark enough, to prevent anyone seeing me. I settled myself down and prepared to wait. It was ten o'clock, and the Angelystor was supposed to start reciting at any time between ten and midnight—although never after.

Occasionally, I would see locals gather near the tree and wait a while before they got bored and went home, taking the non-appearance as a good sign, although I personally thought that was a bit presumptive. *I* was determined to wait the allotted span. I heard the bell strike eleven and owls cry out against the night, but I was warm and a folded rug on a fallen log made a comfortable seat. I was also quite relaxed, as by now I had convinced myself this was a wild-goose chase.

Then I saw something. A dark shape beneath the heavy boughs of the tree.

It was hard to be certain in the poor light of a nearby streetlamp, but there *was* something there. Nobody else seemed to be around so I moved closer, and as I did so the figure's outline sharpened. It was a man, long-robed and wearing a broad-brimmed hat. I could see nothing of his face. He started to speak. A deep voice, steady and lyrical, reciting names one by one. I recognized none and did not hear mine.

A prankster, I decided. Someone who needed unmasking. After all, he was frightening people—frightening them to *death*. I marched up and made to grab his arm but as I reached out, he simply vanished and my hand closed on thin air. I searched around, dumbfounded, but could find nothing. I must admit to being shaken.

Then I considered the other possibilities. One had been auto-suggestion, the phenomenon where people tell you something often enough that you believe it. I had simply seen what I had expected to see. My mind had been playing tricks on me. That was all.

I left the village and returned to London.

When Halloween was again almost upon us, I had a call from Mum. Auntie Cerys had said she was going to the old yew on Halloween. She wanted to listen. Could I go up with her and stop this nonsense?

I was back in Llangernyw, this time walking with my mum and my aunt to the tree. We hadn't been able to persuade Cerys to stay at home, and short of tying her up, there was nothing we could do. The three of us sat on a nearby bench and proceeded to wait in silence.

Again, it got to 11 p.m. and then Cerys suddenly stiffened. Stared straight ahead. "He's here," she said. "Can you see him?"

Neither Mum nor I could see anything.

"He's saying the names," she whispered. "Can you hear him?"

Neither of us could hear anything.

She sat quietly after that, listening and then, with a nod of her head, got up and walked in the direction of home, completely ignoring our presence.

"He said my name," said Cerys, as soon as we'd got through the door.

"There was no one there," said Mum. "You're just imagining it."

I made Cerys a cup of tea with lots of sugar, for the shock. No point in offering her whiskey, as she did not drink. I helped myself to one though.

"I heard him," said Cerys, ignoring the tea. "I'm off to bed."

Then she got up and went without another word. My mother and I looked at each other.

"I'll keep my door open," said Mum, "open hers. Listen out. She'll be fine, though. We'll see her in the morning."

But I could hear the doubt in her voice. We had seen nothing, no Angelystor, and yet…

In the morning, I went into Cerys's room and found her cold.

"The whole of my sister's family," wept Mum. "There *must've* been something there…"

We had a bad eight months, and in the end we couldn't stop ourselves; the following July, we went back to Llangernyw. We weren't the only ones. Others who'd lost loved ones at the supposed summoning of the Angelystor were gathered there, too. Most of us heard nothing, but there was always one who said they had, and after each death, those who had been present felt compelled to return, bringing others with them.

My life now revolves around those two dates, and for the past ten years I have not failed to attend. Mum died five years ago. She said she'd heard her name, although she did not succumb until February. Many died at dates well away from the Angelystor's supposed visits, but they were still attributed to him. I no longer questioned, although I had still not seen him since that first encounter.

It will be Halloween soon, and I am going back to the yew tree. I am fit and well despite the doctor's muttering at my last check-up.

Perhaps this might be my lucky year. Perhaps I might hear my name.

UNDERCURRENT

ALISON CYBE

"I think it all began when I heard about the tunnels under Portsdown Hill," he explained. "Standing at any suitably high point within Portsmouth, you will be able to see the sea to the south and the hill to the north, so even as a child I was always aware of it. The chalk hill, with its solemn white face and old military forts speckled along its top, was always looking over the city and making me curious to see what secrets it held. With the type of military history that Portsmouth has, it didn't take a genius to see that the hill was bound to be the center of many urban legends; after all, it had not only one, but several military forts on its top, even if the larger ones are no longer in service. The talk of hidden bunkers somewhere deep inside the hill wasn't just idle rumor; it was commonly accepted as true. So how could I resist the temptation?

"Urban exploration wasn't really a major thing until I was already in my early twenties. The hobby hadn't hit the mainstream media yet, so it was mostly kept to online bulletin boards and websites. People from all corners of the world would post and chat together, discussing locations that were abandoned, forgotten, or otherwise left to decay, and we would share photographs. Hospitals were a big one, very popular. I was very much into hotels at the time, and there were some amazing abandoned hotels that people had photographed from Russia. Those were amazing—entire massive buildings which had simply been left behind when people had moved out, especially the nobility who had fled their mansions and castles when the revolution occurred. Castles and manor houses and everything in between, left in perfect condition, untouched by time. Those websites were where I first met two of my closest friends.

"Al was the first person on the website that I really got talking to. He used the online name 'End of the Line,' which suited him perfectly due to his love of railway and subway sites. He grew up in London, a city that is almost iconic for its subway system, so I suppose that the interest was second nature to him. He had toured almost the entire underground network, photographing the large number of lost and unused stations that litter the tube lines. Out of the three of us, he had the most experience in urban exploration, being able to navigate in difficult terrain and with minimal lighting with relative ease. This made him something of the leader in our expeditions.

"Dave was the archetypal military fan. His thing was the army, and he was the type of kid who had a massive collection of army surplus. Naturally, his big kick in urban exploration was the unused bases or naval forts, that sort of thing. If a location had a history that was in any way involved with the army or was constructed during any era when a war was going on, he was the man with the info, or 'intel,' He was always so enthusiastic about his hobbies, and keen to be involved in anything that the rest of us were taking part in—he would invite me to his airsoft matches, and would always turn up whenever my band was performing.

"And I guess, having mentioned my band, this brings the entire story over to me. When I finished high school, I was struck with the realization that I hadn't succeeded in making many friends—the few that I did have gradually started to move away, either physically moving to other cities, or socially drifting away from me. I was left with the one thing that had always captured my interest when I was in school: the love of music. I could play the guitar reasonably well, and it wasn't hard to find a band in Portsmouth that was looking for new members—as a city with as many students as we have, there are always many who are eager to perform their music on stage. I answered an advert in the local student newspaper, and before I knew it I had made several new friends who were keen to line up gigs. We played several, all of which were at least somewhat successful, but rarely stood out from the many hundreds of other student bands. Still, the gigs we played in venues like the Wedgewood Rooms were enough to give me a strong sense of satisfaction in my life. Enough, I think, to try trudging through some dark tunnels with a group of two people who were as equally odd as me.

"We planned the first expedition for almost three weeks, reading over the reports that we could find. Dave covered most of the military intel on the forts and bunkers in and around Portsdown Hill, and it wasn't long before we were ready to head in. The experience was, frankly, exhilarating. We moved past the walled-off entryways and climbed our way down a series of old, rusted ladders into a network of barren tunnels that spread what seemed to be for miles in every direction. The passageways were littered with dust and small accrued stones, lined with naval grey walls and heating pipes passing overhead. I wanted desperately to believe that the location had been untouched since the cold war, but I knew this couldn't be true, that other explorers had walked these tunnels before us. We stuck close behind Al as he led the way, taking photographs as he went.

"When we got to some of the actual rooms, Dave was in his glory. Most of the rooms had been stripped, consoles and documents had been removed when the base was vacated all those decades ago, but many of the furnishings remained intact. Bunk beds in the sleeping quarters, the old-style kitchen cookers in the mess halls, the desks and chairs in the command centers, they were all present and accounted for, and were dutifully photographed for posterity. When we left the tunnels, we felt as if we had walked many, many miles; we were tired, exhausted, but satisfied. We began to plan our next expedition immediately.

"Almost a month and a half later, Al led the way into an old, utterly abandoned World War Two bomb shelter. Portsmouth had been hit heavily in the blitz, due to its position as a major naval target, and one of the large bomb shelters located under London Road had been forgotten and left desolate. The entire city had been fortified, anti-aircraft guns placed on the beaches, on the hill and even on large platforms above the sea itself, all to repel the German pilots, but the bomb shelter was still a necessity. Inside there, we feel the enclosed, nervous anxiety of the survivors of the blitzkrieg.

"That wasn't the only emotion we experienced. In Cosham, near the hill, we managed to make our way into a closed-off cinema that was scheduled for demolition. It was a relatively small cinema when compared to the megaplex in the Gunwharf Quays shopping center, and it had long since stopped turning a strong enough profit. The posters of the most recent films that it had been showing when it was closed were still on display on the foyer. The cinema was demolished a few months later, with nothing left of it remaining—except for our photographs.

"Flushed with the buzzing excitement of our successes, we covered other sites as well in the months that followed. Pounds Scrapyard, the abandoned Zurich building, Fraser Range, we covered them all, each with the same eagerness and excitement that grows from having made a genuine accomplishment. For a while, I had forgotten about the relative obscurity of my band, who were still finding only a few small gigs around the local area with no real prospects for signing any major contracts; we were spinning our wheels but not making any progress. This didn't bother me, though—I had the gang. Me, Al and Dave, and our exploration.

"It was Al who had the idea and presented it to the two of us—he had heard the rumors for a while, and wanted to strike it big.

"'We should check out the Nelson tunnels,' he told us one evening while we were sharing a dinner of take-away chicken. I wasn't too sure what the Nelson tunnels actually were, and even Dave only had a few scraps of information, and the websites seemed to be relatively incomplete on their knowledge of them. The tunnels were so named for their proximity to the trail that Nelson himself had made through the city. Only four people on the website had attempted it, and only half-heartedly—the entrance for the tunnels was easy enough to get to, located less than fifteen minutes from Clarence Pier and through an underground manhole sealed behind a door that was inset into the side of the sea bank, but it came with its own particular hazard which most explorers simply didn't care for. The water levels within the tunnels could vary, rising with the tides, and this made planning the exploration extremely difficult. The website boasted a series of photographs, but none of them were especially good, and they only ever mapped the first chamber. For most people, the risk versus reward was simply too far out of balance, and so the Nelson Tunnels was almost forgotten even by our community. Naturally, Al loved the idea. I wasn't personally sold on it, until I realized something—if we were to be the first people to fully map out and explore this tunnel network, the popularity we'd achieve on the websites would be staggering. I'd become a success story, not just in our little group of three, but within an entire bustling online community. My failure with the band would shrink to nothing. So I said yes, it sounded like a wonderful idea. It was agreed, we'd hit the tunnels.

"Planning for this venture would prove to be extremely difficult. We had so little information to go on, so we had to take a lot of care to make sure that all of our bases were covered. Supplies, thankfully, were Dave's forte. Al handled most of the planning, which came down to deciding on the best time of day to make our expedition. He consulted the times for when the tide would be in, and we agreed to make our move when they were at their lowest. The biggest thing on everyone's minds, naturally enough, was to play it safe.

"Eventually the day came, and we met on the commons not far from the entrance to the tunnels. Taking our time to mill around in order to make sure we seemed entirely inconspicuous, playing on our mobile phones whilst we waited for the crowds to clear. It's rather amazing how simply tapping away on your mobile phone renders you somewhat invisible to the people in a crowd. Once the last group, a trio of hipsters with full beards, shuffled along their way, we made our move.

"We hurried along down across the common and found the gate set into the embankment without any trouble. The website had called it a doorway, but in reality it was more a set of metal railings formed into a gateway. Dave made quick work of the latch on it, unchaining it and tugging it open. He was wearing a rather full backpack, decked with every tool that we were likely to need, including a manhole key. He pulled the key out and inserted it to the manhole cover, pulling the circular covering free with a heavy grinding sound. We peered inside to see the tunnel descending downwards, with row upon row of metal hand-rails set as ladders into the damp walls. One by one, we worked our way downwards.

"I was the last to get down the ladders, and the ground was wet beneath my shoes. About half an inch of sea water remained in the chamber and the strong smell of salt filled the air. Al was already switching on his torch, allowing us to see the area around us. The walls seemed to be made of hard-packed concrete, trailing off into the distance. When I looked up, several pipes wound their way along the ceiling, and I noticed that the wall opposite had rusting metal hand-rails set into it at every few feet, no doubt to allow people who had to access the tunnels a good grip to steady themselves from the slippery water surface below. As we started to walk, we noticed that beneath the light splashing of our foot-steps there was a dull crunch; the ground beneath the water was etched with pebbles and grit. This was good, as it meant that our steps were significantly less likely to slide and result in a fall.

"The tunnel went onwards for what must have been ten minutes, gradually turning to the left as it did so. Dave pointed out that the route that we were taking would wind us up along the coast of the beach, leaning slightly towards the sea. It was Al who pointed out that the tunnel was on a rather slight decline, very slowly tilting downwards as we progressed. I asked him if he thought that the tunnel could have been used as part of the sewage system for the city, but he doubted it, telling us that the construction of the tunnels was all wrong for such a use. There was a soft groan in the tunnel's echoing background, a dull rumbling which I recognized as the reverberating bass hum of distant water, and we knew that the tunnel must somewhere empty out into the sea. We were so busy photographing the tunnels that we almost walked right past the metal door that was set into the wall of the tunnel.

"When Al pointed out the door, we pressed around to examine it. It was solid, without any markings or signs posted on it, and it didn't even have a handle to open it. When I knocked on it, there was a resounding echo from the other side. It didn't take long for the three of us to decide that we wanted to push through, and thankfully Dave had just the right tool for the job: a thin length of metal that I thought resembled a crowbar, but Dave called a latch key. Could well have been one for what I knew, I was never technically minded like that, but it didn't even take Dave two minutes to ease the door open. Beyond it, we found another sheer drop, falling into the depths below. Small metal rungs hung on the wall, giving us a clear way down if we wanted to. We turned to one another and discussed the prospect of pushing onwards. We had already come far, and pushing onwards into this deeper tunnel would surely be extremely dangerous.

"It was decided between us all that if we were to make the trip down the rungs, we should take even greater care in doing so. Dave, as prepared as he always was, had a length of rope with him. We didn't have any climbing gear, as we weren't exactly mountaineers, but we decided that if the first one of us to head down along the ladder were to tie the rope around his waist, and latch a knot from the rope onto each rung as he went, it would ensure that if any of us were to fall when our feet were moving along the wet metal of the ladders we would not have far to fall before the rope would catch us. It was an improvised idea, but we thought it would be a solid enough one. Al went first, tying the rope around his waist. He made his way down the ladder, rung by rung, taking his time to secure his way as he went. When he reached the bottom, he called up to me, and I pulled his side of the rope back up and fastened it around myself. I worked my way down; noticing just how wet the rungs felt. Half-way down, I told Al that I thought it would be a good idea to leave the rope here, in case we started to run out of time and had to make our way out of here in a hurry. He was midway through agreeing when I had to pause to wipe some seaweed off of my fingers. I reached the ground and passed the rope back up to Dave.

"As Dave made his way down, I took the time to examine the new chamber. Unlike the one above, the walls here didn't seem to be made of concrete, or any kind of natural material that I could determine. They felt wet to the touch, and hard and somewhat cold, and I thought that we must have found our way into a natural cavern of some sort. I hadn't been paying attention when it happened. One moment I was scanning the new chamber with my torch, and the next a scream split the air. By the time I had turned around, all I was able to see was Dave colliding with the ground. I knew immediately that he had fallen—no, there was a clattering roar that broke the echoes of his fall, telling me that one of the rungs had given way. We hurried over to Dave. He was on his side on the ground, a tangled spread of army camouflage jeans and backpack. He was gasping heavily, letting loud cries of pain out in strong bellows. That was when we noticed his leg, bent double under him, its angle sharply leaning inwards towards his body in a manner it surely shouldn't. I brushed Al to one side and took a look at the leg. It wasn't a simple break; I could see that much. From just above his ankle, a large bulge protruded from beneath his skin, indicating that the bone had snapped and threatened to rupture.

"Dave lay back against the wet rocky ground, struggling to catch his breath. Al was already on his mobile phone, struggling to call for an ambulance. I spoke to Dave loudly, telling him to stay calm, that it wasn't as bad as it looked. It was a problem, yes, but a manageable one. Al started to swear, and when I looked over, I seen him shaking his mobile frantically. 'No signal,' he replied, and asked if I could try mine. I shook my head; I didn't even have mine with me—I've always disliked carrying mobile phones. We reached into Dave's pocket to try to recover his, hoping that his signal would work better here in this subterranean tunnel. When I pulled Dave's phone free, I found that the screen was smashed. Turning it over, its casing was cracked. The damn thing wouldn't even turn on. I threw it on the ground. 'Okay,' I said, 'We're going to carry you out of here. Al, can you unfasten the rope?' I planned to put together a makeshift harness, carry Dave up the ladder into the tunnel above, and from there we were only one step into the city again.

"That was when Al pointed out the rungs that lay broken on the ground. I had thought that there was just one, probably old and rusted from the sea salt. I was wrong—it was all of the ones that the rope had been tied to. Each one had been ripped clear from the crumbling old cave wall and lay in a contorted pile in the torchlight.

"We both tried to figure out a way to get back into the upper tunnel. We spent almost half an hour trying to climb it by hand, or to force the rungs back into place, or to stand on one another's shoulders, but none of our attempts yielded any success. All the while Dave was breathing heavily through his clenched teeth, struggling to bite back the pain he was in. He started talking about his girl-friend, about how much he wanted to see her again—I was single, I had nobody except these two guys with me, and I sure as hell wanted to get us out of here together. I was relying on Al to know what to do, to have some sort of fallback plan for how to get out of this place, but he had nothing. And all the time, we were thinking about the clock, about how long it'd be before the water started to make its way into the tunnel.

"Without any other ideas, we pulled Dave up onto one foot and took his weight between the two of us, supporting him on our shoulders, and tried to make our way onwards into the tunnel. What else could we do? We knew that the water from the sea got in here, so the only chance we had—the only hope we had—was to try to find a way out through that way. I don't know how long we walked for over that crunching, wet pebbled ground, carrying Dave between the two of us. After a while, his pain started to ease—I suspect his endorphins had kicked in, perhaps. He didn't talk about his leg or the pain, but would repeat over and over that he wanted to see his girlfriend, he just wanted to get out of these tunnels and see her, that he didn't want to die without seeing her. We both told him again and again that he wasn't going to die, that was stupid, that only happened in the movies, and that in real life people like us stumbled out of the caves and got found by the coast guard, and that was what was going to happen to the three of us.

"I don't know how long we walked for. The tunnels seemed to turn at different angles, leaning left for a while and then turning sharply to the right. Al, who had until now been able to tell exactly where we should have been, eventu-ally confessed that he had no idea where we were. This announcement brought a new stream of cries from Dave, who began to sob and repeat in fear 'We're going to die down here. We're going to die down here.' I told him again that we weren't, but in all honesty, at this point even I wasn't sure that was the truth. We continued onwards, unsure if we were making any progress at all, not knowing if we were directly under the city or beneath the sea now. My feet started to hurt from the walking, and before long we had to stop to eat. We didn't have many snacks; Dave had brought a few chocolate bars and a tub of ready-made pasta which we shared between us. It was starting to feel very cold in the tunnels. That was when Al finally asked me to step to one side with him, leaving Dave to finish the pasta. We stepped a few feet further down into the tunnel, and Al leaned close to me and whispered something to me, something that I think all three of us had been dimly aware of but had been too afraid to say out loud—the water should have come in an hour ago.

"We pushed on, not daring to mention the time that Al's phone was showing, or the risk of the water. We walked in silence now, with only Dave's moaning breaths to keep the silence from being complete. I don't know how long we walked on for; time itself seemed to lose all sense of meaning, our anxiety keeping us from wanting to see it. I started to grow tired; my eyes became sore, my feet shuffling rather than walking. When Al slipped and fell, causing the rest of us to collapse onto the wet ground, we decided that we should rest for a while. We slept then—I couldn't say how long we slept for, only that it was a fitful and uncomfortable sleep, in the cold and the dampness, on the harsh ground, with only the silence for company. But in the middle of that sleep, I woke. The other two were asleep, but I struggled to get back to rest—something troubled me, and as I lay there trying to sleep, I felt that I knew what it was. A dull sound, somewhere too quiet to be heard even under the white sound of the silence; somewhere in the depths of the cave, perhaps, or maybe I was hearing my own heartbeat.

"We woke eventually, and continued onwards. As the hours pressed on, the three of us found that we had less and less to speak about, so we walked in silence. What could we say to keep each other's spirits up? None of us wanted to look at the clock on Al's phone to see how long we had really been down here, afraid that the time would consume us. We were hungry, all of us. I thought that when we got out of here, I'd get myself a huge dinner. We slept again. We walked onwards. Al didn't speak, he simply pushed on, pausing only to make sure his torch was strong enough to see the way ahead. Dave, when he did speak, only mumbled about how he wanted to see his girlfriend again—he was looking pale, his eyes seemed dark. Sometimes, all he could manage was to say her name to him again and again in a near-whisper. The third time we slept, and I was once more awakened by the sense of the sound of my own heartbeat, I took the chance to sneak a look at Al's phone. We had been down here almost four days.

"Dave didn't wake up that day.

"We tried to wake him up. Al had been shaking him, screaming at him to wake up. Neither of us knew what to do. The entire moment seemed like something out of a dream; I had to check to make sure I wasn't asleep. I didn't want to move on. I had never, in my entire life, lost a friend or family member to death before. Al was certain that it was due to infection, but I couldn't understand that —there had been no puncture of the skin. We almost argued about it, but neither of us could manage to fight. Fighting between the two of us just didn't seem important anymore.

"Neither of us knew what we should do. The ground felt too hard to bury him, and we didn't have anything else we could do. God, we just left him there. What else could we have done? I hated it, I hated myself for doing it, but we just left him there. Al took his backpack, which we dug through to find something to eat, but there wasn't anything there we could use. We just left him there, and continued down the tunnels.

"We found Dave's mobile phone later that day. I didn't even see it; all I heard was this glass-like cracking noise as I walked on, almost stumbling. And there it was, broken and shattered on the ground beneath my foot. I couldn't even think straight—I picked it up, walked over to Al and demanded to know why it was here, this far into the tunnels. How could it possibly have been here? It wasn't possible. We had left it behind, at the entrance to the tunnel, along with the broken rungs. The rungs, which lay scattered at the foot of the wall not far from where we now stood. That was when I lost it; the last scraps of my temper were gone. I screamed at Al, launching myself at him, trying to punch him with the last scraps of my strength. 'You bastard!' I screamed, 'You've been leading us around in circles!' Al was screaming, shouting back at me, and telling me that it was impossible. But I couldn't stop, not after what had happened that morning (morning? When we had woken up, who knows if it was morning?) and not after having left Dave's body behind. It was entirely his fault, it had to be. He was our leader; he was the most experienced one. He was meant to know what he was doing! If he hadn't made such a cock-up of this, Dave would still be alive. I wanted to make Al regret it, I wanted him to pay for this mess, and so I punched him again and again, driving my fist against him. I don't know if he was bleeding or if it was just the wetness of the cavern itself, but soon I had exhausted myself and collapsed, my entire body soaked, and tried to catch my breath.

"When we could both stand again, we continued down the tunnels. Neither of us wanted to mention what had just happened, the fight we had—it had released my anger and Al nursed his jaw and bloodied nose and neither of us could think of anything further to say. We stumbled as we walked, feeling weaker as we pushed on. I think, gradually, we were starting to starve. I couldn't tell, not really. I didn't feel as hungry anymore, but my muscles started to feel weaker, my legs shook as I walked. We slept twice as we continued on, and I started to think that the time between each bout of sleep was growing shorter. Twice, I woke from my sleep certain that the sound of my heartbeat was thumping out in the echo of the tunnels.

"Two days after Dave had died, we found ourselves in a part of the tunnel that seemed entirely unusual. The ground beneath us gave slightly, a little like mud. The walls themselves felt wetter to the touch, and gave slightly when I pressed against them, and we both thought that at this point in the cavern network the water must have weakened the rocks to the point that they were soaked through. We drank as best we could, the foul-tasting salty water all we could manage to keep our strengths up—we had to sip very slightly to resist on gagging on the liquid, and the sensation left me with a headache that pounded in my ears and refused to let me go.

"When I woke again, Al was gone. There was nothing left of him, no marks where he had been sleeping, none of his gear, I figured that he must have pushed on ahead without me. The question of why he would abandon me down here played on my mind as I pushed on. Was he angry that I had lashed out at him? Had he stormed off whilst I was asleep? I didn't know, and I was struggling to think. Time had become a mix of either sleeping or walking forward into the darkness; I couldn't even remember how long ago it had been since I had punched him. It could have been days; it could have been hours. He had to still be angry with me, so he had taken the gear and left. And, God help me, it was the gear that I missed most. Al had the last torch.

"It was so dark. I couldn't have seen Al if he had been standing beside me. Maybe that was his intention, to take the gear and leave me behind. Maybe he had figured I was the weaker of the two of us; that he would make better time without me, have a better chance of getting out of here alive. I had to stumble through the cavern, feeling my way through, making nowhere near as much time as I could have if that selfish bastard had just left me a torch. All I could do was think about how badly I'd fucked this up; how much I'd fucked everything up.

Not just the expedition, but my life in general—how little I had accomplished, how isolated I had let myself become. People would miss Dave, they would miss Al, but who would miss me?

"The ground gave way beneath me so abruptly that I barely even noticed it was gone, sending me tumbling forward. The tunnel was on an incline and I had slipped and lost my footing without even realizing that I had ventured too far. The small rocks and pebbles bit into my skin as I sprawled forward, cutting myself terribly. I hit the bottom of the incline with a heavy thud, and realized that I had fallen down what must surely have been a forty-degree slide into utter darkness. I was bleeding, my body felt cold and I could barely move. I lay there for what must have been hours, until I could finally will my limbs to move once again. I reached out to find something to grab onto, something to help pick myself up and stand upright.

"My fingers groped in the darkness, and found a boot. I grasped onto it, and I felt the bottom falling out from my stomach and I realized who it belonged to. Al lay at the bottom of the incline, his head twisted around, the back of his head matted with black blood and punctured by a hefty jagged rock. He clutched his torch in his hands, and my first thought was to grab it. I powered it on, my hands shaking. I felt cold, even inside my skin I felt cold, and I didn't want to think about Al, whose body lay so close to me. His fingers were wet when I pulled the torch free, and cold. All I could hear was the pounding of my heart, and that horrible echo of it that sounded throughout the caverns. After a few presses, I managed to turn the torch on and shone it around the cavern. Al had, I think, died very quickly. I put it out of my mind—no, I forced it out. I couldn't let myself think about it, not if I wanted to get out of here. And I had to believe I could get out of here, even if I didn't deserve to, even if I had nothing to go back to.

"I couldn't stand any longer, my legs wouldn't support me. My knees swayed when I tried to stand, so instead I crawled, dragging myself through the rough shale and pebbles at the bottom of the soft, muddy floor. The rocks of the walls, which I would occasionally collapse against as I turned this corner and that corner, always felt soft and wet as I laid back against them, reminding me of just how horribly deep beneath the sea I had come. I didn't think about Al laying back there, partly because if I did, I would—oh God, I didn't want to think about how hungry I was. And I knew that if I allowed my mind to go there, even for a moment, I'd never be able to pull it back. I was determined to put as much distance between myself and the corpse as I could.

"I fell in and out of consciousness as I crawled, sleeping sometimes and moving at other times. The echo of my heartbeat was my only companion now, and it sounded loud—so loud, sometimes it drowned out even the white noise of the silence in the caverns. But then, gradually, another sound began to edge its way into my awareness—the soft, churning sound of running water.

"I made my way towards the sound, unable to think, unable to feel. I couldn't reason, I had lost everything that I was as a person, even my awareness of self. I followed the sound of the water, clutching my way along the soft permeable ground towards it, pulling myself along one handful at a time, clawing my way towards the only sense of salvation that I had. At times it sounded so distant, and at times it was drowned out by the echoes of my heartbeat. And at times I didn't even think those echoes were in time with my heart, and I knew that I was losing my mind as well. I cried until my eyes were too dry to see, until my vision was just a blur, but I continued onwards, because the only other alternative was to lay back and die.

"The tunnel opened into a chamber. I clambered along the floor, until the floor gave way, leaving the middle of the chamber as a vast chasm. I could see it below: loud, wet, shining back the torchlight at me. The water was moving, it was so black and I couldn't tell how deep it was, but it was the only chance I had to get out of here. It was flowing; that meant it was moving either into the sea, or coming from the outside and pouring into a deeper part of the caverns. I had no way to know which. I didn't know, I couldn't guess; Al would have known. Maybe Dave, with his military experience, might have known too. But me, I had no way of knowing. Should I make my way down and push against the current, or flow downstream with it? It was a drop of about ten feet down into the water. I could make it down, I knew I could. I was so excited, I realized that I had forgotten to breath. I rolled over onto my back, catching my breath.

"That's when I saw the white stones. I caught a sight of them in the torchlight. They lined the caverns, starting perhaps at the ground, or maybe beneath the ground, and moving upwards to end near the towering cave's top that rose high above me. At first, I thought it was a line of chalk in the caves, but they were too solid. They didn't shine with the rough-hewn texture of the ground; they seemed smooth. They reminded me of columns, arranged almost too neatly in rows across the chamber. And that's when I realized where I was. It was at that moment that every thought in my mind seemed to come together in crystal clarity, and then fly apart. It all made sense, so much perfect sense. I wanted to laugh, but my throat was too dry, too scarred—instead I rolled onto my side, coughing up a wet splatter of blood. My throat burned, and all I could do was to stare at those white stones. Then, without thinking, I pushed myself off the edge of the chasm and fell into the waters below. The water swept me down, and it filled my lungs. I thought, I knew, that I was going to die. And, after what I had seen, I embraced it.

"When I was next aware, my throat was burning and my chest ached. I tried to open my eyes, and was dimly aware of shapes around me. They were moving. Gradually, they started to take form, and I recognized what they were—faces. It took me a moment to understand that I wasn't actually dead, not yet. My chest was sore, I realized, because a man had been pressing down hard against it. I was in Ryde, on the Isle of Wight. The lifeguard had found me. I don't remember being loaded into the ambulance. My memory of the next few days is only a series of fragments.

"I was told that I had swallowed a lot of sea water, that I was suffering from hypothermia and starvation, and multiple injuries and broken bones. I was, they said, lucky to be alive. Gradually, my thoughts returned to me and I was able to sit up. I ached, and they kept me on a drip to help me regain my strength, and they asked me about what had happened. Several of the doctors were concerned about what had happened to me; not simply because I was a John Doe, without any reason for washing up on the shore. They asked me if I had tried to swim from Portsmouth to the Isle of Wight, which I denied. Then they asked me about what I had said to the men in the ambulance, about what I had meant. At first I didn't understand because I couldn't remember the trip to the ambulance. But calmly, one of the doctors explained to me that I had been shouting at them, both in the ambulance ride and in the emergency room. I couldn't remember doing so, not until he told me what it was that I had said; what I had been trying to warn them about.

"When I remembered what I had told the doctors, I tried to tell this man as well. He didn't believe me either, and soon I was talking to other doctors, psychologists, therapists. None of them believed me. But I remembered what I had told them and I cannot forget—it's what I saw after the fall into the water. After I was swept down along its course, in the moments after I had been spat free from the tunnels. I had to warn them that in those moments, before I lost consciousness once again. I had forced my eyes open and looked out at the misty sea water to make sure that I had finally emerged from the caverns. But none of them believed me—none of them have ever, or will ever, believe me. None of them accept that what I saw in the depths of the sea, so far beneath Portsmouth which is built so high above where it lays—I saw staring back at me a giant, colossal eye."

WHERE ONLY THE MOSQUITOES SING

DAN ALLEN

Old folks say it is only a myth to entertain the youth, but if you visit a certain northern lake in the calm of night, when the moon is new, and the loons are silent and a whisper can be heard for miles, you might experience something that will change your mind faster than a bullfrog's tongue snapping up a mayfly.

In a land where you can peel skin off the white birch and each year moose shed their antlers and black flies grow big enough to carry away a squirrel, there is a tale of a star-crossed romance, tender young hearts brought together by attraction and divided by tragedy. At Camp Chikopi, nestled between pine trees on the eastern shore of Ahmic Lake, the boys retell the story, passing it from generation to generation. The legend grows with each batch of new campers, whispered inside musty cabins after the lights are out. Across the gentle waves and just beyond where the cold waters flow from the mouth of the Magnetawan, young girls at Camp Wathahi share a similar tale and keep themselves up late.

The story begins with teens paddling across the lake, gliding over sun-sparkled waters, to visit each other's grounds. Competing like rabid chipmunks, they burn off endless energy in a revolving series of games until darkness fills the eastern horizon and a nightly campfire ends the day. Snuggled close to warm flames, enticed by the sweet aroma of burning hardwood and blanketed by the haze of smoke spiraling heavenward, a boy makes eye contact with a girl, and smiles.

Caught in the trance of hand-holding puppy love, the two scheme to rendezvous at midnight in the cove beneath the cliffs on the thick evergreen-covered north shore, planning to seal their attraction with a first kiss.

When the cabin counselor's snore shakes dust from the rafters and his fellow campers dream of ice cream and cellular reception, the boy creeps away and slips a canoe into the lake. Careful not to splash, he manipulates the paddle with the expertise of a fur-trading voyageur traversing the meandering waters of Algonquin.

He stops halfway and sits abreast Harlow's Cove. His canoe bobs on gentle waves and he watches as the dark outline of his first love approaches. Her smooth strokes slice through the midnight mist and her hair catches a faint reflection of the eyelash-shaped moon.

The boy stands to wave at his newfound love and guide her into the covert shadows beneath a protective cliff that provides the privacy of a limestone curtain. His sudden movement causes a tilt and water threatens to pour over the side. He shifts his weight in a frenzied reaction and the unbalanced canoe capsizes quicker than the flash of a shooting star. Tossed into cold ink-dark water, the boy loses his way and drifts to the bottom.

The young lady, with tears in her eyes and a flashlight gripped in shaking hands, finds only a paddle and the upside-down fiberglass hull. The search is called off after fruitless days of dredging the bottom and poking around the submerged fallen trees and driftwood littered shoreline. The boy is never found, his remains never buried, but each year with the melting of the ice and the return of the robins, boats are untethered and set adrift on moonless nights and paddles disappear from cabin porches as he makes his presence known.

After hearing the story, three young lads with curly blond hair and apple pie smiles escape from their paved-over world of cement and glass and pick the cliff in Harlow's Cove to camp for the night. When their fire burns low and the northern lights shimmer like a dancing green glow-worm, after the cookies are consumed and hockey opinions debated, one restless camper dares the rest to jump off the cliff. In the kingdom of boys and double-dog dares he has no choice but to take the first leap. The darkness hides his descent, but the splash alerts his friends and anything else that might be stirring below the surface. The boy torpe-does deep and struggles to reverse his plunge. Cold hands grasp his leg. The bones pinch his skin and drag him deeper. Terrified, the boy kicks with an urgency only fear can evoke. The hands holding him slip towards his ankles, scratching him with the fleshless tips of decomposing fingers. At last free, his legs burn from spent adrenaline and his lungs, drained of air, threaten to implode like a crushed pop can. He pulls at the water above and thrashes with the frenzy of a cat tossed into a bathtub. Nearing unconsciousness, with one last desperate flurry, he breaks through the surface into sweet midnight air and swims towards shore. Certain his attacker is mere inches behind, his heart pounds faster with each panicked stroke. He senses the creature getting closer and closer, and holds his breath, saving his air for a final death scream. His knee touches a moss-covered stone and he drags himself out into a chilling breeze and scrambles, shivering as he climbs to the safety of the cliff above.

His pals smirk and steal glimpses at each other as he tells his tale, not believing the drama of his experience nor his near fatal escape. Between whispered doubts and muffled chirps, they lay him on a sleeping bag, and their battery-powered torches chase away phantoms and expose shadows. A round circle, like a spotlight on a stage, traces the scratches from above his knee to his ankle. Five distinct ragged marks scar his pale leg and the cuts begin to darken, looking as if they wear lipstick. At the bottom of the longest one, something grey and ugly sticks out of the gash. The pals move in close, their noses almost touching, to see a sight that promises to haunt their sleep. They flinch and the flashlight slips between frozen fingers, blinking out against the ground. Not believing the horrifying implications of the object protruding from the wound, they hurry to turn back on the light. Their fears are confirmed. Hooked under the skin, all algae covered, gnarled and twisted, is an old fingernail.

In the warmth of the early summer, when the mosquitoes hatch and the horseflies swarm, busloads of youth leave behind the monotony of their urban lives and return to a northern paradise, stirring the lake with the roar of laughter. In the dark blue of a shadowed bay, a canoeist's stroke slaps the surface and wakes a dormant spirit for another year of haunting the waters, searching for a lost love and a missing paddle. If you're ever fortunate to stand on a soft blanket of pine needles and marvel at the sight of more stars than you ever could imagine, and if you hear, in the dark moments near midnight, a loud splash that carries over the lake, then put away the paddles, drag up your boat and stay out of the water, for you won't be alone if you dare take a swim on a moonless night, in a northern lake, where only the mosquitoes sing.

THE BOY WITH THE BROKEN TAIL

JO FAIRCLOUGH

He would swim to me every day that summer, disappearing from the golden shore and reappearing as a frantic frothing that slowly made its way towards my rocky perch. All I could see above the writhing water was a little white face, framed by thin white arms that wheeled frantically through ocean and air. Each untrained stroke cast watery rainbows into the sky before smacking back down to the sea with a splash. Body rigid, arms lax, fingers splayed. Artless, graceless, wild. Human.

From the sunny mouth of my cove I would watch him as he flailed his way over to me, my tail swaying gently in the cool waves that lapped against my perch. We were supposed to stay away from them, all of us, but I never could. How the elders could live in ignorance despite knowing that there was a whole other world out there above the sea was a mystery to me. Even the other children seemed uninterested, content with the small, insignificant mysteries offered by our own world, even going so far as to mock me for my own curiosity.

The boy, too, was a mystery to me—a new and exciting mystery that simmered with life and potential. A mystery that I could solve.

Huffing and puffing, he hauled his scrawny form out of the water and scrambled onto the rock beside me. He splayed the two halves of his sickly, bisected tail out over the surface of the warm rock and let his arms fall outstretched away from his body.

Poor soul, I thought. Being forced to rely on such a feeble upper half to compensate for his even feebler lower half.

The boy lay on his back, chest heaving up and plunging down as he stared up at the sky. Each inhale sent droplets of water rolling down his torso to pool on the stone beneath.

"Hey, Mer," he panted.

Mer was the term he used to refer to me—a name, he called it. He said that all people needed names. The fact that I was not a person like he was a person, and that my kind had no need for names, did not seem to make a difference.

"Hello, boy."

He rolled his head to look at me and sighed. "Mer, I've told you, my name is Ben."

I flicked my tail and splashed water over the boy, making him shriek and giggle. "And I've told you, boy, that if you choose my name then I choose yours."

"Fine, choose your own name then."

I thought for a while. What was a name? It was a thing that was uniquely you, though the boy said that many names are shared between hundreds of humans, so I'm not entirely sure what point the whole thing has. What set me apart from the others? Everything. The others define me by my differences, use them as a weapon against me, so why not own them? Why not take what sets me apart and use it to name myself?

"Curiosity?" I suggested.

The boy laughed, which wounded me a little. "You can't have that. It's silly. It's the name of a robot on Mars," he explained, as if this were the most normal sentence in the world. He looked at my blank expression and sat up eagerly. "Which part of that didn't you understand?"

"All of it!" I laughed, the promise of learning quickly banishing the moment of hurt. "Tell me all."

"Robots are machines made from metal and electricity and... other stuff. Humans control them and they do things for us. Curiosity is up in space."

"Space?"

The boy pointed up at the sky and the blazing sun that swam above. "Up there, past the sun and the sky, there are millions of planets—bajillions of planets! Whole other worlds."

"Beyond the stars, too?"

"After the stars and before them. But even with a telescope, they're too far away and too dark, and we can't see them properly. So we fly a robot into space and it sees them for us. One day I'm going to build a new robot, one I can sit inside, and I'm going to fly it into space and drive on, on, on Neptune!" he exclaimed excitedly. "Or a whole new planet nobody has even discovered yet!"

I stared up at the sky, then down into the sea, trying to imagine diving into its cobalt depths and swimming down, down, past the fish and the coral, past the sharks and the whales, down into the trenches where the dark things lie. A nervous excitement spread through my body.

Whole other worlds indeed.

"Curiosity isn't a normal name anyway," the boy continued. "Normal names are, like, Jack and Paul and Chris, Sophie and Sarah and Emma."

"I like Emma."

The boy frowned at me like I was playing a joke on him. "Pick a boy's name, silly."

"But I am not a boy. And I am not a girl either. I am Mer."

"Okay, so Mer's your name then." The boy grinned at me, so happy with his little trick. His grin and his trick made me happy too.

The boy flopped back down onto the warm rock and splayed his arms wide, chest still rising high and falling deep, but slower now. "Man, swimming over to you is still so hard."

"I'm not surprised, considering you are forced to use… well… you know. Your broken tail." I gestured to his sickly lower half, scared to touch it in case it infected me.

The boy laughed and sat up again, looking down at his body. "I keep telling you: they're legs. And they're not broken or weak," he insisted, slapping one hand on each of the long, white, arm-like limbs that protruded from his waist. He grinned at me with pride. "They're full of muscles. My Dad says so. That's why he lets me play in the sea on my own. But I'm not supposed to swim out this far without him, even with my super-muscly legs, so don't tell!"

"I won't tell a soul," I promised, leaning closer to look at his legs. "They don't look full of muscles to me. My tail is full of muscles." I thrust my tail fin down beneath the waves, then scooped up some water and splashed it over the boy to prove my point.

"Yeah, well, we don't spend enough time in the sea to need a tail. We're built for land," he explained, shaking the water from his sandy hair. He looked up and away for a moment, his mouth twisting in thought. "Monkeys have tails, though, and they don't swim. Maybe we could have that kind of tail. That'd be so cool!" Another grin broke out on his moon-round face.

Who or what monkeys were I had no idea, but I didn't care. I didn't want knowledge from the boy, I wanted the type of bond I'd only ever seen from afar. For the first time in my life, my desire to learn was outweighed by my desire to love.

"I've seen you on land, and you're not really fast up there either," I teased, nudging my elbow into his side.

"Faster than you, I bet. You'd just flop around like a big fish!" he exclaimed, collapsing into fits of giggles at the image.

I didn't mind the boy laughing at me, because I pitied him. How heartless the Gods must be to play this cruel joke on humankind. To give life to a body without purpose—a body destined to struggle both through water and over land, never to feel the freedom of perfect design. I am happy to trade his mild superiority on land for my unmatched power in the sea.

Later, as he swam clumsily back to the shore, I watched as each half of his tail broke the waves and then plunged back beneath, one at a time. I laughed and shook my head. How could he not feel the inefficiency of that? How did he not miss his tail fin? He could, with time and a little bit of innovation, learn to swim like me. We could live together, here in the cove, away from the cruelty of intolerances that I'm sure he must have experienced just like me. Just the two of us—two beings who belong nowhere but together.

I began to formulate a plan.

The sun is masked by grey this afternoon, and I fear he will not come to me. I sit on my rock and gaze out over the cloudy seas towards the shadowy beach, willing him hither. Just as I am about to give up, I see him break free of the stubby, kelp-like plants that border the beach and barrel towards the shore, arms and legs flailing just as gracelessly on sand as they do in water. I laugh as I watch him and remember his words of being built for land.

This time, as he nears me, I swim out to meet him. I reach him and he stops short, breathing heavily with exertion.

"Hey, Mer. What's up? Why are you out here?"

I grin at him. "I have a present for you, boy."

His face lights up. "Really? Cool! Thanks Mer, you're so cool!" His smile falters as his mouth dips underwater and he quickly reappears, spitting salt. "Ugh. Please, can we get to the cave first?"

"Oh, you will get to so many more places than just the cave! You will get to coral palaces, and kelp forests, and cities of rock and shell. And you will get there fast and free, just like me!" I cry, before diving beneath the waves. I laugh to myself as I see his little white limbs sweeping circles in his desperation to stay afloat. How strange, to keep your head above water at all times. These poor land creatures have such fear of the sea. It is too much of a mystery to them, but mysteries exist to be explored!

I hear his muffled voice calling for me as I swim towards his broken tail, pulling the length of kelp rope towards me. Around and around his legs I swim, wrapping them tightly together. He screams with laughter above me, so full of joy as he discovers how good it feels to be whole again. His hands grab at my skin and my scales to bring my face to his and kiss me with thanks. Oh, the fun we will have together!

At the end of his new tail I wrap the kelp around two huge, flat shells—poor imitations of my glorious tail fin, but they will do—then tie the rope off in a pretty little bow. The boy is thrashing and flailing now, trying to discover exactly how this new body works. I think he may be scared, but exploring new mysteries is supposed to be scary! I remember the first time I saw the boy. Oh, how he terrified me! A monster with no tail and four arms, like two Merfolk cut in half and stuck together.

The boy finally braves the deep grey sea and lowers his head into the depths. I knew he had the courage!

Swim! I call excitedly to him, mind to mind now that we are in the depths. You will find it so much easier now. Swim!

His eyes are round with excitement and his lips are stretched in a wide O of joyful surprise. Bubbles of laughter escape his lips and rise to the surface, the final breath of land disappearing as he readies himself to take his first breath of sea. I laugh heartily as I watch his poor tail control. Oh, he is like a newborn!

I swim beneath him and grab his new tail, trying to show him how to move it, but it flails wildly beneath my grasp. So proud is this boy—too proud for my help!

His nails scratch my arms as he grabs at them, pulling me closer as his big bulging eyes stare imploringly into my own. He is trying to speak with his mouth, trying to communicate something desperate.

What is it, boy? I call to him. Speak with your mind!

He spasms, he chokes, he screams seawater. But then, all is still. His slack mouth, his limp arms, his new tail. All begin to sink.

I have made a terrible mistake.

I wrap the boy in my arms and whip my tail through the water harder than I ever have before, powering up through the depths towards the grey light above. I burst through the waves and swim to the rock, the boy hanging limply in my grasp, his arms and kelp tail trailing lifelessly behind us in the slipstream.

I throw him onto the rock and wait for him to recover from his exertion. I watch for the rising and falling of his breath, but his body is still. The drops of water on his pale chest are motionless fragments of the grey sky above. His eyes do not move, they just stare blankly upwards into space.

I am cold with dread, shivering in the chill air. I don't understand. What went wrong? The tail should have made it easier, better. The tail should have made him faster, stronger. I built him for the sea! I don't understand. I built him for the sea.

Over the soft rolling of the waves, I hear a voice.

"Ben!"

It comes from the beach, where a man and a woman move along the shoreline, their broken tails splitting and coming together and splitting again in unison.

"Ben!" they call.

I look at the boy's still form. I lay my hand on his chest, now white as bleached bones. The green of the kelp tail is a dark shadow against his skin. His star-filled eyes are blue. His lips are bluer.

"Ben!" they call desperately.

I scoop Ben's limp form in my arms, slide into the sea, and carry him down into the darkness.

TOBY'S SERPENT

K. M. CAMPBELL

Toby held his blanket tight, trying to keep the endless cold from sinking deeper into his bones. On nights like this he felt much older than his forty-two years, yet he still yearned for his mother's protective comfort. The blanket was thin and blue with a baseball team emblazoned on the corners. It was old now, at least thirty years. He kept it close since it was all he had left of his extended family other than strangled, confused memories—the angry grandfather, the outspoken aunties, and the endless, pointless drinking. Perhaps they were dead now. Or perhaps they might welcome him home with lots of food. Toby loved the comfort of food. Then the words of the jumpy little councilor interfered, claiming that family were not always good for Toby's mental health. Toby knew he was an embarrassment. He sighed, his breath coming out in a fog that he instinctively waved away.

The cold had become unbearable. He keyed the engine, glancing at the digital clock. Just five minutes with the heater, that should be enough to warm up and escape into sleep. All too soon he flicked the engine off, still shivering but sleepy now, Toby turned his broken mind to the next task. It was time to head up north where it didn't snow, and he would need his dead mother to guide him.

He hated going so close to his family, not that he had ever seen them while he camped in the bush. His mother had warned him that they were monsters. Toby knew all about monsters; one tailed him ceaselessly. It hid in damp places, slobbering for Toby's soul, determined to suck his poor hurt brain right out of his aching skull.

Before even realizing he had slept he awoke with a start, heart beating hard, making him rub his vast chest. Cold sweat beaded his body.

He started the car, cringing at the muffler that was close to collapse, grateful for the rattling heater that he enjoyed for five blissful minutes. He would get moving soon but he had to be careful; he held no driver's license and had found this car on the side of the road, keys and all. Toby decided it was a gift from God and had taken it. Only God decided who got gifts of luck, and you had to be very, very good. Toby worked so hard to be good. God *had* to send him to heaven.

There were gold coins in the ash tray. Toby licked his lips, imagining a McDonald's burger. He checked the gas needle. It was still on half full, a problem for further down the road.

He wanted to investigate the McDonald's playground, which was a big old airplane parked right next door to the restaurant. But he had learned the hard way that he was unwelcome around children. The government would put him into care again, and he refused to live with weirdos who stole his food money, who cried and screamed and shit on the floor. Toby knew he wasn't normal but he wasn't *that* crazy, and there was no middle ground he could live with.

It was still too early for McDonald's. The drive thru would only offer muffins and dirty brown coffee while Toby needed a burger. They always made him feel better. He rubbed his tears away as he drove to the waterfront to wait, sliding down low in his seat so no one would tell on him. It was a risk being so close to water, but Toby had been safe for long months now. A light fog had settled over the lake. Toby was certain it was really an ocean and no one could explain the size in a satisfying manner, so he stubbornly called it the Sea of Islands. Today grey waves broke on the shoreline. The biting wind howled around the car and loosened the muffler further. He imagined the monster rising from that maelstrom, that hateful, hurtful serpent, pointing a claw and beckoning him into an icy embrace.

The lake and hunger made Toby miserable. His stomach hurt. He couldn't forage since the muffler made him too noticeable and the cold kept him from walking. He'd been finding it difficult to breathe lately, but was too scared of doctors to find out why. Doctors always wanted to send him into 'respite,' which Toby knew was a fancy name for 'lock up with the crazies,' His weight had gone up with his city scavenging; his shirts were sure tighter around the middle, but he got up each day and watched the sun set most nights with a sense of calm acceptance.

Unable to feel his toes, he flicked the engine back into life just as the predawn light gave way to the sun. It peeped over the hills and began spreading orange fingers of warmth across Toby's world. This was the worst time, when the vision of warmth only intensified the feeling of cold.

His eyelids felt heavy as he tried to focus on the gas needle, which never shifted.

Movement caught his attention, and the serpent rose near the center of the lake, almost unnoticed amid the waves. The miserable creature was big but too far away to see Toby, who only relaxed when the black monster sunk back beneath the choppy, dark water.

The sun was high in the sky when something woke him again. It was the serpent, rising from the water right in front of the car.

Toby had been found.

He bit down a scream and covered his head with the blanket, his vision dancing with spots and his chest thudding erratically. He coughed and a huge wad of phlegm landed on his chest. More followed but he managed to swallow, gagging as it slid down his throat like one of the huge shellfish his angry grandfather used to leave in hessian sacks on the doorstep.

As usual, the serpent's bright blue eyes were bulging in rage yet Toby knew if he concentrated on nothing, the serpent would lose the link and look elsewhere. The serpent was always look, look, looking and it was impossible to stare him down. As a child Toby had tried and been left for dead, his head cracked like a sea egg, his existence discarded by a disconnected family, an embarrassed community, and a country hamstrung by impossible utopian ideals.

Returning slowly to McDonalds, so hungry now he thought he might be sick, Toby knew the muffler was attracting too much attention and so denied himself the anonymity of the drive thru and entered the restaurant, gasping at the cocoon of warmth and the heavily scented air.

Young workers studiously ignored Toby as he hobbled to the bathroom, his gammy left leg and weight making him ponderous. He needed to wash his hands and face before eating, and public plumbing was hard for the serpent to negotiate. So long as he was fast, Toby could have a good wash, and at McDonalds there was always free soap. His mother had raised him with manners and he never knowingly let her down over something as simple as hygiene.

Once he was back in line, he carefully counted out his coins. Unable to work out how much food the precious metal would give him he carefully placed it all onto the stainless counter and smiled, anxiety crawling up his spine and settling at the dent in his skull.

"How much food can I get with that?" he asked, working hard to lower his booming voice.

The teenage girl placed a tentative finger on the closest coin.

"I'll get the manager." She turned away, glaring back as if Toby might be ogling her skinny butt. She was deranged if she thought that. Toby didn't like girls or boys. He hated anything sexy; it gave him bad feelings in his stomach. Even the TV shows, magazine pictures, and roadside billboards made him uncomfortable. He hated everyone's obsession with skin and sexy stuff.

The manager arrived, a tall, skinny young man with greasy straight hair and terrible skin. He and Toby exchanged wide crocodile smiles of uncertainty.

"I just want to know how much food I can get with this much money. I'm not good at counting, but I'm real hungry."

"Oh, sure. I can help." He flicked an annoyed glance at the teenager who was busy scowling as she served a young mother and her grabby toddler whose pink tutu was almost in her armpits.

After several enjoyable moments where they discussed Toby's favorite topic, food, the nice man raced to fill his order.

"You sure you don't want a drink?" the nice man asked.

"Nah, I stay away from watery stuff. Dirty serpents are everywhere, even the Sea of Islands."

"Fair enough. I put a little bit extra in." The nice man grinned at the tray as if embarrassed.

"You don't have to do that," Toby said, eyes locked on the stack of cheese-burgers in their pretty yellow paper. "I don't like to be a burden."

"It's no burden. The owner of this place makes a fortune. A couple of burgers won't make a difference. Anyway, we throw tons away. Don't even think about it."

"You like working here?" Toby asked, desperate to be alone with the food but unable to end this human contact, the first kindness in days.

"I started on the floor, and after a few years they paid for me to get educated.

It sure ain't glamourous but it's a start. I wasn't good at school. You want me to ask about a job for you?"

"Nah, thanks. I'm heading up north, get away from this cold and that dirty serpent that's hiding in your sea."

"It sure don't look like a lake, it's so big. Those serpent rumors make the place a tourist trap, which works for me." His eyes clouded with worry. "I'd like to say it's all horseshit but I wouldn't go swimming in there. It just feels wrong. One night when I was walking on the sand, something came after me. I was wasted so musta made it up." But his grin didn't make it to his kind eyes.

"Oh, he's real as me. Just some people don't wanna look at him because he's so scary and angry. He hates the world for things that were done to him and makes the rest of us suffer for it. Like slugs and snails and puppy dog tails, he likes to squash all of it, good and bad."

As Toby took the tray the nice man chuckled, "Fair enough. Here, take a water bottle to wash it all down. It's got a lid so no serpents can sneak in or out."

Toby hesitated before taking the bottle, concluding the nice man was right, the cap made it safe. He felt embarrassed and grateful so turned away, intently focused on the heaving tray. Another young man was standing too close, and there was a heart stopping moment when the tray threatened to drop. His hands sure weren't working well these days.

A strong and youthful grip automatically righted the tray.

"Thank you. Thank you," Toby said with real feeling.

The replying grunt lifted Toby's hazel eyes to find an angry, dark brown glare, and without thinking Toby said, "You don't want to do it. These are good people who don't deserve your rage."

"Get out of the way, old man."

"I got some food we can share. You can even have my water for keeps. It's not opened so no germies." Toby smiled, wide and fake with fear. "We can talk. Thinking's easier when you got a full belly, you ever noticed that? Then you can decide."

"You got any sense in your ugly head, you'll walk out that door."

"You don't got to do it," Toby lamely finished. "You don't got to be all your family think."

"Fuck off."

And Toby stumbled to a booth instead of returning to his car, his mind quickly discarding the angry man with the nasty intention, and returning to his tray which was exploding with color and smell and comfort.

He was two huge bites into his first cheeseburger when the angry man slid into the seat across from him.

"Ya dumb old prick." But there was little menace in his tone now.

"I'm Toby. What's your name? Want a burger? They gave me a couple extra."

"That shit'll kill ya and my name don't matter. It's stupid, like my old lady. She was a bitch."

Toby sighed and saw his mother's reflection in the restaurant glass. "My mom's beautiful. A princess. She died when I was fifteen. The serpent did it. Shot her in the head 'cause she called the cops on him. She wanted to leave him and go back home to my nana's. Just me and her. It woulda been perfect. See, Nana was dying and Mom needed to make sure she was laid out proper. Make sure the land was cleaned up of all the spirits. But my mom liked those white fellas and attracted the old monsters. Those serpents can pop outta anywhere. You notice that?"

After a long pause the angry man smiled, bright and honest, before sliding lower into his vinyl seat as if embarrassed. "You're more messed up than me." But his eyes flickered with uncertainty. "I've heard about a serpent in that lake. It don't feel like a lake. It's too big. There's gotta be something in there. I thought I saw…" His jaw clenched and he refused to say anymore.

"You got a job?" Toby asked around a mouthful of burger that threatened to make him weep with its perfection. "They got some jobs going here."

"What loser works at McDonalds?"

"It's a job. Beats living in the jails or in the government care."

"Government." The angry man spat. "You live on the streets. Don't ya?"

"Sometimes. I don't want the child service people to find me."

"Child services? Holy shit, old man. You got to be in your fifties. I think there's a whole different service for you now. Ain't you got no family to take you in?"

"Nah, the serpent scared everyone away. They was angry at Mom, said it were her own damn fault."

"Let me guess, the serpent's your stepdad?"

Eyes widening, Toby nodded. "Sometimes. Mostly. I don't ever say his name."

"What happened to your real old man?"

"He went over the yellow brick road to Oz for work, never came back. Mom got married real quick after that. She was beautiful. A princess. She got shot in the head by the serpent. He was still just a man then. He made that dirty gun wink right at me too. See this?" Toby parted his thick black hair, showing the deep depression. "Serpent bit me, but didn't get a good enough grip. He took me out to the garden shed when mom was at work, busted me up real good. But I'm still here and Mom called the cops. She picked me over that serpent. Not many moms do that, eh?"

A long pause again. Toby didn't understand the silence and so pushed a burger toward the angry man, nodding and smiling at the stunned expression.

"S'pose your serpent went and blew his own brains out?"

"Hell, no. He got sprayed in the face by the skinny girl policeman. I was bleeding and trying to go to sleep, but the skinny girl policeman told me to stay awake so I saw it all. Man, that big ole policeman with all the tattoos round his big arms, he beat that dirty serpent good after he got the gun off him. I thought that if I never woke up again I'd be in heaven like a happy ole chappy."

"He's still alive?"

"He visits me all the time. Looks like a serpent but I can see it in his eyes. Still wanting to hurt me 'cause I got away and was supposed to be his sacrifice to his evil god. If you see him, you promise me you'll run for your life." Toby stopped eating then and stared hard at the angry man. "Promise!"

"All right, shit, calm down. I promise, if I ever see a serpent I'll run like fuck." He paused, staring at the bawling toddler in her pink tutu who was now grabbing for her happy meal toy. "You need a ride or something? You heading to the city?"

"No way. Me and Mom hate that dirty big dump. I'm going further up, near Mom's grave, and Nana's. It's our land. She was beautiful. A princess. She's dead. Got shot in the head by my serpent 'cause she loved me more than him."

"So you need a ride up there? I've got nowhere else to go."

"Nah, I've got a ride. And you can't stay with me or the serpent will eat your soul right outta your heart. I've gotta travel alone. Get back to Mom. She was beautiful. A princess but she's dead now and I'm just trying to outrun my serpent."

"Yeah, yeah. You said that. I guess you'd get real annoying." He sighed and rubbed tired eyes. "I guess we all got a monster chasing us. You got money?"

"My mom sorts it all, makes sure I get where I'm meant to be, right at the proper time. She's looking after me cause the serpent can't touch her now. Only me."

"You know what? I hope you stare him down one day and blow *his* brains out. I'm so fucking sick of angry…" His lips pursed and he stared into space.

"Then he'd be trying to get Mom. It's better he follows me not her. She was beautiful, a…"

"Yeah, yeah, I know. She was a beautiful princess." He stood to go.

"You gonna ask about a job?"

"Not here. Maybe I'll go south, get away from this fucking mess."

"You shouldn't be swearing all the time, your mom might wash your mouth out with soap. Besides, life ain't so bad, it's short and other than the serpent, it's a beautiful one-shot thing."

"I can't tell if you're a genius or a fucking lunatic. Here, look after this for me." He glanced around and slid a heavy handgun onto Toby's tray. "You got a better chance of getting your problems solved with it than me. Go find your serpent. I'm done. I ain't going to prison and I ain't waiting here to die. I'm gonna find a life, and like you, I'm gonna do it alone."

Snatching the gun, Toby knew immediately that this was dangerous. He hated guns but he liked the nice man at the counter who had given him free burgers. He didn't want him to have a big dent in his head too, so he pushed the horrible cold thing into his dirty underwear and eyed the rubbish bin, certain he would remember to wrap it in burger paper and drop it into the nothingness that lived inside bins. "Alone's only good if you're getting chased by the serpent."

"So go home to your mom's family. Ain't our people always talking bullshit about family and solidarity? I ain't never seen no benefits from my skin color."

Toby laughed. "You kidding? Mom was a princess, a beautiful princess and they still hated her. She warned me about what they'd do to me. That a prince can't be messed up in the head or half-blood. It won't look good to the government to get our land back."

"I thought your mom died when you got shot?"

"She talks to me from heaven."

"Oh, sure. Fucking government ain't giving nothing to likes of us anyway."

"Yeah, government." Toby had no idea what that really meant but didn't want to sound stupid by asking. He was full now, and tired. He had slept late in the car and it must be after midday now. Toby wanted to get some distance from the cold and that freshwater sea where the serpent waited.

"See ya, old man. Hope you kill that serpent one day soon."

"You made the right decision." Toby grinned around another mouthful of burger. "There's a nice boy here what didn't deserve to be shot in the head."

"It ain't a real gun." The angry man chuckled, his smile showing his youth and raw beauty. "But it sure looks like it, huh?"

He sauntered away and Toby knew he should feel pleased the gun was fake, but he just didn't. It sat like a brick in his sweatpants, heavy and obvious, and Toby wanted it gone. As the angry man disappeared, Toby's anxiety ratcheted up. That dirty old serpent liked guns.

Trying to focus on eating didn't work. He wasn't hungry anymore, but he wanted a takeaway bag for his leftovers. If he asked for two bags he could put the gun in one and no one would ever find it. But each time he tried to move someone walked by, kids and their tired parents, groups of teenagers with saggy jeans and spiked hair. The place was full of roaming staff, clearing and cleaning, bored or disappointed.

Without warning a tray dropped and Toby leapt to his feet, crying out.

The gun clattered to the tiled floor.

There was a quiet moment when all heads turned, where people absorbed what lay on the floor and the dirty old man that hovered above it, wide eyed and crazed, snot and food down the front of his filthy clothes, a huge dent on the right side of his head that marked him as different.

The spell broke like a balloon and noise exploded all around. Toby's gaze flicked to the child in the pink tutu that had cried since entering, her cheeks flaming with anger or illness. Now she screamed for her dropped toy on the pristine floor.

Seeing the gun lying there, Toby imagined the serpent aiming it at that indignant little girl and letting it wink. That nasty old monster would enjoy it unless Toby got rid of it fast.

Unable to leave the leftover food behind he stuffed two burgers down his shirt front, his chest heaving with fear and indigestion and something much deeper. He stooped low to snatch the gun, holding it by the winking barrel with his fingertips, like it was a tiny serpent that might bite. He dropped it onto his tray, terrified it would cough and wink all by itself.

As voices began to hurl nasty words at increasing volumes, Toby pushed the tray past the silver barrier and into the rubbish abyss, satisfied at the thud as the gun blended with the other trash. Shivering with relief, he hoped the serpent would chase that gun down into the yawning nothingness and be trapped there forever.

"Nasty old blue eyes," Toby muttered as he hobbled outside, not realizing he still clasped the water bottle until he had to fish his car key from a pocket.

People were following, cursing and holding phones at him. Toby didn't want their phones so kept his head down and locked the door. The car took too long to cough to life and Toby reversed too fast, slamming into parked cars behind him.

Fat tears trailed his face as he hit the speed bump. His muffler finally dropped away. The noise was tremendous, growling and thudding right along with Toby's chest as he burst onto the road, causing traffic to stall and honk. All he could concentrate on was escaping and hiding until his mom told him what to do next.

In his confusion he turned left instead of right, heading him back down south. It took him a long while before he relaxed enough to realize his mistake. By the time he returned to the Sea of Island's shoreline, the serpent was rearing with excitement, keeping pace with the car, slicing in and out of the water like Moby Dick in the book Toby's mom used to read him. Toby glanced at the creature every few seconds, refusing to meet those dirty blue eyes. He gripped the steering wheel hard, expecting the nasty old serpent to leap from the water and force him off the road. Police sirens were screaming, so many that Toby didn't know from which direction. He focused, grateful that all eyes were turned to the McDonald's airplane playground and not his bellowing car.

Soon the engine began coughing once more. Toby tapped the gas meter, which remained stubbornly at the half full mark. Like Toby, the needle was broken.

Desperate, knowing the serpent and the police were close, Toby turned down a narrow dirt track that would be overrun with foliage by spring. He just needed time to sleep and calm down. Then his mom would find a way for him to keep going north.

As Toby emerged into a green paddock, a rainbow pointed to an aged barn. He whimpered at how pretty it was, how safe it all looked. A tune came to him, one his mother often whispered about rainbows and their colors. He couldn't remember the words and hit a palm to his forehead.

"Stupid, dumb brain!" he cried. "Think, you dumb brain!"

He pulled up to the barn, almost driving into the doors in his urgency to hide. Stumbling from the car, he found the double doors unlocked and pulled them wide, certain the serpent had found a way to escape water and would be waiting in the dark. But there was nothing, only an old barn with huge round hay bales packed at the rear. Toby drove in, then imagining he might need to escape, he pulled forward and carefully backed in. It took all his concentration, and even so his plastic rear bumper jammed hard against the wall of hay. Finally satisfied, he flicked the car into silence and rushed to close the barn doors, his chest as tightly packed as the car, a dull pain streaking down one arm.

After long minutes, Toby pressed an ear to a sun warmed wall and concluded he was safe.

"Thanks, Mom," he whispered, but not too loudly in case the serpent was listening for him. He imagined his mom smiling, and he looked forward to shaking free of this cumbersome life and returning to her side. It would be such a relief. He had once tried to hasten God's work and end his own life, only to be bluntly told by a stern white man at the hospital that if he succeeded, he would go to Hell. Toby's mom was in Heaven not Hell, so Toby would just have to be patient and endure.

Sleepy now, he returned to the car. The barn was warm. He would be happy here for a night. Tomorrow he would walk back to the road, poke his thumb out and find a ride up north.

He tried hard not to snooze during the day, knowing it would leave him wakeful in the scary darkness of night. Instead he inspected every corner of the barn, finding mice and abandoned bird nests. It felt important to find things that no one else would ever know of. Toby felt safe. As the sun set and the temperature dropped he snuggled into the car, munching the final hamburger and imagining a ride in a warm modern car all the way to his nana's place.

He awoke with a start in the thick end of night, instantly knowing the serpent was in the car—that cloying, fishy scent, the audible slide of his forked tongue scenting the air. Toby threw the door wide, flicking the overhead light to life and exposing those hateful blue eyes as the serpent arose from the open water bottle. Had Toby not ensured the lid was shut tight? Was he that stupid?

Using all his courage, Toby thought of nothing and fumbled for the lid, grinding it down. But the serpent was strong and the lid would not find the right spot to close. Panic burst out of Toby and he screamed, unthinkingly jamming the serpent into his mouth to stop that hissing sound. As the serpent's needle-sharp fangs sank into Toby's tongue, the gristly head came off in one deft nip of Toby's front teeth. The bottle continued to writhe and jump as the serpent's headless body slid back inside.

Dry retching, Toby held the car door for support and vomited all over the barn's dirt floor. The serpent glared up at him, the blues eyes wide and finally, blessedly very dead.

Wiping his mouth Toby tossed the bottle with the lifeless body as far into the back of the barn as he could. "Find that, you dirty ole bird." He sobbed, wiping his mouth and eyes again and again with one heavy forearm.

It was cold now, and Toby was shivering. "I'm tired and freezing, Mom. Can I turn the heater on for a little while? I'm not going to use the petrol tomorrow anyhow."

Sure, baby. You did real good.

"Did I kill him for real this time?"

It doesn't matter. You get warm and I'll hold you till you get to sleep.

"Thanks, Mom. I'll get on the road tomorrow. Promise."

You are a dream. You don't know how much I love you, my beautiful prince.

"Thanks, Mom. I miss you."

Not long now.

Flicking the car to life and switching the heater on high for the final time, Toby felt his mother's warm embrace surround him. "I love you, Mom."

It was several weeks before Toby's body was found. The police called it suicide by carbon monoxide poisoning, but it no longer mattered. Toby and his mother were finally free of the serpent.

The End

THE ASSOCIATION OF FORGOTTEN GHOULIES, GHOSTIES, LONG LEGGEDY BEASTIES, AND OTHER THINGS THAT GO BUMP IN THE NIGHT

ELIZABETH DAVIS

"The Association of Forgotten Ghoulies, Ghosties, Long Leggedy Beasties" proclaimed the tired banner drooping from the ceiling, one end secured with failing masking tape. Below the block letters someone had scribbled in marker, "And Other Things That Go Bump in The Night." And someone—or thing—had scratched in the lower right-hand corner, "Southwest Ohio Chapter." I watched to see if it would fall—poor entertainment, but better than staring at the ragged "Hang in There" posters on the cinderblock walls. Beneath the end that threatened to fall, a wobbly folding table held a pile of empty pop cans and a donut box with a lonely sour cream donut and the crumbled remains of another. An over-filled trash can threatened to burst. One of the overhead lights flickered incessantly, but the rest shone with cruel fluorescent brightness. Far away, an elevator squealed.

We sat on rickety folding chairs set in something like a circle, all the losers of the supernatural world—and me. I wasn't sure how I had gotten here, or why I was there, or who had slapped the sticker nametag on me. "The Lurker," it said. That wasn't right, not really, but perhaps good enough for here—wherever here was.

No room like this existed in my apartment complex. They were run down, but this looked like something squirreled away at the back of a community

YMCA. I had no reason to stay, but confusion and morbid curiosity kept me in my wobbly, too narrow seat.

And that damn snake was still talking.

"They used to worship me as a god, saw me streaking across the sky," it hissed. Only the head fit on the chair. The rest of its long green body, stinking of mud and grass, curled outside the chairs. "Now the closest thing I have to worshipers are used-up Yellow Springs hippies who try to bury stuff in my body."

"That's at least something," soothed the Facilitator, an old man with a beard that cascaded over his plaid shirt, as thick as his Scottish brogue. He looked and sounded as if he had walked straight out of one of the old sailing movies that played endlessly in Mrs. John's apartment, while I watched from the shadows in the corner.

"It's just not the same," the Thing Under the Trees rumbled. I glanced over at —something that bears dreamed of in their winter hibernation, and woke shivering. Its teeth and claws were the orientating North in that massive body, and all else was darkness and fur. It stank of old blood.

The Snake God opened its mouth wide enough to show the egg in its throat, and started to hiss—but the Facilitator placed his finger on his lips and gestured back to the Thing Under the Trees. No talking out of turn.

"They still fear the woods, tell stories, see me in the black bears—but it's not the same. They don't call me by name. They don't even know the language—my people are scattered to the west, their culture buried in museums." A large sigh shook its mass. "And the forests are so small and fenced away from the sprawling ant cities that humans live in."

"Like my mound." The Snake God slithered over to the Thing Under The Trees, wrapping its green body around the undefined mass with a strength that would have killed the rest of us. The Thing Under The Trees reached up with a paw to pat the coiled body.

I looked away from them, leaving those bygones to their memories. They would never understand how to live in the ant cities, how to thrive in forgotten corners. My body, slender and elongated as the shadows I lived in, was not as strong as theirs. But I had survived. I would always survive, always have my place. Apartments might be remodeled, even rebuilt, but they never disappeared entirely.

"Hah." That was the Canal Monstrosity, a definite her in her fierceness, snorted.

Strong webbed legs gripped the seat as her wide mouth opened, allowing a pythonic tongue to spear the last donut, all the while spritzing herself with a plastic bottle. Her body, mottled in shades of green, blue and yellow, was a colorful contrast to my deep shadows. "Even if they don't remember you properly, at least they still fear you. They never turned against you. You were forgotten by time, I was erased."

"I don't think we have heard this story," the Facilitator encouraged.

She spritzed her tail. "It was after my heyday, when I had climbed boats and hunted the unwise and restless. After the canal was rendered obsolete by railroads. But there were still boats to prey on—until The Great Flood. One great man, determined to remake Dayton in his image, who had listened to the stories from the yellow papers and drunk boatmen, he blamed me for the flood. He thought I had used my powers over the canal to try to infest the city with my young." She drew a deep calming breath, inflating her vocal bag, then exhaling with a slow croak. "He spent twenty-three years campaigning to destroy my home, then filling it in with concrete, and calling the road after himself. It's a good thing my young escaped with the flood. All that is left of their home is a road with a bunch of stupid boat statues beside it."

I wondered if I had seen her children's splashes in the muddy river, swollen by summer rain and winter snow, the one that my apartment complex overlooked. A river I had watched while waiting for the sun to set, and the night workers to nervously walk through the dim lights of the parking lot.

Her mistake was in letting herself become too well known, attracting the attention of the rich and powerful. That's why I was careful, looking for those who were isolated, kids coming home to an empty apartment, their parents still hours in returning. The lonely nights of the young, tired from working all day, too proud to admit their fear as they checked over their shoulder, seeing my shadow in the corner of their eyes. The old, early in the morning, their years of mourning clouding their vision until I closed in.

The Coachman cut in, his voice slow and rumbling. "He wouldn't have dared if it wasn't for those damned railroads, running on the fires of hell themselves. It's so called progress that has done us all in." He brushed the front of his old-fashioned suit, whose period varied with every glance. Fiery red eyes gleamed from under the brim of his hat, the same eyes on the horse behind him—a beast who stood nearly as tale as the Canal Monstrosity, beautiful with a thick mane and sharp white teeth. It was still tied to an overwrought black coach, lit in ghostly blue lights.

Somehow all of this fit behind the Coachman's small plastic chair.

"My name used to be whispered with the greats," he drawled. "The skeletal bride whose racking touch steals youth. Dullahan carrying a jack-o-lantern in their grasp, dragging doom in their wake." His horse looked over at us, giving his hat a nuzzle. "Ladies would faint at the sight of my covered bridge, as the daylight set behind it. The pious who crossed themselves before turning away. The curious who would tread on my bridge with hesitating steps, waiting for me to appear next to them. Best of all was the foolish young men who would come from leagues around, just to race me." He gave his horse a loving pat. "We never lost. Not even when they come with those early sputtering automobiles, convinced that their science would save them."

"But..." He snarled. His horse startled, sending echoes of hooves and carriage wheels around the room. I shrank back into my chair, let the seat shadows swallow me. I dislike loud noises as much as I hate bright lights.

"They could never match us in speed, but those blasted machines took over the road. And they decided that my bridge wasn't good enough. Wasn't wide enough for their bulky monstrosities to drive through, not strong enough for their rubber and chrome, and not beautiful enough to be preserved as historic." He spat on the floor, a steaming plug that flamed. "So called progress is why we are sitting here now."

I was safe. Apartments were always needed, no matter what else that changed—no matter how often they would need to gut the rooms, they were always mine.

"Not all of us," came from the soft voiced Satan's Spawn. She was small, and had the delicate carapace of an insect interspersed with her fur. She sipped the last remains of a pop with her proboscis, watching us in her multifaceted eyes. "Lurker, you're the youngest of us. Have you ever heard of New Burlington?"

The room echoed with the sound of squeaking chairs and dragged chair legs as the rest of them looked at me. I felt my body start to unspool down the chair into the shadows beneath, stretching out to the shadowy corners, where I could climb to the rafters.

"No, I haven't," I said in my whisper voice.

"Not surprised," Satan's Spawn replied, drawing the attention from me. "We were never as popular as Moonville and Helltown. But still, we were known, even as the town emptied out. It never mattered to me as our houses decayed and business moved away. That their stories changed from a witch's curse to a satanic cult lurking among the ruins. I remember the kids who came looking for the ritual circles. It seemed to be the more that New Burlington marched to a ghost town, we were not forgotten." Her antenna quivered and her large foxlike ears turned to catch every nuance of her dramatic silence. "That's why I didn't worry when the last of the townspeople left, those who fought the longest with their lights. I thought without them, there would be nothing keeping foolish thrill-seekers away. Then the flood came." Her leathery wings flopped down, defeated. "There's nothing left but foundations. Sometimes people find them and remember there once was a town, that it had a name, but not me."

There as a moment of awkward silence, as the Canal Monstrosity offered Satan's Spawn what was left of her soda.

The Facilitator cleared his throat. "Lurker, I know it's your first time here, but we would love to hear your story."

"My story?" I exploded in a chorus of sibilant whispers. "I'm not like the rest of you. I'm not forgotten. Everyone in my apartments have felt my touch on their skin, have seen me only in between the flickers of their lightbulbs. For everyone that leaves, there are always neighbors left behind to initiate the new. I am known."

The rest of the group looked away, finding sudden interest in the banners or in their crumb filled napkins. The Facilitator placed a hand on my chair, filling my space with the scent of pipe tobacco. "Don't you remember the tornado?"

ART AND DEATH

PHILLIP T. STEPHENS

I've never experienced vertigo until now, as I gaze upon the Marquette Ore Docks from Dr. Turmella's balcony, from the county's highest peak. The cedars and red pine sweep outward for miles until the land breaks against the water and the pier slices like a dagger into Lake Superior. Blankets of snow whitewash the trees, the ground, as pale as the bone-white winter sky. A boat peels away from the dock, hull rusted reddish brown—a drop of blood drifting with the sluggish current.

A mist collects at the horizon—blacker than the tour guide's dress—portending approaching storms.

The guide's dress wraps her bosom, clings to her hips and to short calves that flow into spool heels with laces, the shoes of librarians and school teachers. She leads us inside and through the den. Mounted stags, boar, and bear overlook solid oak bookshelves that display tomes so ancient the odor of mildew lingers in every corner. Gas lamps, skylights and floor-to-ceiling windows light the room. On a waterfall buffet rests a hand-cranked Victrola.

The cloying scent of fresh-cut jasmine flowers clings to the room.

The museum director zips past. A small fellow with a feminine jawline wearing a pin-striped navy suit with jet black hair—razor cut and slicked back. He puffs on his cigarette like a charging train. His photo's next to the entrance, but she introduces him anyway.

The rubes check their watches, bounce from foot to foot, jiggle keys in their pockets. They don't want introductions; they want to see the lab where the good doctor displayed the trophies of his surgical experiments—children's corpses preserved in alcohol and formaldehyde.

Experiments, if you listen to the rumors, to cure the children of the obscenely rich.

"Dr. Turmella's architectural designs were as famous as his surgical prowess. He designed the neurology wing at Detroit General Hospital, and the London Museum of Occult Antiquities. Many hold him in the same esteem as Frank Lloyd Wright."

When we turn the corner into the portrait gallery, her voice fades. My eyes turn, everyone's eyes turn to the life-sized oil of his daughter Paha. Her translucent white evening gown flows backward into the carpet, clings to curves a father should never paint. Bright red lips match the single red dancing shoe that extends past her gown. She raises her eyes to the skylight. An ebony cigarette holder bridges the tips of her lips and fingers. A portrait reproduced in art books and pulp crime rags—the heiress murdered by the father who painted her portrait.

The heiress who lives in the local folklore, a ghost who steals your children in the middle of the night when you turn out the lights and think they're safe and asleep in their beds. Like all folklore, the story changes every time it's told.

The painting of the girl overshadows the portrait to her right, the first portrait in the gallery. A middle-aged woman with a masculine face perched on a love seat, her nose buried in a book. A masculine face I recognize: my client's missing brother.

She burst into my office like a thunderclap, as ominous as the winter storm that rattled my windows. A wisp, as slight as the first spring sapling, her face hidden by a veil draped in layers from her pillbox hat. Even though her face was hidden, you knew her looks would slap you in the face. Slap you with a leather sap. A sap stuffed with lead and the dreams of angels.

A lightning bolt dimmed the lights. The flash in the window painted her in white and black like an Art Deco print. Thunderclaps shook window sills. It didn't matter. She filled the room with a soft white glow—white as her chiffon dress.

She tucked her heels under the chair, nudged her veil and slipped an ebony cigarette holder between tiny almond lips. Her ring was ebony too, with a triangle balanced on three arrows.

"Mr. Stickwell?"

I struck a match and held it to the tip of her black and gold Sobrane. "Call me Stick. Makes conversation easier. And shorter." The scent of tobacco blended with her jasmine cologne into a heady perfume.

She fished an envelope from a clutch purse the size of a comb, nudged it across the desk with an obsidian nail. I lifted the flap. A photo and two crisp thousand-dollar bills nestled in the fold.

The smoke from her cigarette spiraled toward the ceiling, serpentine and indolent.

I examined the photo. A sucker punch of a photo. Mid-forties male, bald with a Brylcreem combover and wire spectacles. The kind of guy who stops by a diner, orders tea—brewed, not iced, with lemon no sugar—and a green salad. No dressing.

I knew him from Hansome's, a low-rent dinner club in the mission district for guys the upper crust would never acknowledge on the sidewalk, much less join for dinner. Guys like me. But I hadn't seen Geist for months.

"His name's Paul Geist. He's forty-seven, a confirmed bachelor. You, of all people, know what I mean. No one cares he's gone but me."

"And your name is?"

"Not Geist."

She spoke with precision and practice, no jitters or hesitation. I didn't make her for a grieving sister, one that Geist never mentioned. (Then again, men don't join Hansome's to chat about work and family. We drop in for drinks, cigars, chess, and songs around the piano.)

"You won't find him in San Francisco, Mr. Stickwell. He's in Michigan. Worse than Michigan. The Upper Peninsula. He left last spring to renovate a tourist mansion in Marquette. Not a word since Halloween."

For all her femininity, she spoke with a man's cadence. Brisk, almost a bark.

I left the bills untouched. When a dish so hot she'll scorch the kitchen offers a second-rate dick that much dough, they plan to mix both in a bowl and bake us.

I sealed the bills and photo in the envelope, placed it in her fingers and apologized that I couldn't take her case. She left it on my desk. "I'll call your office for updates."

Three days later I stepped off the bus and into the seventh circle of desolation.

Michigan's Upper Peninsula. The only industries are mining, timber, and alcoholism. A bar on every block. Sometimes two.

Half a dick's job is pounding the pavement, but in midwinter Marquette there's no pavement to pound. Just a thick gray slush that soaks through your shoes, your socks, your pant cuffs. Avoid the slush, and snow spills into your collar from an overhang.

My suit is wrinkled and stained from the trip, and my overcoat is useless against Lake Superior's winds. I'd change, but Greyhound lost my bag in Milwaukee. My one stroke of luck—I carry my Minox camera and pen light in my overcoat pocket.

I check in with the local law. The desk sergeant leads me to a half-bagged detective who combs his hair with Crisco. He lobs my license and the photo across his desk. "Never heard of this Geist fellow, eh? Employer never reported him missing, and no sister called for sure."

I sort in my pockets for a Chesterfield, only to realize the snow soaked my smokes. "Could you check your files?"

He props his feet on his typing table, slips his hands into his pockets, and leans back. "You think we're the big city? People go missing. Nobody notices till the ice melts."

I ask the hotel clerk if Geist is still registered. "I can check for sure but don'tcha know we can't give ya information?" No one in Marquette speaks American, or even English. Everything's "ya sure," "for sure," "you betcha," and they punctuate every other sentence with "eh."

I fold a twenty into his pocket. He wears a checked suit and plaid bow tie. The shoulders are too broad and the sleeves too short. Like everyone in Marquette, Sears & Roebuck dictates his fashion sense.

I fold a second twenty. "His bill's up to date, but he's a no show since forever, eh?"

"I work for his sister. Could I see his room?" I fold a third twenty.

No, but he keeps the bribe.

The maid unlocks his room for five dollars.

I rifle through his drawers, the closet, under the bed. Behind his desk I find a hastily-sketched floor plan. Geist scribbled a question mark in the hall behind the administrative offices. But no other notes, no design plans, no architectural sketches.

I toss his suitcase on the bed and flip it open. Packed inside are a pair of gloves and three women's dresses—cocktail, full length evening gown, and housedress. Tucked underneath I find a peignoir and lingerie. Extra-extra-large. Sized for a man.

You might as well know. Sized for me. Stolen from my missing suitcase. Bullets loaded into a metaphoric gun, a gun cocked and aimed at my head.

You may have guessed why Geist and I frequented Hansome's. I've worn women's clothing since my father locked me in my mother's wardrobe. I'd walked in on him bouncing the bedsprings with Mrs. Thompson. The wardrobe and clothes inside bore my mother's scent, my only comfort while listening to my old man pounding my mom's best friend. I hid there every time he broke my mother's jaw and left me behind while he rushed her to the hospital. When they locked him away for killing her, I would cling to her dresses to remember her scent, her warmth, my few precious seconds of comfort in this life.

The bar serves the usual suspects—bourbon, blended, and rye.

I mention Geist when I order my drink. The bartender retrieves a dust-covered bottle of Bushmills from the back of the bottom shelf and splashes it into my glass. "Disappearing's a winter sport. Fall in the lake, pass out in the snow. Half the time, folks catch a bus to Florida and don't bother to leave a note." He leaves the bottle on the bar.

A miner at the end of the bar grabs his beer and sidles into the next stool. Iron dust packs his nails, coats the back of his neck. A hand-rolled cigarette burns his fingers. "This friend? West Coast fella, yah? The one fixing up the Turmella mansion?"

I nod and swallow my drink. Good thing I ordered it neat because it's already half water.

"Bad business that, you betcha. Missing tourists, missing kids, missing all kinds." He runs his finger across his lips like a zipper.

He leans closer. His breath smells of cheap beer and cheaper whiskey.

"No secret, all them kids Turmella killed to make his cures. Queer fella, for sure, like your friend. Don't deny it. Prissy missies. Then you got your daughter. Paha. Crazy parties. Sister of Dorothy. You catch me, eh?"

I caught him, had him dangling from my hook while I fished for a knife to cut the line.

"She was the business brains, him the doctor brains. Built those clinics all over creation to lock away loons. S'posed to cure them, but their parents want them locked away. See, you get crazy kids, people think maybe you crazy too. No one wants them home. Course the kids disappear too, for sure. Folks round here? Cry in their beer, boohoo, the county needs the coin. Whisper at home? Hooray. You betcha."

At first, I think he's referring to patients. He's not. "Both of 'em. Father. Daughter. Poof. Gone." He snaps his fingers. Half an inch of ash tumbles into his drink, but he doesn't notice. "Just like that. Empty clinic. No doctor, no daughter, no kids. Nothing but paintings. Nothing left but ghost stories. Old man or the daughter, depends on who tells 'em, kidnaps anyone who loses their way in a storm to keep the experiments going. Drunks, tourists, kids racing to get home before their parents discover they're gone."

He rolls a cigarette one-handed with Kite Papers and Tops tobacco. "County'd get more coin if they'd sell that building and all that art while people give a shit. Tours, those're chump change."

In the morning the hotel delivers my duds clean and pressed, and my shoes polished to a shine that would shame a marine. All that spit and shine do nothing to impress the city librarian. I might as well have approached her while clutching an open can of Sterno in a paper bag.

In her late forties, with a bun, knitting needle, and multiple layers of VO5, she's as welcoming as crime scene tape. When I ask her to point me to back issues of the local rag, she snaps, "We don't need another ghoul wasting space looking for stories teenagers trade around campfires."

Not that she should worry. Any sensational stories in Marquette never made it to the paper. After my third hour of drilling empty wells, a library assistant drops into the next chair. She slips a phone number under my finger.

The girl wears a plaid skirt with a man's vest and necktie. I'm certain she'd linger at the table, engage me with her doe-eyes and charm, but Mrs. Snotnose returns to the front desk and clears her throat.

The phone number leads me to a local historian—some would say gossip—E. Ikävä Airut, Esq., who writes monographs from his boardinghouse room and publishes himself. He must live on a small pension; I doubt he sells many books.

He brushes the pipe ash from his desk and shows me two of his labors of love. One printed in 1935, the other 1946, both detailing the sordid scandals of Dr. Georg Turmella and his daughter Paha. Both editions display her vignette on the front page, looks so striking Oscar Wilde would switch teams. Bobbed hair, razor cut and oiled. She sports a silk tuxedo. An ebony cigarette holder with a black cigarette extends from her lips to the tips of her long, slender figures.

Airut points to a band on Paha's ring finger, barely visible in the photograph. "That band bears the alchemical symbol for the aqua vitae, or water of life. Orthodox scholars claim the water of life was pure alcohol. More informed scholars know it represents the fountain of eternal life."

Turmella's clinic catered to two classes of children: children of wealthy clients, and castoffs and orphans. He experimented on the castoffs, claimed to cure the rich ones. No one missed the children who died. His clinics expanded and he needed more subjects. So he took them. Healthy children from Ishpeming, Skandia, Rock River.

I wonder how long it's been since Airut enjoyed a decent meal—something other than sardines and instant coffee. The neck of his knit sweater stretches to his shoulders and the sleeves tumble past his fingers. His pants fold across legs that look like broom handles.

He leans forward as if sharing confession. "Paha fared the worst. He molested her, maybe used her for his experiments. That explains her lesbianism and cross-dressing."

I nod as though I share his disgust.

"She hosted lavish, decadent parties. Notorious for the dykes and pillow biters. The old man routinely bribed cops and city officials to keep her reputation clean."

He spins into a diatribe on moral degradation. Blames deviants, homosexuals, and Jews for Hitler's rise to power.

He finally circles back to Turmella. "They disappeared in 1938. Both of them. The estate claims they sailed to Poland for a relief project and the Germans torpedoed their ship." He picks up his pipe, but his tobacco jar is empty. "They fled because the police were closing in."

Airut shows me photographs of four children who resemble the subjects of Turmella's famous character studies. Proof positive that Turmella murdered them. "Thirty-seven children. That's how many I can prove he killed."

He offers coffee. I'm not that desperate. I think his legs will break as he stumbles toward his coffee jar. "His ghost haunts that mansion. He lures unsuspecting tourists to their doom. Like the California fellow the estate hired to renovate."

"I thought it was the girl's ghost."

He drops the spoon next to the jar. "There's the legends and there's the facts. I write about facts."

I thank him and leave. Ghosts don't exist, except for the ghosts in our memory: The ghosts of those we wronged.

Do I think the spirit of a homicidal surgeon trapped and tortures Geist's ghost? No. But I'd like to find a file, a jacket, blueprints, some evidence that Geist worked for the estate before he disappeared. And I hope that scrap of evidence will lead me to Geist, or his body.

Which is why I slip away from the tour and hide in a utility closet until the staff locks the building. When I emerge into the moonlight that shines through the skylight, I notice the snow piling up the rafters and window sills. Tree branches batter the walls from the blizzard blowing through.

I switch on my map light and follow Geist's floor plan, stop first at the painting gallery to snap the character study of Geist. I brace my shoulders against the wall to hold my Minox steady, shoot with 100 ISO and a five second shutter. On the third shot, Paha's face shifts down, in my direction to study me with puzzled curiosity. My camera slips from my fingers and clatters across the floor.

I retrieve it and step backward into the lobby, convinced my nerves spooked me, then follow the fading arrows to the clinic and around the corner to a utility closet door. An innocuous door until you ask why they installed both a knob lock and jimmy proof deadbolt. I beat the rust and both locks in half an hour.

The door pops from the frame and dust billows past, covering my coat, my face, clinging to my hair. I paint the walls with my penlight. The door opens, not to a room or laboratory but an elevator cage, operated by hand pulleys, its moth-eaten ropes unraveling.

The joists resist, and rope fragments pop. The pen light between my teeth illuminates the lower chamber, a cellar hewn and shored from a cave that nature wants to reclaim. Snakes slither down the wall, scattering wolf spiders, jumping spiders, and a brown recluse. The chamber reeks of mildew, mold, decaying moss, decomposing rats and insects.

When I bump the rock floor, the ropes rip the skin from my fingers, and I tumble from the cage. A string of lights runs the length of the far wall, powered by a hand-cranked generator. A chorus of children's voices echoes, "Help us, save me, take me home." I see them strapped to bunk beds that line one wall, kicking and thrashing against their restraints.

But I blink and the image fades. Only rotting mattresses remain, soggy with the water that drips from the walls. Against the adjoining wall, a surgical cart displays a cranial saw, forceps, picks and hammers, trepanation drills and skull punches.

I pan the light across the room. An artist's easel rests in the center with a full view of the chamber. A fresh canvas rests on its shelf.

Someone sits in a wooden armchair next to a dispensing table. I shout, but only their wrist moves. A thick mass falls from the jacket cuff. A rat.

My companion is a desiccated corpse. Geist's. The state of the body surprises me. He should be messier, putrefying, his skin slipping.

I reach inside his jacket to feel for a wallet. I flip it open and shine the light on the plastic window. Geist's driver's license. I drop into a nearby chair. My light climbs the wall and illuminates a triangle over three radiating arrows carved into the stone.

If you ever want a lesson in irony, this is it.

Fingers brush my shoulder. A woman's fingers, with black nails. On her ring finger an ebony band with the water of life symbol. I turn to look back, but the fingers clasp around my ears and lock my head in place. The scent of jasmine and tobacco surrounds me.

"Surprise."

She runs a nail down my cheek. A tiny drop of blood splatters my lapel.

Paha's tux is custom-cut to every seductive curve. She straddles my lap and tugs my tie. "Your mother never taught you to dress. At least not in men's clothes."

I open my lips, but she seals them with a finger. "Don't speak. Give the curare time to take effect." She wiggles the nail that cut my cheek. The murder weapon. "Oops." Then she kisses me, a kiss that draws my soul into hers—long, lingering, addicting.

"Are you alive or a ghost?"

The last words I manage.

"The first time I saw you at the Hansom Club, I planned to lure you here with Geist. A ménage à trois of minds. He's so boring and you have so many levels of regret. A seven-layer cake of despair. Bitterness and buttercream."

She unwinds her legs, stretches, lights a Sobrane. "My father, if you could call him that, thought God cheated him when he made him male. Grandfather threatened to have him blacklisted from medical schools if he didn't marry. When mother delivered me instead of a male heir, my grandfather demanded a second try. Father cut off his penis and delivered it in a specimen jar."

She whispers, "Mother packed her bags and fled to California."

She cranks the generator. The lights reveal an open wardrobe with a white chiffon dress, a navy pinstripe suit, and a plaid skirt with a man's vest. "He never touched me. Couldn't. His one goal in life was to master the art of transmogrification: male to female, female to male. Medicine, alchemy, it mattered little. The children he kept for experiments were children like him—boys forced to be girls and girls forced to be boys. When his methods failed one subject, his interest turned to another. Never noticed they went missing, assumed they returned home."

She strikes a match. The flame highlights the angles in her face. "Grandfather tried to make me male." She touches the flame to her cigarette. "We hunted and fished, he taught me to play golf and bowl, bluff with a busted flush and ten thousand on the table. Dressed me as his grandson and paraded me as his protegee."

Paha leans her shoulder into the wall. Three smoke rings rise toward the ceiling. "I borrowed his taste in women and clothes. But his lust for hunting—that's in the genes." A recluse spider climbs onto her shoulder. She pierces it with her nail and drops it onto her tongue. "How anyone could believe a spineless panty-waist like my father could kill me baffles the mind."

I remain motionless, reduced to a mannequin by her potion. She kneels and slices my vein with her nail. A trough in the chair's arm funnels my blood to an urn.

A body bleeds out in minutes with an expert cut.

Paha mixes blood into the pigments on her palette. "Want to know an amazing secret about blood? It adds depth to reds, a slight desaturation that draws the eye's attention." She holds her pallet knife like a conductor's baton. "My father couldn't paint, either. All those character studies are mine. But they sold for ten times as much with his signature on the canvas."

She applies the paint with broad strokes. "He never discovered the secret of transmogrification. Or immortality." She taps her tooth with the brush barrel. "So easy to kill." She dips the brush into paint and dabs the canvas. "Like shooting a deer in a clearing."

If you take the tour, when you see my portrait in the gallery next to Paha's, please picture the real man and not the clown she painted. A clown in a woman's robe and fuzzy slippers with a red bulb nose, lopsided jaw, and a tear in the corner of his eye.

Did an urban legend survive me? Perhaps a cautionary tale of a cross-dressing San Francisco dick who cruised queer clubs and vanished in 1949? Doubtful. But I hope, when you see my portrait, that you see past the facade, the greasepaint, the wig, the bike horn in my hand, and think: *Here is a soul who lost his self-respect and the respect of his peers.* Ghosts don't dwell in the stories you share at campfires; you pass us on the sidewalks, in alleys, lobbies, and even the streets as you drive. You see past us, see through us, see only the world you imagine to be real.

BELOW THE WATER LINE

CRAIG CRAWFORD

There are worlds within worlds.

It wasn't a hard concept once I got past the crazy. I mean really, each of us lives in our own little world, occasionally coming into contact with others, perhaps sharing part of our world or being welcomed into others. I don't know why the physical world should be any different.

I'm a pretty grounded guy. I get up every morning, go to work in my little cubicle, occasionally go to lunch with the crowd, and just do my thing. I'm not shaking the rafters of the world. I shuffle papers, answer emails, and put in my eight hours. I don't live for the weekends—I do my job pretty well and while a lot of people would consider it boring, I don't mind it. At the end of the day I go home, grab some food, take Harley for a walk and settle in for a book or a show.

I've got a friend who's into the fringe side of things and he's always telling me about aliens and other creepy nonsense. I nod and listen, but I don't buy it. I mean, if there are aliens, real true aliens, then they're either here or they aren't, and it doesn't affect my life one way or another. I've never seen one, and really, I've never run across anything creepy in my life. I've gone hiking but I've never seen Bigfoot, never seen nor heard a ghost, and I haven't crossed paths with any monsters.

Still, I ran into an odd thing recently.

It was Spring Break week at the little university I work for. Most of the students were gone and a lot of the staff, too. Me, I never go anywhere. It's so expensive to fly, there are way too many people in the places I'd go, and really, I like the solitude. I find it relaxing to come into work, the halls empty, supervisors gone, faculty off on some excursion. Nobody hassles me and I can putter around at my cubicle.

I walked into work like I do every morning. I park at a lot about fifteen minutes away from my building. I get kudos for taking the exercise as others tell me how lazy they are and compliment me for being healthy. Hah. I'm not exactly physically fit, and thin is a word that hasn't been used to describe me since I was about five years old.

I like the walk because it takes me along the river running through town. It's always peaceful along the water, and as the seasons change, I catch sight of ducks and geese floating and talking at each other. Honestly, the walk helps me wake up in the morning.

On this particular morning, I happened to see a woman across the bank, strolling along a sidewalk. It's about a hundred yards across, and she was heading toward the same bridge I was. She wore purple hat, which snagged my attention from my usual mental wanderings. It was mid-March and still chilly in the early morning, so I wasn't surprised to see her sporting a longer jacket.

She followed the footpath under the bridge. All at once, she turned toward the river without slowing. I scanned the bank, thinking she'd seen ducks or geese and headed in for a closer look. She was a good distance ahead of me on the opposite bank, so it was hard to see what she'd seen; in fact, all I could see was that she didn't slow down.

Reaching the river's edge, she walked into the water.

At least it looked that way from my vantage point. My pace quickened as I tried to figure out what I was seeing. I remember looking up and down the bank, but there were no other people. Like I said, it was Spring Break, and there weren't many people who traveled this path at the best of times. I was alone aside from the woman herself, so I hurried over, thinking I was watching someone end it all.

Except something was odd. She was sinking down into the water. She didn't seem buoyant at all, but walked as if she was still on the path. At first, I wondered if I was the victim of an optical illusion; because of the distance and the terrain of the bank itself, maybe it only looked like she was walking into the river.

As I sped up, it became apparent that this was no illusion. She strode into the water, now half-submerged, seemingly impervious even though the water had to be freezing in the forty-degree weather. I stopped briefly as I approached the bridge, knowing I'd momentarily lose sight of her if I crossed. I watched until her head ducked below the surface, her purple hat the last bit of proof she'd ever been there.

I ran.

I'm not the most physically fit guy, and I was huffing and puffing to make it across the bridge. I had my phone in my pocket and I fumbled for it while I lumbered, balancing my lunch bag and trying to get eyes on the spot where she'd disappeared.

I scanned the water for any sign of her, but it wasn't pristine and clear like some mountain stream. There was plenty of runoff from the winter, and even on the best days I'd never been able to see to the bottom of it. Hurrying across and down a small set of steps, I ran toward the water, unlocking my phone to dial emergency.

I got within a few feet of the water's edge and stopped. Frantically I scanned the surface, focusing downstream when I noticed the current was strong around the bridge pilings. She had to have been swept away. Yet, she hadn't seemed disturbed by the wash of water, and she hadn't behaved like she'd been fighting the current.

The water was serene and smooth despite a few eddies swirling around the bridge beams. I hesitated. Did I see what I actually thought I saw? Had I somehow imagined it all? It was odd the way she'd appeared to just walk into the water, like she was taking the down escalator at a mall. I wished I'd seen more, but the distance had been too far to see any real details.

My finger poised at the send button to call the police. I scanned the river again, looking for some sign of a drowning. I knew enough to know she wouldn't immediately pop back to the surface once she'd drowned.

Looking down, I saw a shoe print in the soft mud. Smaller than my size twelve, it pressed into the mud, facing the river. Beyond the water the bank stretched out, and I could see a couple of feet down before the murk hid everything.

I thought I could see another print or at least and indentation.

Still I hesitated. It was one of those moments where you trust what you saw, yet can't quite believe it because it's so odd, with the rational part of your brain insisting it could only have been something mundane.

I stood there for several minutes, scanning the water, eyeing the footprint and unsure what to do.

Then something moved in the murk below.

It seemed like a dark shadow, but I caught a hint of white, like a large fish or a sunken chunk of ice. I couldn't make out the shape. I leaned forward, then realized whatever I viewed was coming to the surface.

Two people walked by. "Hey, guy, what are you looking at?"

I jumped. It was two college aged guys in winter jackets, both grinning.

I shook my head. "I don't know, a fish or something."

One of them laughed. "Well, don't fall in." They continued on their way.

My eyes darted back to the water, but whatever I had seen was gone. I studied the footprint one more time. Call me a coward, or irresponsible, but I hadn't seen her surface, and in fact saw no sign other than the two prints that she'd been there at all. In the end, I went to work and spent the rest of the day checking the local news to see if anyone had drowned.

Of course, nothing came up. It didn't mean she hadn't drowned, of course. It might be days, especially during Spring Break, before anyone realized she was gone and even longer before her body turned up.

On the walk back to my car that evening, my eyes were glued to the river. Nothing. I stopped by to examine the print in the mud and the one further on in the water. Nothing had changed.

For the next two days I mulled it over. No drowning incidents appeared on the news feeds, and I saw nothing else. On Thursday I happened on Dane Rogers —my alien guy—and since we were two of the perhaps ten people who'd come to work, he asked me about lunch. I agreed, mostly because of my incident. I wasn't sure if I could voice what I'd seen, but I figured I could see where the conversation led.

We headed out to a deli to grab sandwiches. Dane is a little taller than me, blonde with dark glasses, and he looks normal. Only when you get to know him does his weird side come out. He plopped down across from me and after ordering, we danced through the preliminary conversation. I wasn't sure how to broach my problem; I couldn't just blurt out what I thought I'd seen.

"So, what's new in your world, Phil?" he asked.

"The usual. Jenner's pushing to get as many orders in as possible. Same old. What about you?"

"We're expanding the writing program. I think we're going to get the thumbs up for a studio. You know, let students come in and practice presentations and what not."

"Cool. Hey. I know you're into some weird stuff—sorry, didn't mean it like that, but have you ever come across… people in the water?"

His eyebrows rose. "You mean like mermaids?"

"No. More like… I don't know. Never mind."

But I'd raised his curiosity as well as his eyebrows. "No, it's cool. Why did you ask? There are mermaid stories, but in the last few years there have been reports of something called a 'ningen.' I think it's Japanese, some kind of giant swimming humanoid. There are also theories about an evolutionary line of apes that returned to the sea. Did you see something?"

I opened my mouth, closed it. I tried to start again, but stopped. Finally, I said, "I… you're gonna think I'm nuts." Very original, and I just blurted out the entire thing. I think the incident shook me that much I had to tell someone. To Dane's credit, he sat quietly while I recalled every detail.

When I finally stopped for a drink of pop, he studied me. "Did you take a picture of the footprints?"

I felt like a dumbass. Why hadn't I? It was one of the reasons I didn't believe in the mumbo-jumbo Dane did. People never photographed the things they suppos-edly saw. And now I was just like them. "No. Dammit—I even had my phone out. I was going to call the police, but I never saw anything more than the prints."

"And the girl. Did she look human?"

I shrugged. "I was too far away. The style of the coat and the hat, the way she walked, I know she was female, but I didn't get a look at her."

"And you said it wasn't like she was swimming?"

"That was the really weird part. It wasn't like the water kept her afloat. You know how you get into a pool and the water keeps you buoyant?"

"Yeah."

"It wasn't like that. She just disappeared under like she was walking down a set of stairs."

"Can you show me where after work?"

"Yeah, but it's been… it was three days ago."

Dane shrugged. "Let's go see."

We did. It hadn't rained or snowed during the time. Excitement and dread worked their way into me as I led him to the spot. I wasn't sure I wanted what I'd seen to be real. Walking down to the river's edge I found the place. There was an imprint just at the edge of the river, fainter now from the heat of the sun, but there was a dent in the ground. Further into the water I didn't see anything, but the river ran its steady course.

Dane knelt and ran his fingers over the remains of the print. "Something was standing there," he finally decided. "Have you ever seen anything weird around here before?"

"No."

"Maybe it was an apparition. You know, like the ghost of some girl who drowned in the past?"

"It sure seemed real. And she looked solid."

"Let me do some digging on drowning deaths on the river. I know there have been a few over the years. "

"Thanks," I replied. "I thought I was just crazy."

Dane stood, brushed his fingers off and stabbed one at me. "That's the problem with this stuff. Everyone assumes it's nonsense until it happens to them. There is more going on around us than most people want to believe."

"I saw it and I still can't believe it."

Dane grinned. "I think I'll come back this weekend and check it out. Maybe Saturday night. You want to join me?"

I was curious and it was weird, but hanging out at the river's edge at night was not my idea of a good time. "I'll do some looking on the internet, but I'll leave the investigating to you."

"Suit yourself, but you might be sorry if I find something."

I worked my way through Friday. Dane continued his research. I begged off joining him for a hunt one more time. He was into this kind of thing and eager to look into something close to home. I was content to let him do the footwork.

Hunting on the net, I did discover there had been several drownings over the last eight years. It was as far as I'd traced back. Six in all, and one article talked about the swift current of the river, the bravado of college students, and of course the mixing of alcohol and running water. Neither of the two female drowning victims fit what I saw. The first was taller, close to six foot, and had been a basketball player for the university. I didn't follow sports, though I vaguely remembered the drowning. It had happened three years back. The second had been a heavier girl and she'd done herself in. Some relationship went badly and she decided she couldn't live with it.

There were four other men who'd also drowned, but as I told Dane, I knew the person I'd seen had been female.

I Googled ghosts and other off topic subjects for our area and got all kinds of stuff, but nothing relating to the river. I came across mythology on mermaids and the strange thing Dane had talked about, but the ningen were more related to the ocean and what I had seen had at least appeared human.

I returned to work Monday, eyes trained on the river, but I didn't see the girl and nothing else showed itself. No drownings showed up in the newspaper feeds while I sipped my coffee. I tried calling Dane, but he didn't answer. I sent him an email instead and busied myself with work while I waited for him to respond.

The morning turned to afternoon and I hadn't heard back, which was odd because he ate that stuff up. Even if he'd found nothing, I was sure he'd want to hash over everything. I tried his number again. Three rings before someone picked up. It was one of his coworkers. "Hello?" she asked.

I'd met Shiela once or twice, didn't know her really, but I recognized her nasal voice. "Uh, hi. Is Dane in?"

"No. He's not at work. Can I take a message?"

"It's Phil from downstairs. Phil Jeffries. Is he sick?"

A long pause on the other end. "We're not sure. He didn't call in, but no one can get hold of him. Did you have something to work with him about?"

"Wait," I said. "He didn't come in and he didn't call?"

"No. It's odd. He's really good about it. I tried his cell, but he's not answering it either."

"Uh, okay. I was just calling to say hi. I'll try back tomorrow."

"Alright. When he checks in, I'll let him know you called."

"Thanks."

A chill glided down my spine. I remembered our short conversation Friday, but all he said was he hadn't discovered anything new, so he was going to the river Saturday night to poke around. That was the last time I'd talked to him.

Dane wasn't married. He had a girlfriend, but I'd never met her; I only crossed paths with him occasionally. It wasn't like we were really friends. Still, it bothered me. My brain kicked in with all kinds of reasons why this could only be coincidence, and how he was fine. I was certain he was just home with the flu or something.

It just didn't sit well.

After work I wandered down to the place where I'd seen the girl, and found the prints. I don't know what I expected to find. School was back in session and more people roamed the bridge above and the sidewalk behind me. I tried to look nonchalant as I walked to the water's edge. The original print wasn't much more than an indent at this point, the weather having baked the details away.

I walked along the edge looking, for signs of anything odd in the water. Other than two ducks and floating sticks and debris, all I saw was brown murk. No signs of a purple hat or even a girl, much less any signs Dane had been there. All the way home I puzzled, and spent the rest of the evening scouring the internet for more information.

I learned a lot about mythology and discovered all kinds of references to water spirits, sprites, nymphs, monsters and whatnot. Nothing associating purple hats, though there were some accounts of these creatures being able to walk on dry land.

The next day there was clear concern over Dane, from the break room to the hallways. He was still absent and no one had been able to contact him. I was sufficiently freaked out but kept to myself. I couldn't come forward with my story. It was nuts to begin with and only people like Dane bought into weird things, anyway. I didn't believe he'd been nabbed by some spirit of the river. I did not, however, discount the possibility that he'd fallen in while poking about.

I had no clue what to do.

The following day, the news feeds all shared the same article: *local man disappears*. Shiela had called the police, who went to check on him and found no one at his apartment. Dane's family had been contacted and they didn't know where he was either. The end of the article was the same in every paper: *if anyone has any information, please contact us*, followed by a phone number and email.

Except what could I say? I'd be treated like a lunatic, and probably very quickly end up on a suspect list. Still, they could look for him in the water. I believed he'd had gone to the river that Saturday evening to do just what he'd said. Dane having fallen into the river seemed a real possibility.

I walked to my car that evening, in a conundrum. Should I speak up or not? I didn't like withholding information, but at the same time it had been almost a week. Even if they dragged the river, they were only going to find a body. It wasn't like they were going to find Dane alive.

I was so lost in my thoughts I didn't even hear the click of boots on the pavement, until a flash of color caught my attention.

A flash of purple.

My head snapped up. A young woman passed me on the left. She wore a coat that hung down below her knees and a large knit stocking hat of deep purple atop her head.

My eyes widened, even as I told myself there were probably plenty of people on campus who wore purple hats. I nervously held my breath as she caught up and waited for her to pass me altogether.

Instead she matched my pace, falling into step beside me.

My heart revved.

Her hat was tucked down to the point it crowded her forehead, making it impossible to determine the color of her hair. Large sunglasses covered a good portion of her features. A quick look would have told you she was any student on campus. Except there was something about her skin. Pale in a way that almost glowed, like copy paper. Her lips were thin and when she opened her mouth to speak, it didn't look natural.

"Nothing happened." Her voice sounded strained and high-pitched, like she wasn't used to talking.

"What?" I stammered, adrenaline kicking in.

"You avoided the situation, but it has resolved. Forget what you saw and keep quiet about the man."

"Do you mean Dane?"

She didn't answer.

"I had a friend who came out the river Saturday night. No one knows where he is."

"He took your place," she said.

Fear glided into me. "What do you mean, he took my place?"

She stopped. I did too, struggling to see past her sunglasses into her eyes. It was a cloudy day, and the dark lenses revealed nothing. There was only one other person over a hundred yards behind us, and no one coming our way. She followed my look before opening her mouth. Inside I saw small, pointed teeth, as different from the flat human kind as could be. "You were chosen. I allowed you to see me. Had the other two humans not walked by when they did, you would have come with me. The other man fulfilled your role. Go on about your world. Forget the man. Forget me."

She started walking again, this time more briskly.

I didn't follow. I was dumbfounded, confused and trying to decide if I'd heard what I thought I had. It took my brain some time to digest what she'd said: she'd let me see her enter the water to draw me in. I remembered looking at the footprints and leaning closer to see that shape below the water line.

I remembered the two college guys ribbing me about standing too close to the edge, during which the shape underwater vanished. Sweat trickled down my head.

It had been on purpose. She'd tried to lure me to the water and I'd played the perfect fool. And she wasn't friendly. Dane was gone and she said she'd taken him instead of me. I'm not given to profanity, but a torrent of words rolled around inside my head.

She'd meant to get me and failed, but poor Dane had accidentally given her another opportunity.

I glanced up at her. She was well ahead of me now, the purple hat a beacon across the distance. She must have known because she looked back as she walked. She reached the next bridge, passing a couple walking my way. They paid her no mind, and she quickly stepped off the path and headed for the water.

I didn't want to run, but I walked as quickly as I was able, panting. I watched as she reached the edge, near a bridge support and stepped around it. I lost sight of her for a couple of seconds and I knew it was too late. Passing the couple, I continued on. But as I feared, by the time I could see around the edge of the support, the woman was gone.

I stared at the water for minutes, then hurried to my car. All the way home, I turned her words over in my head. "Chosen," I said aloud, but as I voiced it, I had an idea of what it meant.

Dane's body hadn't been found.

I didn't stop for dinner until the sun had gone down that night—a rarity for me. I got back on the internet digging through websites to see if I could figure out what was going on. I found several stories about water creatures, mostly human-looking ones who lured sailors into the sea, or rivers. All of the stories ended badly for the humans.

Something Dane told me came to mind: There had been several drownings around here over the last few years. I took time for a sandwich and a pop and had my face fixated on my screen until almost two in the morning.

I called in sick to work the next day because I wanted to organize what I'd found and be sure of the pattern I'd discovered. I don't usually call in sick, and when I do, it's been because I'm completely incapacitated. Fear outweighed my guilt, though. I had accidentally happened upon something crazy, the kind of crazy Dane had liked to talk about and catalog. Stuff I had never believed in.

I'd gone back twenty-two years, and learned an awful lot of people had drowned along our river. It was clever though, because they never drowned in the same place, and it never happened every year. One year someone would drown twenty miles downriver. A couple years later, the next would die further upstream. The deaths spread out over several counties. As I searched, I began to discover it was happening in several states downstream. Our river runs a long way, and I doubt the local police ever look beyond the "accident" idea.

Of course, the real question was what I was going to do about it. There was no way I could tell the police that a girl in a purple hat was luring people to their deaths in the depths of the river. And that was the endgame: of the twenty people who'd drowned in the river, all of the bodies had been badly decomposed or partially eaten by small fish.

My best option was to do exactly as the girl had said and just forget the whole thing. After all, a threat had been implied there: I understood that much. I felt terrible that I'd gotten Dane involved—gotten him *killed*—but I was no adventurer. I didn't have a gun and even if I did, I wasn't shooting it off by the river. I didn't know martial arts and I hadn't gotten my butt kicked in a fight since the sixth grade.

Besides, going down there just meant tempting trouble.

Except I'd gotten Dane killed.

In the end, I decided to do the same thing he had, because I wanted to learn more from this girl if I could. I went to a shop and bought a taser. I told the sales guy it was for my niece. He'd only shrugged and shoved it in a bag for me.

I waited for the weekend, work now shrouded in talk about Dane—where he might have gone, what might have happened to him. I kept out of it, only nodding as ideas got thrown around, secretly thankful that Dane and I had had our conversation in private.

Saturday night rolled around. After checking the forecast for rain, packing my taser, and preparing my phone to speed-dial the police, I put on a jacket and headed to the river. I waited until almost ten o'clock before exiting my car.

A faint wind blew. The cloud cover was solid. I couldn't even see the moon. I had a flashlight in one hand and my taser in the other, with my phone in the breast pocket of my jacket. I wore running shoes too; though I wasn't confident in my ability to get very far, I wanted to be prepared.

I understood too this could be construed, in the girl's eyes, as not forgetting, so I planned on not getting too close to the river.

I couldn't help but wonder if this wasn't some big waste of time. Given the vast area in which these drownings happened, she might well have moved on further upstream or down.

It was my secret hope: that I would walk the river a bit, find nothing, and go home.

I went off the sidewalk, keeping my flashlight off in order to avoid drawing attention to myself. The ground was squishy from the thaw, though the temperature had dropped enough that parts of it crunched beneath my shoes. I stayed on my side of the river, away from where I'd discovered the prints; the spot was close to a university building, and I suspected she wouldn't show herself if there was any danger of being discovered.

I headed upstream for a while, keeping a good distance back from the bank, watching the water. It was calm and I could see the reflection of lights from across the river. I could hear the current as the water rolled, but saw nothing surface, nothing in the water to suggest she was nearby. I gave it a good hour, tromping first up, and then downstream. Being a Saturday night, most of the college kids were downtown and it was late enough that no one was out for a walk.

I passed the bridge and continued down toward a tunnel under the roadway that bent along the river. There were lots of trees along the water's edge, and I got a little closer to have a better view.

Suddenly I saw a flash of white in the river. It was several yards away, toward the center, but something had definitely flickered beneath the surface. I stopped. Seconds ticked by, then I saw it again, closer to the bridge. I walked back the way I'd come, keeping my distance.

I was scared and excited, reminding myself I needed to be careful. Whoever she was, she was dangerous in ways I couldn't imagine. I'd read stories of sirens and mermaids who could hypnotize prey. I still held hope there was some rational explanation here, not quite ready to climb down into Dane's rabbit hole for good. But I figured he might not have been completely wrong, either.

I passed the bridge and headed down into the grass, still wary of getting too close. The flash disappeared, reappearing upstream a moment later. It stopped moving. The billowing white spot drifted down, but was soon replaced by two small lights in the water.

My smarter self objected, telling me to get the hell out of there and go home. But I had a taser, a flashlight, and a phone. As long as I didn't get too close to the water, I could get away if I needed to. Besides, this was the first time in my life I'd even been close to something this exciting.

The twin lights floated lazily toward the shore, just below the surface of the water. Curiosity spurred me toward the bank. The lights neared the shore. While afraid, I was mesmerized by them.

A head broke the surface. The twin lights were eyes. *Her* eyes. The street-lamps behind me reflected off them, giving them eyes an eerie yellowy glow. No purple hat this time; long, dark hair stretching out into the water behind her.

She looked far less human. Her pale skin contrasted against the dark water and her face was longer, streamlined somehow, her nose smaller, large eyes reminiscent of a shark.

She cruised within a few feet from shore and stopped.

"Hi," I said, all grace and cleverness gone. "I need to ask you... some things."

Her nose stayed just above the water line. I wondered whether she could breathe both above and below water. Questions bounced off the inside of my head and I had to wrangle them in. "I... uh, Dane—my friend, he's dead, isn't he?"

She closed in on the shore.

"Why did you choose me? Is there some reason specifically or was it just coincidental?"

Her eyes flitted left and right. I checked too, not wanting to give her away if there were other people nearby. But I was the only one in the area. No late-night runners, walking couples, or even staggering Saturday night drunks yet.

She slammed into me, so fast and so hard for such a little frame. I hit the ground, my taser flung behind me, flashlight spinning end over end into the darkness. I mushed into the soft earth, my head slapping the ground. I didn't even have time to react before she was on top of me, large eyes staring into mine.

I saw one of her hands: long, thin, and webbed at the fingers. Each ended in a claw. She brushed one against my throat. "Yell and you die."

I panted, unable to look away from those inhuman dark eyes. I tried to shake my head, but stopped as the claw pressed into my flesh.

"What is your name?" she asked in a low, gurgling voice.

"Phil. Phil Jeffries."

She paused. I saw a pair of inner eyelids pull across her irises, then flip back. "Where do you work?"

Alarm raised; she was trying to find out more about me. "At the university. I'm a buyer for our department."

She paused again. My heartbeat thumped in my ears. "Why did you come here? I told you not to."

"I don't know. I know Dane… he's dead isn't he? I… I've never encountered anyone like you before. I needed to know it wasn't all in my head."

Another long pause, even longer than before. Her eyes never left mine. "You're speaking truth. The man is gone. If I hadn't already taken him, I'd take you too. If you ever come back, you'll disappear. If we read or hear about this, we have ways to find you."

"Read? Wait! Who are you?"

Her mouth stretched wide, revealing a row of thin sharp teeth. "Your kind is so oblivious."

She ran a claw along the side of my neck. It tore my skin, so sharp it cut even though she barely applied pressure. Then, as quickly as she'd struck, she rolled off me and returned to the water. I caught a glimpse of legs, but they looked more like two halves of a fish's tail, coiling together as she slipped into the river.

I lay there on the bank, feeling the blood on my neck and knowing she could have cut me to the bone if she'd wanted. I smelled like the river, and I had slime on me where she'd touched me. But when I looked at the river, it gave no indication she'd ever been there.

Except… the twin lights. I saw them, just below the water line. Then two more. Then another pair and more until six sets of identical eyes glinted my way under the water.

I left. The flashlight and the taser I let lie and got myself home.

The next morning, Dane's body was found downstream. He'd been chewed, was missing fingers and fleshier parts. The article quoted some expert who confirmed the drowning and how even smaller fish will feed on a dead body, making it look like something larger might have eaten it.

I feigned ignorance with Dane. No one had seen him go near the river and no one knew he'd been down there with me, so the authorities assumed he'd been walking along the river and fallen in, succumbing to the current and the cold. Dane's girlfriend came around asking questions of all of us, but I played dumb along with the rest. She knew he was into weird stuff, but would she really have believed me?

I keep reading up on mermaids and the like. I can't see how they're physiologically capable of existing, but obviously they do. I don't think I'll be swimming in open water again, and I'm certainly never taking up fishing or going out on the river. Any river for that matter.

The day after the attack, I changed my parking spot. I took an opening in the ramp next to my building, and quit walking by the river at all.

I think she was right—humans aren't very observant. Either that, or we just choose not to look into very deep into the water.

GHOSTS ON THE BACKROAD

TREVOR JAMES ZAPLE

There are ghosts on these backroads. Everyone says so.

Anywhere a gaggle of kids engage in the art of telling ghost stories—be it around the fire on a farm near the Walton line, along the benches beside the Seaforth post office, or on the haunted promontory of St. Christopher's Beach—someone will inevitably start in on that hoary old chestnut about the spectral apparitions that stalk the lonely back routes crisscrossing the County. In the darkest parts of the night, they say, when the moon has gone into hiding and the stars are bankrupt, you can catch a flickering glimpse of the lives that have been extinguished on these endless stretches of gravel and dirt. In some stories they wail and screech, with viscera flying from their exaggerated gestures and a chill wind heralding their appearance. In others, they are simply spirits, as static as you or I, brief glimpses of lives once lived and lived no longer. They appear, traverse the shoulder of these lonely roads, then disappear to fulfill whatever roles remain to them in the dignity granted to them by invisibility.

Either way, the stories exist, and are told and retold by the kids who ricochet around the County looking for something to do. They're told until they're turned into legend, into myth, and finally into cliché. There aren't really ghosts, the older ones say. Specters don't haunt the laneways of hard-headed European immigrants. They're just memories, reminders of the tragedies that happen all too often on deserted roads, illuminated only by the distant light of an idiot moon. The mute sites of twisted wrecks dot the flattened landscape like pale skeletons in a receding flood.

There are others, like myself, who believe differently; we all have our own reasons. Mine happened on the night of the big orange harvest moon, as she rose like a bloated pumpkin over the most humid week in local memory. Driven outside to the relative coolness of the sweating night, we were desperate. We piled into Ryan Ericson's beat-up old Chevrolet and raced off down Main Street. We hoped to catch relief through the miracle of sheer speed. The post office tower, silent except for the bustling light at the very top, served as an anchor for us as we swung through town streets at dangerous speeds. The Twins held court up there, but we paid it no mind; there was no air conditioning in that peak, and we needed the rush of the breeze beyond anything else.

The main intersection of town was a dream; by the time we left the cheery blue sign on the north side of town behind, we were chasing the wind.

Halfway out to Winthrop we received a text; there was a party going on in the lonely acres between towns. We squealed down the next corner and headed off in search of it. These are the rites of passage on long Friday nights in the County. Instead of endless turns into darkened roadways, we had a destination, a purpose. The languid summer night now felt electric.

We found it down the road from the old gravel pit; a girl in the tenth grade with a keg of beer, a bonfire roaring as though it had been built by pagans, and a decided lack of parental authority. Climbing out of the car, it seemed magical; the low, constant murmur of conversation seemed to hang in the air, spiced on draught beer and smuggled vodka. Here and there it was punctuated with the pops and flares of the roaring fire.

We each took our own paths into this carousal, following our urges as we saw fit. I took a straight path for the keg; the humidity made me terribly thirsty, and my tongue craved the fizz and cut of chilled draught lager. There was a quite a line, but soon enough I had my beer and was mingling through the crowd.

The population was rather predictable; in a town as small as Seaforth, it would be jarring to see anything but the same old faces. You could tell who you were going to see by the place you were at: if you were above the post office, you would see the fancy kids from the subdivisions around the golf course; if you were in the upper apartments of any of the aged buildings behind Main Street you would see a motley collection of stoners and dropouts; on a lonely farm near the yawning gravel pit you would get almost anyone, from the bored and disaffected to the strange folk that wandered the sleeping stretches of Main Street late at night. Half the fun in such a gathering was seeing who you would run into next, and I played that game for a long time.

Within a few hours I became aware simultaneously of two things: first, that I was quite drunk; second, that Ryan Ericson was nowhere to be found. I wandered the farm yard for another half-hour, but neither he nor any of the others that I'd arrived with were anywhere to be found. Eventually I stumbled over to the fire, where a number of hunched figures in black hoodies squatted close to the warmth. They reminded me of huddled goblins, and the looks that they levelled at me did nothing to dispel the impression. I hung around the fire for several awkward moments, contemplating asking them if they'd seen my friends, but cowardice got the better of me. I reeled off into the darkness, hoping to find resolution there. I found only chill blackness, and then a hand on my shoulder. I spun around, frightened. A vaguely familiar face greeted me, floating out of the night.

"We going for a ride?"

I nodded instinctively, unsure of where they were going or why, but also knowing quite simply that I had to be out of there. The night was closing in on me, constricting me, and I needed to make my way home by any means necessary.

"Yes, let's ride," I replied, my breath coming quicker. His face split in a queasy grin. I felt the first stirrings of unease as I followed him across the farm-yard to his parked car. He weaved a little as he walked, stumbling here and there on flat ground. The crickets sang a high, sweet song as we found his car. Once we closed the doors, the interior oppressively silent in their absence.

When he twisted the key in the lock I wanted suddenly to burst out of the car, hit the door with all the force of my shoulder and roll out into the cool, waiting grass.

But I didn't, and he burst out into the night with a jerk and a shove. His driving was no better than his walking, and we were digging ourselves closer into the ditch with each weave as we rushed down that deserted gravel road.

"You wanna find another party?" he wheezed as we gathered speed. I said nothing, gripping the door handle with white-knuckled fingers. I could feel the floor thrumming under my feet, and when I glanced over to check the speedometer, I saw that we were well in excess of the speed limits of a major highway, let alone a deserted backroad.

"Jesus," I said, "how fast are you going? Maybe you should slow down?"

"Nah," he said, "I've got this. These are Huron County roads. I know them like the back of my own hand." He gripped the steering wheel as tightly as I was gripping the door handle. "Have you ever really looked at the back of your hand?" he asked. "Like, really studied it? There isn't much topography on there. You can only really tell by an odd scar, or a mole, or maybe the way that a shadow falls across it when the light is right. There's nothing much there at all, really."

We sped on in silence after that. He made no move to turn on the radio and I was too rigid in my nervous paralysis to adjust it myself. The roar of the engine and the rough gargle of the gravel were the only things to listen to.

A shape appeared in front of the car, a low tan blur with shocked eyes gone tharn. He yanked the wheel to the right; the car squealed out of control, skidded across several feet of suddenly airborne gravel, and rolled over. It scraped along upside down at high speed for forty-five seconds before it struck a tree and came to a crushing, shearing rest.

I came to a moment later, dazed but painless. My face was flush to the ground and a great weight seemed to be pressing onto my chest. I heard the crickets again, a million crickets singing their single note through the darkness.

I tried to breathe and couldn't. Panicking, I began to claw at the earth, scrabbling for a hold I could use to inch my way out. I moved slightly, and was almost able to draw a breath; it wheezed into my windpipe but refused to journey any further. My vision began to darken, and again I clawed at the dirt beneath my hands. But I could not move any further, and my arm collapsed against the calming cool of the grass. *Sleep*, it said. *Restful sleep.*

A hand grasped mine, as cool as the grass but electrifying. It gripped my fingers and pulled, and now I was moving, sliding out from under that car with agonizing slowness, as though I was sliding through a pair of rollers in a factory. The strength in the hand was terrifying; near the end, I was afraid my fingers would snap under its relentless force. In the end I was yanked out, skidding a little. I lay motionless, stretched out in the vast freedom of the humid night air.

For a long time I lay that way, unable to focus my attention long enough to move any part of my body. Finally a great wave of adrenaline washed through me and I rolled onto my back. The unending arc of the summer night sky stretched overhead, glittering diamonds tossed across a great void. A figure stood near me, the owner of the hand that possessed all of the strength in the world. I caught just a glimpse of her: she had blonde hair, cut short, she wore crisp new jeans, and her eyes shone like sapphires unearthed in the darkness of a newly opened cave.

Then she was gone, and I was alone beside the utter wreckage of his car. I began to register a thin, wet wail emanating from the driver's side of the flipped car. It was inhuman, although I was sure that it was originating from the driver's mouth. I was hearing a man fight weakly against the very darkness from which I'd been rescued, and it did not sit well with me. I plugged my ears but still heard him, a distant-seeming hum. Eventually, it stopped.

As the moon set the night grew darker, until I could see no more than a couple of feet in front of me. I pushed myself up, slowly and carefully, and sat up with my hands looped around my knees. A wailing siren shrilled in the distance, amplified by the open farmland. It grew louder as the minutes dragged on. Soon a police car came down the gravel road, followed closely by a firetruck, flashing lights fractured the night into pieces. I numbly watched them approach, park, and get out. They were not moving with any particular sense of urgency. They walked around the scene of the accident, marking off certain areas and taking an interminable number of photographs. Finally, an ambulance arrived, maneuvering down the gravel road with its lights off. Like the first response vehicles, the driver and EMS were in no hurry. They ambled out, bringing out the stretcher, and conversed with the firefighters. Cigarettes were lit, a bottle of water was passed around. The sky slowly grew lighter and they worked together to haul the car back onto its wheels.

The fire crew brought the Jaws of Life out and carefully pried the crushed, compressed car apart. The rescuers recoiled when they first opened the car, but quickly rolled up their sleeves and got to work. It took a few minutes, but they dragged two bodies out of the crumpled wreckage and loaded them onto waiting stretchers. The EMS worker wheeled them into the back of the ambulance and closed the back doors. The driver pulled into gear and the ambulance rumbled off down that deserted stretch of gravel. After finishing their notes and careful plotting of the scene, the police cruiser and the firemen followed. When dawn began to boil out of the east, I was alone again. I sat in the same position, hands clasped around my knees. I'd watched the entire scene in silence, and not one of the first responders had paid the slightest attention to me.

I felt a presence beside me. looked up to see the blonde girl, her sapphire-chip eyes putting the rest of her face into a shameful fade. She stared down at me wordlessly while the sun rose into the humid morning sky. I opened my mouth to speak several times, but before I could utter a word, my mind replace my previously chattering thoughts with a blank hum.

Finally, after hours of this, she spoke.

"Shall we?" She extended her hand, pale, thin, and radiating cold. I took it, and she helped me to my feet. We wandered into the bush running along the edge of the road, hiding from the sharp new discomfort of the dawn.

There are ghosts on these backroads. Everyone says so.

BONES IN A CITY GRAVEYARD

BY SHELDON WOODBURY

She was downtown, below 14th Street, standing on the corner of Bowery and Broome. She'd been standing there for some time, a harsh rain whipping around her. It had only been a four-block walk to the drugstore, but she stopped because she needed to rest. Her legs ached, and the cold rain on her body was mixed with sweat. She glanced at her watch. Almost six o'clock. She was running late.

She tugged her frayed raincoat tighter and thought about how best to allocate the time when she returned back home. First, she would take an extra hot bath to melt away the icy chill. Then the long soothing ritual of oils and creams. Maybe tonight she would even sprinkle a few rose petals in the water for good luck, then put on her makeup by the shimmering glow of candlelight.

Yes, she decided. That would set the mood perfectly.

She started walking again, turning off Broome onto Bowery. Earlier, she had avoided this street on purpose, but was now too tired to take the longer way back home. She kept her head down, dreading what might be ahead.

If the surly bodega owner was slouched in his doorway, he'd watch her like a hawk, then shake his head and spit in disgust. She looked up. The doorway was empty. Beyond that, she saw the upside-down crates where the domino players sat. The rain had kept them inside too. That was good. They loved to shout curses in Spanish and throw empty beer cans whenever she passed. She didn't see any teenagers either, and that was even better. There was usually a small group slouched in front of the pizza shop like scowling dead bodies. They were always the cruelest of all. They'd howl and point whenever she passed, then follow her for a block or two, making "oink, oink" sounds and yelping like a pack of hyenas. Like always, she wondered how hard they'd all laugh if they knew the real joke.

She used to be beautiful.

But she was also another person back then. In fact, she could barely be sure about all the details, because so much about her life had changed.

But she did remember this.

She came from Ohio, because she wanted to be famous. She always thought she was special, because that's what everybody told her when she was growing up. Her beauty sprouted early and propelled her towards a destiny she thought was hers for the asking. She was the head cheerleader, the Prom Queen, and voted most beautiful in the yearbook. *You should be in movies, and on the cover of magazines*, everybody said. It was a small-town chorus she heard so often that it had to be true.

So, the summer she graduated from high school she stumbled up the steps of a bus and came to New York City.

She remembered this too.

She had tried.

She had tried as hard as she possibly could, but the dream never got very far. Audition after audition, meeting after meeting, day after day, year after year, in a city so big and overwhelming it forced the brightly-colored memory of her hometown to get smaller and hazier.

There had been a few small successes, but not very many, just enough to keep the dream alive as the years tumbled by. For most of those years she had tried to be patient, always believing her big break was right around the corner. But the occasional modeling jobs never led anywhere, and the small parts in off-Broadway plays never lasted long enough to get attention from "the right kind of people."

Then, late one night, she finally understood what had happened. The reason for all her bad luck.

It came to her in a nightmare.

Her life had obviously been cursed, and this curse was responsible for everything.

That's what the nightmare told her.

In fact, it was probably the curse that had lured her here in the first place, shrewdly disguising itself as an innocent dream. Pain and punishment, that's what the curse was really all about. What else could explain her brutal misfortune. She had only been in the city a few years when the curse had suddenly killed both her parents back in Ohio. Evidently, the curse loved blood and the sizzling smell of burning flesh, because the accident was a head-on collision in broad daylight.

And that was just the beginning.

Pain and punishment. Punishment and pain. Month after month. Year after year. None of it made any sense, but the curse was relentless.

It brought bad boyfriends and wrinkles, two rapes, and three muggings. Most of all, it brought endless bad luck and missed opportunities, until the only comfort she had left was the little bit of money her parents had left her. It was barely enough to live on, but that was part of the curse's diabolical plan. It wanted her to be desperate. It wanted her of live in filth and darkness. So this is what it did.

It pushed her.

The island of Manhattan was long and slender, jagged on the edges. When she first moved to the city, she found a five-floor walkup on West End Avenue in the nineties. It had friendly neighbors, but the rent kept going up and her succession of crappy jobs couldn't keep pace. Her next apartment was in the fifties, another walkup, but she was only there a few years, unable to afford that either. Her next apartment was farther south, and the one after that farther still. But the curse kept pushing and pushing, until she finally ended up all the way downtown, with the rats and the rubble, in the grimy black shadows of the Bowery.

And lately, the curse had been sending her a brand-new message, whispering it in the gloomiest hours of the night.

Playtime is over, now I want you dead.

She was scared, of course, but she also came up with a plan of her own. The curse had power and cunning, so she needed help. What she needed was a partner. The curse was on the verge of winning, so she desperately needed someone to help her fight back. After all, she kept telling herself, she just needed what most women already had.

She needed a man.

For the past year she'd been placing a personal ad in small magazines and newspapers. The response had been encouraging. Actually, she'd been surprised by the number. But it's a big city, she told herself, so there's probably a large number of just about anything, including men who responded to personal ads. So far, the encounters had been disappointing, but she wasn't about to give up hope.

Her trip down the block had been without incident.

She turned the corner.

The doorway to her building was a short distance away, so she tried to accelerate her lumbering pace. On this block there were no bright lights or passing cars. There was only darkness and dirt, despair and desperation, sordid secrets the rest of the city knew nothing about.

She climbed the two crumbling steps, then pushed open the rusted door of her dilapidated building. The inside entryway was as dark as a cave. The only escape was the shadowy stairway rising up in front of her. She stared at it for almost a minute. This was always the part of the trip she hated the most.

Her rain-soaked foot landed on the first step with a heavy, wet thud. She took a deep breath, then raised her other foot. The zigzagging climb up the six flights of stairs would take another twenty minutes. She took another step, then another, then another. The old wooden boards groaned from the strain, and her legs were already on fire.

Yes, the curse was evil, all right.

It had ruined her life by turning her into the kind of freak drunken old men threw beer cans at. She stopped at the landing, utterly exhausted, but she still had five more flights to go. She sucked in another wheezing breath, then she climbed and climbed, stopping again and again, the shadowy stairway moaning and groaning with each pounding step. When the torturous ascent was finally completed, her trunk like legs were shivering with pain, and her body was a blubbery swamp of stink and sweat.

Why?

Because evil always takes away what you love the most, and this is what the curse had accomplished. It had taken away her beauty by smothering it beneath hundreds of pounds of suffocating flesh. She came to the city with youth and beauty, and she came because she wanted to be famous.

But it was now more than twenty years later, and she weighed almost four hundred pounds.

Drenched with rain and sweat, she stopped in front of the grimy door to her apartment. Her exhaustion and the pain in her legs was so ferocious, the dusty air was swirling in circles. She fell against the wall for support. When the wave finally passed, she took out her keys and unlocked the door. Lumbering inside, a single hope was all that gave her the strength to keep moving forward.

Maybe tonight would be the night she fell in love.

He was late.

When the buzzer finally shrilled, she had been anxiously waiting for almost an hour, but the sudden sound was magic. A tingle washed over her body in a warm rush, and her growing doubts about the night instantly disappeared. She pushed herself up from the sofa and shuffled to the buzzer that would open the downstairs door.

At least she'd put the time waiting to good use.

The apartment was cramped and musty, with a permanent smell that lingered like a fog. Outside, decay was all around, so she treated her meager living space like a private sanctuary she could control. She'd spent most of the last hour sweeping and dusting, obsessively searching for dirt and grime.

Sitting on a small table was a bottle of red wine and a plate with cheese. She always explained that she preferred a quiet evening at home on a first date, and most of the men had readily agreed.

She put her ear against the door, better to hear the footsteps slowly climbing the stairs. Her skin was still tingling with excitement and hope. But there were darker thoughts nagging for attention too.

She felt ugly.

It was a constant feeling she couldn't shake. It was always there, clawing inside her, tearing away at her heart and soul. At first, the weight had come slowly, a few pounds at a time. But then it began to appear with a monotonous consistency, day after day, week after week. It was somewhere around three hundred pounds when the other changes came too, the more drastic mutations in her appearance. This is where the curse had demonstrated its spectacular eye for detail and brilliant talent for punishment. Men worshipped beauty in women, so the curse had gleefully pushed her into a body that was the exact opposite of what men considered beautiful. Her face was now as plump and round as a perfect full moon, and her bright blue eyes had turned murky and morose. The weight of her flesh had bent her spine forward. Even her hair seemed heavy, hanging like a fright wig around her mushy round face.

On the phone, he'd said he was an electrician and he lived in Queens.

The knock on the door was sharp and loud. She opened it slowly, and the sight that greeted her was not unpleasant.

He was dressed in a black leather jacket and a black cowboy shirt. She normally didn't like mustaches, but his was trimmed and neat. What she did like was this: he was still standing in front of the open door smiling. All of this after he had clearly witnessed her size and appearance.

"Hi."

"Hello."

"You must be Phil."

"That's me, all right.

"It's nice to meet you Phil."

"Same here, doll. It's a real pleasure."

Now she was smiling too, because this brief exchange had lasted longer than most of her past dates. Then he followed her inside, which was even better.

This is when her fantasy took flight.

They sat together in the musty living room, he in the chair, she on the tattered brown sofa. He quickly opened the wine and filled their glasses. Yes, she thought, he could very well be the one, her own Prince Charming. He had climbed the shadowy staircase to rescue her like a hero in a fairytale. He was going to fight the curse and win.

Her heart began to soar.

But only for another second or two

He finished his wine in a single gulp, then stumbled towards her. He fell down next to her, mumbling something she couldn't understand. She smelled the harsh stink of whiskey on his breath. He rolled on top of her, shoving his hand under her dress. She felt his calloused fingers crawling between her thighs like a giant spider.

"Stop..."

"C'mon, honey, let's have some fun."

"Please..."

"Hey... don't be a bitch... relax..."

But she couldn't relax. Because now she was scared.

After all these years, she had finally gained a small advantage in her battle against the curse. She could sense when it was near. She felt it now. It was close. It was very, very close. He was still riding on top of her like a drunken cowboy, one hand jammed between her thighs, the other roughly groping her massive breast. She closed her eyes.

It's time, the curse whispered. *It's time.*

The curse snapped her knees shut with a stunning force. The cheese knife was now in her hand. His shocked expression was followed by bloodcurdling screams and death rattle wails as she stabbed him again and again, with the strength that only the curse could give her. The sounds were deafening, but all she could hear was the evil sound of the curse happily giggling with wicked glee.

The two cops had gotten the radio call from the Precinct House a few minutes earlier. The Hispanic super met them at the door. Climbing the stairs, the super continued his story in angry streams of broken English.

Not much made sense, but it had something to do with a fat lady and a locked door. For the past few days neighbors had been complaining about a terrible smell, and the super had finally gotten around to calling the police. At the fifth-floor landing, the older cop stopped to catch his breath. His name was Ramirez, and he knew this much already. He hated climbing stairs, and he hated that smell, because he knew what it was.

On the sixth floor, the super stopped in front of a grungy brown door. He swung a key ring from the back of his pants, and flipped through the keys. The first few tries didn't work. Finally, one did.

The super mumbled angrily to himself as he pushed open the door and switched on the light.

Ramirez turned around and looked at his partner. He was hard to read, which was fine. *Welcome to the graveyard,* Ramirez thought. But that talk would come later. Every job has its own unique rite-of-passage, and Ramirez guessed his rookie partner was about to have his. The younger cop was an Irish kid named Rafferty. He'd just graduated from the Academy six weeks earlier, so he was a virgin with all his naïve assumptions still intact.

Inside the apartment, the smell was overwhelming, thick and musty like smog.

The super was already standing in front of another closed door, pointing out the obvious. The smell was coming from behind this door, but he didn't have a key to open it. The older cop nodded to the rookie. That's why they brought the crowbar. The rookie was a strong kid, a few inches over six feet. He shoved the crowbar in deep at the door's edge. Leaning low, he shoved hard once, then again, and the door popped open.

The rookie quickly straightened back up, giving him the first look at the contents of the room.

When he turned back around, his face was drained and white.

Ramirez walked past the kid, into the room. What hit him first was the stronger smell. It was stomach turning, much worse than the outer room. Then he saw what was lying on the bed. The body was naked and decomposed, rotting into grayness like the carcass of an animal. It was huge, a blubbery mass of human flesh. Right now, only one rat was visible, quietly nibbling at one of the toes, but there must have been others. The nose and ears were gone, most of the fingers too.

Turning around, Ramirez saw the super had already stumbled back a few steps, cursing in Spanish. The kid was still standing in the same place, clutching the crowbar. His face was drained of everything but shock. Every job has its own unique rite-of-passage, and the rookie cop had just had his.

Ramirez smiled grimly, and turned back to the room.

Time to go to work.

Looking around, he saw a lamp on a small table next to the bed. Putting a handkerchief over his nose and mouth, he walked quickly across the room. The sudden light from the lamp didn't make the sight on the bed any prettier, but it sent the rat scurrying away out of sight.

Ramirez walked around the perimeter of the bed, randomly poking the giant corpse with a pencil. The smell was almost unbearable, even with the handker-chief. The skin was tough and leathery, but spongy too. He was looking for evidence. A bullet hole, a knife wound, needle marks, whatever. A couple more pokes, then he stopped.

So far, cause of death unknown.

He turned his attention to the room. Not much there either. A bureau, movie magazines, make-up, plastic bottles, perfume, shoes, old newspapers.

He walked to the closet door and opened it.

What tumbled out was like the pieces of a horrific jigsaw puzzle.

Hundreds of bones spilled out of the closet and clattered down to the floor. Skulls, leg bones, ribcages, thigh bones, every kind imaginable, and all of them, every single one, was completely white and impossibly smooth.

. . .

What Ramirez had to explain to his rookie partner was the legend of "The Graveyard." He did it four nights later at Moran's, the neighborhood bar down the block from the Precinct House.

Ramirez led him through the chattering crowd to the quieter room in the back. Its nickname was "the blue room" because that's where the cops always sat. For the first couple of beers, the conversation wandered over the usual topics: sports, women, precinct politics.

Then Ramirez brought up the events on Monday.

They had already talked over the facts that had accumulated in the last few days. The medical examiner had determined no foul play was involved in the death. The cause was a sudden heart attack brought on by the women's extreme obesity. But the medical examiner had also discovered something else in his autopsy, traces of human flesh in the woman's digestive tract. The connection to the smooth white bones hidden in the closet was horrifically clear. The final piece of evidence was discovered during another search of the apartment. Stashed under the bed, in tightly bound bundles, were letters from hundreds of different men, and copies of the personal ad she'd used to attract them. In the ad she'd described herself as rubenesque.

The rookie shook his head and gulped his beer. "What I don't understand is why the newspapers aren't jumping all over this story."

"Actually, that's what I wanted to talk to you about."

Ramirez glanced around at the nearby tables. It was time to educate his virgin partner, but it wasn't the kind of story he wanted strangers to overhear.

The graveyard was the macabre term the powers-that-be in city government had coined for the decaying blocks hidden in the crumbling gloom behind the Bowery. It was called the graveyard because that's where all the lost causes of the city eventually ended up. Accepting this, the powers-that-be also recognized that what happened in the graveyard was so far beyond the limits of accepted normalcy that it was in the best interests of the city to withhold selected information about the day-to-day crime rate. But the cops obviously knew, because it was their job to contain the problem.

In the graveyard, sick things happened every single day, because some of its inhabitants were known to adapt lifestyles that had mutated far beyond the scope of public understanding and tolerance. It was a place where delusion and insanity were the medication of choice. Simply put, the graveyard was the neighborhood where all the monsters lived.

That was the story he had to tell.

Before he started, Ramirez leaned back in his chair and took a leisurely look at the face in front of him. His new partner was twenty years old. He probably grew up watching cop shows on TV, just like he did. He'd already told him becoming a cop was his childhood dream. But Ramirez had learned a horrible fact in the last twenty years. This was real life, not TV.

And this was New York City, not anywhere else.

"Welcome to the graveyard," he began.

The End.

THE WAYWARD GATE

ETHAN VINCENT

"It is said that the threshold of the Wayward Gate beckons to the unwary with unstable and primitive magicks. That it calls out with enticing promises of unveiled secrets and errant pathways through the unknown and back again."

That's how the elder's story began on the night our caravan arrived in the small mill town of Lorriston on the northern edge of the Arden Forest.

We came up from the southwest in the middle of autumn, following a tree-lined path where the leaves shone bright as freshly lit flames, and the stench of pre-winter rot had yet to fully saturate the dirt. This was my first trip through the Arden, as I was still a young boy at the time. Each day my mother sat with me at the front of our brightly-colored vardo and taught me the ways of the forest. I learned many things during this time, such as how the stripped bark on a nearby tree meant a stag had passed this way, or how the knots in willow branches were created by fairies and symbolized luck.

It was during one of these lessons that I noticed the black stone archway standing a short distance past the tree line. I thought nothing of it at first. Our troupe had encountered many curiosities during our travels, so I assumed that it was a regional monument or marker of some sort. But my mother, following my gaze, told me that the arch was a bit of profane architecture that the locals of the forest called the Wayward Gate.

From my vantage point on the wagon, I noticed how the structure's jet-black mineral seemed to absorb any sunlight upon and around it, creating the unsettling impression that everything in the vicinity sat behind a shadowy veil. As we passed the archway, I could have sworn that I saw something shimmering in midair between the columns, like oil on water. For a moment, I felt as though I could reach out and touch it. But as soon as I confided this to my mother, she stood up and yanked me inside like a sack of potatoes. Then she sat me down and smeared a paste of agrimony and honey across my forehead, an ancient practice for warding off demons and evil spirits. It smelled of candied apricots.

By the time she let me back outside, the archway had fallen out of view, so I went back to looking for willow knots and deer signs.

My first thought upon seeing the town of Lorriston was how it seemed no more than an anthill compared to some of the mountainous cities our troupe had passed through during the summer. It consisted of a town hall, which was the nicest and most well-kept of the buildings, despite being nothing more than a two-story rectangle of wood and thatch, a handful of cottages and houses, and an old lumber mill that sat on the edge of the mill pond like the town's solemn sentry.

The people who came to greet our caravan were dismal at best. Their clothes weren't much better than rags, and I saw their hands were worn and callused from years of heavy labor. Nevertheless, their downturned lips crept up into smiles as Barsali commenced his juggling act from the front of his wagon.

By evening, all eight vardos in our caravan had rounded up next to the lumber mill, and our makeshift stage was erected beside a large bonfire. The townsfolk, eager to pay the half-pence price for an hour or two of carefree excitement, waited outside the ring of wagons until our preparations were complete. Then they made their way to the benches assembled before the stage.

Barsali opened the show with the juggling of lit torches, much to the amazement of the slack-jawed children. Next was a performance of Shakespeare's *A Midsummer Night's Dream* led by Fell and his wife, Charani. Then came various acts of shock and awe, like sword swallowing and fire breathing. After that all ended, it was finally my mother's time to shine. Her thin, soothing voice wound its way through the notes of a song called *The Trees They Grow So High* as I made my best, if deeply flawed, attempt to accompany her on the guitar. And then it was time to introduce the final performer of the night, an elder of the town named Albert Wood.

Ever since I can remember, our performances always end with calling upon a local citizen to recite a bit of regional folklore, or perhaps tell a story about life in their little corner of the world. The purpose of this practice was twofold. First, it made the people of the villages and towns feel honored. Second, it provided we performers a wealth of material from which to craft new stories, poems, and songs of our own.

Albert Wood was a fragile old man, made ever the more obvious when he hobbled up the stairs to the stage. A grey beard billowed off his chin like a storm cloud and his brown eyes were like flood gates holding back wisdom and acuity undiminished by age. Yet his crooked body was bent and twisted, like a scarecrow falling off its perch.

The gaudy decorations of the previous performances were nowhere in sight as he sat upon a wooden stool. The entire camp grew as silent as the waters of the millpond, and every eye turned on the old man. He cleared his throat with a guttural croak that seemed more of phlegm than air, and spat.

"No doubt you have all heard this story before in some form or fashion," he rasped. "But tonight, I shall tell you the full, true history as it was passed down to me from my father and his fathers before him."

He looked out over the crowd while the firelight danced in his eyes. Then he began.

"It is said that the threshold of the Wayward Gate beckons the unwary with unstable and primitive magicks. That it calls out with enticing promises of unveiled secrets and errant pathways through the unknown and back again. These wisps and whispers pour from its void and spill into your ears, filling you with false warmth, ensnaring your mind, and drawing you in.

"To believe there is truly any choice left to you once you are firmly under thrall of the Gate is a lie. Your destiny now lies through that door; the point of no return has long since passed. Fear is less than memory as the cosmic ocean before you crashes against your euphoric mind. Your soul is siphoned from your body like water from a well pump and pulled across the threshold into a realm of roiling chaos.

"Once on the other side, you breathe in the fine film of celestial giants as you remember a time you never knew. Reality opens before you; the non-memory grasps your mind with an intensity you can barely fathom. Both beauty and horror fill your head, balancing the scales of an eternal torment from which you will never escape.

"You might pray for mercy to whatever gods you knew, but the madness offers no respite. And do not anticipate a savior in the form of the Reaper, for you are well beyond death. This is the hell that has been thrust on you, not through any act of your own, but by the cruel and apathetic winds of fate. You are nothing. You are less than a void. Any sense of self left within you only brings forth agony, and loathing of an existence that once was, but is no longer, yours."

Here the fire in his eyes turned to ash. The weight of his story fell heavily across his shoulders and his face became grim and tight. For an instant, I thought his tale had ended.

Then, just as suddenly, the fire reignited and the old man continued.

"Or so it is said. You see, none who cross the threshold of that gate, whether in a physical, spiritual, or mental sense, ever truly return. Thus, we are left without any true knowledge on the nature of what lies beyond it.

"Where did it come from, you ask? No one knows. Some say it simply appeared in that location one spring as the snow melted and fell from the trees. Others may tell you it was built by the hands of the first men to walk this part of the world, a shrine to a god long since lost to time. Still others say that it was forged in the very fires of Hell. Perhaps this true, for the black stone from which it was built has yet to be found anywhere else in this world.

"One thing we do know is that it has a penchant for abducting the souls of children, leaving their bodies vacant and feverish. So many mothers and fathers across the generations have tried to follow their children through the gate, only to appear on the other side, unharmed and whole.

"Now, you may call this story foolish. And that is all very well. It is not my place to judge a man's perception of his reality. But even so, I urge you to not let your children out of your sight past dark, for there is no way of truly knowing what dangers and strangeness hide in this world."

The ominous warning drifted into the night sky like smoke as the old man stood. Somehow he seemed even more bent and rickety than before, but even so he made his way offstage to a hearty round of applause from the locals and troupers alike.

With the final act over, the audience dispersed and the troupe began to break down the stage. As I helped my mother fold the backdrop, I couldn't help but think about the old man's story; it planted in my head a seed of morbid curiosity regarding the stone archway, one I couldn't shake. And by the time we were through cleaning the campsite, I'd made my mind up. I would—had to—test the story for myself.

The summer night was warm and heavy, the air thick with the day's moisture. My mother snored heavily in our wagon as I followed the shore of the millpond to the forest's edge. The midnight waters rippled in a slight breeze that carried the smell of fish and distorted the reflection of the pallid moon. Ahead, the tree line stood dark and imposing, the thick canopy punctured sporadically by moonlight.

With a deep breath I stepped past the first tree, and then the next, and the next. I walked until I could no longer see the moonlit pond, and I spun in a circle ten times with my eyes closed, ensuring I would become good and lost. Then I picked a direction at random and kept walking.

I soon realized I'd done my work too well; I was well and truly lost. My initial excitement was swiftly succumbing to despair when I felt inexplicably drawn toward something to my left. Despair dissipated as swiftly as fog in sunlight, and I realized my feet were moving of their own volition. I was a passenger in my own body, riding upon waves of comfort that pulled me out into a sea of darkness.

After several minutes, I heard music. Piping notes of an ethereal flute drove every thought from my mind, clearing the way for the whispers that promised grand and enticing cosmic knowledge that would outweigh anything I'd learn while shackled to this mortal coil.

I don't know exactly when it was that I came upon the Wayward Gate. All I know is that once I stood before it, the whispers ceased and the real magic began.

The void between the columns was no longer empty. Instead, the gateway opened to the chaos and beauty of a cosmic reality beyond anything I could have dreamed of. Colors of a spectrum I had never imagined blinded me, searing my mind. Screams and deep, hideous laughter deafened me, before being soothed away by the caressing tones of a dying star. The mysterious reality beyond the threshold pulled at me with each euphoric wave of entropic radiation. It pulled so hard that I felt myself dislodge and disconnect from the body that bound me to world of man and for one incredible moment, I became something more than even a god could imagine. I was a man, a fiend, a star, a grain of sand. I was everything and I was nothing.

And suddenly, I woke to the moon's somber face glaring down at me from heights I once beheld. I tried to sit, but my body would not obey. I heard furious talking and panicked shouts, but I couldn't respond. Then my mother's face appeared, blocking the weeping moon. She sat me up and pulled me close with the strength of a bear.

Only after I'd been carried back to Lorriston, and the campsite therein, did I learn what transpired. As it happened, my sneaking about didn't go unnoticed. The town drunk, having chosen to sleep beneath one of our wagons, saw me as I made my way past the millpond and into the forest. Assuming I was simply answering the call of nature, he forgot about me… until I failed to return. An alarm rang somewhere deep in the cotton of his stupor, spurring him to wake the entire troupe who, in turn, woke the town. Minds filled with Albert Wood's warning, the group wasted no time in making their way to the Wayward Gate, hoping to head me off. But they found me there already, standing as a statue, with wide, glossy eyes staring through the empty gate. According to my mother it took five men to tear me away from the gate and drag me to the ground.

Looking back, I realize just how close I came to losing my soul to that terrible cosmic void, so well-hidden behind the veil of reality through the Wayward Gate. While I'm thankful to still be here with my mother and my troupe, part of me still longs to feel that euphoria again.

But for now, I must be content with memory and dreams. Dreams of being enveloped in ever-changing cosmic entropy. Dreams of being everything… and of being nothing.

ROSES

C. S. HELLSTROM

The world is dark and quiet as the Rosas begin to stir, awakening to a new day. Rosa Rugosa blinks her eyes open in the predawn gloom and glances about her familiar surroundings. The spacious open-air temple, with its high roof supported by massive columns of white marble, is nearly silent despite being filled with hundreds of peacefully slumbering girls.

Rosa Rugosa stretches for a minute before she rises noiselessly from the large, soft cushion she has been sleeping on beside Rosa Alba and Rosa Setigera. She inhales deeply, drawing the warm, moist tropical air into her lungs and smelling—no, tasting—the saltiness of the nearby sea. Her stomach rumbles loudly as she stands, so she leaves the still-sleeping Rosa Alba and Rosa Setigera to their dreams and makes her way to the far side of the temple in search of something to eat. Rosa Rugosa tiptoes quietly past the hundreds of other sleeping Rosas splayed out over their various cushions, chaises and lounges. Several of the earliest risers have already gathered the morning offerings and brought them up to the long table that sits along the east-facing side of the temple.

The small gathering of Rosas greets Rosa Rugosa with a unified smile. Some of the Rosas briefly rise from their breakfasts to give her a hug and a kiss on the cheek. Rosa Sericea, her mouth full with a trickle of pink juice running down her chin, points to a bowl of freshly cut melon while Rosa Rugosa scans the long buffet of fruits, fish, and rice cakes for something to fill her empty belly. She smiles, nods her thanks, and proceeds to fill a bowl with multicolored pieces of fruit. Rosa Rugosa adds a rice cake on top and then takes her breakfast out onto the open terrace with Rosa Sericea following behind. They sit on one of the curved white marble benches to enjoy the dawn. The burning yellow orb rises from the ocean's calm surface: the birth of a new day. Far below the temple, out along the sandy beach some two miles distant, they observe the village fishermen engaged in their daily travail. The crews drag the many outrigger canoes into the water and smartly hop in to paddle over the rough surf and out to calm sea beyond the breakers.

The Rosas enjoy their breakfasts in silence, watching the canoes slip one by one over the horizon.

"Rosa Alba, Rosa Rugosa, I come this day to honor you," the matriarch of the village, Attar, calls loudly from the base of the steps, which encircle the temple in concentric rings.

Rosa Rugosa scowls, sets her empty bowl upon the bench beside Rosa Sericea, and descends the one hundred steps of the Temple of the Roses to Attar.

Attar stands at the bottom on the black granite plaza, a waxen smile on her face. None save for a Rosa may mount the circular steps, nor enter the temple at the summit where the Rosas reside when they are not tending to the rose garden or engaging in their daily ablutions.

"Rosa Rugosa, I come this morning to honor you and Rosa Alba. This night is the darkness of your moon, when one Rosa will depart the Temple of the Roses to walk among the stars, whilst the other Rosa will descend the temple steps at daybreak to become a member of the village. Rosa Alba was born one sun closer to this, your two hundredth moon. And so by right it will be Rosa Alba who takes part in tonight's ceremony. Have you given any consideration to a name for yourself, Rosa Rugosa? You must decide on one before you are introduced to the village tomorrow at the welcoming celebration. Or I may choose one for you if you prefer." Attar's waxen smile spreads as she reminds Rosa Rugosa of that which she and every Rosa already know.

"No, Attar. I have not yet chosen a new name nor must I until tomorrow morning, when I am brought into your village. Until then, I remain Rosa Rugosa." Rosa Rugosa says this matter-of-factly in a cold voice devoid of emotion. Attar observes the girl's serious countenance and smiles again, but this time warmly, honestly, perhaps now remembering a time many moons ago when she herself first made the transition from a Rosa to a woman of the village.

"Do not fear, Rosa Rugosa. You will come to accept your new life in the village with time, and you will enjoy it. When I first entered the village, everything I encountered seemed new and appeared strange to me, but it is something that I, and now you, will adapt to. There are several young men from which you may choose a husband, unless you have already selected a certain man? No? Well, you have plenty of time. Your wedding ceremony will be in six moons, when you shall declare the husband you have selected and join with him in devoted service to the village. I am sorry that you will be our sole newcomer this morrow. It is always easier when there are several new members of the community who can help each other adjust to life within the village. I know it is hard at first, to give up the life of a Rosa." Attar speaks gently, knowingly.

Rosa Rugosa answers the leader of the village with a scowl.

Attar continues, "It will not be so hard as you perhaps think, Rosa Rugosa. Every woman at the age of two hundred moons must join the village, save for the Rosa who departs to walk amongst the stars." Attar's countenance resumes the original frozen expression, with its waxen smile and glazed stare.

"Do you have anything else to say to me?" Rosa Rugosa demands, turning her head slightly as a gentle sea breeze plays with her long hair. She shifts her gaze from Attar up to the maroon sun, now fully risen above the watery horizon.

"No, Rosa Rugosa. Not at this time. I will see you again tomorrow morning in the village. May the Lord of the Abyss bless you. I will remain here to honor Rosa Alba when she arises." Attar's smile warms again as she raises her right-hand to the sky with her palm upward, the sign of hello, goodbye, and I love you when speaking with a Rosa. No person save for another Rosa may ever touch a Rosa. Rosa Rugosa turns her back on Attar and ascends the hundred white marble steps of the Temple of the Roses in silence.

The bright tropical sun has risen high into the clear blue sky and quickly banishes the last of the morning chill from the air. Rosa Rugosa and Rosa Alba stroll hand in hand along the center of the long, rectangular promenade toward the white fountain in the distance. The promenade is constructed of polished square blocks of black granite, each a sunken cube measuring greater than fifty yards to a side. The quarter-mile wide promenade rises from the watery depths of the sea, its base covered in seaweed, to proceed six miles inland where it terminates at the top of a round plateau paved with the same mammoth granite cubes.

At the plateau's center, a ring of obelisks extends high into the sky, disappearing amidst the remaining morning fog that boils beneath the powerful bright sun. The massive black stones are smooth to the touch and appear new, save for a thick covering of moss and lichen that extends upward from the base of each to some hundred feet above ground level. Each obelisk is set at a unique angle, some close to vertical while others appear as if they will topple over any moment, though they have remained in their exact positions for nearly a millennium. One obelisk stands out from the rest, with a strangely unnatural appearance that sets it apart from the other eleven; it sits at a perfect right angle to the base of the terrace, standing perfectly straight.

Rosa Rugosa and Rosa Alba smile warmly to their sisters Rosa Phoenica, Rosa Damascena, and Rosa Xanthina as the three skip past, hand in hand and singing a song. They stroll along the center of the promenade and the harmonic trio's sweet melody serenades them until the merry chorus fades into the distance.

To either side of the wide black granite concourse grow countless acres of rose bushes that stretch to the horizon. The various plantings of the different rose varieties combine to form strange patterns over the landscape with their bright blossoms in the colors of white, yellow, pink, red, orange, lavender, and purple. The roses' combined fragrance is ever present, scenting the air with its, sweet intoxicating aroma.

The girls walk unhurriedly in the warm late morning sun until they reach the fountain, set off the center of the promenade at the base of the obelisks. The circular fountain is carved from a single gleaming piece of white marble and contains a large pool of crystal-clear water. It stands out starkly against the black granite of the promenade and the towering obelisks beyond.

The girls sit on the wide edge of the fountain and tilt their heads skyward to feel the warmth of the bright sun on their faces. The merry gurgle of the fountain is the only sound in the world. In the distance to either side of the promenade, near and far, the many Rosas tend to their massive rose garden. The oldest Rosas labor to snip off the past blooms or deadened stalks. Some of the younger Rosas feed the plants with buckets of ground fish and seaweed, whilst the youngest Rosas are engaged in the daily hauling of the countless buckets of water that the acres of roses require to maintain their continual blossoms.

Rosa Rugosa turns to Rosa Alba with a bright smile that seems to flash for a moment from her eyes. Rosa Alba automatically returns her fellow Rosa's, her lifelong companion's, her dearest friend's smile with one of her own. Her best smile, her biggest smile, the one she only smiles when her moon sister Rosa Rugosa smiles at her.

"I love you, Rosa Alba, truly I do, yet I wish with all my heart that it were I going to walk amongst the stars tonight." Rosa Rugosa gazes deeply into Rosa Alba's eyes and her smile fades, transforms, slowly becomes an expression of profound sadness. Rosa Alba's smile disappears along with her friend's, to be replaced with look of concern.

"I am sorry that only one of us may have the honor of departing tonight to walk amongst the stars. It is the two hundredth moon for the both of us, yet I was born one sun closer than you and so the duty and the honor of this moon are mine. I will depart this evening a Rosa, to walk among the stars, whilst you will become a woman and enter the village tomorrow morning. You will be given a new name and you will spend your life as a villager. You will take a husband and you will bear many beautiful Rosas, I have no doubt. I am sorry you will have to enter the village alone. The next moon there are five Rosas, so there will be four new women to enter the village together. They will join you soon. You will be happy, Rosa Rugosa. Do not worry yourself so about what must be." Rosa Alba smiles her warmest smile again and takes Rosa Rugosa's hand into hers, giving it a gentle squeeze before holding on tightly. Rosa Rugosa notices Rosa Alba's palm is warm and damp, whilst her own hand is cool and dry.

"I am sorry, Rosa Alba. I know only one of us may have the honor of going to walk amongst the stars tonight. Two moons ago it was Rosa Gallica who went to the stars, and I promised her then that I would come to her. I love you, Rosa Alba, but I am in love with Rosa Gallica." Rosa Rugosa breaks eye contact, suddenly turning her head to contemplate their reflected faces in the pool's still waters. Rosa Alba releases Rosa Rugosa's hand, which drops numbly to the lip of the pool. Rosa Alba stares at her friend's profile a moment, puzzled, then turns and joins Rosa Rugosa in gazing down at their wavering reflections.

"I am truly sorry, Rosa Rugosa. I love you, but this is my honor, my destiny. Do not be afraid of what is to come tomorrow. I know you will be very happy when…" Rosa Alba replies in a soft, tender voice that becomes a gurgle as her head plunges through the water's shimmering surface, her face briefly meeting its reflection on the way under. It takes all of Rosa Rugosa's strength. It is over in a moment, an excruciatingly long moment.

Rosa Rugosa stands up in a quick, jerking movement and stumbles a few steps backward. Her body begins to shake convulsively, and she almost falls to the ground before she regains her balance to stand hunched over, winded and gasping for air. It is a minute before she catches her breath and straightens herself up to stand tall.

"I am sorry, Rosa Alba. Forgive me, my dear sweet moon sister. But I must go to walk among the stars tonight. I promised Rosa Gallica that I would come to her, and she will be waiting for me," Rosa Rugosa whispers softly as her vision becomes a watery blur. She blinks her eyes, and the first of many hot tears roll down the soft pink cheeks to fall and land with tiny splashes on the cold black granite.

Rosa Rugosa disrobes and slips into the cool waters of the pool. She swims out to the center, then races herself from one side to the other and back several times, pushing herself to swim as fast as she can until she stops some minutes later, thoroughly winded. It was a racing game she used to play with Rosa Alba and Rosa Gallica, a long time ago. She leans back against the smooth granite edge of the pool to catch her breath, and gazes over her sister Rosas as they enjoy their daily ablutions. There are nearly a thousand bathers engaged in loud laughing and giggling, splashing and swimming. Rosa Primula dives into the pool and swims up under the water's surface to Rosa Rugosa, unnoticed from the side. Rosa Primula's dripping head rises from the water next to Rosa Rugosa and she kisses her softly on the cheek.

"Goodbye, Rosa Rugosa. I shall miss you, but I will see you again in six moons, I promise." Rosa Primula's bright, sky-blue eyes flash a smile that perfectly complements the wide grin on her full red lips.

Rosa Rugosa replies to Rosa Primula with a warm smile of her own before she swims to the far side of the pool, exits the water, and dons a clean toga. A sudden flurry of activity on the far side of the pool draws her attention, and she watches intently as the three new Rosas, now aged twenty moons, enter the bathing pool for the first time. Their mothers quietly turn from their former daughters and return to the village, each with a smile on her lips and a tear in her eye. The new Rosas are instantly surrounded by their hundreds of new sisters, who play in the water with them until it is time for the new Rosas to don their first soft white cotton togas. Then, their many loving sisters will help the new Rosas make their initial ascent up the steps of the Temple of the Roses, which will be their home for the next one hundred and eighty lunar cycles, until they attain the age of two hundred synodic months and each fulfill their own destiny.

Rosa Rugosa watches intently as the new Rosas emerge from the water and receive their names: Rosa Moschata, Rosa Canina, Rosa Alba. She breaks a wide smile, turns, and walks slowly toward the promenade when a strong voice devoid of emotion calls from behind. Rosa Rugosa freezes dead in her tracks.

"Rosa Rugosa, I loved Rosa Alba and you took her from me. Mine is the next moon. You will see me again." Rosa Setigera states coldly, dispassionately, with an icy glare that stabs into Rosa Rugosa's back.

Rosa Rugosa raises her face slightly and gazes up into the bright pink-and-marmalade sky. She feels the friendly warmth of the setting sun upon her face, hears the happy buzz of the countless laughs and giggles of the Rosas as they exit the pool behind them. "I loved Rosa Alba, my moon sister, but I did what I had to do. I will see you at the time of the next moon, Rosa Setigera. When we meet, I will offer you my hand." Rosa Rugosa resumes her journey to the promenade at a brisk pace.

Rosa Rugosa discards her toga. It falls silently to the black granite. She raises her face to the stars, smiles, and enters the cool swirling waters of the white fountain that glows brightly in the starlight. Rosa Rugosa cuts her ankles and wrists with the ceremonial implement as she has been taught, then lays back to float peacefully on the shimmering water and stare up into the night sky with its countless stars. The fountain's clear, swirling waters take on a faint pinkish hue that slowly progresses to red as the air fills with a strong, coppery odor.

The ancient one approaches the circle of obelisks, gait slow but moving at a quick pace; each stride of the giant's legs carries the Lord of the Abyss further than the span of one of the massive granite cubes that forms the promenade. Occasionally one of the ancient granite blocks shifts slightly under the Lord's incredible weight. The ancient one pauses a moment beside the tiny white fountain at the base of the circle and inhales deeply, emitting a wet, slushy sound. Then the Lord of the Abyss exhales a gurgling roar that can be heard for miles before entering the circle of obelisks.

The ancient one stands at the center of the circle and remains motionless for a time, staring up at the stars as they make their endless progression through the heavens. Then, as the eastern sky begins to show the first hints of the pink haze of dawn, the ancient one departs the circle and makes its way back along the promenade to the great city located within the ocean's coldest, darkest depths. There is a loud clap from the sea as the ocean's waters surge together to fill the sudden hole left by the Lord of the Abyss' head when it abruptly disappears into the deep at the end of a monstrous stride.

Rosa Rugosa floats on the red waters of the white fountain, her sightless eyes staring up at the stars and a smile frozen in time upon her pink lips. High in the night sky, two Rosas meet amongst the stars and share a tender embrace. When Rosa Gallica and Rosa Rugosa part, Rosa Setigera stands before them. Rosa Rugosa takes Rosa Gallica by the hand and then offers her free hand to Rosa Setigera with a smile. Rosa Setigera pauses, then accepts Rosa Rugosa's hand with a tight squeeze. An unbroken chain of roses stretches across the night sky as the Rosas walk hand in hand together amongst the stars, through eternity.

THE SERPENT OF WOODSFIELD

BY NICK MOORE

My radio crackled to life. Pete, one of my deputies, and he sounded scared.

"Sheriff? You read? We got another one."

I cursed under my breath and closed the trunk. This would have to wait. "I'm here, Pete. What's happening?"

His response was automatic. "Little girl missing, the Fishers, up on Lake Road, looks like…" He trailed off.

Good. At least he's smart enough to keep it off the radio. "10-4, on my way to you." I decided to leave the lights off; word would travel fast enough as it was. At this time of day, the roads were empty anyway, especially in October.

This little slice of heaven, Valley County, is about as nice as you can imagine. I roared up the road, looking at the quiet little houses dotting the woods. But an undeniable tension permeated the community this time of year, one you could sense in the way folks wouldn't meet your eyes. I prefer it when they can't meet my eyes. Better than the eyes that are pleading, praying for a safety I can't promise.

I've been sheriff now for going on thirty years. It's quiet, and the people are nice. Most of them will feel bad when the threat passes. Relief, and then guilt that they feel relief at someone else's grief. They'll pull together. They always do.

If not for the disappearances, it'd be perfect.

Second week of October this year, which meant the families would at least get to enjoy Halloween, though we'd all be on edge. We always are this time of year.

I pulled up in front of the Fishers' place. Cute little house. They'd lived in town for years, four kids. Ted Fisher was outside, chain smoking. I gave him the closest thing I could muster to a supportive pat on the shoulder. He was a good man, hard in a family sort of way. I could see the tears he struggled to hold back.

"Which one?" I kept my voice, low, measured, soothing.

"Emily," he whispered. "She's only six, Sheriff."

I nodded. "We'll find her. We'll get crews out, we'll search the woods."

"You know it won't matter, Sheriff."

"It might, Ted."

I stepped inside. Laurel was sobbing on the couch. Pete got up with a look of relief.

I took off my hat. "What do we know?"

Pete shifted into cop mode, which was good. He was better at this than the emotional side of it. "Emily was in the backyard, kicking a soccer ball against the side of the house."

Laurel interjected, "We've been keeping them inside, but they just got a little stir crazy... I was watching her through the window... it was daylight... she wasn't ten feet from the back door..." She trailed off into a sob.

"No one blames you, Laurel." I tried to be gentle before turning back to Pete. "How long before she was noticed missing?"

"No more than a half hour, Sheriff. Laurel got a call from Mike. He needed her to find some paperwork. She hung up and the kid—" he paused. "Emily, was gone."

I rubbed my chin. "Have deputies set up roadblocks on either end of the Valley. All cars, in or out, get searched. Have the Search and Rescue squad down in the woods on both sides of the lake."

He nodded and got on the radio.

I walked outside and saw the SUV now parked next to my cruiser. Ryan Bergeron stood with a hand on Ted's shoulder, the textbook show of support. I couldn't hear him, but his voice would be the perfect mix of support, confidence, and fear. The closest thing we had to a ruling class around here were the Bergerons. Ryan had been Chairman of the Board of Selectmen since before I came to town as a Deputy Sheriff straight out of the academy.

"Any news, Sheriff?" His voice was perfect for a politician, dripping with what I'd call gravitas. The perfect official voice, I'd give him that.

I nodded as curtly as I could. "We're devoting all our resources to finding this little girl, Mr. Selectman." Our relationship was never personal, but these meetings were always awkward. I didn't have the education or the upbringing that Bergeron wanted to see in a Sheriff. I knew he saw me as a necessary evil, and that was enough to keep him civil towards me. We coexisted here, the apex predators of this tiny political ecosystem.

His eyes narrowed and he nodded. "Well, best carry on."

I walked to my cruiser and looked back to Pete. "Get the units out. Then let's meet back at the station and see what we've got. I have a stop to make."

"It's not going to help, Sheriff."

I turned back towards Ted. The poor man's eyes looked broken. "That serpent got her. We all know it. She's gone."

"There's no serpent Ted," I replied, trying to keep as calm as possible. "Nothing magical about this. The woods are dangerous. We'll do everything we can to find her. You take care of the rest of your family for now."

Anger flashed in his eyes before melting back into sadness. "We're not going to find her, Sheriff. There's something evil in these woods, we all know it." He turned towards Bergeron. "You know it just as well as I do." Then he walked back into his house.

I cut back down towards town, listening to Pete give commands over the radio. He had been a good hire. Former Army, and a true lawman. He still struggled with parts of it, but he was reliable. I needed reliable.

I stopped at the vet to pick up medicine for the K9, and then drove back to the station, parking in the one-car garage out back that we had never managed to get the funding to convert into extra office space. I shuffled gear around in my trunk and looked at my watch, the sun would be set in another six hours.

Once inside, I looked over my office. Small town detritus covered the walls and furniture, a history of a life lived as a rural elected official. I opened my bottom drawer and moved the bottle of whiskey aside, settling for the thick folder underneath.

I opened it up and stared at it.

This file represented decades of personal research. It started with handwritten notes and printouts from cryptozoology websites. Reports the world over about giant snakes, larger than anything that existed on record.

These behemoths haunted the obscure and the historical. The Titanoboa fossils, the basilisk of ancient myth, dragons. Reports of snakes seen by explorers two or three times as long as any confirmed sighting.

Next came records from local Native American tribes in colonial times. Folklore about a great beast living in the caves that dotted the local mountains, a protector of the natural world. A monster said to be large enough to eat a moose, but smarter than any man. The indigenous people would leave gifts so that it might provide them protection and allow them to coexist in its domain.

Next came the photocopies: books and records I gathered over long nights in the Historical Association archives. Folklore about the Serpent of Woodsfield, as this area used to be called. A giant snake that could eat a man whole, but was smart enough to avoid any trap set for it. These were intermixed with colonial-era reports of men disappearing in these woods as far back as the 1600's, simply vanishing without a trace. Trappers, hunters, even a group of soldiers sent to investigate the other disappearances. People had vanished in these woods for hundreds of years, leaving no trace at all. It was as if they evaporated into the trees. The only clues were reports of a serpent so large it could completely encircle a house with its massive body.

Then there was nothing. Time moved on. We forgot.

The file started again in 1985, with a newspaper article about a company blasting at a quarry up in the hills. Things picked up speed quickly. That fall eight workers vanished, several in the middle of shifts. The next fall the attacks started, homes found empty and destroyed, no sign of the families that had lived there. Ten people vanished in 1987, thirteen in 1988, fifteen in 1989, and then one in 1990.

One every year since, too.

Every October, a child vanishes from the Valley, never be seen again. We search all over, but they're never found. We have coyotes in these woods, bears too, even moose, which are a lot more dangerous than most people know. Everyone knew this wasn't normal though. And no trace of the missing ever turned up.

In 1996, Buck Smith and his wife had enough. They made a stink all over town that they were getting the hell out with their kids since no one could stop what was happening. Moved down to Massachusetts, and left a vacuum of uncertainty in their wake. Then one of their kids disappeared that October, first time in almost a decade that no one in Valley County had vanished. Their other kid disappeared the next year. After that no one tried to leave. Whatever evil lurked in the woods would follow you if you did; that had become clear enough.

I flipped through the pages, each photo a smiling face of a child I once knew.

I noticed Pete was standing at the door, and paused. I didn't know how long he had been there, watching me.

"Any news, Pete?"

"Nothing, Sheriff. Just like all the others."

I nodded. "Word out around town?"

He flushed and nodded. "Shouldn't have said that much over the radio, I guess."

I opened my drawer, poured whiskey into two old coffee mugs, and handed one to him. "It's okay, Pete." I tapped the open case file with my knuckle. We both know that no matter what we do, we're adding another face to this file today."

His face sank. "Isn't there anything we can do?"

I grimaced. "I wish there was, but in thirty years on this job I've never figured out how to stop it from happening."

"What is it?"

I hesitated and considered the brown liquid in my glass. "I don't know, Pete. Some people say it's a serial killer, but they don't remember what those houses looked like back in the day, all torn up like they were. Others think an ancient monster roams these woods, some antediluvian beast that we've all forgotten. Some people think it's a curse, the price we pay for living in a place so nice. Hell, I even had some professor of biology say we had a family of bears that had learned to eat humans before going into hibernation."

We sat in silence for a while, sipping on our whiskey.

"You know this is a glaciated valley, Pete?"

Pete looked at me, uncomprehending.

"During the last ice age, a glacier moved through the valley. When glaciers enter a valley, they dig deep. Scour the ground, scrape away the earth that was here before. Who knows what's left when they recede?"

Pete was staring at me now, concern in his eyes. "You okay, Sheriff?"

I closed the file. "Yeah, Pete. Just old and tired of this."

He stared at his whiskey for a minute, then finished it in a large gulp.

"If you don't mind, Sheriff, I'd like to go drive around a bit, see if I can be of use."

I smiled. He had a good heart, and a child on the way. I knew these autumn disappearances weighed heavy on him. "Absolutely, Pete, not a bad idea. I might head up the west side of the Valley myself. You want to take the east side?"

He grinned and jumped up. Atta boy. Just needs to believe there's something that can be done.

I drove down through the center of town. The streets were empty; the news would have everyone lying low until they were sure the danger had passed. I drove out east and up into the hills, weaving my way out far above any houses.

I pulled off the road onto what was little more than a trail, driving into the woods until I could park right behind the SUV that had already arrived.

I stepped out of my car and stared at the man standing next to it. He still had a hell of a head of hair, even if it had gone gray. He would probably call it silver. He was heavier than he had been in his youth, but carried it well.

Bergeron looked up at me. "Hey there, Sheriff."

"Hey there, Mr. Selectman."

He took a deep breath. "I suppose we should get this over with?"

I nodded and popped my trunk. Emily Fisher lay there, sleeping what I prayed was a dreamless sleep. I nodded towards her. "Had to give her another shot of the tranquilizer at the station. She should stay under we're done here."

He grunted a response and picked her up.

We walked up the trail into the woods, taking turns carrying her. We had always done this without ever discussing it, even with the small ones who we could handle on our own. A shared cross that we carried into the wilderness.

We passed a cutoff with a metal sign warning about poison ivy. That had been Bergeron's plan, and it was a good one. Dissuaded anyone from wandering up too far.

We finally got to the mouth of the cave we sought, one with a large hole barely five feet past the entrance, a hole that plunged into the darkness of the earth.

Bergeron pulled out a length or rope and we started tying up young Emily in such a way that would make it easy to lower her down. I found myself remembering the first time I had come out to these woods.

1989 was a rough fall in the valley. Houses were ransacked, and several looked like someone had driven a small train right through them. I was a young Deputy

Sheriff when I got the call from Selectman Ryan Bergeron himself; his uncle's house alarm had gone off and no one was answering the phone. His uncle was supposed to be home alone with his nephew, and he demanded one of us get over there to check it out. I happened to be right down the road, and floored it.

I crested the hill in front of the house and saw the nightmare of the Valley: a giant serpent, black as night, moving out of the house in the deepening dusk and slithering into the woods. I shouted into the radio that I was in pursuit as I raced up the road alongside it, watching as its black skin reflected my emergency lights. I reached the turnoff and flew up the small trail, making my way up into the woods. Sheriff Blake, who'd been a decent man, met me where the trail ended and we set off on foot, following the monster into the darkening woods.

We were halfway up the mountain was Bergeron caught up. He was younger then, and fit. He was carrying a shotgun and swearing he'd help us get the man doing this. If I hadn't seen the thing already, I would have sent him right back to his car. But I knew we would need the help.

We arrived at the cave and stared down the hole, straight down into the depths of the earth. I got a flashlight off my belt and shined it down too, hoping to see how far the abyss went. Instead, I saw a glassy surface. And by the time I realized I was looking at its eyes, it was too late.

The beast exploded from the ground, throwing us all back. I managed to get a shot off, but it didn't have much effect. Instinct took over, and in those moments my reactions were faster than any time before or since, perhaps driven by some memory of Eden and the serpent, or maybe just the fact that I knew this thing had killed fourteen people. I scrambled over a log, barely avoiding its mouth as I tried to find a way to stop it.

I heard other gunshots, the Sheriff and Bergeron trying to make a mark. The beast screeched, a sound I still hear in my nightmares, and rounded on them. Sheriff Blake tried to run at it with a flare, and got flicked back by its massive tail.

Bergeron was still on the ground, struggling to find his feet when the beast turned its attention to him. I watched it draw closer as he tried in vain to propel himself backward to some sort of safety.

In these moments, we do things that can't be explained. And in that moment I screamed at the snake to stop, perhaps the most illogical action a man in my position could have taken. To this day I don't know why I did it; at the time, I never imagined it would work.

To my amazement, it did.

The serpent swung its massive body back towards me and seemed to study me. The intelligence in its eyes was shocking; I have never felt so small and insignificant in my life.

"What do you want?" I shouted.

The serpent stared at me, I imagine with contempt over the idiotic question, but I had no idea what to do.

It was Bergeron who spoke next. "What if we fed you?"

I watched in wonder as the serpent slowly nodded its head.

Bergeron stammered over his words, the only time in my life I've seen the man so shaken. "I'll bring cattle every fall, you feed in the fall, don't you? However many you need."

The beast shook its head. *No.*

I understood. "It has to be human."

It nodded.

Now Bergeron understood, too. "An adult?"

The serpent shook its head again.

Bergon grimaced. "A child, then."

A nod.

Sheriff Blake finally found his voice and swore at us. "Are you really negotiating with a giant damn snake? Move out of the way and let me get a shot off!"

Bergeron ignored Blake and met the beast's gaze. "One child, every October, brought here to this cave. And you do not take any others from this valley."

We all stared in disbelief at the monster as it nodded again.

Sheriff Blake looked at me for support. "This is the craziest nonsense I have ever heard."

The snake looked at Bergeron as if waiting for something else. I didn't understand what.

Bergeron did.

"This year there are only the three of us. You can have one to seal the pact."

The snake turned its eyes to the Sheriff and me, and then looked back to Bergeron.

He pointed a finger at Sheriff Blake. "Take him."

It struck faster than I could see, a blur of black in the fading light. Sheriff Blake screamed only once as the beast receded back into the mountain, and then there was silence. His disappearance would be the fifteenth of the year.

Bergeron turned to me that night, and laid out the agreement that would mark the rest of my life. "We can never speak of this. This will be our sacrifice. I suppose you'll need to get elected Sheriff. I'll do what I can. We have to keep this peace."

Finally, we finished with the knots and began lowering Emily Fisher into the hole.

The first years had been rough. I barely held the community together, until Buck Smith produced an opportunity. Bergeron came to me then, explained that families would leave in droves if they thought it would be safer. No, he surmised. We had to target the Smiths, take both of their kids. One child this year and one child the next, to show that leaving would be more dangerous.

It had worked.

It never got easier, though. Families watched their kids more closely, and it got trickier to grab them without getting caught.

I never married. Couldn't bear to start a family with what I knew. That was my small sacrifice, a way to pay the debt leveraged against my soul.

One October, when we couldn't manage to grab a child, Bergeron provided one of his on Halloween. That was how he paid the debt on his.

We lowered Emily gently until the rope went slack, indicating that she now rested at the bottom. We then threw the remaining rope into the hole. The first few years, the children had been awake. I would hear the screams, followed by the horrible sounds of the beast feeding.

Since we started drugging them, almost twenty years ago now, we had not seen or heard the thing. I presumed it waited for them to wake up before feeding.

We made our way back down to the cars. I stopped when we reached them and glanced back up at the mountain, pondering how many times Bergeron and I would walk those trails, how many children we would offer up to the serpent. How would we pass along this secret? What would happen when we were gone? "How do we know it's still there? We haven't seen it or heard it in years."

Bergeron nodded sadly; it was a thought he, too, had pondered. "We can't know, Sheriff. But if we don't bring a sacrifice, and we're wrong, this whole community will bleed. This is the agreement we have to live with. The price of its protection."

"But," I countered, "if it died, or if it's left, we could have been killing children needlessly for years." I stared at my cruiser. I could get in, drive back to town, continue this cursed tradition for another year. Or I could go back to the cave, wait for Emily to wake up, try to pull her up with a rope. I probably had some extra in the trunk.

I looked at Bergeron, and he met my gaze. "This is our curse, Sheriff. It's the world we must live in. Whatever that nightmare is, we made a pact with it. Now we have to live with that."

I paused for a second, then flicked on my radio, "You there, Pete?"

A moment passed. Then the radio crackled to life, the call and response of lawmen everywhere. "I'm here, Sheriff. Over."

I smiled sadly. "I'm losing the light. Going to head back to the station and draw up a plan for tomorrow. Mind meeting me there?"

"10-4 Sheriff, I'm en route."

I backed my car down to the road and started driving towards town. I glanced up at the mountain one more time as the sun set. *Monsters roam there*, I thought, and shuddered.

THE BREADBOX

BY CECILIA KENNEDY

Long lavender flowers trail the sidewalk where I get the mail in front of my house. When I open the mailbox, I see that it's empty and decide to go back inside, but I hear a familiar voice calling my name, so I turn around.

"Adelaide?" the woman asks.

I realize that the voice belongs to Virginia and that she's wearing a violet skirt paired with a flowing white ruffled shirt. Perhaps I should have dressed better to get the mail—and to hear my name called so brightly into the summer afternoon sun.

"I—I was just stepping out. No mail yet," I say with a nervous laugh in my throat. I wish I wouldn't wring my hands as I talk, but I feel so new, so out of my element.

"My mail hasn't come yet, either. Are you adjusting to the new place?"

"Yes… thank you for asking. Of course, there are always repairs to do and that kind of thing."

"Oh, I sure do know about that. All of these houses around here always need something."

"Mine is very stubborn. It pretty much resists new paint."

"Ah… now there might be a reason for that," Virginia says with a certain spark in her voice that makes me wary.

"What would that be?"

The spark in her voice moves to her eyes, which flash like she's about to tell me a secret that she reserves for only her closest friends. I know better than to be drawn in so foolishly, only to be tricked, but I can't help myself. I want to know.

"Not too many people stay very long in that house you're living in now. They say that some crazy lady—a nurse who worked for the hospital in town in the early '60s or something would poison the kids in the children's ward. Well, she never got caught, but one really irate and distraught mother who believed that nurse killed her daughter while she was staying in the hospital took matters into her own hands. She hacked that woman to death and buried her bones in the yard behind your house."

I must have looked absolutely shocked when Virginia finished her story, because she quickly added that she didn't think anything bad would happen to me or anything—just little annoyances and such that might drive me from the house. And now, I'm wondering if this is how people in this neighborhood get rid of move-ins—without even having met them properly.

I decide instead to put a cheerful smile on my face and tell Virginia that I don't believe in such things. We exchange a few more pleasantries before she slips inside the door of the house right next to mine. I've lived next to that house for two months, and I don't even know the owner's name, but Virginia does. People around here learn the names of those who really matter, it seems.

Turning around and facing the front door of my house, I decide that I just don't want to go back inside right now. I want to know more about the bones, so I walk over to the gate, slip open the latch and get a shovel out of the tool shed in the back of the yard. I have no idea where to begin digging, but there are remnants of a garden closest to the backside of the house. If I wanted to bury someone, I think I'd bury that person in the garden. It would be more pleasant that way, I suppose—no matter how much I might have hated that person.

At first, it takes a long time to just make a dent with a shovel in the hard, cracked soil. Eventually, I figure out a system for shoveling more efficiently, but this work is very difficult, especially in the heat of the sun. But once I've started a project, I like to see it through, so I keep digging. After three hours, I'm convinced that I need to start over again in another part of the yard. I also consider the possibility that Virginia would be delighted to see me digging around for bones, especially if they don't exist.

"Look what I made the move-in do," she would say.

And then I realize that I'm digging in the yard, directly beneath the window of the neighbor's house and that Virginia and Whatever-Her-Name-Is-Next-Door would most definitely be laughing at my expense. When I look up, though, I see that the lacy curtains are closed. So, I get back to work.

Beads of sweat sting my eyes, but I begin to think I see a yellowish-white something just beneath a layer of soil. A hunch tells me to delicately brush the dirt away and look closely, so I do and I begin to see the shape of what I think are bones—long bones of sorts, but I reason that they must be brittle by now and that I should be careful handling them. I tell myself that they're probably just chicken bones, but I've never seen chicken bones like these, so I cradle them lightly and carry them inside the house.

Once inside, I'm not sure what to do with them, so I stick them in the breadbox on the kitchen counter top. The breadbox, I decide, would make a lovely place for the bones and I could visit them every day. They'd be sort of like a new guest in my house.

At night, I think I can hear the bones speaking to me, so I go downstairs and make a cup of coffee and keep them company. Sometimes, I stroke them gently with my fingers as I talk to them.

"The neighborhood really is pretty and the people are nice and all, but I don't know when I'll fit in. I figure I'd join a group or something, but I can't figure it out."

"What do you mean?" the bones ask.

"Well… most organizations have websites with contact names and meeting times and phone numbers, but I can't find anything like that around here. And when I ask the people who walk by, they say they don't know. They say they don't join organizations, but I know they must. There must be a gardening club or something where I could get to know others."

"No. People around here simply grew up together. If they join a club, they do it because someone they already know is there—and they don't need any more friends. They have all the friends they need."

"What happens if those friends die?"

"They don't think like that. You've got to hold your own social events," the bones tell me. "Invite people over here. The women around here love to shop in other peoples' homes. Sell clothing or jewelry from a catalog or something—and serve some wine. It's just the thing to do around here. Don't look outside. Look in."

A Comfort Chic hostess can earn a yearly salary based on home parties alone, I'm told. So I sign on to sell stylish yoga pants and lounging skorts that cost about $100 apiece. "For the stylish, sporty woman on the go," the Comfort Chic website says, and I figure I could *be* that stylish sporty woman with a ton of friends in my Betty Crocker kitchen with the red counter tops and the pink scallop framed cabinets. I could serve casseroles and wine and cozy up to the fireplace. I could hold book club meetings—and feel incredibly fulfilled and satisfied.

"Pick up the phone," the bones tell me. "What are you waiting for?"

A woman named Kelsey handles Comfort Chic sales in my region, and she is more than happy to help me play hostess. She gives me all kinds of sales tips: Every woman wants to try on clothes, even if a piece isn't right for her. Give lots of compliments. Remind them how the Comfort Chic look never goes out of style and can be dressed up with a pop of jewelry, and that the fabric lasts—and is even stain repellant. If nothing else, I'm to get the women "absolutely stinking drunk. They'll try anything on then." Kelsey even helps me pick out a hostess outfit, for which I get ten percent off. Ten percent off of a $200 outfit. And, if I stick with the job, I can earn up to 30% off my outfits. And then there are opportunities for travel and moving up the company ladder—all with home sales parties, so I guess I'll need a lot more friends if I want a Comfort Chic career. Kelsey did it. I could be Kelsey. So, I buy an extra outfit at full price and cake on the makeup before strolling down the sidewalk in clean white sporty tennis shoes, dropping off invitations to all the mailboxes in my neighborhood. I'm letting everyone know that I'm having a Comfort Chic party and there will be wine.

In the local grocery store on the day of the party, I buy up all of the wine and a few bottles of hard liquor for cocktails. I also buy several frozen casseroles—and crackers, cheese, and fruit. I don't want to spend too much time cooking, so everything must be done in advance. That's what Kelsey—and the bones—say.

When I get home, I clean the house and get the oven going. I also have time to put on my hosting outfit and pour a glass of wine, which I sip with the bones to keep me company.

"Adelaide, my dear! How good of you to join me on the day of your party," the bones say.

"Oh, I wouldn't forget about you. You're my honored guest."

"Prove it," the bones say.

The voice though, has changed. There's an edge to it and it makes me feel uneasy, but so far, the bones have been good to me. They've shown me nothing but kindness, so I trust them. If they were once the bones of a nurse, there must be something in their marrow that once truly cared. So what if they went a little wayward in life? Of course, it's no excuse to poison children, but how can I be sure that Virginia told me a true story? These bones are good, I believe. They want me to be happy.

"How would I prove that you're my honored guest?" I tease, while giving the bones a lighthearted tap and a wink.

"I need you to check in with me from time to time, and not forget me or ignore me when I call to you. If you check in with me, I can give you inside advice because I've lived here for a very long time and I know the ropes. I know how you can make good, everlasting friends here."

"I promise I'll check in."

"But that's not all. You have to do everything I tell you to do. You have to trust me."

The voice has softened, and I don't have that unsettling feeling anymore. That feeling is replaced with hope—a hope for everlasting friends, a new stylish career, and happiness. Hope for all of these simple things. It's the simple things that make us happy. The little things.

"Of course I trust you," I tell the bones, and I consider myself a very lucky soul who has just been handed all the "insider's secrets" to making friends in a small town.

Kelsey arrives an hour before the party with several racks of clothing that all somehow neatly fit in her compact car. She unloads everything, and I help her bring the racks of clothing into the house.

"Where are you serving the food?" Kelsey asks.

"Right here—right off the kitchen, on the table I've set up. I can take casseroles out of the oven and place them on the table, buffet style."

"Great! I'll put the clothing racks right here, across from the buffet table."

"But the clothing could get stained—it's right near the food. Shouldn't it be further away?"

"No. The guests need to look at the clothes while they're mingling and eating. And, of course, if they get food or wine on the items—even better! We can show them how stain resistant the fabrics are."

Kelsey has thought of everything, except I see that the rack contains several styles of outfits, but only one of each.

"Shouldn't you have these in different sizes?" I ask.

"No. These are all one-size-fits-all. They're marked as a size 0."

"A zero? No woman wears a zero."

"It's not really a zero. It's a standard size that fits everyone—and I mean everyone. Go ahead. Try something on—anything."

I choose a slim-fitting white cotton skirt and try it on in the guest bathroom. It fits perfectly.

"How does this even work?" I ask.

"I don't know. It just does."

Virginia is the first guest to arrive. She brought a dish with her, and I'm not sure what to do.

"Oh, Virginia! How thoughtful! Thank you—you shouldn't have!" And I mean it; she shouldn't have. I have everything covered and now there's no room on the buffet table for this extra dish, and it's a terrible dish indeed—some kind of brown gravy beef dip served with pork rinds. It doesn't go with anything I've planned to serve.

"I know, but I *always* bring this dish along," Virginia says, in her pink sundress with her orange blossom perfume.

"I'll put it right in the center of the table," I tell her as bitter acid rises and burns in my throat.

Tammy arrives next and she has brought wine, which is all right by me, but now we have too much. Tammy is the woman who lives right next door to me and now I finally know her name. Rose, Peggy, and Barbara arrive together and they're already drunk. They met at Peggy's house beforehand. That's why they're late—and drunk.

While the guests mingle, eat, and look at the clothing on the rack, I hear the bones calling, so I go back into the kitchen and flip open the breadbox.

"These women are so tasteless and annoying. Do you really want them as friends?" the bones ask.

"Well, the way I see it, I don't have any choice. Without them, I'd be incredibly lonely."

"Huh! What about me?" the voice asks.

"Of course I'd never be completely lonely, thanks to you, but I need the company of townsfolk too."

"I know. I get it. So I'm here to help. These women, though, don't want to get to know you. They just want to have a glass or two of wine and try on an outfit and leave. That's not in your best interest. You need to keep them here longer. You need to get them to interact with one another. Here's what I'm thinking: a game of spin the bottle."

"Oh, my! I don't think they'd ever go for that."

"Please—it's not what you think. Whoever spins the bottle picks an outfit for the one it points to. That guest tries on the outfit in your bedroom, and then I'll tell you what to do next."

"Do you think it'll work?"

"I know it will."

When I leave the kitchen, I pull Kelsey aside and tell her about the game I've just invented and she tells me to "go for it," so I do. After downing a shot of whiskey and most of a bottle of wine, I leave the kitchen and announce, "Okay, ladies! Let's get in a circle with an empty bottle of wine and play spin the bottle!"

"Umm. No. We're not doing that," Tammy says.

"It's NOT what you think—not at all! Whoever spins the bottle gets to choose an outfit for the lucky lady the bottle points to. That woman goes upstairs to try on the outfit, and comes back to model it for us."

The women shrug. They look bored, but they gather into a circle anyway. Virginia spins first and the bottle points to Tammy. From the clothing rack, Virginia selects a long green skirt and a striped jersey that matches.

"But I'm short! A long skirt will make me look shorter," Tammy says.

"Too bad. Rules are rules. Gotta try it on," Virginia says.

"The top makes me look like some kind of an idiot sailor, too."

"Ships ahoy!" Virginia calls as Tammy heads upstairs.

The room is absolutely spinning and whirling and I see Kelsey's face and all the others moving past me in a blur, as if I were in some sort of a carnival funhouse. It's difficult to stay standing without holding onto the wall and I feel sick to my stomach, but I think I hear the bones calling from the kitchen, so I push the door open just as I break into a cold sweat.

"Go check on Tammy," the bones say.

The voice sounds more distant this time and the kitchen lights are blinding. The voice seems to carry me away to another place that's at once distant and familiar.

"Check on Tammy, but bring the butcher knife," the voice says.

I feel too sick from the alcohol to even question what the bones say, so I steady myself at the counter and pull open a drawer. I select the butcher knife, which seems impossibly shiny and sharp. I really shouldn't go running around the party drunk, with a knife, but I'm also very susceptible to just doing what I'm told.

Once I reach the top of the stairs, I knock clumsily on the bedroom door and call out to Tammy. She opens up, wearing the outfit Virginia has selected. Sure enough, she looks absolutely overpowered by the skirt and green is not her color. It makes her face look drawn and old.

"I hate this outfit. I am *not* coming down in it."

Before I can answer, the bones take over, whispering in my ear—telling me everything I must do next to keep the party going—forever.

"Are you having fun?" the bones ask.

In my head, I believe I am. The alcohol is fun, though I'm a little woozy. But I finally have all of the popular women in town in my house, and yes, I'm happy, especially at the prospect of new outfits and a new career. Everything is just a dream.

"Do you want this feeling to last?" the bones ask.

Of course I do, so I must do what I'm told and the bones tell me to get rid of Tammy quickly, to tie a scarf around her mouth and gag her and plunge the knife right into her heart and watch the blood flow. Then I can lock the body in the closet and clean up the mess. The bones tell me I'm starting a collection. A collection of friends, and I like the idea of collections—of choices. I must have choices and company. I must also keep the party going, so I retrieve the scarf I used, toss it onto the bed, and stumble back down the stairs to see the guests, who are all pretty drunk by now and laughing loudly at Tammy's expense. They know she'll look ridiculous. And she did. Such a pity they didn't see it!

"Okay, Tammy's deciding to take her time, but let's keep things moving. Let's have Peggy spin this time," I say.

Peggy has to try a couple of times to get the bottle to spin. It finally lands on Rose.

"Ladies, it's time to get risky!" Peggy says as she searches through the rack of clothes. "I'm going for swimwear!"

"Oh, there is *no* way in hell I'm modeling swimwear."

"Relax. I'll pick something that has a skirt on it."

Peggy chooses a very flattering two-piece tankini with a skirted bottom. Rose looks happy as she takes the swimsuit with her up the stairs. Meanwhile, I pour myself another drink because I know what's coming next and I need to remain calm. In my head, I convince myself that the following statements are true: The bones are on my side. They want me to be happy. I want to be happy. If the bones once belonged to a nurse, they can't be all that bad. Not all nurses are bad...

The women turn to each other to laugh some more and talk. I'm not in their inner circle yet, but I will be.

"Excuse me," I say. "I'll just check on Rose—I'll be right back."

"And Tammy, right? What's taking her so long?" Virginia asks.

"I'll check. Don't worry."

The stairs seem to sway as I step on each one, floating up to the room where Rose is turning around in front of the full-length mirror across from the bed.

"What do you think?" she asks.

"Absolutely amazing," I say. "Just one more thing to complete the look..."

I grab the scarf and gag her. She's so drunk she can't fight back, and the blade of the knife slides in easily this time. Effortlessly—like slicing a cake. Then I remember that I don't have dessert. I should have picked up a cake. If Virginia had wanted to bring something, she should have brought cake, not that horrible beef concoction.

I stuff Rose into the closet and come back down the stairs. Virginia, Barbara, and Peggy don't want to spin the bottle anymore, so Kelsey just selects outfits for them to try on.

"One could use the guest bedroom while the others use your bedroom, right?" Kelsey asks, but the bones are protesting:

"Too many rooms—too complicated."

So, I tell Kelsey the guest bedroom is being painted and it's not ready. Also,

Rose may need some help from Peggy, so Peggy can go next to try on some cropped pants and a decorative T-shirt.

When the time is right, I do to Peggy what I did to Tammy and Rose, but now I'm beginning to get sloppy and overconfident. I'm leaving bits of blood on the carpet and I'm not sure I can keep making excuses anymore. I hear footsteps coming up the stairs, so I lock the door.

"Adelaide, your guests are having fun, but they really want to see their friends in their outfits. What's going on? Can I help?"

"I'm doing fine," I tell Kelsey as I shove Peggy inside the closet. The bodies are stacking up and my closet isn't very big. They just kind of fall all over each other, and I have to gather the limbs and throw them upwards.

"That's great and everything," Kelsey says, "but I... they want me to try on an outfit now. A bikini. I'm sure they think that's funny and all—get the head sales rep to try on the merch—but you know, I'm game. I'm a good sport. Can you let me in?"

The bones tell me I should definitely let her in now that the bodies are all safely crammed inside the closet, but I've really got to do something about the droplets of blood on the carpet. I guess I'll just tell Kelsey they're wine stains if she asks, so I let her in.

"Oh, thank God! I'm really curious to see how the others are doing. Where are they?" Kelsey asks.

I'm not even sure how to answer because if I tell her they are all in the master bathroom, wouldn't they be louder? Wouldn't they be laughing and carrying on? And I definitely can't tell her they're in the closet, so I keep dabbing away at the blood stains with the scarf. I can't think of anything else to do.

"Oh—is that wine?" Kelsey asks. "*Every* hostess knows how to get wine stains out of a carpet. Hold on a sec, I have just the thing. I'll run downstairs to get it."

And just like that, she turns her back on me so I stab her hard, in the kidneys, and cover her mouth so she won't scream. With the butcher knife, I finish the job, then run the blade under cold water in the bathroom sink.

"Okay, Bones," I say out loud when I've finally stuffed Kelsey into the closet. "I'm running out of room and I'm getting tired. What do I do with Barbara and Virginia?"

The bones answer pleasantly with a recipe for poison, mixed in with wine.

Virginia and Barbara are ready for another drink, but once their cups are empty, their faces turn blue, then black, as they clutch their throats and gasp for air. Red rivulets flow from their nostrils and open mouths.

The room is spinning faster now and I really want to lie down, but the bones have more work for me to do. I'm supposed to remove the flesh from all of the bodies, reserving just a few skeletal remains—one or two special relics from each friend. I'm supposed to label them so that I can tell them apart. There are important instructions also for cleaning up the house and disposing of the rest of the bodies. But the labeled bones—the relics that I've taken—all go into the breadbox.

In my cozy stone-front cottage with the flower boxes in the windows, I have plans for every night of the week. I select a new outfit from my Comfort Chic collection, bake a casserole, and pour some good red wine. When I open the breadbox, the ladies and I pick up where we all left off: with a rousing game of spin the bottle. Every once in a while, I see the shadow of a figure that stops by to peer through the lacey kitchen curtains. The figure that lurks outside my door surely wants to see if the rumors are true: that a crazy lady move-in has dug up the bones of an evil nurse and made permanent guests of neighbors who've gone missing.

DUSK AND THE FOREST

ARSENI JIGATOV

In the time before now, when the Hunter Lord kept the Cur at bay and the land safe, there was a village in the Old Forest where the men cut tall, strong trees. One such man had a beautiful wife and a beloved daughter, who they called Dusk, as the red of her hair was the color of the setting sun. Many of the villagers were unkind to the child and called her worse things, as the red of her hair was the color of the Cur's fur, which was said to prowl the woods waiting to be called to hunt.

Dusk's father was a loving and wise man. He worked from sunup to sundown and cherished every moment that he had to spend with his daughter. In return, Dusk cherished the wisdom he shared and always took his words to heart.

Dusk's mother was a strict woman short on patience. She loved her daughter, but always tried to prepare her for the cruel and dangerous world, at times with a heavy hand.

Every day Dusk took a basket and her mother's old knife to gather mushrooms in the forest. And every day, her mother said to her:

"Dusk, are you going to gather mushrooms?"

"Yes, Mother," Dusk would reply.

"And are you going to ask for permission from the Earth before you enter the Forest?"

"Yes, Mother."

"And are you going to praise the Old Forest every time you cut one down, for feeding us?"

"Yes, Mother."

"And when you come back to the village, are you going to thank the Hunter Lord for protecting us and giving us shelter from the Cur?"

"Yes, Mother."

And with her mother's approving smile, Dusk was on her way.

She took the path downhill from her house and it brought her to the edge of the village, to the darkest, most shaded parts where the Old Forest was damp and the mushrooms thrived. Before passing through the trees, she dropped to her knees and pressed her knife to her scar-covered forearm, opening her skin to let the offering drop on the ground as she asked for permission. The answer was assumed in the whispering of the leaves.

There was an area in the woods not far from home, where the mushrooms grew in abundance and the safety of the village was a few steps away. Every time she bent down to cut the mushrooms, she whispered her thanks, as a diligent daughter does.

On and on the search took her, deeper into the woods. Her mother had warned her not to wander too far alone, but it rained the night before and the harvest was bountiful. Her basket was filling up quicker than ever. In her excitement, she went far enough that she heard no longer the sounds of the village in the distance and did not recognize her surroundings, as if something unspoken had changed. As if the woods, though once familiar, became a world of their own, both foreboding and alluring.

Ready to turn back, as the basket was full and heavy, she looked around one final time and that's when she saw it. On an old tree stump at the end of a clearing, in the shade of a large pine tree, stood the biggest mushroom she had ever seen. The stem was as thick as both of her arms put together and its head was wide enough to shield her if it rained. Awestruck, Dusk approached, knife in hand, and ran her palm across it. To her surprise, it felt almost as rough as the tree bark. Hesitant only for a moment, she grasped her knife hard in hand and pressed the blade to the base of the mushroom, when suddenly, it spoke.

"Stop, little girl!" it pleaded, but the words came out like a slithering snake. They crawled into her ears and wrapped themselves around her heart. "Stop. Stop... little Dusk. Cut my flesh, and your whole village will feel your regret. I promise. Touch me with your blade and my words will call the Cur that prowls in the dark!"

Shocked, she dropped the knife and, leaving her full basket on the ground, ran as fast as she could back to the village. Having emerged from the trees, Dusk quickly muttered, "Thank you for letting us live and for keeping the Cur at bay, Lord Hunter," and made her way back home.

Another danger awaited her when she returned, as her mother was not pleased.

"The fairies have played tricks on you with that mushroom, Dusk! I have warned you not to wander far into the forest. You must return there first thing in the morning, before the mushroom grows. I need you to bring my knife back!"

"But it knew my name, Mother! And the voice felt like spiders crawling on my skin!" insisted Dusk. The memory of her fear spurred her defiance, but her mother ignored this, leaving little room for argument. The next day, Dusk would have to face her newfound fear.

That night was sleepless. As Dusk laid awake looking at the moonlit window, she heard something uttered on the wind. At first she took it for forest sounds, but with time words began to form until finally, they became a song that flowed from the Old Forest.

"Dusk comes, sun sets on us." She could make out the words clearly now. *"We look for you, at night."* Dusk thought she heard a creaking of the floor-boards from the porch outside as these words came to her. *"What mushrooms want, they always reap."* The image of the Mushroom in the woods returned to haunt her. She saw it clearly now, as if it was there with her in the room standing in the dark corner. *"Carving plight!"*

There was a loud bang somewhere in the house, and with a gasp Dusk hid under her covers, afraid to move or close her eyes.

On and on it went, the same lines echoing and rolling, invading her home and her dreams. In the morning, the voice lingered in her mind, sapping her courage even in the daylight. Dusk didn't know how much she slept that night, but the day after came and went, and she did not return to the forest.

"Where is my knife, Dusk?" asked her mother that evening, sternly. Having nothing to say, Dusk ran from the room and hid in the rafters from her mother's disappointed look. She knew that she could not postpone the return to the woods forever, and yet another day passed riddled with anxiety until her mother's ire left her no options. Dusk didn't know if the song returned that night because, exhausted by the sleepless fear of the past two nights, she slept heavily.

Feeling rested and spurred on by her mother's insistence, Dusk made her way down to the edge of the village. There was no way for her to give a fitting offering this time, as the knife was gone and her mother wouldn't let her have another. Having thought about her options, she reached up and with sudden determination ripped out a handful of her hair, placing it on the ground in front of herself. Whispering the request to enter, she hoped her offering would be enough.

The journey seemed much longer now, and Dusk found herself in no rush to make it to her destination, but she knew that she had to get there. A big part of her hoped that after some earnest searching, she would be unable to retrace her steps and would have to return to the village, defeated. Having never faced the Mushroom again, she hoped she could live with the shame.

Her fears came true instead.

The sight of the Mushroom in the distance caught her by surprise. To her utter horror, it had grown twice in size, but that was not the worst of it.

As she approached the Mushroom, Dusk frantically looked around for her knife and discovered it in the most unlikely of places, lodged in the center of the stem, consumed by the white hard flesh.

"It is mine now, little Dusk," said the Mushroom, and its voice was no longer pleading. It was confident, strong and menacing. "I have the iron of men now. With it I will become the Lord of the Forest. I will keep my people safe from your touch and in time rule this land."

Lost for words and lost for thoughts, Dusk stood still before the Mushroom, helpless. Frozen with indecision and fear, she stared at the thing in front of her.

"Please," she finally said. "O, Lord of Mushrooms. My mother will not let me return home without the knife. Please, can I have it back?"

The Mushroom made a terrifying sound that echoed through the woods. It was screeching and creaking, rumbling and grinding, a sound that went deep into Dusk's core, scratching and stabbing at her heart.

"Leave, little girl! Leave, or I will make you and your mother regret it! With my word alone, I can make your whole village perish! We will dance on your bones once the Cur rips at your flesh!"

Struck by the horrible thought of losing her parents, Dusk turned around and ran as fast as her little legs could carry her. Crossing over into the village, she gave her thanks to the Hunter Lord for keeping them safe from the Cur.

Having no intention to return, Dusk allowed the days to go by. Her mother's frustration and insistence made Dusk feel distraught and distant, making the time spent together unbearable.

"If you put it aside forever, it will grow and become larger than you can ever manage. With every passing day, it will be harder and harder for you to go back. Don't make it worse than it is. Face the Mushroom." And every time Dusk made a promise to heed her mother's words, but as every new day came, she found new excuses to put it aside till the day after. The Mushroom Lord ruled her heart and pulled on the strings of her fear.

One day, her father returned home early and sat Dusk down on his knee. She told him her tale, and he listened intently.

"Your mother is right. We can't put it aside any longer. The fairy folk are cunning and will take advantage of every day that you give them. The Mushroom Lord will never forget you. We will go together, sweet daughter, and face your tormentor together."

With hours left before sunset they set out, her father performing the ritual when stepping into the forest. Dusk knew the path well by now, but with every step they took, confusion set it. Though the woods were the same, the dreaded clearing was nowhere to be found. An hour of wandering revealed nothing.

"I fear this is a lesson that you will have to learn on your own," said Dusk's father as they turned back and began their journey home, giving the appropriate gratitude upon their return.

"The path that was revealed to you is denied to me. You will have to walk it again, alone. But there is a way, though you will not like it. We have told you never to enter the woods at night, as the moon hours are the time of the fairy and it is no place for humans. Well, I tell you now, Dusk. Go there this night, when the Mushroom least expects you. Go there and use his arrogance against him. As your mother said, never put aside cleansing the fear that grows in your heart till tomorrow. Strike it down."

With the blessing of her parents and strengthened by their love for her, Dusk vowed to make the trip that evening. She packed a basket to take with her, with a gift to the Mushroom King.

Dusk made it to the edge of the village and stopped, having almost forgotten the offering and permission. The worry that her hair wouldn't be enough the second time crept into her mind. Certainty came only with blood, so she bit as hard as she could into her forearm. Her small, sharp teeth pierced the skin and the offering ran down her lips, dripping onto the ground. Whispering the request to enter, she crossed the boundary of the woods, wincing from pain.

The sun was teasing the horizon when Dusk began her journey to the dreaded clearing. Every step felt heavy to her, like a fear swamp dragging her down while the voice in her head begged her to return home. The Old Forest was silent, as if making room for the words yet to come. At first there came a scratching, crawling sound as if something menacing was hunting her in the tall grass. It came from far and near, ahead and behind her. Crawling into her ears like spiders, spinning a web of meaning. "*Dusk creeps*," it repeated, again and again. "*Dusk creeps, dusk creeps. Sun sleeps, sun sleeps.*" The words were picking up in volume and determination, becoming more and more clear. "*Dusk creeps, sun sleeps. Forest weeps, mushroom reaps, mushroom reaps!*"

Reaching the fateful clearing, Dusk saw that the Mushroom was the source of the chanting. Bound to the ground no longer, it paced around on long roots like spider legs protruding from the bottom and the sides of its body. Each branch of the spider root was almost as tall as Dusk herself, sharp and menacing.

"You should not have come back, little Dusk! There is nothing for you here now," it said before Dusk could even come near. Its words did not make her hesitate as she continued her approach.

"I have brought you an offering, O Lord of All Mushrooms!"

Hearing this, the faceless Mushroom stayed quiet. It liked being addressed that way, and being given an offering seemed very regal to it.

Dusk stopped a few paces away and waited patiently. "Please, keep the knife. And take this offering so that you do not make my village perish with your words."

"You may approach, child. What did you bring me?" asked the Mushroom, pleased with this arrangement. It bent its root-legs and lowered itself to her, leaning forward to accept the gift.

She stood at the foot of the mighty fungus and looked up. Her heart beat like the wings of a tiny bird as she reached inside the basket and spoke.

"The iron of men, O Mushroom Lord."

And with these words, she pulled her father's hatchet from the basket, grasping it in both of her tiny hands and swinging it high above her head. She chopped as deep as she could into the heart of the mushroom's stem, where her knife was. The fungus let out a bellowing scream that rang through the forest, but uttered not a single word, lost in its pain. Again and again little Dusk plunged the blade into the mushroom, cutting a deep hole in its flesh. Her foe whimpered and whined, but the girl was lost in the moment of bloodlust.

"I offer…" she muttered breathlessly as she pulled back the axe. "Gratitude…" Another blow was struck. "For giving us…" Again and again, the blade cut deeper into the mushroom. "Nourishment."

It was dead silent, then.

Dusk stood above the toppled fungus as it lay on the ground, broken at its base and hacked at its core. The glimmer of metal betrayed her knife lodged inside of its body. With both hands she reached in and pulled it out, a grin of triumph on her face.

Throwing her tools into her basket she collected what she could fit of the Mushroom Lord.

The elation of victory coursed through her veins like poison. It was the first time that she faced the danger of the Old Forest alone at night, and she had come out alive. Rushing home, she ran up the path that led to her house to find her parents waiting for her on the porch. Her mother was pleased at the return of the knife, and her father was impressed by the bounty and his daughter's bravery. Exhausted, Dusk couldn't wait to get to bed. Her mother came to tuck her in.

"Dusk, I am so proud of you. But tell me, did you ask for permission today when you entered the Old Forest?"

"Yes, Mother," answered Dusk with a smile and a yawn.

"And did you offer gratitude when you took from the Old Forest?"

"I did, Mother," she answered dutifully, closing her eyes.

"And did you thank the Hunter Lord for keeping us safe from the Cur when you left?"

No answer broke the silence of the room. Fur red as the setting sun.

ASURI

C. E. CLAYTON

Tck-tck.

Tck-tck.

The clicking sound next to my ear was so loud that whatever made it had to be nearby. I picked up my pace, but the sound persisted, causing my hair to stand on end.

I started to run.

No one was out on the street at this time of night. The houses moved farther and farther apart as I ran for the hill that would lead me back to more familiar ground.

The sound finally faded, as if its source was disappearing into the distance. I put my hand to my belly, feeling the little kick of the child within, and took comfort that it was at least doing well despite my terror.

A rustling sound had me glancing around the unlit street. The few houses were dark; the residents in this part of town were elderly and tended to turn in early. I glanced to the sky and saw what I thought was the tip of a wing disappearing in the tree above me. Not wanting a bat to get stuck in my unruly curls, I walked—or wobbled, really—as fast as my quivering legs would allow.

The chill returned, teasing my spine, as I sensed something watching me just out of sight. Glancing up at the quivering tree branches above, I didn't pay attention to where I was going. My sandal caught in the sidewalk. I toppled forward, my outstretched hand to break my fall before my belly could.

But I never hit the ground.

I felt claws around my arms, scratching and tearing my skin like a rusty razor. I tried to scream. Then, hands—*oh God, were those hands?*—covered my mouth. I smelled a pungent mixture of rotting eggs, a full porta-potty on a hot day, and a drop of musty perfume.

I gasped and squirmed. The claws tore my arms. There came a lip-smacking sound behind my ear that had me gagging and, in conjunction with the stench, I vomited against the disgusting hand over my mouth. My heaving was answered with a sharp pain at the base of my skull. Bright white stars flooded my vision.

The smell hit me first: that same rotting egg stench mixed with rank feces and a dash of stale, sickly-sweet perfume. Then there was a sound.

A sucking, slurping sound, like a messy child scarfing down noodle soup. Before I could make sense of the smell or the sounds, pain overwhelmed me.

My arms burned where the thing's claws had torn into me. The wet stickiness told me they were covered in blood. My belly was contorting, clenching in painful cramps.

NO!

My eyes snapped open, my hand scrambling over my belly and between my legs. I felt nothing, and hoped once I calmed that my cramping would cease.

Then the slurping noise invaded my ears once more. Even in the near-darkness I saw the source: an elongated, snout like organ protruded from the blackness, clamped over the remnants of... *something*. It looked like an enormous leech, long and moist, dark and trembling, sucking away at flesh that I couldn't identify.

The owner of the proboscis appeared to be a human-sized bat that had gone through a fire. Its skin was grey and covered in scars that looked like old burns, its lips pulled back in a twisted snarl around the tongue-like organ that stuck out from its long fangs.

Its hands were more like claws; the dirty talons clamped over chunks of meat. Its backwards facing feet were pressed against a nearby wall, tensed to spring. I only got a glimpse of its wings—a cross between a crow and a bat—before the creature noticed I was awake.

Its eyes suddenly locked on me. I opened my mouth to scream, and it lunged, sinking its talons into my shoulders and lifting me just enough to slam my head against the ground.

I woke, shivering so intensely my teeth rattled in my skull. Everything came back to me in fetid flashes of dark shadows and glints of wet, snake-like appendages. Bile inched up the back of my throat, but I clamped my hand over my mouth, afraid that whatever demon brought me here might still be lurking.

That's when I realized I couldn't see anything.

It's cracked my skull hard enough to make me blind!

I began to cry. My hands slid over my belly, trying to determine whether the life within was safe. A weak tremble from my child was enough to reassure me.

I tried to take stock of my situation. I was in pain, abducted by a thing straight out of a horror story—*no*. Things like that don't exist. I had been abducted and knocked on the head. I was seeing things, and nothing more.

"Demons and devils aren't real," I whispered.

At that moment, I realized I wasn't blind. Faint light came from somewhere above, thin cracks of gold outlining a door. My captor left me in what looked like a basement, but it was colder than any basement I'd ever been in before.

I tried to focus on the things that made sense, rather than the hellish memories that defied explanation. Humans are capable of enough depravity; we don't need beasts ripped straight out of folklore to add to the mayhem. I couldn't seriously believe that a creature from the deepest pit of hell was plaguing my new home.

My courage temporarily bolstered, I tried to stand but slipped on something sticky. I stifled a cry. It wasn't that the fall hurt, but I didn't want to consider what I slipped in. I didn't want it to be my blood; while I knew my arms were a mess and my head wound bled, there was too much on the ground to mean anything good.

I got back to my feet and inched forward, hands outstretched. Just the thought of what might be lurking in the icy basement with me was enough to make me whimper. I bit my lip so hard that I wouldn't be able to scream, even if I wanted to. Which turned out to be a good thing.

My fingers trailed over something cold and fleshy. Something that felt like it might have been alive at one point.

I heard creaking above me, the slow whine of the floorboards marking the path of the thing above. Terror gripped me. I couldn't move. I couldn't even duck, or prepare to spring for the door. I was paralyzed, unblinking eyes aching as the shadow blotted out the golden rim of light that I so desperately wanted to be my salvation.

The door opened quietly. Just a slight suction sound, like you'd hear when opening a refrigerator door, so faint I could barely hear it over the hammering of my heart.

Framed in the light was a shape, small in stature and painfully skinny. I couldn't tell if it was a man or woman. What I *could* tell: it wasn't my abductor. Regardless of what my concussed mind may have conjured, the thing that grabbed me would have had to be far larger than the petite form above me.

The figure moved. A light flickered on overhead. Just a normal halogen bulb, nothing supernatural about it. I thought I might cry for joy.

Standing at the top of the stairs was a little old woman.

It took me a moment to recognize her as the owner of the Filipino market and delicatessen. I'd gone to the shop just the other day to pick up barbecued pork for a party.

I remembered the little lady behind the counter: her face like wrinkled, soft leather, her wispy charcoal grey hair, her small, red-rimmed eyes hesitant as she peered at me shyly. I remembered how she smiled at me when I made an offhand comment about my baby twitching in response to the delicious smell wafting through the deli. And now, somehow, I was in the basement of her market.

"Help me," I croaked. "Please, I don't know how I got here. Something… some*one* took me. Call the police, call… anyone. Please!"

The woman cocked her head. Her dark eyes flashed like coals as they slid to the side, as if looking at someone I couldn't see. I tried to crawl toward her, to inch my way up the stairs. That's when I finally realized where I was: a meat locker. It explained the cold and the slab of unidentifiable meat I'd touched. It also explained why I couldn't feel the manacle around my ankle. I only noticed *that* when my forward progress was abruptly halted.

My eyes widened. Sweat collected on my brow as I stared at my restraint. My hand floated to my belly once more, out of habit now.

The movement caught the old woman's eyes. She shook her head and forced a smile, reaching for the light switch once more.

"No! You have to help me! Is—is someone forcing you to keep me here?

Please, I'll make sure no one knows you freed me. I'll pay you, anything you want, whatever it takes!"

Shaking her head again, she mumbled something in a language I didn't understand and glanced to the side once more. Then she flicked off the light and shut the door.

"*NO!*" I scrambled as far as the chain would allow. But the cold and blood loss made my attempts feeble, and without the light, I couldn't even see my restraints well enough to try and pry them off.

But it didn't stop me from trying.

Despite my exhaustion, I didn't sleep. I couldn't.

I was too afraid that if I shut my eyes for even a moment, they would never open again. I suppose that wouldn't have been the worst outcome, considering what I'd witnessed, but I wanted—I *needed*—to get out. I needed to escape to have any hope of saving my baby.

I knew the little market was open on the weekends. I knew the smells of the traditional dishes would bring in customers all day long. So I screamed and screamed and rattled my restraints, and screamed some more, hoping someone would hear me and do something.

But nothing happened.

Wherever the refrigerated basement was in relation to the customers, I was far enough away that my cries were hidden beneath layers of fans and traffic. But I didn't give up. I screamed for hours and hours until my throat was raw and it hurt to even open my mouth.

Time slipped by. Eventually the store above closed, its patrons shuffling back to their homes with a delicious dinner to share with their families, oblivious to the woman chained beneath their feet.

Long after the store had closed, I heard the floor boards creak above me once more, groaning under a weight that I knew was disproportionate to the little woman's size.

I crouched against the wall, hoping she would venture close enough for me to grab her. If she was being threatened to keep me here against her will, I'd promise again to protect her or... or something. But I had to get out of here!

The suction on the door released. A flood of light entered the room. Too late, I realized I wasn't hiding behind anything, but it didn't matter. The form at the top of the stairs was not the same little grandma from earlier. It was bulkier, but I couldn't get a clear view, not with my eyes adjusting to the sudden bright light.

My heart seemed to stop for a moment, frozen in terror, before it began beating painfully in my chest, each thud like a hammer against my rib cage as my heart tried to flee my body. My breath had been stolen from me, and nothing I did could capture it again.

The creature that abducted me stood at the top of the stairs.

Its greyish, burned body glistened like it had just crawled out of those alien pods you see in the movies. There was a faint twinkle as its dark eyes peered at me, its fangs flashing in a wicked smile. Its bat wings with their tattered collection of black feathers quivered as it tossed a bundle down the stairwell, followed by a body that bounced along the stairs before coming to rest not far from where I clung to the wall. My fingers ached, nails digging as far as they could go into the grout.

My stomach clenched as the creature slunk down the stairs after its prizes. It didn't turn on the overhead light, but the glow from the room at the top of the stairs seemed sufficient as it crawled towards the body.

I couldn't stop myself. I looked.

It was a child.

A young boy, maybe five or six, emaciated and bald, as if he'd had cancer when he was alive. He was clearly dead, and judging by the chemical stench wafting from him, he had not been dead long.

The beast crouched in front of me. Its stench assaulted me, and I couldn't even scream or look away, sweating so profusely that the moisture stuck to my lashes. I watched as it reclined on its backwards facing feet, claws digging into the ground, and pulled the child—and the sack—toward it. The demon didn't look at me, but still I felt like it was watching me, observing my every frantic breath and delighting in the accelerated beating of my heart.

The proboscis slithered out of its mouth, avoiding its rows of razor-like teeth. Its moist black body snaked toward the child. I tried to scream at it to leave him alone, to let the boy have some dignity in death, but it barely came out as more than a squeak. My muscles twitched, trying to obey my body's instinct to shove itself through the thick wall in order to get away from this monster.

Monster… I can't believe there really is such a thing!

Its tongue-like appendage pried open the child's mouth, slid down the boy's throat, and disappeared deep in his body. The proboscis grew in size as the beast *ate* something from within the deceased boy. There was no reason for the beast to eat near me; it didn't need to scare me any more than it already had. But as it fixed its gaze on me, I got the sense it was observing every detail of my face, memorizing me. I felt as if it needed me for something, something I didn't want to think about...

Fear and filth and disgust overtook me, and I vomited.

The beast didn't seem bothered by my sick all over the floor, splattering the animal carcasses nearby. It simply busied itself with the sack as it continued to feed. Out of the sack came a variety of plant materials: parts of tree trunks, palm fronds, grass and weed clippings, and other things you'd find in compost heaps.

The creature's scarred, claw-like hands began to emit a faint green light that curled and twisted around its muddy talons like cemetery mist. The claws moved with surprising dexterity, and seemed to be knitting the plants together; weaving something that began to look humanoid.

The pile of twigs, tree parts, and leaves slowly became something I recognized: it became *me*!

My grotesque doppelganger slowly transformed into something more life-like, its eyes turning from black beads to a chocolate brown, its grassy hair transforming into thick brown curls. It even developed a swell to its belly.

As the green mist evaporated from the beast's claws, my facsimile's mouth opened and shut until finally it croaked, "Hello. My name is Rachel."

The voice was raspy, like a rough breeze ripping through dead leaves. It coughed, and tried again. "Hello, I'm Ra*chel*. Rachel. I'm Rachel."

"No," I squeaked. "*I'm* Rachel. You're just a pile of rotting compost!"

It turned to me, brown eyes gleaming. Then it smiled. Seeing that grin on the demon's creation made my body convulse.

The facsimile studied me for a moment and then adopted an expression of pain, clutching its fake, pregnant belly. "Oh no... No! My baby! Something is wrong!"

It turned to its creator. The beast nodded in approval, clearly pleased with its performance.

"There's nothing wrong with my child," I said. "Let me go!"

Both ignored me.

The beast leaned back on its backwards facing feet, and my doppelganger wobbled up the stairs, vanishing into the night. With a sinking feeling, I realized the demon was covering its tracks. By unleashing its creation into the world, no one would come looking for me. No one would know anything was wrong... and if the doppelganger were to die, then no one would *ever* look for me.

I began to weep. Everyone I knew would all think I was fine, or had grown sick and died. None would know a hellish beast had kidnapped me, kept me in the basement of a Filipino delicatessen, and for what?

"Why are you doing this? Please... let me go. I won't tell anyone about you, I swear!" I begged.

It slurped the snake-like organ back into its mouth, and a deep rumbling filled the room, as if it were laughing. Its red-rimmed eyes found mine, and I tried even harder to shove myself through the wall at my back.

Then it sprang at the dead child, ripping apart the hollow remains of the boy before grabbing me with its sharp claws once more. I screamed. The putrid smell of rotting flesh made me gag.

I tried to scramble away, but my feet slipped over the gore on the floor. Its claws dug into my flesh as it forced me close and shoved me down. Then it straddled me, the black tongue-like appendage snaking out of its mouth again. It looked down at me, brown saliva dripping from its razor-like teeth.

I continued to thrash, but it was no use. The demon's rumbling laughter filled the room once again.

It shook me. My teeth rattled in my skull, and dizziness overwhelmed me. Its proboscis slithered over my belly as if making a promise. I screamed. It slammed my head back down on the floor.

I came around sometime later. The monster was gone, and the door at the top of the stairs was closed. My fingers trembled as they prodded my abdomen, reassuring myself that my child was still safe. For now. I shivered to think what the beast had in mind for me and my infant after watching it eat and dismember a dead child.

I began to cry.

I don't know how long I lay there weeping before the door at the top of the stairs opened again. The tiny silhouette of the little grandma appeared. Flicking on the light, she peered at me from the top of the stairs before glancing off to the side, again at something I couldn't see.

Looking around the basement, I noticed with a shudder that the dead child was gone. Nothing remained but a shred of his clothing, telling me that what I witnessed was not a fevered dream.

"Please, you have to let me out of here!" I pleaded as the old woman walked down the stairs. She didn't even glance at me. Trying a different tactic, I said, "My name's Rachel. Can you tell me what's happening at least? What's your name?"

She finally looked at me, dark eyes rimmed in red as if she had been up all night. But her eyes...

My breath hitched, and a shiver ran down the length of my body.

They looked just like the beast's. How could this little old woman and that beast have such similar eyes?

She finally spoke. "Asuri."

"Asuri? Is that your name?"

Her thin lips twitched as if she would smile, and she shook her head as if I were a child. She gestured vaguely at the basement and the rooms above, then rested her wrinkled hand on her chest. "Asuri."

She shuffled away, deeper into the basement to a wall of refrigerators I could barely see.

It was then I understood, fully and completely, that this woman was not going to let me go. Whatever her relationship was with the monster, she could not, and would not, free me.

I glanced around, taking advantage of the light while I had it, and spied the meat I bumped into earlier. The unidentifiable animal was in the process of aging for whatever dish it would become, but still possessed its rib bones.

Sparing one last glance for the old woman, I tiptoed to the hanging meat and dug my fingers into its leathery surface, trying to pry a bone loose. I hadn't managed to do much damage when I heard the woman begin to make noises: a ticking sound as she continued to rummage in the refrigerator.

My heart nearly stopped. It sounded so familiar to the *tck-tck* I heard the night of my capture.

I forced my thoughts back to the present, then tiptoed between the wall and the hanging carcass. I did this as many times as I could, counting the steps and memorizing my path so I could get back to the slab of meat and continue my work in the dark. Once I felt confident I had memorized the path, I took better note of my ankle and the manacle around it.

The manacle was nothing fancy, but even so, I had never picked a lock. All I knew of the practice was what I saw in movies, and I didn't think those were accurate. I fingered the metal links around the manacle. If I couldn't pick the lock, perhaps the bone would be strong enough to pry off the chain links. If I could get those off, then I could leave! As long as the woman didn't lock me in. Since I never heard a latch any time the woman or monster entered, I figured it was a precaution my captors felt unnecessary.

The grandma shuffled back toward me, her lips forming a faint smile as she drifted up the stairs, her arms laden with supplies. My heart hammered in my throat. Even though she took no notice of me, I feared she could guess at my plan, or had heard my shuffling and suspected *something*. But if she suspected anything, or noticed any damage to the aging meat, she gave no indication as she flicked the light off and left, the door suctioning closed behind her.

Once my eyes adjusted to the darkness, I counted the steps back to the hanging meat, and began prying the bone free.

By the time I pulled the bone out, my fingers were slick with animal fat and drying muscle tissue. It smelled awful, but I didn't let that deter me. I went to work, trying to pry apart the chain that held my manacle in place. The bone slipped once, stabbing my ankle and eliciting an unwelcome hiss of pain.

The floorboards above me creaked like they always did when the woman walked overhead. I hiccupped in fear, thinking she heard my cry of pain, but she never came down the stairs, and I went back to work.

My fingers were slick by the time a chain link finally opened enough for me to pull my ankle free. I bit my tongue to keep from screaming in elation, then crept to the stairs, hands outstretched to keep myself from stumbling.

I waited at the foot of the stairs. I couldn't hear anything, no faint sounds of music or the busy shop above. I couldn't hear the floorboards creak, either. I had hoped to finish before the store closed; that way a Good Samaritan could have helped me.

I wasn't sure what time the old lady left for the night, or when the beast returned. I could only pray I had enough time left to make it out. Taking a deep breath, I went up the stairs, cringing each time the stairs groaned in protest.

I pushed open the door and peeked around the corner.

There was nothing. The store was definitely closed. The white light of the moon shining through the high windows was my only light source as I hobbled toward the front entrance.

I made it to the market and I ran as fast as I could. I only looked down once, noting the slight slickness of blood from where I'd stabbed myself with the bone.

The front door, unsurprisingly, was locked. But it was locked with a mere deadbolt. I unlatched the door and pushed my way outside, silently wishing for an alarm to blare so the police would come, but I had no such luck.

I turned in circles, trying to orient myself. I'd been to the market once, but the city looked different at night, and I was too new in general to know where anything was. Finally, I found a street that looked familiar, and ran.

Never before had I lamented the loss of pay phones. Surrounded by empty shops, I'd have given anything to have access to a phone!

As I limped down the tree-lined sidewalk, a familiar sound stopped me cold. *Tck-tck, tck-tck* coming from above me. I frantically scanned the tree above, but saw nothing.

But that did not mean the beast was not there.

Tck-tck.

Tck-tck.

I ran.

The clicking sound followed me, so loud that I feared it would descend upon me at any moment.

I tried to scream but my throat was too raw, my breathing too labored to make much of a sound. Not that I was close enough to a residential area for anyone to hear. I tried to run faster, but I could only go so fast on my bare feet, lightheaded from blood loss and lack of food as I tore down the sidewalk.

Finally, things began to look familiar. I saw my little bungalow on the corner. I just had to get inside and I, and my baby, would be safe.

The *tck-tck, tck-tck* began to fade. I slowed my pace, sucking in a much-needed lungful of air as I approached the last of the trees and the long lawn leading up to my front door.

It was only when I heard the rustle of wings that I remembered the ticking sound had sounded farthest away just before the beast struck. My hands shook as I looked into the branches above me.

The demon smiled, lips ripping on the razor-like teeth. Its eyes flashed in the night, back haunches twitching like a cat preparing to spring at its prey. My stomach sank as a growing sense of dread filled me. I lurched out from under the tree, desperate to get to my front door.

Where are my keys?!

I heard the rustle of wings and the deep rumble of laughter as my feet slipped on the dewy lawn. The beast may have not intended to let me leave, but it clearly enjoyed hunting me down. Toying with me. I was never going to escape. I was never going to save my child.

My hands trembled as I desperately tried to find my house keys. I'd throw myself through the front window if I had to.

I never got the opportunity.

Its filthy talons sunk into my collar bone, lifting me off my feet as they scrambled for traction. I opened my mouth to scream for help, but its snake-like tongue slithered down my throat, suffocating me as it carried me off into the night, back to my refrigerated tomb.

IF I HAD A HEART

M. BRANDON ROBBINS

They found the young man's body at 8:19 on a Saturday morning. He was stripped to the waist, his shirt and jacket scattered around him. There were no bruises or lacerations on his body and no signs of a struggle—except that his heart had been ripped out of his chest. A gaping cavity was left where it used to be, and his torso was caked in dried blood. He had no doubt been laying there for quite some time. None of the residents reported any loud noises, shouting, or anything else out of place. There were no eyewitnesses to what happened. It was a mystery.

But I know what happened, because the same thing almost happened to me. I could come forward and tell my story, but nobody would believe me. I have doubts about what happened myself, but in the cold hours of the night when I can't sleep and unwelcome memories come creeping back into my conscience, I remember what happened with frightening clarity. The only thing that could have caused that man's gruesome death was the same terrible encounter that almost caused mine.

I was walking home after a night out with friends, slightly drunk and riding the high of actually getting a girl's phone number for once. I kept my hand in my pocket, clutching the slip of paper I had written it on as if my very life depended on it. It was the best night I remembered in some time, made all the better by the fact that I didn't have to work the next day.

I decided to take the long way home. The weather was nice, it wasn't too late, and I could use some time to sober up a bit before trying to go to sleep. I enjoyed living downtown; there was always something going on, and taking the long way home never seemed like a bad idea.

But it was quiet that night. There were no bars hosting live music, no night-clubs with lines spilling out of the door. There were no couples enjoying sitting outside the cafes, and the bookstores and record shops had long ago closed up for the evening. It was a rare night that saw an eerie hush fall over downtown, and I soon regretted my decision to not walk a direct path to my apartment complex. The quiet was unsettling, and made me uneasy.

I had just turned a corner to put myself back on the short way home when I heard a voice singing. It was distant, almost like an echo, but I could make out every word. I still remember the lyrics to this day.

> *I could feel love*
> *I could feel pain*
> *I could smile in the sun*
> *And dance in the rain*
> *I could laugh*
> *I could cry*
> *I could live*
> *I could die*
> *If I had a heart.*

Though the voice was soft and clear, the song did not put me at ease. It kept changing in pitch, making it impossible to pin down as masculine or feminine. All I know is that it sounded hollow and stripped of emotion. Hearing it made me tense up, every muscle tightening and my throat feeling as if would close. I quickened my step and dared not look back.

I heard the singing again, closer this time. I feared the next corner I had to turn, not knowing what I would find there as all rationality left me behind.

Thankfully, nothing was waiting for me. I hurried, nearly jogging, desperate to reach the safety of my apartment. I could see my building at the end of the block.

I heard the singing again, closer and louder this time. I started to run.

Just as I was coming up to the door, my keys already in my hand, it came around the corner. The creature was tall, with spidery limbs and ivory skin. It was covered in tattered rags and locks of stringy black hair drifted around its head. When it looked at me, I only two glowing white eyes set deep in its skull, as if the skin had been stretched tight or even ripped away.

I froze. I tried to command my body to move. I could have reached out and touched my apartment door, but my arms were stuck to my side. I tried to scream, but couldn't make a sound; I'd lost all control of my body.

Without moving its mouth, the creature sang once more.

I could feel love
I could feel pain
I could smile in the sun
And dance in the rain
I could laugh
I could cry
I could live
I could die
If I had your heart.

The change to the final line did not escape me.

The creature crept toward me on spindly legs and reached out with one bony, elongated hand. As it reached for my chest, panic spread through me. The creature put its hand directly over my heart and let it rest there for a minute.

I heard the thing speak, even though its mouth never moved. Its voice was raspy and raw, as if every word was a struggle, completely unlike its singing voice. "Your heart is full of joy. Your heart is full of life. I like your heart so very much. I think I'll make it mine."

It was then that I heard laughter from around the corner. The thing jerked its hand back and looked toward the sound. I could suddenly move once more. Immediately I dashed inside my building and slammed the door behind me. I heard a woman's voice scream, "Oh my God! Did you see that?"

I didn't stick around to find out what happened next. I ran up to my apartment and locked myself in. Sleep didn't come that night, and I would have nightmares for weeks.

.   .   .

I drove everywhere I went after that encounter, and made every effort to be home before dark. My friends started to worry about me. Before that night, I loved going out with them, whether to listen to live music or catch a movie. It was a long time before I was able to do those things again, and even then, I made myself some very strict rules. Not only did I drive everywhere, but I always parked as close as I could to the entrance of my destination. And if I had to be out after dark, I made sure to be in a group.

But now, the monster has found a heart. Maybe it will be able to rest now. And maybe my life can be normal again.

Or maybe it will need a new heart one day.

All I know is that if you're walking home at night and you hear something singing about what it can do if it had a heart, you'd better run as fast as you can. The creature may find your heart full of joy and life.

And it may make it theirs.

DID YOU FEED THE SHADOWS?

NEALA AMES

I'd heard the family legend for years before it became my own.

My Aunt Grace particularly loved to tell the story, and would do so anytime someone even mentioned shadows. Every old house has its share of legends. This is especially true where families have occupied the same property for generations. It was true for us.

I never understood why my father hated that story so much. He would become almost apoplectic each time he heard it. But when he disappeared one evening in the middle of January and it became my responsibility to fill the role assigned to our family's firstborn child, I finally understood his hatred.

My brother Elliott was afraid of shadows. He'd been that way even as an infant. It was for this reason that I made him come with me every day when I fed them. I always fed them as early as possible; if they ate any later than sundown, they could become dangerous.

When I stepped into the bedroom to get my brother, several small, thin shadows slid before me. He looked up when I entered the room. "Is it time to feed them?" he murmured.

I nodded.

The shadows were already gathering. We made quick work of feeding the ones crouching in our bedroom, then walked out into the hall. We stepped as close as we dared to the shadows there. Quickly we forced our breath into the corners. After the corners were fed, I opened the playroom door.

Shadows skittered swiftly across the floor to the farthest wall. We stepped over the train set in the middle of the room and dodged around the rows of plastic soldiers frozen in their battle positions. The little shadows thrown by the toys were not dangerous. Cautiously, I approached the larger shadows crouched in the corner, waiting.

Taking a deep breath, I shot my breath toward all the shadows. Beside me, Elliot did his share. I blew one last time. Then I bolted from the room before they could catch me.

Even so, I felt cold tentacles snatch and fail to hold my left ankle. Elliot was already in the hall. Together, we continued the feeding.

We fed the shadows underneath our mother's bed and the ones in all the closets. We fed the shadows lurking in the corners of the downstairs rooms. By now it was almost dark, and we still had to face our biggest challenge: the basement. Even before I got to the door, I could hear grumbling coming from the area below me.

I gathered my courage, snatched the door open, and flicked on the basement light.

Deep shadows clustered in every corner, under the stairs and beneath the arms of the large furnace. Quickly, we breathed bursts of air toward the shadows under the stairs so that they would let us pass. Then Elliott and I marched together around the perimeter of the large area, sending puffs of food into all the corners.

By the time we reached the shadows thrown by the fire, we were panting. Our food was gone; we had been too generous to the corners. But it was dangerous to make the furnace shadows wait much longer. Clenching my jaw, I pushed my brother toward the center of the room.

Though the light seeping from the overhead bulb was dim, I could tell Elliott was terrified. Thrusting him aside, I leaned over and drew in as much air as my lungs would hold. Forcefully, I blew into the shadows. They growled menacingly.

"Help me!" I gasped to my petrified brother. Frantically, I drew in another long breath. I inched toward the shadows thrown by the glowing orange flames. The fire flickered inside the monstrous furnace. Long, finger-like shadows reached outward from the grinning maw. They grew even larger, darker. Another growl escaped from deep inside the largest charcoal body. The individual shadows gathered together in one roiling, dark mass. Desperately, I drew a half-dozen quick breaths and blew into the darkness. The shadow was not diverted. I tried to back away, but the cold concrete wall was a barrier behind me. Elliott shrieked and darted toward the stairs as the enraged shadow billowed over me.

Mother found my clothes on the floor of the basement later that night. Elliott, white-faced, told her I had run away. He knows that is not true. Now my brother, though pale and shaking, must do the feeding alone. He is afraid. He fears what he will find within the darkness.

I am waiting with the others. The sun is low on the horizon. I hear Elliott approaching. Softly, I growl. It is time to feed the shadows.

THE CURSED ISLE

MANDY BURKHEAD

The minor fiefdom of Brouillard was situated on the shores of a small lake. From the town's fishing dock, one could look out over the waters to an island. It was this island that the townspeople believed to be haunted. For many years they dealt with strange occurrences and tragedies in their town, all of which, they claimed, were centered around the island.

On two different summers in the past two decades, giant swarms of bloated locusts had flown in from the island, destroying all of the crops in Brouillard. On many nights, inhuman screeching could be heard coming from the island, and it lasted for hours. Dogs or horses that came too near to the edge of the lake went insane; they either turned and sprinted into the waters where they drowned or attacked their owners. From time to time the waters around the island would turn red as with blood. And then there were the deaths.

For all of these reasons, the island was dubbed L'île Maudite, the Cursed Isle. It was to investigate this island and claims of witchcraft that saw Father Antoine and Brother Dominique at Brouillard on that fateful day in 1709.

They arrived at the sleepy little town towards dusk, after a long day of travel in their modest open cart. They were only four days into the new year, and the air was bitterly cold. Thus, the townspeople were all tucked inside their homes to keep warm.

They passed the charred remains of the recently burned down Church, and

Father Antoine said a prayer before they continued on.

The town was too small for an inn, so the lord had offered to keep them in his own home. He came out to greet them, sending his son to care for their horses while he led them inside. He was a nervous little man named Guillaume, with thinning hair and a rotund form. Seating them in his parlor, he immediately began to speak on the subject of the hauntings.

"You have no idea how happy I am that you have arrived, Father," he began.

Father Antoine indicated Brother Dominique beside him, who had taken a roll of parchment, a quill, and ink from his pack. He began to quickly scribble down notes. "Brother Dominique has joined me to observe the happenings here and transcribe them all. While I know some details from the letter you sent, would you perhaps be willing to tell us all of the particulars of what your towns-people have experienced, starting at the beginning?"

"Of course, of course." The lord nodded as his wife poured them each a cup of tea. "I'm not sure I can pinpoint exactly when it all began; before I became seigneur, certainly. There have always been rumors that the island is haunted. But I can nevertheless detail those events that have occurred during my tenure, which began two decades hence.

"On three separate occasions, townspeople have gone missing. The first was a fisherman named Jean who did not return home to his family one evening. The next morning, as he was still nowhere to be found in town nor was his boat at the dock, we searched the lake. His boat was found on the shores of the island, and… not too far off, was his body."

"How did he die?" Father Antoine asked.

"He was hanging from a tree by a noose," the lord replied.

"A suicide, then?" Brother Dominique clarified.

"So it would appear." Seigneur Guillaume frowned. "But his wife claimed he was a happy man. They had two healthy children and were doing well that year. She could think of no reason for him to take such an action."

Father Antoine indicated for the lord to continue his story. "Well, the next was a young boy who drowned. It was summer, and the children were swimming in the lake. When questioned separately, they each claimed the same thing: that they had felt a hand under the water grab at them and try to pull them under. They all fled, leaving the slowest and weakest swimmer behind, who drowned."

"Perhaps a prank gone wrong, and the boys did not wish to get into trouble?" Brother Dominique wondered aloud.

"Perhaps. I could find no wrongdoing or mischief on their parts, as it appeared to be naught but an accident." Guillaume took a sip of tea before continuing. "The most recent, some five years ago, was the worst. A young man and woman fell in the love, but the girl was already betrothed to another. Knowing that their families would not approve, they ran away together. A friend of theirs was discovered stealing a boat full of food and other supplies in the night, and I realized that he must be bringing the supplies to the lovers. Under questioning, he admitted that they had hidden out on L'île Maudite, knowing that they would be left in peace there.

"The families went to the island to retrieve their children, only to discover that in the short time they were missing, they had somehow become completely feral. They ran around the island naked, covered in dirt and blood. The blood, it was discovered, was from rabbits and squirrels they'd killed and eaten, despite having plentiful supplies from their friend. They did not speak when the families demanded them to return home, and instead attacked them, scratching and biting like beasts. In the chaos, the young man was killed. The woman was brought home, but never recovered her faculties. She had a miscarriage some months later that took her life as well. The midwife who delivered the stillborn babe claimed that it was deformed and monstrous."

"I see," Father Antoine said. "And all of these culminated in the most recent event which you spoke of in your letter, the midwife who was accused of witchcraft. Can you detail what happened?"

The lord wiped nervously at his brow with a handkerchief. "A fortnight ago, our Church caught fire in the night. Many of us went out to help put it out. While we were able to keep it from spreading to the rest of the village, our priest perished in the fire.

"The first person on the scene was Giselle Leclère, our local midwife and apothecary. However, she lives at the edge of town, near the lake. The next day a mob came to my door, claiming that there was no reason for her to have been at the Church in the middle of the night, and that she must have been the one to set the fire in the first place. They demanded that I arrest her on charges of witchcraft. I had no other choice but to do so, but without a priest to judge her, I have kept her locked in a cellar in town, awaiting your arrival."

Brother Dominique scribbled furiously as the lord spoke. In truth, this was the real reason that he had convinced Father Antoine to allow him to join the priest for this mission. He had read of historical possessions and modern witch

hunts. In the 1640s, the famous witch hunter Matthew Hopkins had been responsible for executing nearly three hundred witches. And not two decades ago had
been the horrific witch trials in the New World, in a town called Salem.

Brother Dominique firmly believed that such things were the result of mass
hysteria or corruption of government, and thus he did not approve of witch
hunts. After hearing news that a woman was set to be tried for witchcraft, he
begged Father Antoine to investigate the hauntings in the hopes of calming the
townspeople and clearing the name of the supposed witch.

After all, Brother Dominique was a man of science. Like many other monks
and priests, he enjoyed the study of Heavenly bodies. His study of science led
Brother Dominique to the belief that when common folk deemed a place to be
haunted or a person to be a witch, there must be a rational explanation behind it
waiting to be discovered.

And so he was determined, with Father Antoine's help, to prove to these
simple folk that they had merely been beset by a string of odd and tragic coincidences, and were now searching for a scapegoat on whom to take their revenge.

"Things have gotten much, much worse since her imprisonment." Guillaume
rung his hands nervously. "I am beginning to wonder if perhaps she is a witch."

"How so?" Father Antoine asked.

"Whereas before the paranormal events had been limited to the island and
waters around it, now they seem to have spread to the whole town. Daily I have
townspeople coming to me, telling me that they are hearing noises in their
homes. Doors slamming, footsteps, even chains rattling. Some told me of their
livestock or pets going missing. And others have seen things, inhuman things."
Guillaume appeared more and more agitated as he spoke, and Dominique began
to grow irritated. It seemed they would get no rational or sensible accounts from
the man.

"What things do they claim to have seen?" Father Antoine asked politely.

"Shadows. In the middle of the night they will wake up to find shadows
standing around their beds. One man, returning home late from the fields, said
that a shadowed figure followed him until he reached his home. Another, a
woman, swears she saw spirits in the graveyard."

Brother Dominique could no longer contain his annoyance. "It is not
uncommon for one to see shadows in the darkness. Especially when one is
already of a mind to believe that there are supernatural entities afoot. And those
who woke to such things were likely still dreaming."

Guillaume shook his head. "I was once the same, believing these events to be coincidences, believing that people were frightening themselves. But I too have begun to experience these hauntings of late, ever since our priest was murdered. I believe with his presence gone, the malevolent force has grown bolder!"

Dominique opened his mouth to speak again, but Father Antoine held up his hand for silence. He obediently held his tongue. "I believe that the towns-people here are haunted by something," Father Antoine began. The lord perked up. "But whether it is a matter of the mind or the soul is what I must determine."

The lord nodded. "Just wait. After a week here you will believe that it is the work of the Devil!"

It did not take a week. That very night they both encountered something unnatural.

Father Antoine and Brother Dominique had retired to their guest room to sleep. Father Antoine took the bed, and Brother Dominique made himself comfortable on the floor with pillows and blankets.

"Why do you encourage the lord?" Dominique asked as Father Antoine read his Bible in bed, as was his nightly ritual. "Is it not clear that this is merely a case of people frightening themselves? We should demand that they set the accused witch free and go about their lives rationally."

"They truly believe that what they are experiencing is not of this world. They are frightened, and yes, perhaps their fright has led them to escalate their predicament. It is very likely that they are causing their own haunting with their fear." He turned a page. "But you are young, and have yet to experience the work of the Devil. I have. I will know with time if this is the former or the latter, and if it is the latter, I will exorcise the town and the island that they believe is the source." He glanced over at Dominique. "Just as God is in Heaven and we do His work, so too the Devil and his demons exist."

Brother Dominique did not bother to argue. Father Antoine blew out the candle and told him to get some sleep. He wasn't sure how long he had slept before Father Antoine woke him, shaking his shoulder gently. Brother Dominique sat up groggily, confused to see that it was still night, moonlight filtering in through the window.

"What is it, Father? Why have you woken me?" he asked.

"Shh. Do you hear that?" the priest asked. Dominique listened. It didn't take long to realize what Father Antoine was referring too: he could hear laughter.

But it was not normal laughter. It was somewhat between a giggle and a cackle. He could not determine the gender of its origin, but it was incessant. He wondered how the person managed to take a breath.

"Now, I want you to look out the window and tell me what you see," the priest commanded.

Dominique stood warily, making his way over the window where the priest stood. Father Antoine pulled back the curtain and stepped aside for Dominique to look.

There was a figure walking down the street. In the dark, Dominique had trouble making out any detail, other than it was a person who appeared to be naked and walked with a limp. The person also appeared to be the source of the laughter. "They are hurt. Perhaps violated. We should go help them." He turned towards the priest.

The man shook his head. "Not yet."

Brother Dominique found this odd, but did as he was told, turning to look out the window. The person was now standing in front of the lord's house, swaying backward and forward. How they had gotten there so quickly, he could not say.

Then suddenly the stranger fell backwards and began crawling on all fours. Dominique watched in horror as it crawled up the wall with no regards to the laws of physics.

The cackling grew louder as it came nearer. Battling it was Father Antoine's voice beside him, praying in Latin. Brother Dominique also took up the prayer, but was startled to find the room shaking, as if in an earthquake. He heard paintings falling off of the walls in other rooms, the sound of dishes crashing downstairs.

And then suddenly the creature was there in front of them, on the other side of the window, its back to them. Its head rotated like an owl's, all the way around on its body, so that it could gaze through the window at them. Brother Dominique nearly fell as he fought the urge to get away from it. Only Father Antoine calmly chanting beside him kept him standing as he stared into the face of something so unnatural.

For it had no face, at least no human one. There were only empty black hollows where its eyes, nose, and mouth should be. When it opened its mouth, its jaw extended down, down, almost to its chest.

He saw movement beside him, and Father Antoine flung holy water at the window, demanding the creature to be gone. It screeched like a cat and crawled back down the wall. Dominique watched as it scurried down the street and disappeared into the darkness.

The house's shaking had stopped. Father Antoine was panting. Dominique's own heart was racing, and he promptly turned and vomited into the chamber pot.

When he finished, the priest stood beside him with a flask. "Have a drink of this," he commanded.

"But Father—" Dominique began to protest when he smelled the spirits.

"I assure you, God will understand," Father Antoine told him sternly.

Dominique took a swig, grimacing at the burning sensation, but it did help to calm him somewhat. "What was that thing?" he asked. "It was not... natural."

"A demon," the priest replied, grimacing. "It would seem that the hysteria of these townspeople is not unfounded."

"But you have driven it off, yes? Then they will no longer be troubled by it?" Dominique hoped.

Father Antoine shook his head. "That entity was weak, most likely drawn here by the fear and death. The demon at the heart of these hauntings will be much more powerful. Tomorrow we will question the supposed witch, then exorcise the village."

Dominique did not sleep the rest of the night. He had no clue how Father Antoine managed to calmly lie back down and close his eyes. The man was unwavering, no matter the circumstances. Dominique, on the other hand, stayed up through the night with his Bible and Cross, his back to the wall, eyes glancing between the window and door. He prayed the Rosary for many hours, but it did little to calm his frazzled nerves.

He tried to think of some earthly explanation for the thing he had seen, but came up with none. He began to wonder at his own hypocrisy, that he worshipped the Holy Trinity and yet had never truly believed in spirits or demonic forces.

Finally, dawn broke and Father Antoine woke with the sun as he always did. They went downstairs to break their fast with the lord and his family.

Brother Dominique expected to see the house in disarray, paintings on the floor, dishes shattered. Instead everything was intact. The family seemed no more upset than they had been the night before. Not once during their meal did Father Antoine mention what they had experienced, until Dominique began to wonder if it had all been a bad dream. But as they departed the lord's house to question the accused witch, the priest fell some distance behind the lord to speak with Dominique in private. "I did not wish to panic them further. Thus, we will hold our tongues regarding anything else we experience while we are here. Fear only makes demons stronger."

Brother Dominique nodded silently, both filled with dread that it had not been a nightmare and relief that he was not alone in what he had seen. They followed the lord to a storage building; the town was much too small for any sort of jailhouse. Moving past shelves of provisions, they descended stone steps into a cellar. The seigneur unlocked the heavy chains holding the door closed and allowed the priest and monk to step inside.

Besides barrels and bottles of wine, the small room was dark and empty. "Who else has a key to the cellar?" Father Antoine asked.

"No one! I'm the only one. And it was locked. How... how did she get out?" He shook his head, eyes wide. "Maybe she really is a witch..."

Father Antoine pursed his lips. "Never mind about that. For now, we will begin blessing the village."

Dominique followed the priest through the village, carrying the Holy Water and Bible while Father Antoine recited prayers in Latin and sprinkled Holy Water on the door of each hearth. The people came out of their houses and stood, receiving the blessing and making the Sign of the Cross in their wake. With each person and house that was blessed, Dominique could feel the dark cloud of dread begin to lift from the town. Within the hour they had covered the entire village and reached the edge of the lake. The island loomed in the distance. It felt as if it were watching them, a sentient and malevolent being.

"Take us to the island," Father Antoine commanded the lord.

Guillaume turned to him with wide eyes. "You... you want me to take you... th-there?"

"Are you not the seigneur of this town?" Father Antoine asked harshly. "The people must see you confronting the evil that haunts them. If you do not do this, they will lose all respect for you."

The man looked as if he was going to protest, but the crowd of townspeople watching quieted him. He nodded sullenly, stepping onto the dock and leading the holy men to a small boat. Brother Dominique rowed them to the small island.

The lord already looked as if he might pass out at any moment, and he did not wish to overexert the man.

It took but a few minutes to reach the island's shores, yet a heavy fog hung over the waters, obscuring the town. All sound seemed to cease; they heard neither the sounds of life from the town nor birds chirping or squirrels rustling in the leaves. Even the wind was still, as if the earth held its breath.

"Let us begin," Father Antoine said. They formed a line and proceeded to the heart of the island as they had through the town, with Father Antoine blessing the rocks, trees, and ground as they went.

"Do you see them? In the trees?" Seigneur Guillaume asked from behind Dominique. He turned to admonish the lord for interrupting Father Antoine, but paused when he observed what the lord pointed to. Hanging from a tree was some sort of strange knot made of twigs. He looked up and around and saw several of them hanging throughout the trees. He just nodded silently to Guillaume and continued to follow Father Antoine.

The wind began to pick up the further they moved into the island. It was strange, for it hadn't seemed that large when observing it from the shore of the lake, and yet they had walked for ten minutes or more without emerging on the other side. The foliage was so dense as to block out the sunlight, and in the perpetual twilight he could see shadows at the corners of his vision. Whenever he turned to look at them fully, they seemed to dart off into the darkness.

And still Father Antoine continued forward, unperturbed. The wind grew stronger, as if a storm had blown in; the trees above them danced in the breeze. They began to hear a howling that Brother Dominique suspected was not the wind at all.

And then that laughing began, the same endless cackling they had heard the night before. Guillaume was now gripping Brother Dominique's shoulder so hard it hurt. The lord's eyes were manic and his whole body shook with fear as he jumped at every movement around them. "You must not show fear, Seigneur. It makes demons stronger," Dominique explained, but this only made the man panic even more.

And then they emerged into a clearing, a perfect circle in the trees. In the center of it stood a woman.

"That's her!" The lord exclaimed, pointing at her. "That's the witch!"

"Stay back," Father Antoine commanded. He stepped into the clearing, continuing to chant and fling holy water.

The woman inside it was also chanting, though not in Latin or any language that Brother Dominique could understand. Her appearance surprised him. He wasn't sure what he had expected. An old crone perhaps? Or a demonic form, with warts and disfigurements? What he had not expected was a beautiful young woman, perhaps a few years his junior, with her arms flung wide and her eyes rolled back so that they appeared completely white. She was surrounded by strange items: a book, a dagger, and a bowl, and she had drawn in the dirt a star inside a circle.

The priest approached her, and it was if the two began to spar with their chanting. The wind whipped the trees about wildly. The sky had turned red though it was not yet midday. Thunder rumbled in the distance, and lightning struck all around them. Dominique saw the lord flee into the forest, and then heard a bloodcurdling scream from the direction in which he'd fled. He grimaced and said a prayer for the man's soul before returning to the spectacle before him.

The woman began to rise from the ground. Her chanting cut off, but she continued to move her mouth. It was as if there were something before her, something that Dominique couldn't quite see. He rubbed at his eyes and peered closer, and its form became more distinct. It was a dark mass of shadow and smoke that exuded hate and malice, neither human nor beast, its shape indefinable, seeming to shift before his very eyes.

It held the woman by her neck, and then it tossed her as if she weighed nothing. She came soaring towards Dominique, hitting a tree and collapsing to the earth beside him. Father Antoine now stood alone with the thing. The witch was no longer able to strengthen the demon, and yet as the moments passed it seemed to grow more solid, more real, before Dominique's eyes.

The witch moaned beside him, and Dominique tore his eyes from the Holy battle to glance down at her. She sat up slowly, rubbing at her head. "What..." she glanced first at Dominique, then at the priest. "No!" she screamed. "Stop him!"

She jumped to her feet and leapt forward, but Dominique grabbed her, holding her back. "Silence, witch!" he commanded, clamping his hand over her mouth to prevent her resuming her chant. She struggled against him as the maelstrom raged. Father Antoine held forth his Bible, glaring into the eyes of the demon.

Suddenly the witch bit his hand, causing Dominique to let go of her mouth. "Stop him! You have to stop him! He is ruining the spell!"

"That is the point, witch! He is casting the evil from this island," Dominique responded.

"You don't understand! It's a binding spell! *He's going to release it!*"

Dominique had difficulty hearing her over the now screeching wind. But it mattered not. They were going to destroy it, to cast it back to Hell where it had come from. She was only trying to trick him.

And yet... it looked larger, more powerful with each passing second. Brother Dominique felt an overwhelming sense of dread as Father Antoine yelled, "I command you to leave this place, in the name of the Father, and of the Son, and of the Holy Spirit!"

The creature began to laugh. "As you wish." Its voice sounded like a thousand anguished screams.

With a deafening *crack* it disappeared in an explosion, throwing Dominique and the witch backwards with the sheer force. Dominique felt a wave of cold wash over his entire body. When he managed to sit up, the entire island was covered in ice, radiating outwards from the place the demon had stood moments before. Dominique pushed himself to his knees and managed to stand, limping to where Father Antoine lay on the ground in the center of the clearing. He rolled Father Antoine over, gasping when he found the priest dead, his body coated in frost, as if he had perished in a snowstorm. The priest's eyes were wide with fear and mouth open in a silent scream.

"You did this. You ignorant fools!" Dominique looked up to find the witch glaring at him. "You've doomed us all. For generations my ancestors kept it trapped here, away from humanity. And now you've freed it."

He was having difficulty understanding all that had transpired. "We were trying to get rid of it. What—what will it do?"

She gazed into the distance. "Wherever it goes, it brings with it a cold so bitter that livestock freeze in their pens and children die in their sleep. Seas will turn to ice. Crops will wither and people will starve by the thousands."

She gathered her instruments from the clearing, then set off away from him.

"Where are you going?!" Dominique yelled after her.

She paused, then glared back at him. "To prepare for the hunt. I will chase it for as long and far as I must to trap it once more. Go home, monk, and pray that your God forgives you for your ignorance."

Dominique gazed after the witch's retreating form in horror.

What had they done?

THE BEAST ON LINCOLN WAY

CHRISTINE DRUGA

I

I'm an idiot. I should have listened, but I'm stupid and stubborn. When someone tells you not to put your hand on the hot stove, you listen, right? And if you don't, you get hurt and there is no one to blame but yourself.

It started two weeks ago. My buddies and I had rented a cabin near a lake for the opening weekend of trout season. We fished, we drank beer, we cooked over the fire... We were having a great time. That Saturday night, as we sat around the fire with drinks in hand, we started telling ghost stories. Most of them were old urban legends, some of them were personal experiences. Others were "scary" stories that ended with a hilarious insult to someone's mother. It was all in good fun. Until Max told us about Lincoln Way.

Lincoln Way was a residential street in a town near where we lived in south-western Pennsylvania. We were all familiar with it. My parents used to have a friend that lived in the last house on the dead-end road, so I spent a good portion of my time there when I was a kid. The street was something of an oddity, because every single house there was now abandoned. No one seemed to know why the residents of Lincoln Way just seemed to get out of dodge, leaving behind food, furniture, and even cars. A local group of "urban explorers" had recently posted an article on their Facebook page about it, finding that the houses still had the same owners as they had as far back as the '70s, but no one was willing to live on the now-overgrown street. Most people assumed that the residents of Lincoln Way had moved because of the poor economy taking its toll on an already poverty-stricken area, but Max claimed to know better. He claimed to know the *real* reason that the residential street no longer had any residents.

According to Max, something lurked in the woods that surrounded Lincoln Way. Something not human, but not like any animal we had ever seen or heard of. He claimed that this creature had tormented the street's residents. Pets would go missing, only to be found some days later mutilated at the wood line. Backyard gardens would be torn up by paws too big to belong to rabbits or dogs. People would be kept awake at night by things scratching and banging on the side of their home, or snarls and howls that seemed to be right outside of their window. Supposedly, no one had seen the beast causing such trouble on Lincoln Way. At least no one who had stuck around to tell anyone about it. Max claimed that the street was abandoned out of fear, each occupied house being left after its inhabitants were spooked by an escalation in the creature's torment. That would explain why most, if not all, of the houses still contained so many belongings. You don't take the time to load furniture into a U-Haul and empty your fridge if you're scared out of your mind.

I was skeptical of the story, as any reasonable person would be. Lincoln Way might not have been surrounded by other residential streets, but it was right off a main road. That main road had a gas station and a bar less than a minute down the road one way, and an entire town less than two minutes in the other direction. Surely, if there was some terrible creature in the area, it wouldn't stick to that one road and the patch of woods that surrounded it. My parents' friend had moved out of that neighborhood almost twenty years ago, so my argument that "he had never had a problem with Bigfoot" was almost immediately swept aside. When I suggested that we go check it out the next weekend, I was met with horrified stares and exclamations of disproval: "You can't go there! I just told you that something horrible lives there!" "There's no way in hell I'm going there. I'm too pretty to die." "Dude, even if there isn't some weird monster there, I'm not risking getting arrested or hurt by wandering around a street full of houses that are probably falling down. And there are probably a lot of rats. I hate rats."

These were just some of the arguments I heard.

Only one person, out of the five other guys that sat around the fire with me that night, was willing to explore with me. His name was Sam, and he was a big guy covered in tattoos. Sam was arguably the biggest badass in our group, but behind the beard and drawings of skulls and other crazy shit that was inked into his skin, he was a great guy and a loyal friend. The only reason he agreed to go with me was because he didn't want me to go by myself. He saw that I was determined to debunk Max's story, and told me, "I'm not letting your dumb ass go in there alone and get mugged by some hobo squatter or some weird shit. Your mom would be pissed at me, and she's way scarier than Bigfoot." So the next weekend, last Saturday to be exact, Sam picked me up when he got off of work, and we drove to Lincoln Way.

Sam parked his blue pickup truck in front of one of the houses at the beginning of the street. It was still light outside, but it was later in the day, so we brought flashlights with us. We didn't know how long we would be there, or how dark it would be inside the dilapidated houses that we were determined to explore. We decided to walk along the wood line first, which meant walking through the overgrown backyards of the houses. We tried to look for evidence of digging in the yards, but the grass and weeds were so high that it would have taken forever to scan the ground it grew from. We walked the length of the street through the backyards, crossed the street at the dead end, and walked down the opposite side through those yards. When we were confident that nothing was going to jump from the trees and grab us, we started looking inside the houses.

Sam and I weren't comfortable going into many of the houses because of how run down they were. The ones we didn't enter, we looked at the insides through first floor windows. Every house on the block was full of belongings, and most of them looked like they had been ransacked. Furniture was overturned and thrown against walls, photos were strewn all over the floors, the curtains that still hung were shredded, and pillows were torn open. Out of all of the houses, there were only four or five that weren't tossed, and those houses were more disturbing. The houses that we entered that didn't look like a hurricane hit the inside looked like someone could have been living there, minus the dirt and grime. Pictures still hung on the walls, books were still on the shelves, beds were made, and dishes were in the sink. One of the houses had food on the table, though it looked like some small critters had munched on it long ago. It looked like the previous residents literally just up and left in the middle of dinner, without bothering to take anything with them. One of the houses had a garage.

Its door looked like it fell off the track long ago, and it still had a car parked inside.

The sun was almost completely set when Sam and I exited the last house. We were thoroughly creeped out by our findings, so we decided it was time to call it a night and go home. We were walking toward Sam's truck when we heard it: *scraaaaatch, scraaaaatch, scraaaaatch...* BANG.

We froze, standing completely still in the middle of a cracked road, and listened to the sounds for a minute or so. It was coming from behind the house to our left. Sam whispered that we should get the hell out of there, but I wanted to prove Max wrong. Like I said at the beginning, I'm an idiot.

I slowly made my way toward the noise, keeping my hand cupped over the front of my flashlight. I was about to round the corner into the backyard when it stopped. I listened for a few seconds, standing completely still. I could hear something coming toward me slowly, something big creeping through the tall grass. I pressed myself against the side of the house, and looked back to see Sam still standing in the middle of the road. A deep, guttural snarl made me turn back to the yard, and I saw it.

It stood on all fours, and was as big as a horse. Thick, black hair covered its massive body. Its muscular front legs were tipped with claws longer than my fingers, and its mouth was full of too many razor-sharp teeth. The few people I've described it to reasoned that it was a bear or a large wild cat far from home, but it didn't look like either of those. The beast's head almost resembled a massive dog, except for the horns on either side. I stared into deep red eyes, rooted to my spot with terror, as this creature slowly made its way closer to me. Another growl escaped from its throat, and I began to shake so badly that I dropped my flashlight. The sudden movement and flash of light seemed to startle it. I took my chance and ran back to the street, screaming for Sam to get into the truck and start the engine. I could hear heavy paws hitting the ground not far behind me as I ran faster than I ever have in my life. I launched myself into Sam's truck, and he threw it in gear and pulled a U-turn to get us the hell out of there. The truck's headlights illuminated the beast for a moment as it stopped in the middle of the road to avoid being hit. What I had thought was fur was actually closer to a mass of thin porcupine needles, and every one on its back stood straight up as the beast crouched to spring at the truck. Sam was speeding toward the main road when we heard the howl of the creature. It sounded pained and angry, as if it was starving and upset that it was denied a meal.

We now know why Lincoln Way was abandoned. The people were harassed, maybe worse, by some kind of monster that resides in the woods, waiting for someone to investigate a strange noise so that it can attack. It's hungry and vicious, and it's not alone. I know this, because when Sam was turning the truck around during our great escape, his headlights briefly pointed into the woods. That's where I saw at least three more sets of deep, shining red eyes.

II

"Watch out for Bigfoot!" Tara called out as I was putting on my boots.

"Come on now, that silly urban legend is just that. Silly. The only thing lurking around those houses are bums and bugs."

I know I sounded confident in my response, but there was a hint of anxiety building in my chest.

There were always rumors about why everyone seemed to just drop everything and leave their homes on Lincoln Way. A few years ago, the story shifted from "they were paid to leave" to "they were forced out by a monster." Skeptics debated and argued and joked about it on Facebook while believers traveled to explore the mysterious abandoned street.

The local cops hated their town's newfound fame. They suddenly went from occasionally having to check for vagrants squatting in the empty houses to being forced to patrol the area regularly to chase off urban explorers and ghost hunters.

A lot of people were relieved, and a lot of them were disappointed, when it was announced that all sixteen houses remaining on Lincoln Way were going to be torn down. It wasn't all that surprising, really. There had been two pretty big fires on the street since its popularity soared, and the already-dilapidated houses quickly became even more rundown from all the foot traffic and vandals. It was dangerous, and the risk wasn't keeping anyone away.

I was just happy for the work. The company I normally worked for wasn't doing so hot, so the "winter layoffs" came to some of us a bit sooner than normal. Unemployment was helping to keep the power on, but I could see the stress building in Tara's eyes every time we planned a trip to the grocery store. She normally had a few more months to plan for my seasonal bouts of occasional side jobs and more frequent couch surfing.

I pulled up to Lincoln Way around six a.m. The boss wanted us there early so he could lead a safety meeting before we began. I had grown up just across the river, so the area itself was familiar and comfortable, but I had to admit that the decrepit buildings behind the ginormous "NO TRESPASSING" sign held an eerie air around them. That anxiety in my chest bubbled a bit more for a moment.

After hearing the same spiel about hardhats and shit that I've heard a million times before, we got to work. I won't bore you with stories of operating machinery and lewd jokes among working men (although I did learn a few new ones). All you really need to know is that everything was going smoothly. After a few days on the job, I was no longer concerned about giant dogs attacking us on our lunch break.

The first Friday on the worksite wrapped up, and some of the crew were planning on meeting up at a bar just down the road. Lenny, a hulking goofball in his mid-fifties, insisted that I come along.

Two hours and quite a few brews later, Lenny and I were the only remaining crew members there. I was searching for an opportunity to cut out, eager to get home to Tara and a hot shower. Lenny had other ideas.

"What d'you think about that rumor? About the beasts? Do you think it's true?" Lenny asked as he carefully put his mug back on the bar top.

"I doubt it. I mean, we haven't seen any evidence, right?"

"Ah, but that's the thing!" His eyes lit up like he had been anticipating this conversation from day one. "We're only there during the day. Every story I've heard about it, the monsters only come out at night."

I chuckled and shook my head. "I didn't peg you as a believer in boogeymen."

"I'm not. But you have to admit that it's creepy and interesting. I'd've been down here exploring myself, if I wasn't afraid of getting arrested for trespassing." He looked at me rather expectantly. I was getting the hint, and it made me kind of uncomfortable.

"Haha, the cops scare you more than the monsters, huh? We'd still get arrested for trespass—"

"Ah, but here's the thing! All we gotta do is tell them we work there—that's not a lie—and that we forgot something onsite and were going back to get it!" Lenny was practically bouncing out of his seat at this point.

We went back and forth a bit before I finally gave in, mostly because I didn't want Lenny to get hurt or in trouble drunkenly stumbling around in the dark all by himself.

I swear the "No Trespassing" sign was twice as big at night, but it was probably just my guilty conscience and the alcohol messing with my head. The barriers blocking the road prevented cars from entering Lincoln Way, but really didn't do much to stop someone from just walking on in. That's exactly what we did.

I blamed the goosebumps on the chill in the air, but there was that nagging feeling of fear itching at the back of my mind. There was a reason that the urban legend took off the way it did: this place was fucking creepy.

We stumbled around for about twenty minutes, watching the best we could for tripping hazards and wishing we had brought flashlights. Just as I started to tell Lenny that we were wasting our time, he shushed me.

"Did you hear that?" he asked in a loud whisper.

"I didn't hear anything, Lenny. We should go."

"*Sssssh*! There's something in the woods over here."

Before I could respond, Lenny took off toward one of the houses that was still mostly standing. I stood as still as I ever had, trying to hear anything other than his clumsy footsteps. I was torn. It was reasonable to believe that any noise Lenny had heard was just a racoon or something, but the hair on the back of my neck and the sick feeling in my stomach were screaming at me to run. While I stood there and debated just how good of a friend Lenny was, I noticed he suddenly got very quiet.

"Lenny?" I called out to the dark. "Quit screwin' around!"

Silence.

"Lenny!" I called again as I started moving toward the house. I was stopped mid-stride by a high-pitched shriek.

I couldn't see a damn thing, but I could hear everything.

Branches breaking, frenzied movement, a low rumble of a growl, then an angry snarl followed by Lenny begging God for help.

Help! That's what I needed to do. I broke out of my terrified stupor and rushed around the side of the house. On my way to the backyard, I grabbed a broken piece of wood that was leaning against the building. I was about to piss myself in fear, but damn it, I was going to defend my friend.

At least, that was my intention until I turned the corner.

Lenny was backed against the back wall of the house, trying to slowly inch his way toward where I was standing. In front of him stood the biggest dog I have ever seen.

Except… was it a dog? Dogs don't get that big, and they don't have horns, but it looked like a dog. A mean dog… with a lot of teeth.

I couldn't stop the whimper that escaped my mouth. In a split second I went from a knight in shining armor to a terrified child. The sound drew Lenny's attention, and he was about halfway through saying my name when the "dog" attacked.

My bladder emptied as the first bite tore into Lenny's stomach. His intestines stretched from his belly to the beast's mouth for a moment while it swiped its massive paw across Lenny's chest, knocking my friend to the ground and leaving dark streaks across what was left of his shirt.

The monster began to eat, and I was at my car door before I had even realized I was moving.

I drove for about five minutes before I had to pull over to vomit on the side of the road. I sat in wet pants for a while and debated what I should do next.

The cops probably wouldn't believe me, and I didn't want to go to jail because they figured I saw an opportunity in the legend. I could just drive home, grab Tara, and run far away from that cursed street, but that plan relied on her believing me.

The only thing I knew for sure was that I was never going back to that job.

Tara was already asleep when I got home, so at least I didn't have to explain the state of me. I didn't sleep at all. I checked and double checked and triple checked every door and window in the house, then got my hunting rifle from the safe and sat in the living room until the sun came up. I took a hot shower, slipped into bed, and waited for my wife to stir.

Tara's a wonderful woman. I could tell that my sudden extreme change in demeanor worried her, but she didn't ask questions when I insisted I was just not feeling well. I called off work on Monday and Tuesday, and quit on Wednesday. I watched the news and scoured the internet every chance I got, expecting to find some news about finding a body behind an abandoned house on a haunted street. The only thing I ever found was a Missing Person post on a friend of a friend's Facebook page. I stared at Lenny's smiling face in the photo for entirely too long before I shut my laptop and cried.

The houses are all gone now, replaced by broken pavement and growing grass. I ignored any and all phone calls from my former coworkers, and the police never came, so I'm assuming no one suspects that I was involved in Lenny's disappearance. There was no news of any mishaps or anything on the job site, but there was no news on Lenny either, so I guess that doesn't say much.

There's talk of a housing development replacing the rows of abandoned houses, but I pray that it never happens. Whatever's out there, I doubt that it left the comfort of the trees where it's apparently lived for years.

Who knows, maybe it did. There are plenty of new hunting grounds in the area.

Regardless, I don't think we've seen the last of the Beast on Lincoln Way.

THE BLIND SPOT BULLY

WATT MORGAN

Theo's left eye was half-swollen shut and covered in an opaque greenish goop that crusted around the edges. He wiped the goop off with a wet piece of paper towel and poked at the lid in the mirror. It didn't appear to be a bug bite—there were no punctures in the skin or red marks—but he wasn't ruling anything out.

Over the course of the morning, the swelling receded some, though even by noon he'd noticed his reflection in the glass of one of the soda coolers and had to admit it still looked pretty bad. The regulars gave him funny looks, but very few mentioned it outright. And anyway, what was there to say? *Yeah, I woke up like this. No, I don't know what happened. I hope it goes away, too. Can I see out of it? Sure. Things are a little blurry, but I'm sure it'll be okay. Yeah, right, I'll go see the doctor. 'Cause I can totally afford that.*

By evening, his vision had cleared up completely, but the eyelid still had a pink, puffed appearance to it. He poked and pulled at it in the mirror, but there was no sign of what had caused the aberration. He gave up, slouched on the sofa with a beer, and vegged out to cooking competition reruns. As eleven rolled around, he forced himself to his feet and plodded to bed, hoping that the eye issue was behind him and tomorrow would turn out to be just like every other day.

As he leaned over his pillow to flick off his bedside lamp, something dark caught in the corner of his vision. He turned to look, but there was nothing there.

Just the pale, water-stained walls of the apartment. Sighing deeply, he doused the room in darkness and drifted to sleep.

"The problem is that nobody can see the world the way it really is," Plaid-man said. "We only see the way we want the world to be. Our entire visual field is skewed by the perceptions of reality we have in our heads. Can we even say that there's any truth at all?"

Theo shrugged. This was a conversation he'd participated in with Plaid-man over and over again for the entire year the guy had been coming to the store. In its various forms, the argument was that everyone is wrong about everything, and that made facts worthless. "Sure," Theo said. "Isn't that what science is for?"

Plaid-man waved his hand. "Whatever. Science. Yeah, you can even use science to demand that people see the world the way you want them to, by developing numbers and statistics that skew toward your personal perception. Science itself is based primarily on taking measurements of an experience. And we don't even get to see the results of the experiments." He was holding up an old lady with a short stack of tuna cans in her hand. Theo tried to signal for Plaid-man to move over, but the guy was oblivious. "All that we common consumers get to see are secondhand articles interpreting the data. Look, even the bloggers are skewing the science further to their personal point of view."

Theo leaned around him, signaling to the old lady that he'd scan her items. She smiled and handed over the cans. "Well," Theo said. "So you're saying there's no truth at all?" Beep. Beep.

"No. No, of course not. There has to be *something* that's true. Something is holding all of reality together, right? I mean, even if all of this is some kind of illusion, and I'm the only real human here and I'm imagining it—Descartes, you know?—then at least there's an I Am at task for all of this."

"Eleven ninety-three." The lady balked as if she might argue, then hung her head and unsnapped the hasp on her purse. Theo turned back to Plaid-man. "But what's the point of even arguing over it? If this is real, then we have to agree it's real. If it's not real, then…"

"What's the point? What's the *point*?! Your whole life is constituted by decisions you've made based on the assumption of truth. If the truth isn't true at all, then we've all got a hell of a lot of—oh, shit. Is it really after ten already?"

Theo looked back at the clock. "Yeah."

"I gotta go. I'm late. See ya tomorrow, man!"

"Hope so!" Theo called back sarcastically. The old lady was trying to pass him a few paper bills and some coins. "Oh, sorry," he said, taking them from her. She smiled, took her change and cans, and left.

Finally, he was alone. The morning rush was over. Sure, there would be some stragglers here and there; the store never quite stopped moving. But now he would get time to himself to restock the shelves and enjoy a little mediocre silence.

Going out to the stockroom was his least favorite part of the job. No matter how much he mopped, wet spots formed on the floor, spreading rusty, staining liquid across the already scuffed and chipped tile. Even when new, the fluorescent ceiling bulbs worked dimly, flickered often, and buzzed like wasps. And for some reason it was always bone-chillingly cold, even on sweltering summer days. The thought of going back there made him shudder, so Theo spent as little time in the stockroom as he could, and had a system in place so that he could rush in, grab product, and hurry out.

With a deep breath, and a plastic shopping bag in hand, he pulled the creaking metal door open and peered inside. As always, it was so dim he could barely see the back of the room from the door. No matter. He was the one who stocked the store, he was the one who stocked the room, and he could locate every item in here even if he were blind.

First up was the chips, on the right side of the room. He consulted his mental list of what brands needed to be restocked and then hurried in. The heavy door slammed shut behind him. Instantly, claustrophobia gripped him. His palms became clammy and he shivered. Glancing around to make sure the room really was empty, Theo raced to the boxes of chips and shoved them into his plastic shopping bag one at a time, until the bag was overfull. Once he had what he needed, he turned back the way he had come.

As Theo moved toward the stockroom door, he caught sight of a dark spot in the corner of his eye. It was familiar. Had he seen it before? Almost human in form. He could make out the shape of a head and shoulders, one arm raised up and holding something in its grip. He gasped and turned toward the vision, but it was gone. He shivered so violently that a couple of the packages fell from his bag, scattering across the floor. He cursed.

The lights went out.

His mouth felt tacky and dry. Dreadfully certain that he was going to die in here, he dropped to his knees and felt around for the bags he'd dropped, his fingertips searching the cold, damp floor. His breathing felt labored, and he became acutely aware that something was in the room with him. He was sure of it. Standing in the corner, watching him struggle with the chips, waiting for him to move closer. Waiting for him to come within reach. Waiting and ready to snatch him up.

Theo gasped and whined, and finally found one of the chip bags. His heart raced as he felt around for the other one. Small whimpers pushed their way from his throat. He wanted to leave, wanted to get out of here and into a place where it was light, warm, and alive.

There was a sound: someone was breathing in here. And it wasn't him. Long, rattling deep breaths coming from the corner of the room where he had caught the shape out of the corner of his eye. Whatever it was he had seen was still there. Still standing there in the corner and still holding onto the object in its hand.

And then it began to shuffle toward him. Drawn-out, dragging steps across the tile. The rattling breaths growing louder.

Theo's hand bumped the last chip bag. He reached out to grab it, but the plastic packaging slipped from his wet fingers and fell to the floor again. Closer the dragging steps came, swishing the musty water around the floor. Closer came the rattling deep breaths. Theo felt his body shaking. *Screw the chips*, he thought. *Screw them, I'm getting out of here now!*

He climbed to his feet and leapt toward the door, sure of where it was yet unsure that it would still be there. The shopping bag full of chips fell from his grip and he heard the upended sack spill its contents. He didn't care. Getting away from here was foremost. He'd worry about the stock later. He had to escape. If he didn't go now, he would die.

He reached for the handle. Tried to turn it.

His wet hand slipped off. The door pulled open, offering a knife slice of light, then fell closed again. Behind him, he could hear the dragging steps moving closer. Moving faster. The long, rattling breaths getting louder. So close that he swore he could feel the breath on his neck, warm and dry and reeking of sulfur and cherry. An odor that made Theo choke.

He swiped his wet hands on his pants to dry them off the best he could. Cold fingertips brushed the back of his shoulder. He reached for the handle again and tugged.

The lights came back on. No flickering.

The room was empty. Chip packages littered the tile floor. He didn't stick around to pick them up.

Theo was still shaking when the evening shift came in to relieve him. Plenty of customers had come and gone by then, but he refused to restock anything. He made an excuse to Tawny that he'd felt sick all day, could barely hold in his breakfast, didn't even attempt lunch, and that was why he hadn't done any work. She rolled her eyes and asked him to at least hold the door open for her while she stocked.

"The back room gives me the goddamn creeps," she said.

Theo agreed.

It was almost dark by the time he got home. He hated winter. It was always like this. Dark on his way in to work, fading to darkness on his way back. The sun seemed like an angel that blessed the few who could afford a day off. His experience inside the stock room only made it all worse.

When he got inside his apartment, he turned on every light, flipped on the television, turned the volume up loud, and started a cup of noodles in the microwave. Sitting on the couch in front of some blaring gameshow, he tapped out a post onto an occult forum. "True story:" he wrote into the title field, "dark figure in the corner of my eye." Then he proceeded to recount the entire experience in as much detail as he could remember. Retelling it raised goosebumps on his skin and chilled him so much that he drew a blanket across his shoulders.

After he was done, he hit *Submit* and set his phone down on the cushion beside him. His knee quivered restlessly. He hoped someone would see his post and respond. He hoped it would be soon. He refreshed the page. Nothing. He refreshed it again. Nothing. He tried to watch the gameshow, playing along with the contestants as they responded to lowball trivia questions, but the knot in his stomach wouldn't let him enjoy it, so he got up and paced. The microwave beeped.

When he got back to the couch with his cup of noodles, there were several messages waiting for him.

The first one read, *Great, now I'm never going to get some sleep haha. Great story, dude. One for the creepypasta books.*

Another: *Oof. You should write professionally. That sent shivers up my spine.*

The last one made Theo's heart stop:

Hey, that sounds like something my cousin went through. He started experiencing these weird hallucinations during the day of someone or something approaching him. A dark figure like you describe. He complained about it constantly. Everyone brushed it off cause he was always kind of like that. You know, trying to be the center of attention all the time. We just thought it was another one of those. But he wouldn't stop, and after a couple days it was clear that something really was up. He'd gotten pale. Stopped eating. Looked like he wasn't sleeping. His body shook uncontrollably.

Then he disappeared.

Nobody knew what had happened to him. Where he'd gone. But we searched everywhere for him, and after forty-eight hours the police set up a manhunt.

They did find him eventually. His eyes had been gouged out of their sockets. They wouldn't let us see it, but the mortician had to use glass eyes to replace his real ones.

We tried to find out more information based on what he'd told us. We didn't find much, but there are a few accounts from others whose family and friends had similar experiences.

From what I can tell, people have taken to calling him the Blind Spot Bully. Did you have any weird swelling in one eye before all of this started? That's how he marks you. Then he hides in your blind spots so you can't see him, but if you're paying attention, sometimes he's not fast enough and you can catch sight of him when you're turning your head.

That thing he's holding? It's a big spoon with a serrated edge. Have you ever seen a grapefruit spoon? Imagine that but bigger. Rounder. Like the size of a fist. It's what he uses to dig your eyes out. Nobody knows what he does with the eyes. None of them have ever been found.

I don't know much else. There's no other information. No occult mythology describing a demon like this. We searched everywhere after my cousin died. That's all we know.

Jesus, I'm sorry, man. I'm sorry to have to tell you this. But we couldn't find anyone who'd survived an encounter.

I'll pray for you.

He didn't fall asleep until two a.m., and even then it was fitful. When his alarm woke him, the bedsheets were soaked in sweat. Swinging his head back and forth, he tried to catch sight of the Bully, but there was nothing.

At first, he considered just lying there in bed and giving up. *Let the Blind Spot Bully come to me,* he thought. *If I can't get away from him, then what's the point?* But he knew he wouldn't do that. He knew he would get out of bed and live as though nothing was happening.

Maybe nothing really was going on. Maybe he just needed a day off. Some time for himself. Go relax on a beach somewhere. Get a tan. And anyway, nothing was ever proven true by being posted on the internet. Sure, he'd been experiencing something weird, but there was no proof that it was some grape-fruit-loving demon.

He started to smile a little, then laughed to himself, imagining a wrinkled old demon shuffling around a nursing home with a grapefruit in one hand, trying to get his morning bowel movement started. That was all Theo needed to get out of bed and into the shower.

"Can I ask you something?" It was the first time he had tried to get Plaid-man's opinion on anything. It felt wrong asking, really. Normally, Theo dreaded the Plaid-man's daily appearance, but today he'd been itching to talk to someone, anyone, about what had been happening to him. He knew Plaid-man would have plenty of words on the subject, and he hoped some of them would be soothing.

"Yeah, shoot." Plaid-man gnawed on a bit of beef jerky he hadn't paid for yet.

"Is it possible to be, I don't know… haunted by demons?"

Plaid-man paused, a knot of dried beef halfway to his lips. "Why?" He dropped the meat back into the package. "Something happen?"

Theo cringed. This wasn't going to go well, was it? Well, too late, now. Time to pony up the details.

Plaid-man listened, his jaw clenching and unclenching, as Theo explained his eyelid, the shadow in the corner of his vision, the unexplained experience in the stock room, the internet omen. "I mean, only yesterday you were talking about how our realities are based on personal perceptions, right? So it's totally valid that what's happening to me is just a result of stress. Right? Like, I'm just over-worked and underpaid, and all of that bullshit is coming out in some hallucinatory way. Right?"

"That wasn't quite what I meant to—"

"It's possible? Please. Tell me it's possible."

Plaid-man set the package on the counter and shifted uncomfortably. "Hey, I believe in the power of the mind as much as anyone does, but listen, man. Whatever you're experiencing. That sounds like some deep dark voodoo. It was Descartes, right?"

"Huh?"

"Descartes. That believed his reality could be illusory."

"You'd know better than I would."

"Yeah. I would. But the thing about Descartes was he believed in demons. He thought it was totally possible that a demon could be tricking him into believing that his reality was the truth when it wasn't. His whole deal was that there was only one thing he could know for sure. Which was that he existed in whatever form, as a soul or as a series of electrical signals in the old grey matter, as long as he thought. He knew that much was the truth."

"Sure, so you're saying that I probably am being haunted."

"I don't know, man. But I do think that you believe you are."

Theo shook his head. He felt even more confused now than when he'd started this conversation. He wished he'd never brought it up.

"Do you?"

"Believe that I'm being haunted?"

Plaid-man nodded.

Theo shrugged. "I don't want to. But…"

"Don't doubt yourself, man. Don't doubt your reality. That way lies insanity. Or, at the very least, apathy."

"So what do I do?" He hated begging.

Plaid-man glanced at the clock behind Theo. "Shit. I don't know, man. Fight it if you can. Or, you know, enjoy the life you have left. Didn't you always want to do something?"

Theo shook his head. "Not really."

"Then he's already got you."

"Who?" Already knowing the answer.

Plaid-man picked up the package of jerky and popped a knot of beef into his mouth. "The Blind Spot Bully, that's who."

Another night at home with the lights on in every room. Another night at home with the television on full blast. Another night quivering uncontrollably from fear, waiting for the serrated spoon to come and carve out his eyes.

The alarm woke him. He'd slept through the night with a remarkable restfulness, with no dreams. Instead of lying awake shivering, he'd collapsed to sleep at around midnight, and stayed that way until soft cello strains played him awake.

Theo opened his eyes. It had now been a day and a half since his scare in the stock room. He shook his head and smiled. It was an illusion, then. He'd been hallucinating. There had been no Blind Spot Bully; that was some online urban legend designed to scare him. And he'd let it. He'd let him scare himself. He chuckled and leaned over to dismiss the alarm.

The Blind Spot Bully was there. Kneeling by the side of the bed. The serrated spoon in one hand, some of it glinting in the morning sunlight, the rest of it covered in what could be rust or what could be dried blood. Deeply inset eyes stared joyfully back at Theo. A mouth was open, revealing a row of yellowing and sharpened teeth. That smell was back, the odor of sulfur and cherry, filling his nostrils.

Theo screamed and leapt away, scrambling from the bed to the floor. His leg caught in the sheets, tangling into a knot around his left ankle. He looked back at the Bully, but there was nothing. The sound of drawn-out dragging steps made their way around the bed toward him. He could hear the low, rattling breaths.

The sheets wouldn't unravel no matter how hard he kicked at them. The floor creaked under the weight of the Bully he couldn't see. Theo tilted his head to and fro, trying to catch a glimpse of the demon in his blind spot. Saw enough to know he didn't have much time. Kicking at the sheets only made the knot around his ankle tighter. He reached down with his hands and tugged, trying to tear the knot down off the heel of his left foot. An invisible hand gripped the sheet and began to pull, wrenching him toward the foot of the bed where the Bully stood.

Theo rolled around, digging his fingertips into a slit between the hardwood boards. With his right foot he pressed on the knot that had snared him, trying to push it off. He was ripped backward. One of his fingernails tore out between the boards, the pain of it rippling down his forearm. He screamed. Blood smeared onto the floor. He kicked again, felt the knot slide off his heel, and scrambled away.

Tripping over the door sill, Theo was thrown against the far wall. Something cracked in his shoulder as he hit, and he slid back to the floor. He looked into his room, shifting his vision back and forth, trying to get the Bully back into the blind spot, but he couldn't find him. Pain tore across his back and chest from his shoulder. His fingernail hung on a thread of skin. Shimmering red blood pooled at the wound.

Dragging steps again, moving across the floor of his bedroom. That sulfur and cherry smell got stronger. Thicker. Choking in his throat. Something muttered and cackled. A floorboard creaked.

Theo rose to his feet and rushed down the hall and into the kitchen. He fell against the countertop, too much weight on the wrong arm sending shooting pains through his shoulder. Groaning, he pulled the utensil drawer open and grabbed a steak knife from the bin.

His lungs burned and heaved. His knuckles went white as he gripped the steak knife. He stumbled to the corner of the room.

The dragging sound stopped.

The sulfur and cherry smell faded away.

The long, rattling breaths disappeared.

Theo crouched in the corner, glancing back and forth, trying to get a glimpse down the hall with his blind spot. Trying to see where the Bully had gone.

Seconds passed into minutes. Nothing happened. His body shook uncontrollably. Heavy, soggy sobs wracked him. The minutes dragged on uneventfully.

After a time, Theo rose shakily to his feet. Inching forward bit by bit, he held the knife in front of him, ready to swing at any sign of movement. His vision swayed, trying to catch sight of the Bully.

Nothing in the hallway.

He continued down to his bedroom door, shaking his head in all directions as he looked in. There was nothing to see. Just the sheets dangling half-off the mattress and a dribble of blood trailing out the door.

He lowered the knife, took in a deep breath, and exhaled.

Cold fingertips dragged across the back of his neck. The smell of sulfur and cherry returned. Theo spun around, steak knife swinging in an arc.

It stopped midair, held away by an invisible hand.

In his blind spot, something slightly shiny and rust-colored pressed against the cavity where his eye sat. He felt the serrations sink into his eyelid. He screamed. The spoon dug in. Blood oozed out, running down his cheek. Theo dropped the knife. Heard it clatter across the floor.

The spoon dug deeper.

THE ROUGAROU

ANGELIQUE FAWNS

My husband Benoit was moving the two of us up north, where the summers are short and the winter creates frostbite patches on your skin. Being originally from Louisiana, my Creole blood didn't like the cold. This was Canadian logging country, in one of the least inhabited areas of Ontario. Grocery shopping was a day trip, and the closest neighbor was an hour's snowmobile ride away.

Our romance started at a big television network in Toronto. I sold commercial airtime and Benoit was the creative lead in the marketing department. More than just our ad campaigns clicked. I was instantly attracted to this burly man with an amazing imagination. We also connected through our French Louisiana roots. His ancestors were run out of Nova Scotia and settled there before migrating back to Quebec, and my descendants came from African slaves brought to work on French colonial plantations. We both loved reading the history and colorful superstitions of our New Orleans culture. We made an odd couple, my petite frame and tanned skin next to his hulking body and red-headed paleness. He proposed to me by piercing an arrow through a voodoo doll's heart with a ring attached to it.

There was great content on Netflix that featured legends of our people, including some spine-tingling horror movies. Unfortunately, we weren't the only ones who loved Netflix. As more and more TV viewers cut the cord and cancelled their cable subscriptions, conventional television suffered. We were both let go when the company's shares sank to penny stock level. The owners filed for bankruptcy protection, and hundreds of people were walked out the door without severance packages.

My husband had an odd weekend hobby where he liked to drive into the Canadian Shield forests and strap chains to Belgian horses (because Belgians are the strongest breed of heavy horse) and skid logs out of forests. Wealthy landowners found it a novelty to hire him for a weekend. It put a few dollars in his pockets and kept him in incredible shape. Environmental horse logging was a dying art, but his grandfather had cleared land with draft horses for a living up in the Gatineau region of Quebec, so Ben came by it naturally. When his grandfather died, Ben took the two old horses and boarded them at a stable north of Toronto with big grassy fields. He said working with Betty and Bob the Belgians reminded him of his Acadian roots.

We'd put off starting a family to focus on our careers and now neither one of us had a job. Toronto was an expensive city, and full-time work was in short supply, so I couldn't say no when he found a lucrative job as a logger almost four hours northeast. He was hired to clear trees near Bon Echo Park for a rich family who wanted to open a private campground. Using horses to do the logging made sense to keep the trails and land undamaged.

Part of Benoit's pay was free furnished accommodation on a small acreage with a barn for Betty and Bob, his grandfather's Belgians. We were renting a condo in downtown Toronto, so we broke the lease and sold all our furniture on Kijiji. If I thought that process made me miserable, I had no idea what was in store for me. We packed up his pickup truck with the bare essentials, our American Bulldog Daisy, and started the long drive north.

I'd thought cottage country was wilderness. Wrong. Once we got into the County of Frontenac, it was obvious why no one had settled here after the early logging boom. The land was hilly, harsh, and truly remote. For the last hour, there wasn't a restaurant, store, or even a poutine stand, only a few old lonely shacks here and there.

After what seemed forever, Ben pulled into a two-acre property with an old double-wide trailer on blocks. It backed onto a huge forest so it would be easy for him to hitch up the horses and get to work. But I couldn't see anything else good about it. The house had aluminum siding, a crooked porch, and small windows. Smoke billowed out of the chimney and a pile of logs sat outside. Great. Probably no central heating.

"Ben, you've got to be kidding?" I asked as we turned onto the snow-covered property.

"Hey, it's not that bad! It's only for a year, Louisa. Think how much fun you're going to have keeping the fireplace stocked with wood." He gave me a big grin and reached over Daisy's back to give my short black hair a ruffle.

I kept my mouth shut. There was really nothing he could do about it. And I loved him, so I was going to endure this. We unpacked and settled the horses into the small barn. At least the stables were quaint, with an old-school hay loft and a wide aisle down the middle.

Going back into the trailer-house, I turned the tap at the cracked ceramic sink to get a glass of water. It was an odd yellow color and smelled like sulfur. Good thing we had some bottled water. There wasn't a fireplace, but instead a black wood stove that ate logs voraciously. Mysterious stains marked the walls.

I could get used to the rundown furnishings, well water, and wood stove. What I couldn't get used to was the howling. Every night, the eerie serenade of a wolf made my blood run cold.

"Ben, do you hear that?" I asked, shaking him awake the first few nights after he crawled into bed, exhausted from logging.

"It's just the January winds. They pick up coming down the mountainside," he said, giving me a hug and promptly falling back asleep.

Laboring all day in the freezing cold made him sleep like the dead. Benoit got up with the sun and took Betty and Bob out to pull down oak and ash trees. He didn't return till sundown. Then he had to bed down the horses and give them grain and fresh water before coming in himself.

There is nothing quite like the smell of man-sweat mixed with horse, manure, and chainsaw oil. Ben would take off his wet boots and hang the insoles by the fire along with his damp pants and jacket. The whole house would be permeated with the foul odor. One more thing I had to learn to tolerate. I didn't sleep well at night, and it made me edgy. I was sure the howling was intensifying. That was not the wind. I took comfort from Daisy's big warm body draped over my feet. I'm sure my one-hundred-and-forty-pound bulldog could take on a supersized wolf. Or at least distract it while I ran away.

After about a week of huddling in the house and trying to make it homey, it was time to brave the cold. I hadn't ventured into thigh-high snow yet, but by now Ben and his skidding equipment had made a good trail. Shivering with teeth chattering, I got out of bed and bundled up with sweat pants and three sweaters.

There was coffee left in the bottom of the pot, so I poured myself a cup of the now thick sludge and pulled on my boots, snow pants and thick down jacket. The puffy coat along with three sweaters made a scarf redundant. I could hardly turn my neck already, doing my impersonation of the Stay Puft Marshmallow Man.

Daisy and I headed out the back door and started following Ben's footprints to the barn. The real path would start there. The cold made my nostril hairs freeze and my lungs started a long, slow burn. When I got to the barn, I pulled open the sliding door and went in to warm up for a minute. The horses truly lived in nicer digs then we did. Climbing the wood rung ladder, I went up to explore the hay loft. There were spiderwebs coating the window at the end. Rubbing a hole in the dirt, I peered out at endless miles of trees up the mountain. A gorgeous sight with the sun reflecting off the tips of the fir and pine trees. I made a plan to get cross-country skis next time we went to town.

Looking down to the side I saw a big indentation in the hay, like something had been laying there. Bending down for a closer look, I saw some rough black and brown hair. Bear, maybe? But no; picking up a clump, I saw the coarse mass certainly wasn't bear. The thought that it might be the wolf I heard howling made me shiver, even in the warm barn under my layers. I noticed the hay still felt warm. Getting up quickly, I hustled back to the ladder. Just before my head dropped past the loft floor, I saw two masked black eyes staring at me.

An enormous raccoon strolled out from behind a round bale and settled back in her spot. I felt a little ridiculous. What kind of monster was I imagining, anyway?

Daisy was in the aisle waiting for me. We headed out of the barn, but my unfounded fear had coated me in sweat, and I didn't want to catch a worse chill. I abandoned the winter walk idea and decided to tell Ben that we had a raccoon issue when he got home. The creature was probably stealing all our horse grain.

Except he did not come home that evening. Our spicy seafood stew sat untouched in the slow cooker.

Daisy and I waited by the back door, staring down the trail as the sun sank behind the mountain. I tried to will the old Belgians and Ben to appear, but nothing happened. Cold terror crept up the back of my spine.

Rather than sit still and let the very last rays of light disappear, I put on all my warm gear again and grabbed an industrial-sized flashlight. This time Daisy and I rushed all the way down the footpath, past the barn, and onto the horses' skidding trail. As soon as we entered the forest, the little bit of light from the sun was obscured. It was really dark. I couldn't tell if the icy chill I felt came from the cold or from dread. Walking as fast as I could, I tried not to look into the black trees on either side of me. Daisy scampered eagerly through the undergrowth, her nose guiding her. This was her first real walk off the property.

"Benoit! Are you out here? Ben! Call out if you need help!"

For a long time, I heard nothing back. But then a long slow howl filled the air. I stopped in my tracks and my heart thudded to an awful stop. Daisy nudged me and a low growl emanated from her throat. I heard the eerie howl again and my feet moved me forward before I became paralyzed with fear. I rushed forward into the black night, with only the thin light from the flashlight to stop me from tripping over roots.

Up ahead, I could see a clearing made by Ben's logging efforts. Charging into the wide-open space, a glow came from the full moon cresting over the trees. A big chestnut horse burst out of the trees on the far side and came galloping across the clearing. By the white stripe on her face, I could tell it was Betty. She had her hauling collar on but was missing the rest of the harness and chains. She came straight at me but luckily, she slid to a stop before trampling me and I raised a hand to her cheek. Her eyes were so wide that the white showed all around, and sweat coated her body. A froth covered her chest and neck.

"Whoa, girl. Where's Benoit?" Where's your partner Bob?" I stroked her neck.

My eyes quickly assessed her body. I noticed blood on her side. Uh oh. Before I could take a closer look, the howl started up again, and this time it sounded very close. Betty reared up and galloped down the path towards home.

Now I knew something terrible had happened. Was the team attacked by a wolf pack? Where was Benoit? He would never leave his horses. Up ahead I saw a dark form lying in the snow by the edge of the clearing. Daisy charged ahead of me and started whining with joy. *It must be Ben!* Running at full tilt, I crashed into the snow beside him and pushed Daisy back from licking his face.

"It's me! It's Louisa! Are you okay?"

His eyes were open and he stared silently at me.

"What happened? Are you hurt?" I scanned his body for injury, but couldn't see anything immediately wrong with him until he pointed at his leg. His chainsaw pants were ripped and I could see blood underneath them.

"Did you cut your leg with your chainsaw? Can you walk?" I gasped, trying to get the dwindling glow from the flashlight close enough so I could take a better look.

"I… I didn't cut my leg. I was bitten."

"What? Bitten by what?" I said, trying to keep my panic under control.

Just then the low howl echoed through the woods, and Daisy turned and took off into the trees.

"Daisy! No, Daisy come back!"

"Let her go, Louisa, and help me up." Ben grabbed my arm. I tried to get his massive frame off the ground. After a few minutes of slipping and grunting, we were both standing.

"Where's Bob?" I asked as we slowly start walking towards home. He was limping, and leaning heavily on me. "I saw Betty on the way here."

"I'm sorry, honey, but Bob is gone." Deep sadness choked his voice.

"Gone? How?" I clung to his arm and focused on putting one foot in front of the other.

"He was attacked by this *thing*… when I tried to defend him, it bit me. Then it dragged him away, chains, harness and all. Betty shook free and took off." His French accent was strong, as it always was when he became emotional.

"Bitten by what? A wolf?" I looked down at his bloody leg. It seemed to have clotted up. Thank goodness an artery hadn't been hit.

"No. Not a wolf. Did your grandmother in New Orleans tell you tales of a man with a wolf's head? The Rougarou? Mon dieu."

"Yes. If I didn't go to church, she told me the Rougarou would come for me. Every kid in my neighborhood was terrified into good behavior with those stories. So you're trying to tell me you were bit by what? A Cajun werewolf?"

I heard the rapid pounding of paws behind us, but as I turned, ready to fight, I saw it was just Daisy. Thank goodness.

We were almost home and Benoit was picking up the pace. "Louisa, I'm not imagining anything. It had a human body with long claws on its hands and a wolf's head."

I didn't respond immediately. I tried to remember the story my grandmother told me, always trying to frighten me into going to those long boring Catholic services. Some part of the story was niggling at my brain.

We were at the barn now, and Betty was waiting at the door. I leaned Benoit against the side wall to let her into the barn and her stall. Luckily her heated bucket was already filled with water, so I just tossed some hay at her. She calmed down as soon as she started eating. But her eyes flicked in confusion at the empty stall beside her.

Grabbing ahold of Benoit again, we staggered into our house and I set him down on the couch. He pulled off his chainsaw pants and snow gear while I got some warm water, iodine, and bandages. It *did* look like a creature had taken a chunk out of his leg. After cleaning and disinfecting it, I dressed him in his flannel pajamas and gave him a glass of scotch. I rarely drink, but I got one for myself as well.

I remembered my grandmother's story more clearly then. The heat of the whiskey cleared my mind and boiled in my mouth.

"Do you remember the rest of the legend, Benoit? The part about how the Rougarou is under the spell for one hundred and one days? Then, after drawing human blood the curse is transferred to his victim?" I took a big gulp of my scotch and looked at him.

His eyes grew wide, and a new shiver rippled through me.

STRANGE CREATURES

EVELYN DESHANE

Emma blinked once. When the purple skin, slit by gills, remained in her line of sight, she set her binoculars down by her side. There was no way she was looking at what she thought she was seeing. There was simply no way. First of all, the Turtle Lake Monster was a water-creature and this one was on land. Secondly, the skin was purple, and everyone knew that the Turtle Lake Monster was green, or at least, dark blue. Lastly—and most importantly—that creature was not *real*. It was an urban legend, folklore perpetuated by townspeople and internet conspiracy boards. Even if she *was* a so-called cryptid hunter and spent the bulk of her life on those boards or spinning her own theories on YouTube, none of this was really real, right?

Right?

Emma took a deep breath and looked through her binoculars again. The creature was still there. The skin was still purple. Turtle Lake was twenty feet away from the thing at most, making it nearly forty feet from her position behind a bush. She was pretty far out, so maybe this body was just a doll or prop that fell off a boat. Maybe this was left over from a movie shot in the wilderness, someone trying to make hoax footage like Patterson-Gimlin. She briefly convinced herself the body was a stock prop from *Supernatural* or a practical joke left behind—it was April 19th, after all—but by the time she closed ten feet of distance, her heart sank.

The body of the creature was lifeless. The gills did not suck in water or air. A fetid, rotting smell hung around the body. The creature was definitely dead—but that meant it had once been alive.

"This can't be real," she said, barely above a whisper. The dusk air seemed to whisper back a confirmation. *Real, real, real.* She suddenly became aware of her prone position, alone at the edge of the woods. The nearest town was miles away. Most of the cabins had tourists inside who minded their own business. No one would hear her scream. If something did happen, she'd be just another trans woman to add to a missing list and not investigate further.

But the feeling didn't stay. Curiosity and the thrill of discovery replaced the fear, leaving her with the body of a creature she would call the definitive Turtle Lake Monster on her YouTube channel. With its corpse in front of her, she didn't want to default to genus or origin stories from folklore. She wanted to know who the creature had really been.

The investigator side of her personality, the one that grew up watching *The X-Files* and *Outer Limits* and who disdained the melodramatic turn that *Supernatural* had taken, emerged. She hunched down by the body with her flashlight and shone against its skin. Most lore said the Turtle Lake Monster was like a large sea-horse with a curved body, scaly, and with a canine head. But this creature resembled the gill-man from the B-movie about the black lagoon. It was fish-like with humanoid features such as arms and legs, which indicated that it had the ability to walk on land as well as swim in the water.

At least, she figured as much. She used her encyclopedic knowledge of cryptids to decipher the creature's life before its untimely end, while also categorizing and updating her knowledge on the lore itself. The eyes of the creature were harder to place; they seemed reptilian, not human or fish-like, since they were more on the side of its head. Perhaps it was a creature that migrated? Maybe it was evolving? She considered all these possibilities without touching or moving the body; she had no idea what killed it, or whether the cause of death was contagious. She saw no wounds—but then again, it was out of the water. Lack of air could have killed it, but if it had flipped to the surface, surely it would have crawled right back in.

She raised her flashlight to the lake. The sun had set. The wind was colder. She rose and examined the area of grass spanning between its body and the shoreline. It smelled like the damp part of her dad's basement; the cleaning supply closest at the hospital where her dad finally died; and the stale smell of vitamins that her mother insisted she take when she was six or seven to make her a 'strong boy.'

Emma walked towards the lake with her flashlight in one hand and her Swiss army knife in the other. She wasn't exactly sure what she could fight off with a corkscrew or a small blade, but it made her feel better. Always be prepared was the Boy Scouts code, even if Canada didn't exactly have the Boy Scouts, but rather a kind of No Name Brand imitation. Her training came back to her in a whirl, warped with the cryptozoology and *The X-Files* episodes she kept on repeat.

The water lapped against the rocks on the shoreline. A few signs had been erected, declaring the lake a part of Canadian National heritage. A smaller sign followed and apologized in a whitewashed way for taking indigenous land. The park was located on a large swath of land just outside of a reservation in rural Saskatchewan. The area had been repurposed into a tourist trap that held dozens of cabins for people looking to get away. Whenever Emma made the two-hour trek from Saskatoon to hunt for monsters here, she'd only end up finding adults making out like teenagers in the bushes. She'd stopped filming her trips altogether because of it.

"The one time I find a real monster. The one damn time…" she muttered under her breath.

She heard a twig snap behind her. Emma turned around so fast she worried she'd knock off her own glasses.

Her flashlight barely illuminated the darkness front of her. All she saw was a slick line of goop running from the shoreline to where the body of the Lake Monster had been.

It's gone.

A chill slammed down Emma's back, lodging deep in her abdomen. *Oh, God. The one time I find a monster and I don't have a camera… and the monster gets up to leave.*

Emma picked up her binoculars and scanned the area, but it was too dark now. She should have left fifteen minutes ago. She saw nothing, only blackness, until purple glittered under the twilight. Stars had come out, along with Venus, and directed light on what Emma thought was a moving creature. No… a dead creature being dragged. She remembered the way her father's body had been limp yet stiff in death. Those jerky movements were unmistakable, even on a cryptid; the Lake Monster was now being dragged toward a rock-face several hundred feet ahead. The rock wall seemed to shudder. Then all the purple scales, glittering in starlight, disappeared.

Emma put down the binoculars. The wind that had once seemed so comforting warned her. *You are not alone here. All of this is real, real, real and you are in danger.*

She stamped down her fear long enough to take a sample of the gloop on the grass. Then she ran, faster than she ever remembered, for her car.

Alana was home when she called, but Emma spoke so fast that she hung up. Emma called back within seconds and held her tongue between her teeth so she didn't lose her mind.

"That was *you*?" Alana balked. "I thought someone was crank calling me with your phone. Sorry."

"You have no idea what I've discovered." Each syllabus felt like a stone under her tongue, slowing her down. "The Turtle Lake Monster. It's real. I found it tonight. It looks like *The Creature from the Black Lagoon*, but it's the Turtle Lake Monster. I swear."

"Uh-huh. And who donned the gill-suit this time around?"

Emma huffed. "You know I never hire actors for my videos. I just don't shake the tree of doubt."

"And you capitalize on smudges."

Emma huffed again, but didn't argue. Her YouTube channel had gone viral when she claimed to have found Old Yellow Top on a trip to Niagara Falls. She'd taken a photo in the woods on a whim and soon noticed a strange shadow and blonde fuzz in the background. She'd then showcased the photo in a confessional YouTube video, embellishing her vision of the Sasquatch-like cryptid known to haunt Ontario—but only a little bit. Her photo was like a magic eye painting; some days, she saw it and believed her story fully. Other days, it made her feel nauseated by straining her eyes too long with no payoff.

Regardless, people believed her enough to frequent her channel and demand more from her. And Emma coveted the attention. For once, internet fame had come to a trans person from something other than a before and after gender montage set to some sentimental song. Trans women could have other damn interests—like cryptozoology. Her trans identity was incidental to her belief in strange creatures. No one wanted to hear about hormone injections and surgery rejection letters, about transphobia in her workplace and getting sir'd at the bank. They craved Old Yellow Top, a dozen different versions of Igopogo, and her adventures in Saskatoon's national parks, looking for other creatures not yet discovered. Her audience knew she was trans—she hated to say it was kind of obvious judging by her jawline and the cadence of her voice when she got excited—but it didn't matter. For once, people didn't care what was in her pants. They cared about what was in the damn woods.

"I don't need to have smudges anymore," Emma insisted. "Not when I have the real thing."

"Yeah, uh huh. Sure." Alana's bored voice was only half an act. Her role on the show had always been to play the skeptic to Emma's true believer stance. In a way, they were the inverse Scully and Mulder in terms of the roles they played and who they most resembled. Before Alana had transitioned, she'd been a tall and brooding boy who exchanged a dozen letters with penpals about monsters in the wilderness, sort of like a *Red Shoe Diaries* and Fox Mulder hybrid. Though Alana tried to play to Scully's sceptic, she also wanted to believe so deeply. She just never wanted to let go of her skepticism until she saw the proof.

Until she saw the damn body in front of her—like Emma just had. In another burst of excited chatter, Emma tried to tell Alana the whole story from beginning to end. The whole truth. She emphasized that point several times before it finally seemed to sink in.

"Wait," Alana said. "So you're not reading from a script?"

"Again, I don't have scripts or actors. Just talking points and smudges."

"So you actually found something? And you weren't fucking filming? You whore."

"You bitch," Emma replied playfully, then sighed. "But no. No filming."

"Well, you have photos, right? With your phone?"

Emma's silence made Alana huff. All the excitement had now drained; she didn't even bother to trade spars back and forth. "So you still have nothing. This is still a wet dream, like us ever getting our licenses to match who we are?"

Emma laughed, though the joke was awful. It hit her in all her most vulnerable places. She grabbed the spare sheet of paper out from her jeans pocket. The goop was in the center of the page. "I have a sample. From the body. There have got to be chemicals in it. My cell reception always goes wonky in this area. It's part of why I was looking here earlier tonight. I figured it was going to be aliens if I found anything at all, but now we have a creature."

"No, we literally have the creature's wet dream. Ugh. I hate you so much right now."

Emma smiled. Alana was this close to believing. Just one subtle push and—

"All right," Alana said. "Show me where you found the body. I have to see this for myself."

As soon as Emma pulled into the parking lot, she felt like they were being watched. It was half past midnight, and all the stars that had been so bright seemed dimmed. Even Venus was no longer visible.

"I don't think this is a good idea."

"Now you're getting cold feet? You know," Alana said, shaking her head, "I'm starting to think you're a fake. Like the *National Enquirer*."

"Hey now. Those magazines actually do report stuff. Serious political issues and cover-ups. They just bury it next to Batboy's baby mama so it's not taken seriously."

"And now you're the Lone Gunman. All in one." Alana rolled her eyes. "Soon you'll start talking to me about chemtrails. And *then* we're going to have a serious issue."

"First of all, how dare you."

Emma and Alana locked eyes for a long, extended moment before bursting into laugher. Alana started to mimic the infamous InfoWars segment about frogs turning gay, tying it to their own transition. "If only the water really gave us boobs," Alana said forlornly, "then we wouldn't need doctors at all."

"But this conspiracy," Emma said, once again feeling the gravity of the situation. "What if it is real? What if I actually found something that would have been buried in the *National Enquirer*? What if...??"

"You're given a Pulitzer in crazy talk?" Alana laughed again. "If that's the case, we're sharing it because that snot bubble you trapped on paper is nothing. We're getting more, okay? And then we'll talk about it, especially if that means we're given the keys to the InfoWars castle. God, can you imagine?"

Alana continued to chuckle as she got out of the car. Emma opened the backseat and gathered the lab equipment they'd lifted from Alana's veterinarian's office. She could test the sample there come morning, and soon enough the lab would report back with some kind of certainty as to what they'd found. Alana had already theorized that it could just be normal guck from lake life that had been warped through plastics and other chemicals. It didn't even have to be a new kind of animal; scientists were discovering new bacteria all the time. So maybe they *would* get an award for all of this. It only depended on what audience they wanted the most.

"Ready?" Alana gestured to Emma's phone. "You better tape us this time."

Emma nodded. Her binoculars were around her neck, her Swiss army knife and backup hand-crank flashlight in her belt loops. She used the flashlight on her phone to guide her. As Alana walked towards the lake with her own light, Emma flipped open the camera and started the intro shot.

"Hello, Tubies. We're on a secret mission. Alana is convinced that I'm wrong about finding a gill-man corpse tonight, which could be the infamous Turtle Lake Monster. In spite of her skepticism, and how my creature differs from the standard lore, I'm still pretty sure I'm right, and what I found is real. It disappeared the moment I turned away, but who knows what still lingers in the water? Come on."

She turned the phone away from her face and held it out to illuminate the path. Her voice had taken on the cadence of a performance: part circus announcer and part confessional queen. Yet a deep fear lingered within her, something that Emma hadn't quite faced. She didn't tell Alana *how* the body had disappeared. Only that it did.

Emma glanced towards the rock face several feet away. Nothing glittered. Nothing glinted. But the sensation of being watched was still so acute.

"Here?" Alana asked. She dropped her kit and examined the grass. "I think I see the purple goo. You getting this? I'm not doing this twice and I'm definitely not staging anything."

"Hush now. We never stage."

"Uh-huh. Just tell me I'm in the right place."

"You are. That's where I found the body."

Emma filmed as Alana took out tweezers and plucked blades of grass. She dropped them into baggies. When they reached the water, the trail of purple goo had faded, most likely washed away. Rocks littered the ground nearby, interspersed with what looked to be egg shells. When Emma pointed it out, Alana shot her a look.

"I saw them. It's not my first rodeo." She sighed with what Emma thought was fear as she knelt to collect the shells. "This is probably nothing. So many people camp in this area, it's probably just leftover breakfast. But I'll collect it anyway. Anything to prove you wrong."

Emma made a noise of feigned pain. She turned the camera on herself once again. "Well, everyone, what do you think? Are those egg shells from omelets, or something else? Does the Turtle Lake Monster actually sleep out here? Will it come back and rescue its babies? Or will this video be too dark to upload it and force me to scrap all this effort tonight?"

Alana laughed as Emma cut the camera. Emma slipped the phone into her pocket before kneeling beside Alana, who examined the eggshells through the plastic baggie, brows knit in confusion.

"Are you okay? You seemed... spooked. Or dare I say, like a believer."

"This is really strange, Emma." She extended the bag to Emma, who looked at the shells. They were striated with lines, faintly purple on the inside. Not familiar, not omelette eggs. Not even close. When Emma looked up, she swore she saw the same shade of purple glittering by the rock face. There and then gone. The lapping of the water and wind was all she heard.

"It *is* strange," Emma agreed. "But is it real?"

"I think we may actually be onto something. For once, this might not be a hoax."

After two weeks and testing the samples twice, the results came back as inconclusive. Unfamiliar. Strange. Not even Alana's boss understood what he was looking at, and he was an expert in tropical fish. He had no idea what the two of them were doing, but he wanted to publish whatever they found in an academic journal. More people were spiraling into this story, all without warning. Alana had been talking to her former penpals who were now email buddies about monsters once again, causing Emma's channel to explode overnight. A new audience was already pre-emptively setting up to wait for the big reveal. The cryptid and conspiracy community beckoned her. The screeching mantle of InfoWars would pass to her. Full acceptance. A captive audience. Everything she ever wanted. She had wanted to believe, and now she could believe.

But the video remained on her phone, untouched and unedited. She didn't want to upload the scene because it still felt lacking. She was the only living witness to the gill-man, the Lake Turtle Monster; everyone else was the friend of a friend, the second stage. They were the ones keeping the lore alive—even

Alana. She claimed to have a front seat to the evidence, but she didn't see the body. She only saw the goop.

As far as Emma was concerned, this was *her* cryptid. And her cryptid still seemed so distant to her, even though she had been so close to his death.

When Alana called for the sixth time in one night, Emma finally let her phone power down. She didn't want to talk about the types of tours they'd do now, the books they could write, or even the podcasts they could do. Fuck being a cog in the conspiracy. She never wanted to be on a panel of experts or screech about what was in the water. When she was a kid and first heard about Bigfoot, she had wanted to go out and meet him. She'd been a scared camper on a Boy Scout trip, listening to urban legends and fearing that she'd pee her pants. But when those campers finally delivered the punchline in the scary stories, the monsters seemed more like her friends. They were more like herself, in her strange creature form, waiting to emerge into daylight.

Emma got into her car and drove to Turtle Lake.

A well-worn pathway in the grass directed her to the rockface, where another pathway, lined with small evergreens and black pebbles, led her to the top of a steep hill. When she felt along the rock for edges, her finger dipped into a crack that led her fingers to a doorknob. She turned it and heard a sharp grating sound. Not a knob, but a bell. She stood in front of the fuzzy door and waited. Someone would come, she was sure of it. She needed to reveal herself in order to be revealed.

"My name is Emma," she said after a moment. "Emma Bryant."

The door quaked and slid apart. An older woman with a sharp nose and thin lips appeared. Her hair was dyed a monochrome black and pulled back into a ponytail so tight it seemed more like a hood than hair. The lines around her mouth revealed her advanced age, and the ones near her eyes spoke wisdom. She smiled when she saw Emma.

"No friend tonight?"

"No. Just me."

The woman ushered her inside. The steep hill had been hollowed out, making Emma think of the first plans for Mount Rushmore. On a road trip to see her cousins, her father took her to the monument and told her all about the crazy inventor who'd wanted to keep important records inside the Presidents' heads.

He died before it was complete, so the rocks stayed piled up and nothing was ever stored inside. Emma could sense, from the smell of decay and printed paper alone, that the woman had managed to succeed where the man had failed. The scope of her records became evident once Emma's eyes adjusted to the low light.

Each wall was covered in photographs, many of them amber with age. Emma recognized many from her cryptozoological studies. There was the original 1947 image of Caddy, a sea serpent in British Columbia, a visual rendition of the Igopogo lake monster of Ontario, and a frame of the famous Bigfoot footage from the 1960s, mixed in with other cryptids from around the globe. She even saw her own photo of Old Yellow Top, the one from her YouTube channel that adorned a dozen postcards in her online shop. Emma was about to ask the woman how she knew of these images when she spotted a framed photo of the woman, much younger, standing next to Old Yellow Top himself. Emma paused, blinked several times, and then pressed her face so close to the photo that she could see lingering fingerprints on the glass. This was Old Yellow Top. Not a costume, but very real. The woman's records weren't just a wunderkammer of crypto-scientist wet dreams. They were her records, like her own family photos.

"Tea?"

"No, thank you," Emma said. She sat on the chair the woman offered to her. The kitchen was also filled with photographs, along with knick-knacks and trinkets which took up every spare shelf and mantelpiece. A stuffed jackalope hung over the stack of tea mugs. The woman brushed the head of the jackalope, as if for luck, before pouring herself some tea.

"I would appreciate it if you do not expose this place," the woman said.

"Oh. Um."

"I know you have a channel. And I know you take this seriously. But you can't."

Emma buckled under the criticism. She always hated it when people told her what she could and couldn't do, especially with the occult. The only thing that irked her as much as prohibition was when people told her what to do with her gender.

"I..." In spite of her anger, the woman's cool gaze made Emma bite back her tone. "I don't see how that matters to you."

"Not to me. But to the animals and creatures, it matters a lot."

"What do you mean?"

Before the woman could answer, small hissing noises filled the room. Emma thought it was the kettle, but the woman had already poured her tea. The woman rose from her seat and opened a door next to the kitchen. Several small purple creatures nestled together in a makeshift bed. They were small, lizard-like, but with humanoid arms and legs. Their skin looked gooey, almost like raw chicken… except that it was purple.

"Oh my God," Emma said.

"Yes," the woman answered. She opened a drawer and removed a plastic bag that seemed to skitter with life, and shook live beetles into the baby Turtle Monster's nest. The creatures ate quickly. "These are what remains of the Turtle Monster you found two weeks ago."

"It… it can have babies?"

The woman smiled. "How do you think they reproduce? They are not created through thought forms, like the tulpas. They must breed, like you or me."

"Obviously. I mean. I just…"

"What you found on the grass was afterbirth. The mother laid her eggs, but she died in the process. It happens every so often."

"Oh, okay." Emma bit her lip, pretending to understand. In no textbook or strange small-fonted website on Angelfire had she ever found this kind of information. Everything was familiar—yet brand fucking new. "I'm glad her babies survived."

"I am too. But you must respect them." The woman placed the paper bag back on the shelf and shut the door to the babies' room. Light flashed before the door was shut, and Emma assumed a hot lamp on a sensor turned on once the door was closed. The hissing died down. "So I do not ask that you hold back your video for me, but for them. For the generations of cryptids like them."

"Like Old Yellow Top? You have to make sure he gets busy and breeds, too?"

When the woman nodded, Emma held back a laugh. No way this was real. What was this woman, the cryptid whisperer? Was she proficient in cryptid husbandry? It made no sense. It was like some strange erotica found on Amazon and written by a crank author. She was about to say as much when the woman held up her hand.

"You will find this foolish. But there is something dire happening here. When the land is destroyed, so is home of all wildlife. You take care of the caribou, the cougar, and the sea otter, while I've taken care of the cryptids. I'm not alone, but I'm the best."

"I have no way of checking that citation."

The woman smiled. She grabbed a worn leather book from a shelf and extended it. The name Phoebe Cavanagh was written on the bottom. "That's me. I've been doing this a long time. I started out as a doctor. Then I noticed that my patients in one particular area kept getting ill. So I investigated. I learned they weren't becoming ill, but being pushed out by a native species. The Thetis monster wanted its water back. It needed the reserve. So I gave it him."

Emma opened the book. A photo of a creature that looked similar to the purple one she'd found was on the front page, followed by newspaper clipping from the 1920s that described the first sighting of the Thetis Lake Monster, and the sickness that came after and killed seven people. The second newspaper clipping was from the 1950s, during a second wave of sickness. Phoebe was quoted in a newspaper article from the 1950s, and pictured in an image. She somehow projected an air of stoic wisdom even back then, in her youth. Her hair was dark and her eyes were bright. In the book, Phoebe detailed how to treat the Thetis's water so it could still live and thrive, and the town would no longer need to steal, but be able to share the resources.

"My patients got better soon after we implemented a better system," she said. "And the land got better too, because the cryptids were happy."

"And now you're taking care of the woods?"

She nodded. "All of Canada has monster problems. I've been all over—but here, in Saskatoon, there seems to be an influx of creatures dying. I'm still trying to figure it out. Luanne wasn't the first patient I've lost, but at least she laid eggs this time around. At least there is another generation."

Luanne. Emma repeated the name inside her head. It was strange to think of that name fitting that creature, but it somehow did. Emma wanted to be like the monsters. She wanted to understand them. This was the best way to understand them, learning their names and habits. Yet despite an overwhelming feeling to bond and learn, she looked at the scrapbook in front of her with skepticism like a shield.

"Let's say all of this is true," Emma started. "And that my silence helps these creatures maintain their privacy so they can go on reproducing. What's stopping me, really, from taking this scrapbook back to town as proof? Sure, most people will call me crazy and walk away. But a handful will come. And a handful will destroy this place, and possibly make me rich in the process. There is nothing stopping me from uploading that video."

"Except a conscience."

"Fancy word. Doesn't mean anything."

"But Luanne does. Names do. And you know them now."

Emma shook her head. Phoebe may have been right, but that wouldn't stop Alana. Emma may be more sentimental, but Alana was now on a mission.

"I can help you, you know. With your predicament."

"My predicament?" Emma laughed. She gestured to her body in a derisive manner. "Oh, sweetheart, I'm born this way. Haven't you heard?"

"I've heard a lot of things. And I've learned a lot of things. Flip to the back of the book."

With a curious head tilt, Emma examined photos from a mid-century circus with Lobster Boy and a The Fattest Man. Then of a woman and man hybrid called Donna/Donald. As the photographs continued, Donna disappeared and Donald emerged. There were more sequences just like that, spanning from the early 1950s to modern times. Each image of a smiling face was familiar to Emma in spite of never knowing these trans people personally. She'd seen these before-and-after cascades on YouTube so many times; all that was missing in Phoebe's version was a Coldplay song.

Emma closed the book. "I don't think you have what I want."

"Are you sure?"

Emma wanted to get up. Leave the weird, hollow stone house and post her video for all the glory. But she stayed rooted in her chair.

Phoebe noticed and went on.

"I ask and offer these services to you because I know we can only live in two worlds for so long. We either embrace the supernatural and let it consume us, until Lake Monster eggs are quotidian and we know the skin is purple and never was another color, or we turn our backs on this world and never look at strangeness again. We forget what's hidden and we become normal."

"Being normal is overrated," Emma said.

"Being normal is what's been denied to you. So you embrace the odd. That's fine. I embraced the odd. I wanted to help—but I'm helping creatures stay normal, too. To have babies. To repair broken bones or amputate limbs caught in bear traps. This is my normal. This is not a freakshow to me. You have to decide if you want to be normal with humans, or if you want to be normal among cryptids. You can't have both anymore, Emma. That's reached an end now."

Emma wanted to argue. She wanted to yell back like a child and complain that no one could ever tell her what to do. About gender. About the occult. The two most important things to her felt taken from her by an old witch—but finally, they also felt explained. Emma had wanted to be a monster because she felt like a monster as a child. When she realized she didn't have to be a scary boy eating vitamins to grow strong and follow in his dad's footsteps, she said fuck it. She left that world behind—only to be stuck in this one. Being trans without ID. Without a license. She did the YouTube stuff because the ad revenue from blurry photos paid her bills. She waited and waited and waited for surgery that would make her normal, while knowing it would probably never come. So she'd decided to stay with monsters.

But these monsters were normal. It was different, but there was a normal here. They had photos on their walls. They posed with their friends and families. Their doctor. Phoebe was a doctor, just like the ones that acted as gatekeepers to Emma. Except that Phoebe provided her with a door to a normal life. Not one living as a freak in either realm.

But she had to choose.

"Are you sure you can do this?"

Phoebe nodded. "It's kind of my specialty."

Emma didn't want to ask how or why. It didn't seem to matter. She closed the book and handed it over. "Okay. I won't post."

"Thank you." Phoebe rose from the table. She set out another pot of water to boil and took down another jar filled with herbs. When she offered tea this time, Emma said yes.

The darkness came faster than she thought possible.

"Hey, Tubies," Emma said into her phone. It was daylight. Her body ached, but she was alive. Her smile was wider, her mind clearer. And her license was brand new in her purse. She could do anything now. She climbed up the rock face across from Turtle Lake and made sure the door to Phoebe's world was hidden in her video. "I wanted to let you all know that this will be my last update. Ever. Alana will be taking over, though, and she has some amazing things to tell you guys."

Earlier in the week, Emma deleted the previous footage. When Alana had asked why, she claimed it was too dark. Alana had been frustrated, especially since the vet's office had been broken into the night before. The sludge that was really afterbirth was now gone. No records of the strange lab experiments remained. Even Davis, Alana's boss, somehow had an explanation for what they'd seen that day, categorizing it as an obscure fish disease. He no longer wanted to publish.

But Alana couldn't let it go.

That was okay, though. Phoebe had assured Emma as much. Alana had never seen the Lake Monster up close. She only saw the traces, the edges of the monster. She only had the lore. There was no face to face contact, no crossing into another world. Alana was always going to be skating close to that edge, but she would never get inside unless she was lucky. It was always a million and one chance to be that lucky.

Emma had used up all that luck. As a parting gift, she handed over her YouTube Channel, now bursting with subscribers, to the person who would carry on the lore—but the lore only.

"So, I'm moving to Ontario," Emma said, still looking into the camera. "Not just because of Old Yellow Topper, but because there's a lot cool things in Toronto. Boring things for you, but cool for me. I really did have a blast doing this show, guys. Probably more than you can even imagine."

Emma's smile hurt. Her heart swelled. When she signed off, she gave her standard peace symbol with her fingers, but for the last time. She closed the camera on her phone. She would upload it when she had a signal again. She wouldn't even need to edit it.

Then she would move. Her life would start over, utterly normal.

She rose and stood next to the door. It would not open for her again. But when she pressed her ear against it, she heard sounds of life on the other side. Hissing and fussing. Baby cryptids, and a mother that would keep them safe.

A minute later, Emma walked towards her car and headed for home.

THE CAVERN

A. L. KING

Because a regular stare would not do, Victor glared at the hole in the ground. Should he have heeded his mother's advice and flown his drone nearer to home? She would surely say that she told him so. Was it that cavernous pit's fault that he flew the device until its charge died and it fell like debris from a failed space launch? Most certainly not. But he needed something to blame for his newest toy being stuck in the rocks of that deep, deep cavern, and he was looking at it, *glaring* at it.

He dropped to his knees for a better view, wondering how far down that hole went. Best to find out *the easy way*, rather than taking an uncalculated risk and discovering *the hard way*. He snorted, puckered his lips, and let a long string of snotty saliva drip into the pit.

He waited. He listened. He heard nothing.

Victor was preparing to stand and find something with more substance than a loogie to throw in and test the depths, but before he could stand, there was a deep roar, as if that almost perfectly vertical den in the middle of the West Virginia woodlands were somehow inhabited by lions. A sudden *whoosh* of air billowed upward, blowing the Berkeley Springs Bulldogs cap off his head. He watched helplessly as his favorite memento from little league baseball did a series of backflips before flitting downward into the cavern. It passed his still-visible drone and disappeared.

"Son of a whore!" he yelled.

"*Son of a whore! Son-of-a-whore! Sonofawhore!*" the hole echoed.

The earthy burst of air had been warm, but Victor shivered. The smell it brought upward lingered, reminding him of the time his dog Daisy got loose and devoured a sizeable husk of roadkill. The scent now was like her breath then, a hot fragrance of death.

That sound, though. At first he thought of it as a roar. Now he realized it was *coughing*.

As if to confirm this wild notion, another grumble and gust bowled upward —a series of them, each one lighter than the last, like the hole was a giant throat clearing itself.

The going-on-summer sun slid out from the shadow of a few clouds, spreading a fresh gleam over the colossal pit. Those rocks, including the ones between which his drone had wedged itself, showed familiar grooves. He was looking at *teeth*. The stalagmite and stalactite dentins traveled as far into the abyss as he could see. It was like staring into the mouth of a shark. A giant land shark!

Victor had gone from glaring at the hole to staring in utter horror. He fought the paralysis of shock, but could barely manage to avert his gaze to the scene around him.

That's when his wide eyes spotted several landmarks he recognized—the big oak tree he liked to climb, and the fire pit where teenagers older than he left crushed and partially drained beer cans. He had been hiking to that clearing in the woods since he was eight years old, and never before had there been a giant mouth in the ground.

Except maybe the hole had been there since he first found that clearing, since before he was even born. He could keep his own mouth closed, so it stood to reason that the crevice above which he currently kneeled had until then concealed whatever passed for its lips. How many times had he treaded those pursed slips of earth and thought them a mere crack in the ground?

The young man screamed, the echoes reflecting his boyhood. And then there was something more than reverberation from the depths. A dry sound, like laughter.

He looked back at the dark center to see an elongated form writhing there. Had he still been under the impression that he had happened upon a normal cavern, he might have considered the moving thing a large snake. In the midst of

West Virginia woods, an anaconda would have made more sense. However, he knew better. There was an enormous mouth in the ground, and it was wagging its tongue as it laughed.

The hole was *mocking* him.

"Shut up! Shut up! Shut up!" Victor yelled.

He waited for an echo, but this time there was none. Something else began rising from those depths instead. A voice. Words.

"I've been shut up. *I've been* shut up *for longer than you can fathom. I awaken to no feast and no praise, and you spit in me! Where have my worshippers gone? Who are you?"*

Victor recalled upperclassmen saying they occasionally met in the woods to ingest magic mushrooms and "trip balls." He wanted desperately to convince himself that he had somehow stumbled upon some of their leftovers and tried them out—as he occasionally did when they abandoned half-empty liquor bottles around the nearby fire pit—but he knew better. He was not tripping balls. He flew his drone for too long, so it fell, and he found it lodged between the teeth of a giant hole in the ground—a huge mouth demanding answers of him.

He still could not bring himself to move, so he contemplated its questions. Were those worshippers native to that area? Had they provided a *feast* whenever the thing beneath the earth awoke? How did it know English?

"I-I don't know where your worshippers w-w-went. I'm Vi-Victor."

A pause. Then: *"How many Victors are there?"*

"My *name* is Victor, but there are plenty of p-people."

"Ohhhhhh!" Its voice was as deep as its seemingly infinite throat, like a million throat-singers harmonizing at once. *"How many* people *can you spare?"*

The sun further escaped the clouds, providing greater illumination into the pit. The moist and glistening tongue stretched upward. Victor suddenly realized what it meant when it spoke of a feast. He understood just how close he was to becoming an appetizer should that tongue decide to lick the dry lips upon which he crouched.

He thought about trying to get up again and perhaps run, but it would be pointless. Just as he could widen his own mouth, he figured the thing speaking could do the same. Or maybe it could stick out its tongue extremely far, like a monstrous Gene Simmons.

Victor looked away from the hole and toward the fire pit where teenagers liked to party. Then he gave an approximate answer to that last question.

.   .   .

Victor listened to jabbering, vulgar sounds and the droning of music, waiting for the right moment. Then his fully charged drone lifted skyward, drawing their attention. They pointed and marvelled. Some—mostly the young men—laughed. Others—mostly the young women—cried out fearfully. But when Victor made his taunting, underclassman presence known, they all gave chase.

They thought it was *their* land. They thought *him* a trespasser. But as the mouth opened and stretched and they fell into oblivion, their thoughts ceased to matter.

Standing on the other side and listening to deep echoes of digestion, Victor came upon a truth the previous tenants of that land had understood: the land belongs to people only when it is sleeping. When it awakens, the opposite is true.

He landed his drone, picked it up, and carried it home.

BRIDEY'S BRIDGE

LINDSAY KING-MILLER

The cold air felt good on my flushed cheeks as I strode, barely stumbling, out of Mikey's Place. I had been drowning my sorrows since sundown, but they just kept floating back to the surface. It was time to walk my drunk ass home.

There's a gay bar on the other side of town, but Lauren was probably there with her coven of harpies, all buying her drinks and congratulating her on kicking me to the curb. Mikey's was more my speed, the kind of place where there's no cocktail menu and lots of motorcycles outside. The kind of place where guys who know your girlfriend just moved out clap you on the back with heavy palms and keep your glass full until closing time and don't ask you about your feelings. And, not for nothing, the kind of place where there's never a line for the ladies' room.

Of course, that meant there'd be no question who had punched the mirror and broken it, even though I'd been thorough about washing the blood off my knuckles. Mikey was going to want me to pay for that. And it would be hard to afford now that Lauren wouldn't be helping with the rent.

Could you please control your temper, Andrea? I could hear Lauren asking in my head, the way she did any time I broke something. Her passive-aggressive calm voice, like she was trying so hard not to sink to my level. Sometimes her eyes would fill with accusatory tears.

My apartment was only a short walk from Mikey's, just on the other side of the river. There was a wide, well-lit pedestrian lane along the highway overpass, but to cross there I'd have to go several blocks out of my way. The more direct route lay across a narrow footbridge the locals all called Bridey's Bridge, because a couple hundred years ago some logger's wife jumped off it to her death. Bridey's Bridge had no lights, and in the dark it was kind of creepy.

Lauren, of course, loved it. Even with all the weird shit that happened there, and the stories about ghosts. She thought it was mysterious and romantic.

But I was not going to take a twenty-minute detour in the middle of the freezing cold night just to avoid being reminded of Lauren. I stepped out onto the bridge. Who cared how much it creaked? It hadn't fallen down yet, and it wasn't going to tonight.

I had only taken a few steps when I heard the woman crying.

There are all these stories about Bridey's Bridge, like I said. Supposedly the ghost of the logger's wife still walks back and forth across it, tempting people to join her in death. I don't really buy ghosts. I think there's a much simpler explanation for everything that's happened here, which is that the bridge crosses the river right where the ravine is at its deepest. From the center of Bridey's Bridge, the surface of the water is at least fifty feet below you.

So if you're in the mood to jump off something high, this is the best spot in town.

And someone was sitting on the railing, right in the middle of the bridge, weeping.

Shit. I'm not proud of this, but it was my first thought. *Shit, what terrible timing.* If I'd only been a few minutes earlier or later leaving Mikey's, I might have missed this sobbing woman entirely, and she'd be someone else's problem. I was hardly in the frame of mind to talk someone off the ledge. It probably wouldn't take much to get me right up there next to her.

I slowed, contemplating turning around and taking the long way home, but the woman had noticed my presence. I heard her sniffle, trying to swallow the sound of her crying. There was a long moment in which I could feel us both wondering if we could pretend we hadn't seen each other and continue on our way.

A car drove past behind me, the rumble of its engine making us both tense. For just a moment, its headlights shimmered off her hair, the kind of glossy black that makes you think of deep water. I couldn't see her face, but that hair was beautiful.

I stepped forward.

Even in the dark, I could tell by her shoulders that she knew I was coming closer. Still, she didn't say anything.

"Hey," I said, my voice uncomfortably loud. I couldn't hear any cars anymore. It was just me and the crying woman. I had the eerie feeling that bridge was growing, that if I looked over my shoulder I'd no longer be able to see the ground behind me.

She didn't say anything, and I spoke again. "Hey, are you okay?" As if anyone ever sat on the railing of a bridge in the middle of the night crying because they were okay.

"Of course," she said, not even attempting to hide the sob in her voice. "I'm just enjoying the fresh air." She hiccupped.

Her voice was like a river over rocks, cool and throaty, with an undercurrent of danger. I wanted her to keep talking. "Why don't you come down from there?" I said cautiously. "You can enjoy the air someplace a little less, um. You know." My drunken brain fumbled for a word. "A little less up." I laughed at my own awkwardness, but she didn't return the chuckle.

"I like it here," she said instead. I could still hear her sniffling.

"People have fallen from that railing," I said, taking another step toward her. "Maybe I should help you—"

"Back off," said the woman, and this time there was no tearful quaver in her voice. "I don't need help. I just need to be left alone."

Even through the thin, grimy layer of clouds, the moonlight on her hair shimmered. If I could see the river below my feet, I knew it would be the same rippling black.

I wanted to touch it. Her hair, not the water.

"What's going on?" I asked. "You can talk to me. I want to help. Whatever it is, we can fix it. You don't need to do anything, um. Extreme."

She shifted her weight, still not looking at me, but making me think she was considering it. "Have you ever done anything extreme?"

It was funny. The haze of tequila had obscured the pain in my hand, but when she said that, my knuckles throbbed. I held my hand up in front of my face, remembering the crunch of the wineglass under my fist.

Not a glass. A mirror. I had broken a mirror tonight.

But I couldn't picture the mirror shattering, my own reflection smashed to pieces. All I could see was the wineglass, and Lauren's face. Red wine pooling on the floor, almost black. Her dark, wet eyes.

I took another step, and the bridge wobbled beneath me.

No, the bridge was solid. Steel and lumber, built to last. I was just swaying the in the wind of my own inebriation. "I think I got extremely drunk," I said to the woman, to the curve of her shoulder and the waterfall of hair that hid her face. I wanted so badly to see her face.

"You should go home and sleep it off," she replied.

"I'm not going to leave you here by yourself," I said. Something tickled the fingers on my right hand. For a moment, I thought it was some kind of insect. Then I realized it was a fat drop of blood winding its way down from knuckle to fingertip. I was bleeding again.

It didn't matter. I was going to bring this girl back to solid ground if I had to carry her in my arms. I could almost feel it now, all that black hair spilling down over me, her face rising out of the darkness like a smooth rock from the center of a stream. Smiling. Grateful. Alive.

It was so quiet on the bridge that I could hear a drop of blood fall from the end of my finger and burst against the weathered wood.

"I want to be alone," said the woman. I heard the tears in her voice, but something else too, a rumble of determination. "Please go away."

"Hey, I get it," I said. "It's hard to ask for help. You're strong. I see that you're strong. It doesn't make you weak if you need a little bit of help." I thought again of her in my arms, the weight of her body relaxing into mine. Even strong women needed to be carried sometimes. I had tried and tried to explain that to Lauren, but she never so much as leaned on me. The tension never left her shoulders.

This woman's shoulders curled in like wings, like they were trying to protect her. I wanted her to unfold them. Let me in.

"You think you can give me what I need?" Her head turned toward me, just a little. Not enough for me to see her face.

"I want to try," I said.

She turned away again, looking out over the river. I saw her arms tense, hands pressed down on the railing as though about to shove herself off it.

For a moment, I lost my breath completely. No. She couldn't. I couldn't lose her. Reaching for her, I had a desperate flash of a vision—her body floating through the air, as though she had all the time in the world to reach the water's surface—and then my fingers closed around her wrist.

"I can," I said frantically. "I can, I can, I promise."

She didn't answer. She was crying again, her shoulders shuddering. I thought again of wings trying to take flight, but she didn't pull her hand away from mine.

"I can do it," I said. "I can give you what you need." Still grasping her wrist, I reached out with my other hand and brushed her black hair away from her cheek.

Touching her hair was like plunging my hand into cold, rushing water. I was too startled to scream. A river gushed between my fingers, the current dragging me in. There were *things* in that water. Twisting, clutching things.

Now I saw her face.

I couldn't move. In the river that was her hair, something twined its slippery body around my arm and pulled. Her face looked slick and spongy like an algae-furred rock. Her eyes were much too big. Her mouth was unthinkable.

"Help me," she sobbed.

She was growing taller, pulling me up at the same time that she was dragging me slowly underwater, *into* her. My hand on her wrist was sinking, as though into deep, sucking mud. I tried to kick her away, but my shoes scrabbled uselessly against the bridge's railing, now somehow below me.

"Lauren," I screamed. But she was nowhere. I was alone up here, so high and yet so very deep.

The black-haired woman drew me in for a kiss, and the river rushed into my mouth and carried me away.

THE TRUTH ABOUT JADE

PETER NINNES

I sit with my back to the windows, facing the direction from which they might come. Sometimes even the innocent need to run from the law. The gate lounge information sign shows three hours until boarding. There's still time to record my version of events before I leave this dismal country, email the story to my contact in Australia, then delete it from my laptop in case they nab me before the plane pushes back from the gate. In case I accuse myself of imagining the unimaginable.

It's my first visit to the country, and I have good reasons never to return. Evil lurks in every corner. Everyday activities have appalling consequences for the unwary. Jade's body may or may not be found, may or may not still exist. She read me a newspaper story two days ago, sitting on my lap. It said the country's police may hold suspects without charge for up to sixty days. They are notorious, claimed the article, for using that time to extract confessions, regardless of the quality of their evidence. People like me can't risk falling into their hands.

Jade Garnett took my class in discrete mathematics as an elective in the final semester of her Asian studies degree. "I need a break from gods, gargoyles, and goblin gangs," she said. Smart and diligent, she dropped into my office to thank me for her final grade. She deserved the high distinction, and I thanked her in return for the thought and effort she'd put into her work.

She twirled a strand of black hair around one finger, resting all her weight on one of her long, bronze legs. "Margaret"—the local students loved using my first name, while the international students preferred Professor Coombs—"would you care to go for a drink? I mean, it's okay if you're too busy, but I just thought…"

My body and brain were worn down by twenty years of the academic grind at Bondi University. That first afternoon at the campus bar was a small step for her, but it was a giant leap for this lonely fifty-something, craving rejuvenation.

By the end of the summer, Jade had fully inducted me into the topsy-turvy logic of her desire, and we'd had more thrills and spills than the Tamworth rodeo.

I started to think it was more than a fling, but the affair stalled as February's heat leaked over into March. Jade dropped a bomb in my lap, announcing that she would take up a teaching job in the northern hemisphere.

"You can come and visit," she declared, as we kissed at the airport a week later. I lay on the beach that afternoon, obsessing about Jade, hoping she was content with her decision. She was swimming free, forty thousand feet above the water, while I buried my face in my towel, as forlorn as a stranded cetacean.

Three months later, I lifted the window shade on the rising northern sun. A slight bump and the growl of reverse thrust welcomed me to the country Jade called home. A further four hours in the express train found me reeking of long-distance travel as I spotted Jade on the platform. I fell into her arms only to be pushed away, exhausted and confused. "We can't hug in public. Wait until we get to my apartment."

On the seventh and final full day of my stay—Jade only had a week off between school terms—we decided to go hiking in the mountains above the town. We both needed to get out of the one-room apartment, where the harsh words of our quarrel the previous evening lay scattered on the floor like razor blades.

It started with a ring of the doorbell. Jade was in the shower, so I opened the door to find a young man in a UCLA t-shirt.

"Ah, you must be Mrs. Garnett. Nice to meet…"

Jade burst out of the bathroom, wrapped in a towel.

"Jason, I said I was busy until Sunday night."

After mistaking me for—or being told I was—Jade's mother, the young American added insult to impertinence by giving Jade the most hangdog, lovesick look that ever oozed from between the covers of a cheap romance novel.

Jade pushed past me, shut the door in the fellow's face, and turned the lock. Without meeting my eyes, she disappeared back into the bathroom.

That evening, we made such a racket shouting at each other that the upstairs neighbor knocked on the door to check on our welfare. In the end, I pretended to believe Jade's protestations. "He's just one of the English teachers. A bit of a pest, actually."

"The view of the valley is amazing on clear days like this." Jade strode ahead, her ponytail beckoning my wounded heart to follow. We'd woken at nine, and the late morning heat sent sweat running down my spine like a river. We followed a creek, crossed a small bridge, and began a steep, zigzagging climb up a ridge. Enormous pines shaded us from the harsh summer sun. My heaving chest reminded me that Jade's lungs had been functioning for three decades less than mine.

"I joined a hiking club, and we came up here a couple of weekends ago." Jade paused where the path widened and levelled out. "The first rule of the club is, 'Never walk more than an hour without a snack.'"

She handed me a rice ball from her day pack, and stripped down to her singlet. At the sight of her gym-toned upper arms, I decided to keep my overshirt on.

"What are those stones?" I asked, pointing to the engraved slabs lining the path.

"Prayers for dead children."

I shivered. "To bring them back to life?"

"No. My friends told me that they ensure the children don't spend too much time in hell before being reincarnated."

"Children go to hell? What an appalling concept."

"Only for a little while, and some of the hells aren't so bad."

"And what's that dog at the end of the row of stones? It seems to have more than one tail."

"It's a wolf. In this country, they're messengers of the gods. They can shapeshift into humans, so some people take them as wives or lovers."

I guess I'm a bit of a scaredy-cat, but the thought of wolves changing into humans sent goose bumps across my arms. The temperature dropped as a heavy cloud blocked the sun, and gloom darkened the forest beyond the path.

"People here still believe in supernatural wolves and multiple hells? I thought this was a developed country, not some superstitious backwater."

Jade laughed. "It's all nonsense, of course. The stuff of fairy stories and tall tales."

Despite her reassurances, the forest seemed grimmer, the track narrower, and the gathering clouds more threatening.

My spirits lifted when we reached the grassy plateau of the summit, which dropped into the valley. Directly across from us, a great triangular peak stood sentinel over the town spread out below. A brown snake of river bisected the agglomeration of beige and grey houses, factories, supermarkets and bulk-goods stores.

"Hello!" Jade shouted. Her voice bounced back to us and away down the valley.

"Many people here believe that your voice sounds different when it comes back because the echo is really a mountain spirit answering your call," Jade said.

"Stop it! You're giving me the creeps."

We sat in the shade on the steps of a small shrine at the back of the clearing. The shrine lacked a front wall, and a long, tasselled rope hung down from a bell at the top of the steps. An altar at the rear of the plain wooden floor housed a corroded bronze statue of some god or other staring blank-eyed into infinity.

Jade looped her arm in mine and lay her cheek on the top of my head.

"I'm so glad you came and could see all this. Are you feeling okay?"

"I guess so," I said. "Everything about this country is different. The color of the buildings. The smell of the forest. Even the air feels strange, bulkier, more—what can I say?—populated."

"It's the humidity. It saps your energy. Speaking of energy, do you have any left? I think we need to make up." The electricity flowed again in my veins as she pushed me gently onto the bare boards.

Later, I realized that we shouldn't have let matters develop from that point. According to Jade, even the two of us embracing in public was outrageous. If I was superstitious, I'd believe that Jade's actions as her emotion reached its peak might have contributed to the disaster. She inadvertently grabbed the shrine bell rope and tugged on it repeatedly, sending news of our mutual achievement echoing across the mountains. Later, as I fled back to town, I realized we were no more than a pair of stupid foreigners whose sense of decency and respect had drowned in a tsunami of lust.

The clouds closed in. We danced in the rain thrown down in great torrents that cooled our overheated bodies and soaked the clothes we'd abandoned on the grass. Eventually, we retreated to the shelter of the shrine, wrung out our clothes and dressed again. We shook with cold like a pair of mice who'd nibbled through an electric cable. Jade made tea using a gas burner from her day pack, and we belatedly ate our sandwiches.

The rain stopped, but thick clouds still obscured the peak opposite. Wisps of fluffy white scudded across the clearing. "Let's take a quick nap, then head back down before it gets dark," Jade suggested. We curled up together and soon fell asleep, despite the hardness of the floor.

"Don't freak out, but I think we have a visitor." Jade's whisper woke me, and for a moment I felt disoriented. When I opened my eyes, Jade was propped on one elbow, looking out at the clearing. From my position on the floor, I could see the front eave of the shrine, and beyond that only a greyish-white mist, as if we'd entered a zone in which neither day nor night existed. The trees on the edge of the clearing had disappeared in the fog, so I raised my head a little to see this visitor.

"Oh my God!" I threw myself behind Jade's back, forcing myself to stare at the figure. Five feet from the shrine stood an old man. His bald head bulged above ruddy, wrinkled jowls, and his beaked nose pointed at the ground. His eyes were fixed on us. One was large like a horse's. The other could have been stolen from a snake. He wore a long cloak the colour of the cloud enveloping the shrine, which made it seem like he was both there and not there at the same time. His garment was impossibly clean for being on a mountain recently soaked by a downpour. His skinny arms emerged from deep, dark sleeves, and twisted fingers grasped a long, knobbly walking stick. From below the ragged hem of his cloak protruded a single pale, hairless leg, and his five bare toes splayed out like an eagle's claws.

Every hair on my body was upright and trying to tear itself away from my skin.

"Who the hell is he?" I whispered in Jade's ear.

Jade had a facility for language, and she spoke to him in the local tongue, seemingly unfazed by his appearance.

He did not answer at first, but continued to stare at us with such intensity I inched back further towards the altar. Then he strode to the bottom of the shrine steps. The back of my neck tingled. The way he walked smoothly on one leg was uncanny, as if his other leg was merely invisible. He began to speak, voice so soft that Jade moved forward to catch his words.

"Not so close!" I hissed.

"I can't quite catch it. He's speaking some kind of dialect, but I think he wants to know who called the spirits."

"What?" I had no idea what the fool was talking about.

Jade leaned closer, and said something to the man. He spoke again. Suddenly he shouted so loud that I leapt up. He dropped his stick and lunged at Jade, grabbing her by the neck. He tried to throw her onto her back on the wet grass, but she broke free and ran towards the edge of the clearing, invisible in the fog.

"The cliff!" I shouted, and she stopped, cloud whirling about her.

The one-legged man ran towards her. Jade's skin was whiter than the man's robe, and her eyes bulged with fear.

"Go left," I called, directing her to the track down the mountain, but she went right, the ghoul close behind, his stick raised above his head.

"Get away from me!" Jade yelled.

I grabbed the day pack and threw myself off the edge of the shrine platform. I dashed after the madman and swung the bag at his raised arms. It went straight through both limbs. He brought the stick down toward Jade's head. She saw it coming and ducked, fell on the ground, and rolled away as the stick flew at her again. I aimed a kick at his backside, and my foot went right through him. I tried to grab his shoulders, but I found nothing to grasp. I ran after him as he dashed off in pursuit of Jade, who circled back to the shrine. She dashed up the steps and grabbed the bell rope, pulling it repeatedly, as if to reverse her earlier tolling. The old man stopped and let out a yell that drowned out the ringing.

I fumbled with the day pack, trying to get at our fruit knife for reasons that escape me now. I swore as the zip stuck. The man turned and stared at me, his stick poised again above his head. Jade took the opportunity to flee towards the track down the mountain. She took two or three steps, and she stopped. She let out a scream that could have been heard on the other side of the distant mountains. The cloud started to swirl and writhe like a witches' brew bubbling in a cauldron. A great roar filled the clearing. From behind the shrine building bounded a cat. It had the patterning of a regular tabby. It had two ears and two cat eyes. The body sprouted four legs with four paws. But I screamed, because the beast was at least ten feet high at the shoulder.

The fantastic feline bared its dreadful fangs and lunged at Jade. She evaded it with another drop and roll, but it romped after her. The old man chased the feline, his stick at the ready. Blind with fear, Jade ran into the fog rolling across the clearing, and vanished. Jade, my lover, my friend, who'd ignited my worn-out body with her youthful zest and lifted my spirits with her endless joy. Jade, with whom I'd fought so wilfully the previous evening, and with whom I'd experienced unparalleled ecstasy that afternoon. That same Jade was swallowed by the cloud.

I held my breath, willing Jade to reappear. All that emerged, however, was an ear-splitting scream. Even as I write this, the sound of Jade's cry as she plummeted over the cliff freezes the marrow in my bones. I lean my spinning head on one hand, recalling the sickening *crack* that followed.

The old man started to lay into the cat, striking it over and over with his stick. The cat swiped at him with its paw, but, like my attempted blows, it had no effect. I ran to the top of the path, barely visible in the mist and fading light.

Branches lashed my face as I half ran, half fell down the soggy track. I nearly missed the bend below the summit. I had every intention of looking for Jade, but a commotion erupted back up the track. I turned and saw two green eyes flashing among the trees. I hope Jade—wherever she is—forgives me. The giant cat snarled and crashed closer, so I turned and ran.

Then I glanced over my shoulder, and stopped in my tracks. The cat was sniffing around in the bushes. Then it lifted its head. Even though I paused for a mere fraction of a second before resuming my flight, that ghastly scene is burned into my brain as if carved by a surgeon's laser. Yet, I can't bring myself to describe it.

The ground staff announce boarding for first class passengers, platinum miles members, and parents with young infants. There is no sign of authority figures hunting a fugitive white woman. Perhaps it is too early for Jason to report Jade missing, too soon for any other hikers to discover Jade's remains. I pull my jacket tighter, wondering if, in fact, there are any remains to find.

If Interpol tracks me down in Sydney, so be it. At least I can expect a fair hearing in my home country. In this country, overflowing with evil spirits and ghouls and monstrous animals, a white woman's tale of the supernatural will be laughed out of court. No judge in his right mind will see it as anything other than a middle-aged woman's lame excuse for murdering her young girlfriend in a fit of jealousy. I'll be painted as some kind of pervert, or a predator, or I won't have a chance to tell the truth because police will beat a false confession out of me.

Now we are all onboard, and I'm settled on the aisle in 9D. My palms sweat as I type. The purser announces that we'll be departing shortly, after they finalize the passenger manifest. But now there's a disturbance at the door. A police officer appears. And another. One male, one female, dressed in serious navy-blue uniforms. They talk to the purser. They look down the aisle. I still have an airport Wi-Fi signal. I must remember to hit save, and then switch to the new message awaiting an attachment. In a moment, I'll email this story. Then delete it from my laptop. So, for now, goodbye.

EVERY TOWN HAS HAUNTS

ZACHARY FINN

We all thought Tom was a piece of crap, which made his disappearance a little less burdensome than it might've been had it been someone we did *not* view as a piece of crap.

Sure, the school counselors and principals had the little remembrance ceremony—they even offered private counseling sessions that I'm almost certain nobody took advantage of—but it was just going through the motions, and everybody knew it. The school administration knew they had to pay lip service to the fact he was gone and most likely dead judging by the fact that his torn bloody shirt, smashed cell phone, and (at least according to Kate) a voicemail message sent to his mom begging for help. Needless to say, things weren't looking to promising for lil' Tommy.

Kate's father was the officer in charge of investigating Tom's disappearance, which gave her all the supposed inside info. The bloody shirt and phone were found at the abandoned subway station (that much we *did* know for certain), so everyone assumed some weird drifter probably did to Tom the things that weird drifters do, and nobody *really* cared. The official writeup was that he ran away. The blood on his shirt was too contaminated to positively identify as his, and based on his personality, he was a likely flight risk anyway.

Tom sucked. Teachers hated him because he was awkward and stupid. Underclassmen hated him because he was always saying weird stuff to them that was only funny (or made sense for that matter) to him. Girls hated him because they thought he was a creep. Boys hated him because...

I could go on, but I'm sure I've painted a sufficient picture. When Tom fell off the face of the earth, his mother was likely the only one who didn't mutter a celebratory "good riddance." If he was added to some weirdo's face collection, well... *karma can be swift* seemed to be the general consensus.

He didn't belong here anyway.

That should have been the end of it. Tom should've become nothing more than a distant, obnoxious memory that *maybe* somebody *might* bring up years down the road at a future reunion party, or an urban legend sixth graders tell each other before visiting the abandoned station.

But that wasn't the case.

Tom's disappearance revealed one of those seams that every town has, hides, and prays to God never comes to light. That's what Tom did, though. Even in disappearance, he couldn't just leave us alone and go to that distant abyss out of sight and mind. No, he had to reveal the ugly of this town, which now holds so many of us in its grip.

I know what you're thinking: small, backwoods New York town has its ghosts? Big surprise. But don't forget that every town, no matter how big or small, has that shadowy past tucked away. Take New York City for instance, with its dark side streets which lead to only God knows where and have seen only God know what. Or Washington D.C., with its soul-sucking politicians who walk around with blood on their hands amidst the center of the world. Head west and visit the port towns that saw sailors shanghaied. Not to mention all those backwoods communities that had something horrible happen, and afterward tried to ignore it.

Some towns hide it better than others, and some towns can't hide it at all. Those are the ones you don't visit because they don't *really* exist except to those who are trapped there.

What happened here, though, had simmered and festered *just* beneath the surface for so long that all it took was Tom to rip that veil away. Then, like a dam had finally given way, it poured out into the streets and the houses and the shops like a flood meant to wash this place clean... or maybe just to show how dirty this place really was.

. . .

My dreams started not long after Tom went missing. I didn't realize the two were intertwined until later, since dreams were easy enough to explain away. I was stressed out getting ready for the SAT and trying to figure out which college I'd be indebted to for the 10-20 years, so a few nightmares might be expected.

These dreams were particularly disturbing, though. I woke up night after night drenched in cold sweat as moonlight poured through my window and illuminated the town in the distance. The dreams were always so vivid—so lifelike —but I told myself it was the stress coupled with what we'd been learning about in history class, all blending chaotically in my subconscious.

That was how I explained the sound of the gathering mob that filled my dreams with an angry, electric energy whenever I closed my eyes. Or the screams of accusation that ripped through the murmur like bolts of lightning, or the subsequent pleads of innocence which only provoked the crowd further.

It was always hazy in my memory—almost like droplets of rain blurring my glasses—but ahead of me I could always see the crowd, all of whom seemed to be more shadow figures than physical human beings.

I remember the way they would shiver and ripple like the surface of puddle, radiating toxic energy of simultaneous hatred and guilt. I remember seeing the flames, the tree. I remember hearing the desperate, distant voice claiming innocence. Then the rain would start, thick and heavy.

And warm.

I would look down at my hands and see them awash in scarlet, and I'd realize it was raining blood.

That's when I would wake up, covered in sweat with the moon filling my window with a soft white light that partially illuminated the city, yet was too weak to reveal the darkness that lay beneath…

Sue was next and unlike Tom, her disappearance caused a stir. Everybody liked Sue, me included, which meant community-wide searches through the surrounding woods, posters with her face plastered on every store front, and hushed conversations about what might've been. That must have burned Tom's mom something fierce. However, she used the interest sparked by Sue's disappearance to get people thinking about Tom again at the next town hall meeting.

"See, I told you Tom didn't run away! I bet he's alive somewhere, being held against his will."

No one answered.

"He's been kidnapped! Same with this Sue girl! There's somebody in this town who knows what happened!" Tom's mom gazed around accusingly, her eyes pinpointing a few suspect individuals with laser precision—mostly former teachers who had had issues with Tom.

Her anger had me rethinking my decision to attend this particular community meeting; I was only there in the first place because my Civics teacher had offered extra credit to any student who attended a local government function.

"There's no proof of that," the mayor said, though it was clear from the way he glanced around the room that he was looking for somebody else to speak up. Somebody, hopefully, who could back up his claim with concrete evidence. But the room stayed silent.

Toms mother interpreted the lack of response as support, and screamed, "Some sicko has my sweet son and nobody cares!

Normally, it would be all I could do not to bust out laughing at hearing Tom referred to as "sweet." But truth be told, I felt for his mom. It was difficult to watch her stubbornly advocate for her missing son at a meeting that had been called together to discuss Sue's disappearance.

"... we of course understand your frustration, but with no concrete evidence of abduction, and his history of truancy... the police report..." It was a lazy answer, which we all knew was far from satisfactory. "We're doing everything in our power—"

But before he could finish, Tom's mom burst into an expletive laced tirade about the mayor, the school, and the town's personal vendetta against her son. After a solid five minutes she seemed to tire herself out, eventually plopping down in her seat.

"Well then..." The mayor sounded like he was about to pause, but seemed to realize any break might set Tom's mother off again. So instead he picked right back up: "We need to have a serious discussion about what's happening to our town's young people and whether these are connected. For a town our size, no matter what is happening here... runaways or not... it is of course our utmost concern to get these young folks back safely!"

He kept talking, mostly saying a lot of nothing and gripping the podium like he was a *real* politician and not someone elected because no one else wanted the job. A soft murmur drifted through the audience as he spoke, growing slowly louder until somebody had the confidence to stand up.

It was Sue's father.

Everybody turned to face him. There were deep, dark bags underneath his eyes, and his voice quivered as he spoke. I'd only met him once before, at the powderpuff football game the school hosted every year. It looked as if he had aged a decade since.

"The police haven't found a trace of our Susie, and it's clear this boy Tom was trouble. If the two are connected, I doubt *he's* an innocent victim." His voice hissed, venom seeping into each word as he turned to face Tom's mother. I think everybody in the room braced in their seat, bracing for an explosion of epic proportions.

But Tom's mother only stared back for a moment. Then she grunted, stood up, and walked right out.

The room watched in thunderstruck silence as the doors swung shut behind her.

"She went ballistic!" Rich told everybody the next day. Those who weren't at the meeting gathered around to hear the firsthand account of it, news of which was sweeping through the hallways like a forest fire.

"Then Sue's dad stood up, pointed at her, and said 'it was probably your son who kidnapped my daughter!'" Which was of course an exaggeration, but Rich wouldn't let that get in the way of a good story.

For the most part, the general consensus was that Sue's dad might be onto something. I mean, Tom's disappearance—with the bloody shirt and broken phone—looked staged upon closer inspection. He'd have had to smash his phone if he wanted to disappear so the GPS couldn't track him, and all he'd have needed was a little cut to get some blood on the shirt and make it look like something sinister.

The assumption had changed amongst the high school population: now Tom was just a runaway likely hiding out in some dilapidated house as a squatter, and he might—no, probably was—responsible for Sue's disappearance. He was a creep, after all; it had only been a matter of time before something like this happened.

The dreams continued.

Dreamscapes of burning corpses, gleeful faces, and screams of agony filled my nights, each one less surreal than that of the previous night. The screeches weren't always the same: sometimes they were the husky, drawn out screams of men; other times they were the grief-filled shrieks of women. But no matter what, they were always audible over the hum of the mob.

The mob would change too. Sometimes their faces would be covered in dirt and sod, clothes worn down to rags. Other times they would be dressed well in suits and dresses, with canes and shawls. There would be children with them no matter what, and the crowd seemed to go on and on, a sea of bodies.

I'd wake up as the blood started to rain down, and look through the window to see the town sitting in the distance.

After a week there was no new information about Sue or Tom, so a few of us decided to go to the abandoned train station—ostensibly to help search for Tom and Sue, but in reality for shits, giggles, and a dose of excitement.

The abandoned station sits where the edge of town used to exist, back when there was actual money coming in and before all the businesses left. Once those were gone, the town shrank down to a small main street with a few surrounding stores, while the train station was surrendered to nature and the elements.

It was a quick hike to find it, but of course, we'd all been there before as part of a middle school coming-of-age ritual so it wasn't too hard. It was me, Rich, Harold, and Anne who set out that night. We'd been friends since preschool, and what with everyone planning to attend different colleges we realized this might be the last thing we all did together.

As we made our way out, the sun was softly setting, casting a warm, orange glow through the springtime growth.

Rich was hitting on Anne, joking about how he'd always be the one who got away since she was heading upstate for college. Harold and I were discussing what we might stumble upon at the train station, drawing on a vast library of crappy horror movies to frame the possibilities.

"Maybe Tom melted into the train station, becoming some weird, symbiotic parasite that attacks all who enter it's domain!"

"God, that would be fitting," was Anne' response to Harold's hypothesis. She'd caught up with us, leaving Rich a few feet behind us, whistling loudly.

"Yeah... he was definitely something," I agreed.

"He was always messaging us girls. You should've seen what he sent. A few of us had a group chat where we'd share all the screenshots. He was *relentless*. I mean, no matter what you told him he just wouldn't stop. They were always weird too. Not like he was trying to get with you, just… bizarre. *"*

Me, Rich and Harold all laughed at the thought of Tom badgering Anne, but she stayed stone-faced and continued talking.

"It was desperate. I almost felt bad for him. Like he didn't know how to *actually* talk to a girl—or anybody for that matter—so he was just reading from a script and being weird."

"He was just an asshole. We all know that," I chimed in. Anne only let out a soft sigh as we walked down the overgrown path.

Even in the twilight, the late spring landscape seemed so alive and vibrant. The neon green overgrowth magnified the colors of the fading sun, and the path through the woods glowed beneath its last rays.

We all grew quiet as the chirps of night birds and crickets filled the dusk. My mind began to drift. Amidst a pleasant daydream involving Anne, a startling flash of deja vu ripped me from my thoughts. For a second I was back in my nightmares: the mob, the screeches, the blood from above… they were all there, happening, as real as could be. Only they were familiar now. The voices… I *knew* them…

But before it could all click, a voice cut through the dreamscape.

"I think that's it over there—" Rich said.

I snapped to the present and shook off the strange vision, which was easy to do when I saw the station ahead.

It was a tangled mess of concrete and the natural world trying to reclaim it: crumbling concrete structures, foliage, and faded graffiti all blended together in a jumbled heap of the past. It felt like we had stumbled on an ancient monolith.

"I wonder what Tom was doing here by himself?" I asked. Rich shrugged and Harold threw his hands up, but Anne answered.

"He was lonely." She almost sounded sad, which made me feel bad for him. Until that moment I'd hated him, and truth be told, there are plenty of times I've hated him since… but the thought of him hanging out at the crumbling structure, all alone, was almost too much to bear.

"You're overthinking it. He probably just came here to jerk it."

Harold laughed at Rich's comment, but it was hollow, forced.

Looking to change the subject, I began rambling about the history of the place. I'd spent the better part of my eighth period study hall researching the station. Although the town was small, urban explorers trickled through to capture the decaying station in their blogs. The local history office had an interesting writeup, too.

"It shut down in 1932 because the Great Depression did a number on this place."

I expected to be made fun of, but everybody seemed interested so I continued. "Everybody who could leave went and left. But once this station shut down, people were kind of stuck here. There wasn't a lot of money or food. Seems like they were some pretty dark times."

We were only about twenty feet away from the station, but everybody seemed rooted to their current spot. Now that we were close, we could see everything. All around us, the forest looked poised to engulf everything except the station in its circular clearing. While overgrown, the grass and vegetation within it was thinner and paler, almost like everything was just barely clinging to life.

I finally willed myself forward. The crunch of the dried weeds beneath my feet seemed to snap everybody to the present, and they were soon following behind. Nobody spoke. Whether due to reverence or fear, I don't know.

The silence was eventually broken by loud *caws* as nesting birds exploded from the station. The flurry of dark bodies was so startling I almost lost my footing. Anne gasped behind me.

As the birds disappeared, we all began to laugh. There was something freeing about laughing at the fear we'd all felt from a few birds; it lifted the ominous veil that seemed to cover us.

We marched to the grime-smeared platform. The graffiti sprayed throughout was either racist, or looked like the handiwork of an unexceptional fourth-grader. Some appeared to be a disturbing mix of the two. Still, something about the graffiti demanded our attention.

We were staring at an anatomical anomaly crudely painted on one of the walls when I noticed it. In a hallway that seemed to lead nowhere, the original destination having been ripped away for building materials decades ago, a colorful world bloomed within the darkened portal.

I walked over without a word. Anne, Rich, and Harold followed. The graffiti —no, not graffiti—the *paintings* here were marvelous. Bright worlds and scenes I can barely describe filled the doorway, all beautiful. We looked on them silently. No jokes, no smartass comments, just awe.

"Do you think Sue did these? She took an art class with me, I think," Rich said as we entered the hall.

"Maybe Tom did. He spent a lot of time here," Anne said.

No one responded to either question; we were too enraptured by the drawings. Some of the scenes depicted the natural world with swirling, colorful galaxies exploding behind them. Others were local landmarks—restaurants, shops, the school—but those were just entryways, doorways like the painting-covered hall we'd just entered. Some showed happy scenes with bright colors, while others were dark and chaotic. But all of it grew from the doorways of those well-known sites, hinting at a world just beyond the familiar.

When the sun set, our flashlights came out. We couldn't pull ourselves away from the murals on the decaying doorway.

The rest of the night is a blur. We stayed out at that abandoned station for hours. At one point I sat down on the platform. Anne joined me. Rich and Harold were tromping around the back somewhere, which gave us a moment to talk.

Of course, the subject was Tom.

"The messages weren't that bad. The ones Tom sent." Her voice sounded sad. Regretful. "I mean, they were weird… but they weren't creepy or pervy like we made them out to be. He never said anything like he was hitting on us. He was just so weird… and he wouldn't stop sending them."

"He shouldn't have kept messaging you if it was clear you didn't want to talk to him. That's still, I don't know, *aggressive*."

It was the best answer I could give. Anne was a good person, so good she was blaming herself for something that wasn't her fault. The guilt was in no way earned, but I knew I would never convince her. Sometimes being a good person means you have to bear more weight than you deserve.

She leaned her head on my shoulder. After a momentary electric shock, I relaxed. It felt right. Natural.

And as the stars unfolded in front of us and she rested against me, the smell of her perfume enveloping us, I truly understood the beauty in the artist's paintings.

We finally began to make our way back to town. Rich suggested we walk past Tom's house. We didn't ask why; we just did it.

I expected the streets to be quiet at the late hour, but as we approached, I realized the town was alive with a festival-like hum. Even as we emerged from the woods far from the center of town, we saw lights bouncing around the street like fireflies, a clear indicator that this night was abnormal.

Something was going on.

I looked down at my phone: 11:33 pm; yet it looked like Halloween night. Roving groups of teenagers, most of whom I knew, moved in packs with their hoods up. Adults stood in their doorways or on their porches, overseeing whatever was happening.

Rich sprinted ahead of us like a kid rushing into a carnival. "I told you we'd want to come back this way! Sarah texted me and told me we need to get down here. Wait till you see the house!"

Anne looked at me anxiously. I felt her apprehension; the pit of my stomach seemed filled with battery acid, and for the briefest moment I was back in my nightmare, surrounded by an angry mob as blood rained down.

Then I was back on the street, walking past groups of people I knew strolling through the streets toward Tom's old house.

We heard it before we saw it: a soft howl that fluttered through the night like wind. It was guttural yet soft. Tension flooded me; I had an inkling of what I would see when we turned the corner, and I didn't want to see it. I wanted to turn down a side street and sprint to my house before I saw what this town was capable of.

But I didn't run away. I turned that corner with Anne, Rich, and Harold, and for the first time in my life, the veil rippled. I saw what lay underneath—and it was ugly.

As we stared at the monstrosity of human anger, Anne moved closer to me. She didn't want to see this, either. Yet here we were.

Tom's house was covered in eggs and toilet paper. But that was just the start. Someone had scrawled blood red graffiti across the house, words and phrases that would make a sailor blush. Violent threats wove through the vulgarities, but they looked different; instead of the puffy, blurred lines of spray paint, these seemed to streak in choppy lines, as though smeared on by hand.

Kill the monster.

The Freak will burn.

When we find him…

Beneath that was a crudely drawn noose wrapped around the neck of a stick figure. Crude, caveman-like drawings, but they drove home the point that if Tom came home, he was in for a bad night.

For a split second the house rippled, shifted, and contorted to something different for a second. The front yard was filled with toiling shadows. They weren't human—not quite—but somehow I knew that they had been, once. Some of smeared more writing on the house, while others peered through the window with the fascination of a small child. Normal people, most of whom I knew, mingled with them, seemingly unaware that they weren't alone in painting threats.

"You hiding him!" a rattling voice hollered. I instantly recognized it as Tom's father, who sat beyond the picket fence, overseeing it all. He continued to shout, much of it incoherent. Whenever he yelled, those shadows seemed to ripple and darken, seeming to coalesce into a void.

I grabbed Anne' arm and ran. I couldn't bear to watch it anymore, and I couldn't bear to leave her behind. I wanted to get Rich and Harold out of there as well… but they seemed enthralled. I could have sworn I saw them making their way towards the house as we sprinted away.

We ran past growing crowds and amused spectators as we made our way to my house. Neither of us spoke; we just ran. And when we finally arrived, bursting through the front door like we were going to call the cops—though even then we knew there was nothing they could, or would, do)—my house was silent. Whether my parents were upstairs asleep or back in town I'll never know. Either was, my house wasn't empty.

My grandmother sat in her usual rocking chair, looking out the living room window. "They're busy tonight…" she said in a harsh whisper. "Normally they don't start this early… normally it's not till later in the night. But I guess it's been a while." She shifted into a more comfortable position.

"This happens… regularly?" Anne's voice raised in surprise and horror.

"Not quite regularly. Every few years. Can't remember the last one…" She paused to think. "Started awhile back—before me even—with some fellow, some drifter, around the time the train station closed. Came into town pretending to sell property rights or bonds or something… can't quite remember how the story went. But he swindled a bunch of folks of what little they had. The town was in bad shape already—people froze to death that winter, it was so bad—and before he could leave, well, they caught him."

The rocking picked up. The increased motion of the chair sent her into a coughing fit. The dry rasp echoed around the dim room like a chain dragged on concrete. Finally she managed to stop, and the story continued.

"They made him pay. For the scams, of course... but it didn't stop there. They made him pay for the businesses leaving. For the starving families. For every small, petty wrong anyone in this town ever felt. They buried him out by the train station. And that was the start. Did you see 'em?" She posed her question with a devious little chuckle, a laugh I'd never heard before.

"The shadows... I saw them." Anne was brave enough to answer, to recognize and say it aloud. I just nodded, which was the most I could muster.

"They've been around for as long as I can remember. Wandering, causing trouble. Can't say I know what or who they were. Maybe it's that original mob that killed that scammer. Or maybe it's all the souls this town swallowed with it, like those two missing children. Can't say I know. What I *do* know is that they like stirring up trouble till someone dies. And I guess that boy's mother is the next one."

My grandmother shrugged, and before we could process what she'd told us, she was softly snoring.

Anne slept over that night. There was no way either of us were going back out into town until the morning, especially knowing that what we'd seen at that point was just the tip of the iceberg.

It wasn't how I'd pictured it happening growing up, but I guess it rarely is.

That morning, Anne convinced me to walk back into town to see the aftermath of the night. It was early, much earlier than I'd normally be up and walking on a Sunday. *Now* it seemed like we were walking into a ghost town. A soft fog obscured the edges of the main street. No one walked the paved paths that had been abuzz with activity only hours before. It was like a dreamscape, reality softy blurring into the ether. The fact that it was a town—a world—that I thought I'd known filled my stomach with an acidic burn.

"Do you see it?" Anne asked, her voice a mix of wonder and horror. I looked at her and her eyes, those livewire blue eyes that could stop my heart with a sideways glance, stared off in the direction of Tom's house. I didn't want to follow Anne' gaze, but I knew I had to. And when I finally turned to look at it... well, I'd liked to say I was shocked. But I suppose the dreams had prepared me.

A procession of shadows surrounded the house. The towns ugliness was splattered across its facade like the obscene graffiti in the train station. The shadows stood patiently, flickering and wavering as if they might disappear. It was clear they were waiting for something.

They didn't have to wait long. The sudden explosion of a gunshot echoed through the foggy morning. Tom's house seemed to reverberate and shake from the burst.

"She did it. She's the victim they were looking for." Anne said what we both knew. Together, we watched the shadow mob disappear one by one.

I never left.

You might think that once I saw what I did that night—how evil this place could be—I'd be on the first bus out of town. Put as many miles between myself and my hometown as possible. That's what Anne did, after all, and who can blame her?

And that's what I was going to do, I swear. But every time I almost brought myself to leave, a wicked thought would cross my mind:

If your small town has these skeletons in its closet... what will the next town have waiting for you?

And every time that question crossing my mind, I decide I don't to find out. Sometimes, the evil you know is better than the one you don't. Or at least that's how I justified staying here, even after I saw the mob return a second time, then a third.

Those dreams still haunt me. And now I see those shadows everywhere I go, constantly, no matter what time of day; they're no longer contained to those nights when the monsters in people emerge.

I never found out what happened to Tom or Sue. Maybe it was the ghosts of this town looking to stir up some trouble. Or maybe they both did what I haven't managed to do; just upped and left this place. Who knows?

What I do know is I've spent countless nights at that old abandoned station, staring deep into those paintings that show what *might* be out there, where Anne is now, beyond the buildings and storefronts and shadows I now know so well. I *want* to know if those worlds are out there—the beautiful ones existing just beyond the town that has swallowed me.

But I don't think I ever will.

SEPTEMBER HARVEST

MARCIA SHERMAN

Once every twenty or thirty years or so it happened. Out of boredom, or on a dare, or after some particularly strong cider, a group of idle boys would take it into their heads to steal from that orchard. Despite the whispered warnings: do not ever get caught at the Smith farm after dark! No matter the stories told at bedtime: that is what happened to them when they stole from the Smith trees! In defiance of the punishments promised: if you are bad you will be sent to pick at Smith's!

So it was that this group of six abandoned their after-dinner chores, met up by the clock tower, snuck past the darkening woods, oh so quietly slipped through a gap in the fence pickets—look how easy that was!—and began tossing apples into their sacks. Apples they just knew would taste so much better from being stolen. Eagerly filling bag upon bag, laughing and joking and shushing one another, they lost track of time and wandered far into the crazy, twisted maze of aged, gnarled trees. They never noticed the setting sun drifting into dusk.

When the town clock began to chime seven, they all froze for just a moment in disbelief, then began to run. Uneven ground gave way to uneven cobblestones and they fled up the path in panic, pushing one another out of the way, racing the clock. Where had this wind come from? Red and orange and yellow leaves blew around their brown leather shoes. When had it become so cold? Their homespun gray cloaks were suddenly no match for the dip in temperature. Every chime from the clock tower slowed their escaping footsteps. The heavy bags of pilfered fruit stuck fast to their hands and weighed them down. They only made it as far as the edge of the Smith property, where the road divided the last orchard from the town square. No longer able to lift their feet, their vision blurred. Wide eyed with fear, everything in sight was abruptly overlaid with a green haze. The six heard the last chime of the clock and then... nothing.

The next morning brought much wailing and weeping, shouting and sobbing. Six boys gone, apparently out for a lark in the early evening, they were last seen headed out of town towards the orchards. The orchards? Not the Smith orchards! Every able-bodied man searched day and night for a week. Nothing, not one thing, was found—not a cap, or a shoe, or a scrap of fabric. Lucky mothers of boys who had decided not to go apple picking avoided the unlucky mothers. And those six unlucky mothers tried to convince themselves their boys, bored with the slow little town, had set off for a life in the big fast city.

With a sinking heart, and little hope, Sheriff McIntosh walked to the edge of the town square, carrying the last of the notices listing the names of the missing: Arthur Turner, Johnny Voun, George Carpenter, Harry Masters, Milo Gibson, and James Grieve. He knew exactly how their families felt, having lost a relative in a similar manner. His great-uncle had disappeared long before the Sheriff was born, but the story was often told—a part of his family lore. Grandmother Braeburn talked of little else now that she was so old and frail. Harvest times especially seemed to agitate her. Everyone believed it was just a part of her senility, the tale of how her brother was swallowed by the trees. Imagine. The family just let her ramble, and humoured her.

Had this tree always been here? Right here by the cobblestone road, between the town square and the boundary of the Smith property? Well, of course it must have been here, trees do not grow overnight. In a town with so many trees and so many orchards it was hard to remember every one. The Sheriff raised his hammer, and the tree almost appeared to shrink away from him. When he drove in the nail, he thought he heard a cry. He shook his head. Crazy what lack of sleep will do, make you see and hear things. McIntosh wearily gazed up the rolling hill at the ancient farmhouse beyond rows, and rows, and rows of trees. That Smith family sure had a way with growing apples. A flicker of movement caught his eye and he turned quickly... perhaps? But no, it was just Granny Smith, with her shears and picking basket, collecting fruit from one of the half-dozen trees at the edge of the orchard.

THE DANCER IN THE CORN

ERIC NIRSCHEL

Nathan's reflection was pale, gaunt and miserable-looking. His eyes, dulled from lack of sleep, were sunken and lifeless. It was a poor reflection of a man, and for once, Nathan Drecker was thankful for it. There was no way of knowing what lay in the darkness beyond the window. No way of knowing, perhaps, but Nathan had a better idea than most.

Nathan turned away from the glass, drawing the curtains, mercifully shielding himself from his own weary reflection as darkness slowly closed its skeleton fingers around the Iowa countryside. The gentle swaying of the train sloshed his brain around inside his skull, a dull ache growing feverish and insistent. Nathan's hands trembled as he shook a pair of round white tablets into his palm; their texture was chalky and the residue left faint white streaks on his skin. Dollar store aspirin. There was no telling if it was even actually aspirin at all, but that didn't stop him from popping both tablets into his mouth, chewing without the usual grimace one would expect. It was not his first rodeo. The tired-looking man with the stylish, round spectacles capped the small plastic bottle and tucked it into the breast pocket of his brown corduroy field coat.

It had been more than a week since the funeral. Nathan had outlived them all: his parents by a little and his brother by a lot. Of the trio, his brother was the only one that he missed. It was why he'd waited a week before leaving; he had no intention of seeing to the business of planting his mother's casket in that moldering earth. She'd have plenty of company in the sad little plot overlooking Ash Fork from the hill where Barth & Sons funeral home stood its silent vigil, waiting for more of the dearly departed to pass its gates. She could rot right along with the old son of a bitch. Some departed were dearer than others.

Like Riley, and Trevor, and... Nathan rubbed his eyes, internally chastising himself for dredging up the old hurts. There would be plenty of time for that once the train arrived. Outside, row after row after row of midseason corn would rush past in the darkness, sentries standing silent watch as if awaiting his return. He couldn't help but wonder if something still danced between the rows in the dark, waiting for its own harvest. He'd seen it twice before, out there in the fields. They'd called it 'Skinhusker' without a hint of irony.

His headache intensified.

"I've got to admit, I never thought you would come back. Not ever. Can't say I'd blame you."

Deacon Blithe hadn't aged as well as Nathan; his hair was thin and greying, and his gut hung out over his worn leather belt with more gusto than it ought. Deacon's face was pocked with small scars racked up over the years, most likely from welding without a proper mask. Deacon was something of a handyman, though his steady job was at the grist mill. Everything in Ash Fork revolved around corn in one way or another. Everything.

"Wish I could say I was glad to be back, but..." Nathan trailed off.

"Oh, I know, believe me. Things've never been the same, since... you know." Deacon's face contorted as if he'd smelled something rotten, and he took a long pull from his glass, though it seemed more reflex than thirst.

"How come you stayed, Blithe? I mean, not that I'm not damn glad to see you again, but why stick around?" Nathan rubbed his chin, feeling the scratch of stubble against the back of his hand.

"Darcy, mostly," Blithe responded distantly.

"Darcy... you don't mean Darcy Ray Stevens?" Nathan was nonplussed; Darcy Ray Stevens had been crowned homecoming queen the year Nate left town, and went on to win the state beauty pageant the following year. Blithe wasn't an ugly kid back in those days, but he wasn't homecoming material, either.

"One and the same." Blithe beamed, his faintly sullen demeanor melting away for a moment as pride took over. "We hooked up, God, two years after you got out. With her here, I couldn't much fly the coop. She didn't want to leave family, and I couldn't exactly tell her about... y'know. So, I stuck it out. Eventually I guess I grew roots."

"Well, shit, Blithe, I'm happy as hell for you. Punching above your weight like that!" Nathan laughed for the first time in days, but Blithe didn't join him.

"She, uh..." Blithe stammered for a moment, staring down into his beer. The din of the bar around them seemed to fade into the background, and Nate almost reached the realization before Blithe told him, "She died, Nate. Year back. Cancer."

"Jesus, Blithe... I'm sorry. I didn't know."

The two stared down into their respective mugs in silence for a long moment.

"It's this town, Nate. Nothing good lasts in this place. Not without blood. You know that." Blithe looked up from his mug, eyes wet. "Seeing you again is a great thing, Nate, but you promise me you'll do what you need to do here and get the fuck out. You were right when you left. You were always right."

The old farmhouse had started its life as a classic European-style I-house sometime in the 1840s. The first settlers in the Iowa Valley brought many traditions with them from the old country (some more innocuous than others), and chief among them was their architectural styling. Now, as Nathan looked at it, the old house had little left of its original design. Two rooms had been added, a porch had been tacked on, the roof had been reshingled and the siding replaced. There were new gutters and the old shutters he remembered had long been removed. The house was a different color than he remembered it, but somewhere beneath the changes that had been made in the twenty-three or so years since he'd left, the same skeleton remained.

Nathan could only offer a sigh; he was too tired to be angry and too distanced from his family to be nostalgic. The things people try to hide beneath a coat of paint. He plodded around to the side of the house, casting his gaze back toward the rear porch. There, roughly twenty feet from the back steps, stood the old swing set. Two seats swayed gently in the morning breeze, the chains creaking slightly. Two seats for two brothers, Josh and Nate. Beyond the swing set, a wall of green, tall stalks ebbing and flowing like a great green sea. Nathan shuddered, suddenly feeling cold despite the morning sun, and went inside.

Little of the interior had changed in twenty years, and amidst the stifling still-
ness and the drifting motes of dust catching the sun cascading through the side
windows, Nathan wasn't sure if that was a good or bad thing. A rush of memories hit him hard enough to take his breath away, and he closed his eyes, wincing
as though struck. He fished around in his pocket and scooped out the bottle of
aspirin, chewing and swallowing. For a moment, Nate was reminded of old Jack
Torrance, chewing on Excedrin. Nathan was no alcoholic, but he sure felt like a
drink. He also felt like someone had taken a croquet mallet to his head, but that
was neither here nor there.

His old room looked much the same as he'd left it; save for the layers of
dust, everything was where he'd put it last. The walls were bare, old yellow and
beige floral print wallpaper faded and greying with time. During the last year
Nathan still lived there, he'd taken down most of his decorations and packed
most of his things. His father had railed, but his mother was less overt in her
objections. "We can't leave," she'd tell him. "We owe this town more than you
could ever know. We have roots here." His parents thought it was a phase and
that he'd grow out of it. He didn't. Roots be damned.

Laying down on his old bed felt wrong, yet familiar. He remembered lying
awake at night, listening to the rustling of the leaves. Cold winter mornings
when the snow came in hard. Those were the best mornings to sleep in,
knowing school was cancelled. Back when he was a kid and he hadn't yet
peeked behind the curtain, everything had been much more pleasant. Surprisingly decent memories, and yet... the truth has a way of changing memories.
Once-pleasant thoughts take on a red tint and the copper smell of blood. Good
memories get linked to bad. People die. Things kill them. Nathan had
promised. Promised himself almost daily for years that he'd never set foot in
this house again. Promises like that were easy to make as a teenager. Even
into his twenties. Now that his parents were really dead, though, there were
adult responsibilities. There was an estate to manage, and, God willing, a
house to sell off. He felt responsible, and if handling this business himself
could finally close that chapter of his life for good, he would do it. Maybe he
could finally bury Joshua... and Riley, and Trevor, and yes, maybe even
Haley.

Nathan sat up and groaned. His eyes were watering. From the dust, surely.

. . .

"So, how long are you in town for?" Sheriff Darby took a long drag from his cigarette, his eyes hidden behind mirror aviators.

"Only a week or so. Just long enough to get things in order. Soon as I'm done sorting through the paperwork, I'm heading back east."

"That's probably for the best. Shame to see one of the old families go, but maybe it's time this town got some new blood."

"You mean that literally or figuratively, sheriff?" Nathan grimaced, loading the last of his grocery bags into the trunk of his rental.

Darby's face soured, his lips pursing into a fine line.

Darby was a large, well-built man with worker's hands. His jaw was square and cleanly shaved, and the edges of his black hair were only now beginning to grey. Darby had been two years ahead of Nathan in school. His father had been Sheriff before him.

"Don't go digging up the past like that."

Nathan closed the trunk. "That would imply it ever got buried. You're not going to going to give me the 'let sleeping dogs lie' speech, are you, Sheriff?"

Darby grimaced, dropping his cigarette and grinding it into the asphalt with his booted heel. "More of a 'be careful what you say' speech, really."

"Wouldn't happen to be intended as a veiled threat, would it, Sheriff?"

Darby sighed, shaking his head. "Not from me, no. I got my own feelings about how things went down, but I'm a lawman. My feelings got no place in what I do. Leastwise, they're not supposed to." Darby took off his hat, running a hand through his hair before replacing it. "So, no, not from me. But the Wolfram brothers might beg to differ. Fitch and Spyer might have something to say about it, as well."

The Wolfram brothers, Earl and Carl, had been bullies in their day, and from the way Darby talked about them, they hadn't much changed. Arlington Fitch was the son of Ash Fork's longest serving mayor. He'd finally been voted out not long after Nathan left. Jimmy Spyer was his father's son, taking over the butcher shop on the main line. None of the apples fell far from the tree. The more things change, the more they stay the same.

"There's been talk," Darby continued. "Talk of finishing the business."

Nathan nodded grimly, fumbling with the keys in his pocket. He was uneasy, but not entirely because of what Darby was saying. The feeling crept up on him, slowly at first, and then rapidly, like a swirling grey shadow passing across the sun. He felt like a teenager again. Like he was right back in that long, hot summer when the town turned on itself and so many died. Somehow, it suddenly seemed to Nathan as he stood in the parking lot of Greely's Market, that nothing at all had changed. The people passing by may have different faces now, but deep down they were the same. Everything was the same.

There was something cold in the room with him. It wasn't an external cold, not like an icy rain or a biting wind. It was deeper, older, and more profound. It was a cold that radiated from inside, as if your bones had turned to rods of ice. Nathan shivered, clutching the blankets close even though it was the middle of the summer and he could hear the crickets and cicadas outside. The cold was brutal, aching, and above all, unnatural. He'd felt it before. It was the cold in the skinhusker's eyes, black pools so clear you could see your reflection in them as it peeled you, raking your skin back and opening you up like an ear of corn. Art imitates life, and life imitates... long, arachnid fingers capped with razors, teeth like knives. Black eyes. Nightmare eyes. Eyes full of hatred and terror and revenge. So much revenge. Eyes that were looking down at Nathan while he slept...

Nathan sprung to life, leaping out of the bed and snatching his revolver from the end table right as he fell, careening to the floor, rolling frantically. He wheeled around, frigid sweat plastering his hair to his forehead. The gun was a cold lump in his hand, his fumbling, numb fingers frantic for the trigger. They found it, and Nathan took aim above the bed... and there was nothing. No dark shape. No black eyes. Only empty wall where a Nirvana poster had hung when he was in high school.

Clouds drifted lazily overhead, backlit in blue and white. But out over the corn, darkness gathered. Fat, bloated grey clouds roiled over the horizon, and faintly, thunder rumbled.

"It's been a long time, Nate," Callum said with a sigh, taking a long, slow pull from his pipe.

"Not long enough, if you ask me," Nate replied, leaning on the banister of the new back porch. 'New' was subjective; it had probably been there for a decade.

Callum and Maddy Pierce were some of the last people Nathan expected to still be in Ash Fork. Well into their nineties, he'd given both up for dead long ago. Nathan could count on his fingers the number of people he still had any respect for in Ash Fork, and the Pierces were chief among them.

"Lord, ain't that the truth," Callum grumbled, shaking his head. "Though I expect the good Lord hasn't got much truck with this place nowadays, if he ever did."

"How come you stayed, Cal? You and Maddy were the first people I'd have expected to get out of Dodge."

"Spite, mostly." Callum sighed.

"We wanted to leave. After they took her… after what happened to our girl… with Haley gone, it didn't seem right to stay." Mrs. Pierce looked wistful.

"Then the fires came. Started in the old theater and spread down the whole left side of Main street. After that, the draught. Six straight years of it. Seeing the look on all their faces year after year was the closest thing to revenge I was liable to get." Callum grinned wickedly; it was a malicious look, cold and vicious and old. An anger nursed for decades, packed tight like a diamond. "After the draught killed off the corn crop so many years in a row, it was a gasser to have the rains do it the year after."

"The town's suffered a lot since you did what you did. Deservedly, too, mind. Old Providence bridge collapsed one summer a few years back. Killed the mayor's daughter. You know who got the blame."

"I kept the rifle, you know," Callum said grimly. "Picked it up when no one was looking and stowed it away. I've got it hanging on the mantle. It's not quite the head of a 'god,' but its damn close."

Nathan fidgeted nervously. He could still feel the rifle in his hands. It was heavy, an old .308 Remington bolt action fit for a bear. Back then, it wasn't odd for teenagers to hunt or target shoot. They'd all been packing heat that summer. Riley had a shotgun. Nathan could still remember how satisfying racking the slide had felt. The sound… it sounded like vengeance. Trevor had a double barrel, an over-under he used to hunt duck and skeet, respectively. Blithe had lifted a Colt 1911 from his old man. And Nate had his rifle. His fingers tingled, recalling the grain of the wood, the rough etchings in the stock. He'd spent a month researching, reading, learning. He etched every symbol, every charm, every sigil he could find into the wood. A powerful spell. He hadn't been hunting bear that summer. He'd been hunting a god.

And he'd killed it.

. . .

The gunshot quaked through Nathan, a bolt of lightning that suddenly made everything seem real, complete with its own thunder. He'd been on autopilot. At some point, Nathan realized, he'd come to the understanding that it would end in blood. It was a slow, creeping realization, and, like a frog in a pot of boiling water, Nathan hadn't jumped. He was too tired, too fed up with it all. He'd been carrying the memory of the friends that had died at his side, of the girl he couldn't save, for too long to jump.

A man he didn't recognize stumped through the doorway, the front door hanging on one hinge. Nathan pulled the trigger again and he jerked spastically, his body wheeling against the frame and down to the floor, crimson streaks against the old wood.

He'd heard the engines rumbling up to the old I-frame just before two in the morning. Trucks and vans loaded down with townies bent on dragging him from the house. He didn't know most of them; many were younger than he was, ginned up with lies about how good and kind the 'Watcher in the Rows' had been to the town. About how the harvest god had blessed them and how Nathan Drecker had ruined everything. They wouldn't be reasoned with, and at this point Nathan didn't much care to try. Just seeing them done up in their fine green sashes and ritual face paint was enough to make his blood boil.

He fired again, moving toward the back of the house, the acrid stink of gunpowder filling the hall between kitchen and living room. Another figure, a woman, clutched at her face with a stuttering cry, her cheekbone shattering with a spray of gore.

Nathan was out his back door and across the grass, his bare feet soaked instantly with condensation. To his right, the corn stood menacingly, still and tall and silent. It may as well have been a brick wall; nothing would convince Nathan to go into the corn again.

He wheeled around the side of the house, slipping on the wet grass, his pockets clinking with the sound of unspent .357 bullets. Good that he did; a club swung high, aiming for his head and smashing against the side of the house. They'd been waiting for him. Nathan lurched back toward his attacker, jamming the barrel of his revolver into the man's gut. He pulled the trigger twice, the green sash the man wore rising as the bullets came out his back, spattered red.

The others circled him, more joining their number. The others who'd gone into the house now circled around behind him, penning him in. Nathan's hand shot into his pocket. Brass clinked. He was surrounded, and this time there were faces he *did* recognize. The mob closed in, far more than his six round revolver could dispense with, even if he was a crack shot.

That didn't stop him from pulling the trigger six more times.

The clearing had been cut for this purpose. In the dancing titian haze of a massive bonfire, Nathan's bleary eyes slowly focused on the swaying throng. Dancers cavorted around the flames with wild, ecstatic glee. There were songs being sung, though Nathan didn't know what they were saying. He recognized the sound of the words; the old tongue, they called it, but he didn't know what language it truly was. He'd never learned it. Never wanted to.

Nathan was only briefly surprised that he wasn't tied up; the pain arcing through his legs was enough of an explanation as to why. He wouldn't be running anywhere, broken as they both were, quite deliberately and below the knee. He'd been propped up against a bale of hay, facing the fire. To his right stood a podium, and on the far side he could see Blithe, beaten and bloody, crumpled against his own bale.

"Guess... I should've... kept working out, huh?" Blithe sputtered, blood oozing from a split lip. His breathing was ragged. "I should've known, Nate, I should've..."

"Don't. There's no fault in not thinking like a crazy motherfucker," Nate interrupted.

"I thought it was done..." Blithe groaned.

"Of course you did, you dense son of a bitch." Earl Wolfram turned toward Blithe with a toothy grin, much of his face obscured by the heavy green hood he wore. "You honestly thought you could kill a god because you're a goddamned moron."

"Fuck you, Earl. You always were a prick." Blithe spat.

Earl, for his part, exhibited remarkable self-control, given what Nathan knew about him, and only kicked Blithe twice.

"That's enough, Earl. You don't wanna get on Fitch's bad side. He wants 'em mostly in one piece," Carl chided from the crowd.

"I thought you two were supposed to be the muscle around here." Nathan forced a laugh, even though it pained him. He thought that maybe a rib was broken, as well.

Earl moved toward him but stopped, waved off by a cloaked figure stepping up to the podium. The figure drew back its hood and Arlington Fitch revealed himself, balding head and thick, coke bottle glasses glinting in the bonfire's light. Nathan hadn't seen him in decades, but Fitch had always been a whiny little brat. And now, looking at him in his long, flowing green robe, Nathan couldn't shake the feeling that anywhere else, at any other time, Fitch would be a nobody. Middle manager at a department store, maybe. Here, though, Fitch was the big kahuna.

"They are not afraid of me, Nathan," Fitch said with a shyster's grin. "They fear that which I represent. The great Sucellus!"

Fitch's voice raised at the annunciation of his god's name, and the gathered throng cheered the sound of it. Women swooned and men whooped and hollered. Fitch was a rock star.

"It's been a long time, brothers and sisters!" Fitch raised his arms, pausing for a moment as the high-pitched feedback died from the nearby speakers. "It's been a long time, but finally, the hour is here! The moment we retake our land from the blasphemers and chancers! From the false saviors who condemned us to ruin more than twenty years ago! For the first time in two decades, we are poised to regain the favor of our great and beneficent god! Sucellus! Karmanor! Berstuk! Blessed are the many names of He Who Dances in the Corn!"

More cheers. Frantic, unhinged laughter. Nathan had heard it before, all those years ago, when he'd watched from the edge of the clearing. That was the night his brother had died. The first time he'd seen the Skinhusker, it peeled Joshua like an ear of corn. The second time he'd seen it, it was over the iron sights of a Remington. This would be his third time.

The shape rose slowly from the corn to Nathan's right, long and gaunt, arachnid limbs lifting a bulbous frame up above the top of the stalks. It stepped forward with a long, lumbering step met with gasps and stuttered prayers in the old tongue. In the light, its gnarled frame looked like a mockery of a man, twisted bark-like skin layered with greasy ridged leaves pretending to be flesh. The thing's face, if one could call it that, was a misshapen lump of strange flesh, twisted around and around like taffy, from which a gaping maw opened, ringed with dagger-like teeth. Its eyes, black as midnight, caught the flame and flickered, dancing like candles. They settled on Blithe first.

"Witness now the fate of those who would do battle with a god! Look upon the flesh laid bare! Nonbelievers and defilers, obsessed with their paltry flesh. A fool is parted from more than his money, my friends!"

Fitch's tirade continued, arms gesticulating wildly for effect, his face beading sweat behind partly fogged glasses. His fervor grew so he could be heard over Blithe's screams.

By the time the screaming stopped, the blood had flown so thick that it pooled on the damp earth.

It was a festival. The creature walked among its flock like a king, holding out strips of flesh to the congregants. They cheered and offered breathless thanks, their lips staining crimson as they accepted the offering of 'the Generous One, He Who Walks in the Corn.'

The thing reveled in its station, capering between the robed figures with jerking, spastic motions, joining the dancers around the bonfire. Periodically, it would stop, reaching out to gently run a loving finger over the cheek of a pretty girl. Its sharp caress left a crimson line, and the girl would titter and giggle as if its fingers weren't capped with razors, as if she weren't bleeding. Mindless, engulfed in the monstrosity's vain worship.

Nathan was mostly ignored in the throng, left to his own devices beside the podium. Without his gun and with two broken legs, he wasn't going far, even if he'd intended to make a run for it. Fitch wasn't far away, still standing at his podium, ranting and raving, inciting his little cult. Nathan began to fade; he wasn't sure how many times Fitch had gone over the same script. The lunatic dialogue with himself all blurred together into a droning that was easy to tune out. It wasn't until the dancing stopped that Nathan became aware of the eyes on him.

The gaunt figure of the skinhusker; Sucellus, Karmanor, the Dancer Between the Rows, whatever it chose to be called at any given moment, strode through the crowd, standing easily two heads above the tallest man. Its black eyes focused on Nathan. Nathan, for his part, was dimly aware that it was taunting him. It wanted Nathan alive to see its triumph. More than twenty years after Nathan and his friends had squared off against it in the corn, it was alive, and all of his friends were dead. They'd gone to war with the old, the evil, and they'd lost. It wanted Nathan to know it before he died.

Fitch raised his arms. "And now, brothers and sisters, Sons and daughters of Yum Caax! Now witness the truth of things! The truth is that no man may stand before a god without reverence! No man may raise a fist to a god without retribution! No man may—"

The gunshot hung in the air for a long, tense moment, and no one, not even the abomination staring down at Nathan, seemed to realize it had happened for several frozen seconds. Arlington Fitch's face caved in, the back of his head exploding in a geyser of shredded tissue and bone. His arms remained raised as he fell, the faceless body splayed backward in the dirt.

The first panicked scream broke the spell. More gunshots came from the corn, muzzle flashes illuminating the rows briefly before figures changed position. Nathan could hear voices. An old man's voice, raspy and grim, calling out from the corn. "It's been twenty years coming, you son of a bitch!"

Callum stepped into the clearing, working the bolt on Nathan's old Remington .308. The slide was smooth, and Callum's gnarled hands were poetry. He racked the bolt, chambered another round, and fired. The skinhusker shuddered and lurched forward, hunching over Nathan with a screeching roar. The pain in its black eyes was real. It remembered the last time it had been shot with that gun. Nathan had spent months researching, reading, learning. He etched every symbol, every charm, every sigil he could find into the wood. A powerful spell. This time it was Callum, Haley's father, who was hunting, and he wasn't alone. There were other voices. Nathan recognized Sheriff Darby among them.

The chaos unfurled around him. Robed cult members screamed as Darby, Callum, and the others rained lead into their ranks. Darby moved into the clearing alongside a pair of deputies. A clerk Nathan recognized from the grocery store was there with a rifle... the good people of Ash Fork finally making a stand.

The monster would not be deprived its revenge, however. It reached down, grabbed Nathan around the head and lifted until the two were eye level. They stared at each other for a long moment, and for the first time in his life, Nathan was unafraid. Here, now, staring the creature that had taken so much from him right in the eye, a sense of completion swept over him. Completion and calm. He screamed when the razor-tipped thumbs of the skinhusker plunged into his sockets, but he was not present for it. He was too focused, too deep inside himself to be cognizant of the pain. He willed his arms to move, and his hands came up to grasp the sides of his nemesis's head. His own thumbs found the black pools there, and sank deep. The skinhusker screamed with him, and the two danced a wild jig, screaming together before careening into the bonfire, spilling flaming logs and cinder. The flames leapt high into the sky, smoke billowing into the blackness above.

The fire burned for days, jumping from one corn field to another. Every time the fire seemed squelched, flames would flare up in another field, until, finally, all the fields around the town were charred black and lifeless.

That was the last summer Ash Fork ever tried to grow corn.

LOST AND FOUND

J. B. TONER

Midway along the journey of this life,
  I found myself alone in a dark wood...

— THE INFERNO, DANTE ALIGHERI

It's a weighty thing, walking east at nightfall. Behind you, the rising streetlight-yellow meets the sinking crimson sunlight in a turmoil of purple and orange, but with every step, you slide the black canopy across that seraphic pandemonium. And nobody takes Darkwood Road except at nightfall.

As Sarah Crofton walked swiftly along the weed-cracked asphalt, the town capsizing into shadow at her back, two strong and slender figures glided along at her right and her left. The right-hand figure was a lady in blue, robed up to the chin but with a waterfall of dark hair that swept down her back, unstirred by the evening breeze. Her face was solemn, beautiful, untouchable. The left-hand figure was identical, but her robe was red and open at the throat, and a tiny smile curved her lips. None of them spoke.

The gibbous moon was in the treetops when Sarah came to the edge of the woods, and the cold conflagration of the starlight had begun. She passed beneath the branch-roof without slowing her stride. The lovely ones held position at her flanks. In silence, I followed.

Soon they were deep enough into the wood that hardly any light could be seen through the boughs. Then Sarah turned left and departed from the road. The shadow enfolded her, and no mortal eye could have tracked her movements any further. But her entourage kept pace, and did not snap even a single twig along the way.

"Why, Sarah?" whispered the lady in blue. "You can seek yourself in other ways. Better ways."

"No, Sarah," whispered the lady in red. "This is the way: the pathless way. In losing yourself, you will find what you seek."

She moved slowly, her hands out in front to push away face-biting branches. Her feet stumbled over rocks and roots, but she kept her balance. Above her in the leaves, owls murmured.

"You might as well turn back, Maryaela," the red lady remarked. "She won't be needing you out here."

"Here more than ever," said the other. "What she thinks she wants isn't what she's truly looking for."

"She wants the Numinous, of course. The mysterious, the otherworldly. You could give her that, but you won't."

"And you would give it, but can't. Yours is a false mystery, Monika. Glamour without substance."

"We'll see."

In silence, I followed.

The night air grew cool. Sarah proceeded on her way awhile longer, finally coming to a halt in the trackless depths. Then she raised her hands to unbutton her blouse. On her sleek skin, a single beam of moonlight glimmered pale. Her hands sank lower, slipping her skirt down over her feet.

"Yes," Monika urged. "Open yourself to the secret. Give yourself to the darkness. Find your soul."

"Sarah, you're losing yourself," Maryaela mourned. "You're losing everything."

Naked in the shadows, Sarah raised her arms above her head. Stretching exultantly toward the skies, letting her hair fall free. Wide open to the spirits of the night. Around her, the air grew dense with the Numinous.

Monika hissed: "*Yessssssss.*"

It was time. I came ponderously from the dark tree trunks, reaching. My parts encircled the two robed ones, and they saw me too late.

"A Numivore!" Maryaela cried.

Curling tightly around their bodies, squeezing them like ripe fruit.

"No!" shrieked Monika.

Lifting them high above me, high above my maw. I squeezed and squeezed, till the essence burst forth and dribbled down my slavering chin. The powers of light and darkness mixed in a delectable vintage. Squeezing, squeezing. Every drop.

Sarah lowered her hands, frowning. She looked around as if coming out of a trance. She scratched her head and spoke. "Hello?"

In silence, I departed.

THE LAND OF LORE

MELODY GRACE

"The most merciful thing in the world, I think, is the inability of the human mind to correlate all its contents. We live on a placid island of ignorance in the midst of black seas of infinity, and it was not meant that we should voyage far," I said into the darkness.

I was recently cast the narrator of the theatre's adaptation of *The Call of Cthulhu*. I'm a frequent flyer when it comes to these plays, and therefore given access to the theatre after close to practice my lines. I find a special calmness in its solitude.

I flipped the pages in my hand, staring out into the nonexistent crowd when something caught my eye. In the fifth row of chairs from the stage, almost in the middle, sat a lone book that I knew hadn't been there earlier. Was someone in there with me?

"Hello?" I called out into the dark. Silence answered me in return.

I sighed and made my way off the stage and toward the chairs. "Fine, I'll bite," I mumbled as I reached the right row. Scooting through the tight space, I finally reached the mysterious book and gasped. It was one of my childhood favorites: *Abadeha: The Philippine Cinderella*.

I smiled, hugging the book tightly to my chest as memories of my mother reading it to me as a little girl came flooding into my mind. The nostalgia quickly vanished once I opened it up. Pictures of dark creatures had replaced the story of Cinderella. It was a whole different tale, with the only similarity being the cover itself.

Closing the book, I turned toward the stage only to find it gone. In its place stood a lonely red door encased by nothing at all, simply a relic in the void. I looked around the theatre to find that it too, was part of this black hole. My legs began to tremble as I slowly walked towards the crimson beacon. With shaking hands I reached for the knob and turned it gently.

Creak.

The door responded in protest as it opened wider. My heart thudded rapidly in my chest as I peeked inside. I was met with the earthy smell of pine and dirt. I sighed, giving one last look to the emptiness behind me before stepping through.

The forest was brighter than the theatre at least. The moon hung low while the trees were blanketed by a thin layer of fog. I glanced down at the book in my hand and shivered as I opened it again. This time the pages were blank. What was happening?

Before I had time to truly question my surroundings, I heard the cry of an infant off in the distance. My feet started moving towards the sound as my maternal instincts kicked in full force; I needed to find that baby.

I pushed through the brush as the child wailed, my compass in the night. This went on for a good ten minutes before the moon cast a glow onto a hole in a tree. I glimpsed the corner of a blanket within. As I approached, the crying stopped.

With shaking hands, I reached into the hole and wrapped my fingers around a lump covered by a soft blue blanket. It squirmed at my touch as it began to coo at the embrace. "Who the hell leaves a ba—"

My heart stopped.

Staring up at me was not a child. I'm not even sure it was human. Red eyes and sharp teeth sent my adrenaline rushing. My breath sharpened like the wind. The monster grinned, then leapt out of my arms and onto a tree branch above my head. It was ready to devour its prey.

I took off running into the night, the devil baby on my heels. "Zigzag, Kathy, come on," I chanted, out of breath.

Then a building became visible through the trees: a small hut just off in the distance. I raced towards it.

I reached the door and barreled through the door—no time for niceties. Luckily, it was empty. The creature scratched hard on the side, letting out a loud shriek of betrayal. I looked down at my hand and realized I was still holding the damn book from the theatre. But something seemed off.

I opened the pages to reveal a picture of the demon child and the word *Tiyanak* scrawled above it in red ink. What the hell was going on? I could feel the panic rising in my chest.

Then, something moved within the cabin.

My wide eyes scanned the empty space before they stopped on her: a small lady sitting in the far end of the room. She was silently rocking back and forth, as calm as could be.

"Kathy, so happy you could join me," she croaked as she extended her bony hand towards me.

"H-how do you know my name?" I whispered.

The old woman looked at me and smiled with two rows of yellow crooked teeth. My stomach churned. "Oh, my dear, I've been *waiting* for you for ages."

I gave her a once-over before folding my arms tightly around my shivering body. "Where am I?"

"Why, you are in the lost land, of course!" she bellowed. "A place where stories go to die. Not for much longer, though. Soon, soon they will all know."

With a wave of her hand, the woman began to chant in a low, muffled tone. I couldn't make out the words, but I knew they meant trouble. Within seconds, the floor beneath me began to shake with a fury. Bugs began to pour through the cracks, little black creatures with beady red eyes that seemed to jerk in all directions.

The lady stood from her chair and as they surrounded her, she let out a maniacal laugh. I stumbled backwards, tripping over a stool and landing on my back just in time to see the shrew lock eyes with me.

"Ipasok," she mumbled, and the bugs turned towards me. Before I had the chance to move, they began to enter me. My eyes, my ears, my mouth; I couldn't breathe as they filled every orifice.

Eyes closed, my whole body began to ache as I pleaded with the witch to make it stop. She cackled at my agony for a long while before she raised her hands in the air, causing the bugs to retreat.

I looked up. The woman smiled at me with the most sinister expression I could imagine. I closed my eyes once more and then she whispered, "You better wake up, Kathy. Wake up. Before you forget how to…"

My eyes burst open when I felt the last of the bugs leave my body. To my surprise, I was back in the theatre. I frantically patted my arms and legs, feeling myself out to make sure I was okay. I let out a long sigh of relief when I didn't feel any bugs.

Then the book caught my eye.

I crawled over and opened it, revealing a picture of the old woman. Her haunting smile caused a feeling of dread to wash over me. Above her picture was the word *Mambabarang*. I flipped to the next page, hands trembling as a loud popping sound began to fill my ears. My heart sank into my gut as I read the words:

A Mambabarang is an evil witch who conjures spirits in the form of insects. Once they enter the body of her victim, they will terrorize every inch with immeasurable pain. Only when they leave the body will the victim be free.

Unless, of course, they left behind eggs...

CAIRN LAKE

JOHN HIGGINS

Deep in the North Woods of Maine, skirting the western edge of the vast forest was Cairn Lake. The mosquitos, black flies, and hordes of no-see-ums were too bothersome for all but the heartiest of hikers. People who found their way back to the lake never stayed more than an hour or two, and never at night, when the insects really swarmed. Snakes seethed on its shore, and thick moss grew over every rock and up every tree within twenty feet of the waters. Some claimed it radiated tendrils of life even in the deep freeze of winter—although deep snow made for impassible roads, so no one really knew what Cairn Lake did in the colder months. It was just a story people told.

For nearly 200 years, loggers have encroached on the land—and in fact, the Cooper Brothers Logging Company had owned the land for as long as loggers had been in this part of the country. But they could never get within a quarter-mile of Cairn Lake.

When the loggers got too close, machines broke down, saws grew dull, axe heads flew off the handles, and in many cases, people died—usually by a dead-fall. The ones who didn't get crushed succumbed to a sickness that by the mid-1800s was known as the "Cairn Lake Cough"—a mild understatement for men who would be suddenly short of breath in the morning, then blue, cold, and dead by nightfall.

But since only loggers were afflicted, most folks never heard of the sickness.

In 2003, the logging business in Maine began its long death march, losing out to competition from Brazil and China. It was then that the Cooper Brothers decided it was time to unload that useless tract of land, which would make enough money to keep the business going for another couple of years.

Dan Miller and Teddy van Buren were freelance surveyors sent up to stake out the land and prepare it for the real estate market. Dan was a few years older than Teddy, and had a boatload more sense than his partner. Dan made the deals. Dan shook the hands. Dan made the promises, and Dan signed the contracts. Teddy mostly drank his money and otherwise barely kept the roof over his head. They had been childhood friends, but as far as business partners went, Dan wished he had a few more folks to choose from. But Teddy was the only other certified surveyor Dan knew, and of course that entanglement of being friends for twenty years complicated matters.

It was 8:30 on a Monday morning in August, while on their way to the site, that they encountered their first obstacle.

"Holy shit," Dan muttered, bringing the pickup truck to halt deep in the woods. They had been riding on an old logging road—little more than two ruts worn into the earth—when the road abruptly ended in a stand of trees.

"What?" Teddy roused from the passenger seat. He had been dozing, hoping to sleep off a hangover. His eyes burned as he opened them. "Where the hell is the road?"

Dan sighed and put his cigarette out in the ashtray. "It just fuckin' stops." He looked up at the barrier. "Those trees gotta be a hundred years old, at least. Big fuckers."

"Well where the hell does the land start?" Teddy reached down and fumbled through the portfolio lying on the dirty floor of the fifteen-year-old Ford. He pulled out a satellite map. "Look." He pointed at a spot on the map and shoved it toward Dan. "You can see the road ending right here." He lifted his index finger to the trees in front of them. "That's where it starts."

"Shit." Dan groaned and looked around at the corridor of forest. The narrow road was barely wide enough to accommodate their pickup. "That means when we're done, I have to back all the way out. That's like two miles." He dropped his head. "Son of a bitch."

"Look, it's a two- or three-day job, anyway. We'll set up the tent back here, start on the edge and work our way in. Worry about getting out later. I got a hatchet, so I can probably take down a few of these smaller trees on the side to give you a turnaround before we go."

Dan nodded. The trees on either side were younger and smaller than the ones blocking his path. With a little elbow grease, they could manage something. It wasn't typical to camp out for a surveying job, but for remote areas like this, it had to be done. It made for a long couple of days, but the pay was fantastic. He had planned on being able to drive into the site, but the hike wouldn't kill them. "Let's get started."

They set up their tent behind the truck, sprayed on their bug repellant, put on their face netting, and grabbed the survey equipment along with a backpack full of ribboned stakes.

Everything went according to plan that day. The bugs were thick, the air was humid, and both men had their share of mosquito bites despite the repellant. But they were ahead of schedule and damn tired when they bedded down for the night.

Dan woke suddenly to the utter darkness of the North Woods. He had the vague impression that something had woken him. He sat up and listened to the droning hum of tree frogs and katydids… and Teddy's soft snoring from some-where in the darkness.

Nothing sounded out of place.

He tucked into his sleeping bag again when he heard a sound from the woods —a slow crashing and a thump, like a big tree falling. It was distant, but loud enough to probably wake him.

"Widow-maker," Dan whispered. The sound of his voice was a small comfort. *Probably some deadfall*, he thought.

Teddy snored, unfazed. He had brought a bottle of vodka in his duffle bag to "help him sleep," as he said. It seemed to be working.

But Dan's heart was pounding. He had camped countless times in his life, but the noise out here was something he'd never experienced. The droning, croaking, and buzzing of the insects against the tent walls seemed to press in on him, as though it grew louder the longer he listened.

He closed his eyes and tried to relax his mind, to drift away from the anxiety. It was nothing but the sounds of the woods. It just seemed louder because he was keyed up. Maybe it was a dream that had woken him.

Branches snapped.

Wood creaked.

Crash.

This was still distant, but closer.

Dan held his breath and listened. He could believe it was another deadfall, but it would take some convincing. Deadfalls weren't all that common, especially on a calm, clear night like tonight.

Something scurried past his tent on small feet, maybe a raccoon. It doubled back and came close to the tent wall on Teddy's side. Other scurrying feet followed and slowed as they approached.

Dan could hear them move around the edges of the tent.

Something low to the ground pushed on the front tent flap. It was zipped, but a corner at the top left was left undone, exposing the screen layer. Dan had left it that way to let in the night air.

He tried to get a handle on how many tiny feet were moving through the dry leaves around the tent, but could only guess. *Probably sounds like more than it is,* he told himself.

Distant wood creaked, branches broke, another crash to the ground.

Closer, now.

"Okay," Dan muttered. He patted his hand around in the dark until he found his .30-30. Only a fool would camp this far out without some kind of protection, either against wildlife or humans… and Dan prided himself on not being a fool.

He sat up and pulled the bolt back as quietly as possible to chamber a round.

The scurrying noises in the leaves stopped. Again, Dan held his breath.

One by one, the sounds of the creatures walking the perimeter of the tent receded into the surrounding woods. Maybe it was the human sound of the gun that the animals recognized. Dan waited several long minutes for the creatures to retreat into the night, until only the sounds of the droning katydids and tree frogs remained.

He settled back down and listened to the night for another half hour before drifting off to sleep.

"Hey, get the fuck up. Jesus." Teddy was at the entrance of the tent, kicking Dan's foot.

Dan woke in the same position he had been in when he'd fallen asleep. He sat up, muscles stiff. Bright sunlight streamed in through the open flap. "What time is it?"

"Like, seven-thirty. Dude, I've been waiting an hour for you. C'mon, let's get this done and get the hell out of here. These bugs are killers."

Dan stood up and pulled on his boots.

Teddy handed him a mug of coffee. "That's all that's left. I saved it for you."

"Shit," Dan said after taking a sip. "It's like coffee syrup."

"I didn't say it was good."

Dan finished the gritty liquid and left the tent. He scanned the ground to get a clue of what might have been out there. There were no tracks he could see, and he didn't want to crouch down and get a real good look, because then he'd have to tell Teddy what had happened… and in the light of day, his terror from last night seemed ridiculous.

The men didn't say anything as they gathered their equipment and headed out for the lake. The closer they got, the more aggressive the insects became. No-see-ums were starting to get into the protective face masks, and clouds of mosquitos came at the webbing in what looked to be almost organized sorties.

"Christ," Teddy said after a while. "Who the hell would buy property out here?"

Dan shook his head. "This land butts up against some huge tract of private property on the other side, and I think Cooper Brothers is hoping to get it sold to whoever owns that land. Who wouldn't want to own a lake?"

"Goddamn mosquitos will drain your dry before you get there. I ain't never seen it like this. These bitches are hungry."

"Oh," Dan said as they crested a ridge. "That's why it's called Cairn Lake." He pointed down the hill.

Teddy met him. "I don't even know what a fuckin' cairn is, but I see the lake."

"There," Dan pointed again. "That big pile of stone. That's manmade." There was a mound of stones standing over ten feet tall about twenty feet from the lake. Dan headed toward it.

"Hey," Teddy said. "Did it rain last night?"

Dan stopped and turned around. "No, I don't think so."

"Look at that." He pointed to a spot on the path down the hill. It was a large, muddy puddle about six feet across. The top of a tree had snapped and was now lying nearby. Teddy's eyes went up to where the tree had been broken. "I've heard of tornados doing something like that, but we damn sure didn't have a tornado. That break is fresh and nothing else is wet around here." He studied the ground. "Check that out." He trundled down to the broken tree top. "Wood's still green."

"I heard something last night," Dan grunted. "That must have been it."

"Weird."

The men continued down the hill and saw another large puddle and a tree that had been bent over so far that the trunk had splintered halfway up and fallen to the forest floor. They didn't spend much time examining it, although both men were unnerved.

The cairn was a tight piling of stones, carefully fitted together but not carved. Some of the stones had small pictures carved into them. "What the hell are those?" Teddy leaned in. The shimmering clouds of bugs made it difficult to clearly see through the netting.

"I don't know," Dan said, trying to get a good look at the small petroglyphs. "People, animals... I think."

"This shit is old, like native American or something. Micmac."

Something moved on Dan's periphery. He turned and saw someone run along the edge of the lake and disappear into the trees. "You see that?"

"Uh-uh." Teddy straightened and looked out at the lake. "What'd you see?"

"Somebody," the word trailed off as his left his mouth. "I think."

"Who the fuck would be all the way out here?"

Dan stood still for a while and watched for any more movement. "I should have brought the gun."

"I got some bear repellent and I think there's an air horn in the backpack." Black bears were pretty skittish, and loud noise was usually enough to drive them away.

Dan muttered an agreement, but he wasn't so sure it was bears that worried him. After a few more seconds of scanning the woods, Dan shucked the backpack, pulled out the map, and started working out a pattern for them to follow for the day.

"See that?" Teddy said as Dan crouched over the map.

"What?"

Teddy pointed to the lake. "I see someone out there, in the middle. Do you fuckin' see that?" He walked down toward the shore.

Dan stood and looked out across the placid waters. He slowly walked down and stopped next to Teddy. "I don't..."

"Yeah," Teddy said, resigned. "I don't see it anymore. Maybe it was the sunlight or something."

Dan's gaze dropped to the clear, green water. He placed his hand on Teddy's back.

"What's up?"

Dan's mouth went dry as he lifted his eyes to the other man. "Look." He nodded his head in the direction of the water.

"Jesus Christ," Teddy said as he scanned the shoreline.

Beneath the surface of the water, in the shallows and stretching out into the deepening murk, were piles of bones, large and small, coating the lake floor. Human skulls also littered the shallow water. Dozens of them.

Trees creaked behind them.

Teddy turned to see the trees bending and weaving themselves into a barrier, preventing them from leaving the water's edge. The wooden walls writhed and shifted, coming closer. Bark flaked off in chunks, revealing naked flesh under-neath—skin, bone, blood. Each great tree that bent to form the barrier sloughed its bark to reveal a tangle of flesh beneath.

Teddy choked back a scream and Dan felt his breath seize in his chest.

The thick tendrils pressed closer. Dan and Teddy pushed back, but the wall continued forward, shoving them relentlessly along the muddy banks and into the shallows.

Dan turned to run further up shore, but saw that all the trees around the lake were bending, stitching themselves into a woven wall around the water.

"What the fuck?" Teddy shouted, futilely shoving back against the trees. "*What the fuck?*"

Then a creature rose from the center of the lake, as tall as the trees, pale and shimmering. Bestial mouths and eyes covered the living slime from which many tentacles seethed; hundreds of teeth snapped at the cool morning air. With each mouth stretching, each jagged fang glinting in the sun, it reached for the two terrified men.

SEAGULLS

DMITRY KOSTYUKEVICH - TRANSLATED BY OLEG HASANOV

"Ruslan! Stop feeding them!" Aunt Masha grabbed Ruslan's thin wrist, and the boy nearly dropped the cookie. He pursed his mouth and looked plaintively at me.

I stroked my son's hair: never mind, it's just Aunt Masha's nature to boss people around, she's quick to temper and she tolerates no dissent, deal with it, kid, we're her guests here.

"They will fine you for feeding the seagulls here. These creatures aren't afraid of anything. It's simply unbearable. They can rip it from your hands."

A fat seagull was walking on the beach three feet away. I had never seen such big ones: they were well accommodated here on the Baltic Sea, and it was not a big deal that they were forbidden to be fed. They take a dive and they come up with their beak full of fish. Playing a sneaky trick on tourists is a piece of cake for them. They'll always get it their own way.

"They have a breeding season now," Aunt Masha said, glaring at the seagull. "They have to feed their young. That's why they're getting pretty brazen."

The bird clicked greedily with its yellow hooked beak. On its mandible was a red spot, like a ripening berry or a drop of blood. The seagull came a few steps closer on its webbed feet.

Ruslan pressed himself to my leg and hid the cookie behind his back. No chance for this winged fisher to have a Belorussian treat, left over after our trip from our hometown of Novopolotsk to this seaside German resort. And rightly so: I didn't feel like feeding this monster anymore. Obviously, they made a decent living on the shellfish, shrimp, and garbage.

I squawked and raised my hand. The seagull made a shrill shriek and soared upward. A long, wide shadow began sliding over the fine yellow sand and then over the wet shore.

"Wow." I whistled appreciation. "What a wingspread."

"It can extend to two meters," Aunt Mash said in a teacher's tone. She actually had worked as a teacher before moving to Germany. "I've read about it."

I took my cell phone and asked Google about seagulls. I followed the link "Attack of Seagulls on People" and ran my eyes over the article. "One of the explanations of seagulls' aggressive behavior is formic acid. After consuming flying ants, seagulls get drunk and become extremely badly-behaved…" I put the phone away. I leaned towards Ruslan and whispered in his ear. He brightened up and raised his inquisitive eyes to Aunt Masha.

"What's the German for seagull?"

"Möwe," Aunt Masha said, stretching the vowel "ö" out.

"Möwe," Ruslan repeated.

I couldn't help but tousle his fair hair again: he was a really smart boy. He should socialize with his peers more to integrate himself into society. But he was very sensitive, and I knew it would be hard for him at school.

"One more!" Ruslan exclaimed.

A seagull sat on the barrier of a tribune, which had been built to celebrate some occasion or other. Another one sat nearby. Dark spots on the head and wingtips, a snow-white belly, yellow and green feet, a short tail. Plump birds, good birds… good… this word seemed inappropriate.

"They make nests here on the roofs," came another fact from Aunt Masha. "Smart as dogs. Some of them distract you, imitating an attack, while the others calmly fly up and snatch food. Usually from children."

"Acting in cahoots," I said.

"Are seagulls dogs?" Ruslan asked.

Aunt Masha patiently began a thorough explanation.

I took out my camera from the bag, zoomed in, and captured its beaky profile.

Ruslan was already dying to run to the sea. Aunt Masha lay on the towel wearing a swimming suit and blouse. "It was in the papers that a week ago a woman was attacked by a seagull. Her head was pecked all over and her face was scratched."

I thought that a five-year-old didn't need to know such details, but I said nothing, as usual. We were her guests here (it was beginning to sound like a mantra). Though I hardly believe that our relationship would have been different in Novopolotsk, for instance, which Aunt Masha and Uncle Roma had left twelve years ago. Dragon ladies don't change patterns of behavior.

Aunt Masha and Uncle Roma were my school friend's parents. Their Jewish family had embraced the German citizenship entitled to them according to a program. My friend had gone off the grid, but a year ago he showed up, found me on the social media, and invited me over. To my amazement, I agreed. My wife Ksenia then insisted that I wake Ruslan with me to Rostock. The salt air would be good for him. She couldn't go with us because our summer vacation times didn't match.

And here we were, in the nice Hanseatic city of Rostock. We had gone by train to Berlin, then on to Rostock from there. Uncle Roma met us at the railway station. We left our suitcase and backpacks at their home, hopped on the train with Aunt Masha to Warnemünde, which used to be a fishing town and was now a seaside resort. Now we were admiring the Baltic Sea, which seemed to support the cloudless sky.

I never got to meet my friend. He suddenly had to fly off on a business trip to St. Petersburg, but he assured me that his parents would meet us, and show us the city.

And that's how it happened. It seemed that those twelve years had not passed. Uncle Roma still constantly made jokes. This was why Ruslan liked him right away. Aunt Masha was the leader and mentor.

"Don't play in the water too long," she instructed. "It's still too cool. Do you understand, Ruslan?"

Ruslan lowered his eyes and nodded.

"Good boy. When you come back there'll be a candy waiting for you."

"What should you say?" I asked my son.

"Thank you."

"You're welcome," Aunt Masha said with contentment.

I looked at the tribune. The barriers were empty. Huge *Möwe* were circling over the sun loungers and playgrounds.

The shoreline curved like a crescent. Along its entire length were people, sunshades, and loungers. Somewhere at the tip of the crescent I could see sunbathing nudists. On that score, the Germans were more relaxed. They were also crazy about getting tattoos. The scourge youth, as Aunt Masha put it. They covered their bodies with tattoos from head to toe.

On our right, two Frauen were drinking cocktails. Tattoos covered virtually all of the skin exposed to the salt air and hot sun. One of them was slim and beautiful. The other one was plump, her hair the color of swamp mud. Lesbies, by the look of them.

On the left was a man practicing yoga. On the wrong side of forty, lean, big-nosed. Smooth movements, closed eyes, dark shorts, white T-shirt. The lesbies nodded at the yogi, giggling.

Between us and the foamy edge of water, there was a badly sunburnt dad, who watched with a smile as his kid destroyed someone's sandcastle. Nearby, a group of teenagers smoked hookah.

Aunt Masha talked to a girl from whom a seagull had stolen a sandwich. The girl had come here from Georgia to work. I didn't hear more of their conversation as I ran with Ruslan towards the first sea he'd ever seen.

Within ten minutes, I almost had to use force to get Ruslan out of the salty happiness. His blue lips were a signal for that. I didn't have a chance to swim properly myself because I was backing up Ruslan during his fight with the waves.

"Wipe him dry," ordered Aunt Masha. "Put the dry underwear and the sunhat on him."

I wish Ksenia were here, I thought. I would sprint as far as possible and take cover in order to avoid the explosion caused by the inevitable altercation between her and Masha.

"We'll take a walk."

Aunt Masha nodded, propped herself up on one elbow above her towel, wiped the sand off its edge and began scolding Uncle Roma over the phone: why he had forgotten to give them the beach umbrella, and the buckets and spades for the kid wouldn't hurt. Poor Uncle Roma... Though why poor? He's comfortable... he is so unpractical on the surface, so soft and kind, he so reminded me of... myself.

I sneered internally and said, "Well, where shall we go, traveler?"

"To the rescue station!"

"Deal."

Narrow paths winded between the vacationists. I looked for stones of unusual shape to make Ruslan happy. Here and there we stumbled upon topless young, and not so young, Frauen who had obviously been reluctant to go to the nudists' area. A fair-haired and big-breasted woman was taking selfies, her boyfriend sitting beside her and drinking beer.

I focused on searching for the stones. I found one that looked like a bird wing and wanted to call Ruslan, but couldn't see him anywhere. My heart skipped a beat, the strong muscle painfully straining. But then I saw the familiar red sunhat flashing ahead, and it was over.

What a panic-monger I am, I cursed myself, but it was hard to overcome hyper-protection—it's always the same story.

Ruslan, milling around the two-story rescue station, peeked into the open door. The floorboards there were shining with soap. A beefy girl clad in shorts and a tennis shirt was handling a duster. Silly ideas about Pamela Anderson from the "Baywatch" TV show popped into my head. I shook my head and without thinking put the stone into the pocket of my swim shorts, having forgotten to show it to Ruslan.

There was noise and flapping sounds up above.

A seagull came down on the rails of the observation deck and froze proudly against the backdrop of a lonely cloud.

"Möwe, Möwe, Möwe," I beckoned like they beckon pigeons —coochie-coochie-coo.

The seagull scowled at me with black beady eyes. I groped in my pocket for the stone, just in case.

"Dad, what are these things called?"

"What things?"

"Over there… like life jackets, only not really life jackets. The rescuers wear them."

Ruslan pointed at something inside the room. Finally, I understood what he meant.

"I don't remember what it's called." I was upset: Dads should know everything. I wanted to Google it, but I had left my cell in the bag (internet roaming was the only thing that I concealed from Ksenia during the trip). "This thing is like a lifesaver. A buoy, I guess… Rescuers throw it to those who are drowning, and drag them to the shore."

Ruslan heard me out, then rushed around the corner. He spotted a beach quad bike.

I looked back to see where Aunt Masha was. We had walked a good distance off; the tribune was the landmark, quite far away.

Ruslan was not to be seen around the beach vehicles. Maybe he had found himself a new object for investigation; they were quad bikes, after all!

I walked around the building, found myself near the open door and began worrying.

The sounds of the seashore changed. They became restless somehow, almost hysterical. I brushed this thought aside. There were more important things to think about.

Ruslan was nowhere to be found.

I felt a lump in my throat. My heart strained again. Not one muscle, but three, five…

Right and left, people were screaming. A heavy wide shadow crawled on the sand. I didn't look up, didn't turn back at the screams. My eyes registered a red ball, a red backpack, red swimming trunks… My eyes deceived my brain. My ribs seemed to squeeze my trembling weak intestines.

"Ruslan," I called, running around the rescue station for the second time. "Ruslan! Ruslan!"

I ran into the damn quad bike.

Someone screamed. Shrilly, grievously, womanlike.

What the hell was going on there?! I jerked my head around.

A stout elderly woman pointed her finger to the sky, her bulldoggish cheeks shaking. One after another, the people around began paying attention to what was pointing at.

I followed the woman's finger, wishing to get it over with as soon as possible and find my son. He couldn't have gone far. Maybe he was hanging around bouncy castles or slides…

And then I saw.

Ruslan.

Ruslan, hanging from a crooked flat-sided beak of a gigantic seagull. His little round mouth opened and closed. This only happened when Ruslan was very scared. Once, he'd run onto a road and found himself engulfed by the sounds of car horns and screeching brakes. No screams, no tears, only his mouth, opening and closing.

The bird, the damn Möwe, was monstrous, unreal. Not a seagull but the Andean condor from Jules Verne's "In Search of the Castaways." No, much bigger, with wider wings. A prehistoric bird, Pelagornis or… but whatever it was, surely it was too small to carry a child up into the air! My Ruslan! But it had picked him up, picked him up and flown off. How? How could it be possible? What was it? Magic or antigravity?

The seagull struggled to gain height, now falling down, now going up with a jerk. Jerk, falling. Jerk, falling. With prey. With my son.

A man jumped up and tried to catch Ruslan by the leg but he couldn't reach him. The bird was cruising along the shore, but could fly away into the sea at any moment. Ruslan's sunhat dropped off his head and glided down on the sand like a red spot, a wound without the body.

I ran after the seagull with its wings curved slightly into the air, noticing that the black feathers made it look burned. The sharp hook of the beak dug in my son's T-shirt collar. I guess I shouted something, wild, incomprehensible threats to this monstrous Baltic thief.

I couldn't see Ruslan's eyes anymore. No sooner had the realization hit me than the Möwe turned towards the sea after all. A little more and it would…

Almost without thinking, I grabbed the first thing within my reach and threw it at the seagull.

The folding seat made an arc in the air and landed right on the bird's back, hitting its wings and spine. I jumped up in surprise and joy. Though it was too early to celebrate just yet.

The yellow beak opened. Ruslan fell in the water.

And immediately disappeared under the arriving wave.

I rushed to him, struggling through the cold resilient water, trying not to lose sight of the landing point. I assured myself that it was not deep there, only up to Ruslan's neck. I prayed that somehow, by some miracle, he wouldn't panic and splutter, he wouldn't…

I cried and rammed through the waves. Just a few more feet. Just a little bit more.

For a brief moment, there was a question on the edge of my mind. It quickly disappeared in the slimy seaweed. The beach, I saw, had nearly disappeared from view.

I dived, opened my eyes and saw a pale spot. Ruslan's shirt! My hand came up against Ruslan's back. I came up and pulled...

On my chest, his head over my shoulder, he began coughing and then crying. "Dad... da... will everything be all right?"

"Sure, little man. It's all over. Now everything's going to be okay."

I turned to the shore and understood that my promise was premature.

Seagulls attacked the beach.

Sweeping wings beat heavily in the air. The birds swooped down on the people, pinched and pecked them. Two seagulls lifted into the air a boy about seven or eight years old. He was coughing, arms and legs twitching. I had no pity for him left in me, no pity for anyone, except Ruslan.

A huge seagull hovered over a girl wearing an orange swimsuit. Attacked, pecked, and scraped. The girl raised her hands to protect herself and screamed. Her rangy boyfriend jumped up and struck the bird with his fist. In revenge, the smaller birds immediately descended upon him. The younglings with black beaks and striped bodies assaulted the couple with a shrill, blood-curdling yapping.

A wave hit me, and my knees buckled. I realized that I was standing and staring at the feathery hell. Standing just like those people in the sea when Ruslan fell in the water... Why didn't anyone hasten to rescue him? This was the question I'd thought of and then instantly forgotten, just moments ago.

We looked at the shore. At the crazy Möwe and their new hunger for human flesh. I noticed someone, trying desperately to hide from the swooping seagulls in the water.

Ruslan twined his arms around my neck so hard that I was suffocating.

"Close your eyes, son."

"I already did," he said seriously. "Why did the bad birdie attack me?"

"It's gotten too much sun." I made a joke but, of course, there was nothing to laugh about here. Nevertheless, Ruslan giggled into my shoulder. I wish I were so brave...

I wanted to close my eyes just like my son. To avoid watching seagulls ripping juicy bright pieces off the face of a girl crumpled near an overturned lounger. To not see the people in swimming trunks and dripping suits running to their neat hotels where gulls surged on the balconies, surging around the helpless guests like bees around a burning hive. To block the sight of the big-nosed yogi crawling our way, his T-shirt torn on his back, his eyes wide open but blind, mangled by the beaks.

Without putting Ruslan down, I leaned down and picked up a folded sunshade. Using it as a stick, I drove off a seagull from the back of the man's neck. There was nothing else I could do for him.

A shadow dashed from above and scraped my head, bringing pain. I touched my right temple. There was blood on my fingers. The wretched creature had torn off a piece of my scalp!

Everything was swarming under my feet. Salt stung my eyes. It was hard to see where I stepped. A crumpled towel, a smashed plastic cup with a pink umbrella on a toothpick, the fat tattooed frau sprawled between rows of roofed beach chairs. The seagulls were all over her—tearing and spitting out her tattoos. Her skinned and bloodied body shook convulsively, her green hair matted with blood.

The sky screamed and roared with rage.

I hid Ruslan's head on my chest. My hand came across an umbrella. I opened it and ducked under it. This didn't stop the seagulls, but at least they were ripping not me but the nylon, beating against the dome.

For a few moments, I lost direction and found myself in front of a stone breakwater. I whirled around, having no idea where Aunt Masha was, or if I should be looking for her at all. The main thing was to get Ruslan out... to save him...

Aunt Masha found us herself.

"Come on! Follow me!"

She dragged me by the elbow—a short, strong-minded, and resolute woman. The left side of her face was stained with blood and wet sand. For the first time, I sincerely believed that everything would be all right.

"Where?" I said, gasping.

"To the lighthouse!"

The old lighthouse earned the city two Euros per person. We had planned to explore it and other places of interest tomorrow.

"Dad, have the birds flown away?"

Ruslan could hear that the answer would be negative, but I lied. "Almost."

"I want my mommy."

I did too.

There was a man lying on the wooden boardwalk. The birds had stolen his face. Bit by bit. After pecking his eyes out, they even took a few of his teeth.

I turned around to avoid looking at the prone bodies, and regretted it immediately.

My heart nearly fell out of my mouth, as Ruslan once put it.

Between the shore and the horizon, I saw was a motionless ship on the waves. A flesh red color inscription "GOTTX" ran across its side. The vessel reminded me of a rusted hopper train car with a T-shaped mast, above which the seagulls circled. Hundreds, thousands. Some of them could have been gigantic Tolkien eagles.

As I watched, they formed a horrible cloud.

The cloud shrieked. A devilish sharp sound, in which you could hear laughter, crying, whining, and the creaking of forgotten doors.

Some of the birds flew to the cloud. Others flew out of it towards the seashore. To the feast.

I stumbled. I was saved from falling by Aunt Masha.

The lighthouse door didn't budge. Aunt Masha drummed on it with her mighty fists. She shouted something in German and in Russian, beating and kicking the door.

And it opened.

A scrawny gray-bearded old man let us in and bolted the door shut.

I put Ruslan on the floor and slumped down against the wall.

Space inside was terribly cramped. In the well of the lighthouse, there was only enough room for a table and a stand with souvenirs. A spiral staircase stretched along the walls, so narrow it would be hard for people to pass each other.

"May I open my eyes?" Ruslan asked.

"Yes," I said unwillingly, as if a longer answer would kill me. My arms hung listlessly. My breathing was labored.

My son looked at me. There was fear in his eyes, the worst fear in the world, a child's fear.

Far above our heads, there was the sound of broken glass. The seagulls beat against the narrow windows and attacked the observation deck.

Aunt Masha was asking the old lightkeeper about something. She wanted to know under what conditions we would have to hold the line.

Round lamps illuminated the inside of the lighthouse. The light was sickly yellow.

How much time till sunset? And what would it bring with it?

The black, oily, foreign word "GOTTX" was circling inside my head.

Aunt Masha put her bag by her side. I saw my cell phone sticking out between the hastily rammed clothes.

I took it and asked Google at what time do seagulls go to bed.

SOME OLD PEOPLE IN MY VILLAGE DON'T HAVE FINGERS

MOHAMMED KHAN

Some old people in my village don't have fingers. If you were to ask them why, they'd tell you the story of Bobo.

Bobo was a cruel man, born with a black and twisted soul. But Bobo was also gifted. He was gifted with the love of all who saw his handsome face or heard his gentle voice

When he was young, he would steal gifts from his friends. Later, sometimes that same day, he'd show the stolen item to them, surrounded by his companions. When the victim voiced his villainy, Bobo would refute, "No. This is mine. You must be mistaken."

His friends would trust him faster than a heartbeat and turn on the accuser. Poor old Bobo, constantly under attack. Why couldn't they leave him alone?

This was Bobo's game in youth. As horrible as it was, Bobo got bored. So, as he got older, his games got messier.

In his village, very occasionally, a child would go missing. The next night their parents would be invited to dine at his mansion.

They'd be served lavish meats, meticulously garnished and marinated. Midway through the meal, he'd tell them the truth. He'd tell them they were eating their own children.

You see, his voice was so magical by now that he knew he had nothing to fear. When he asked them to continue eating, they would. The parents would laugh and joke with Bobo as they fed on their progeny.

Bobo played his games many times in the village. No one could stop him, or even bear a grudge against him. Who could hate his voice?

A drunk.

A drunk hated him.

This drunk had been one of the victims, and lost his daughter to Bobo's games. In sobriety, he loved Bobo like all the rest. Only in his drunkenness did his true feelings surface and bubble over into drunken tirades for all to hear.

One day, his tale came to the ears of a Judge: The Red Judge of Paris, who said, "Bobo must hang till death."

Upon hearing this, the drunk sobered up and began to weep, begging the judge for leniency for his daughter's murderer. Grabbing onto the Judge's leg, he hollered, "Please! I swear my soul to you, spare him! "

"All right. I promise you. Bobo will not be arrested."

With that, the drunk fell to the ground in a relieved stupor, leaving the Judge to think.

The old Judge knew that arresting a man so charismatic would be impossible for him. That did not mean he'd forgotten, nor forgiven. Already, a plan for Bobo's punishment had formed.

The Judge visited the house of an old woman. She had been a seamstress in her younger days, and now lived alone in her hut at the edge of the great forest.

The Judge gave her instructions for the punishment and in return, gave her a single copper coin. "Take it as the soul of the drunkard. A sin coerced is a sin nonetheless. "

The woman swallowed the coin and gave the Judge a smile, baring blackened teeth and brown gums, like gravestones in a cemetery. The Judge did not return it.

That night, when Bobo was in his bed, the window to his bedroom flew open. In crawled the old woman on all fours, moving like a thing that had forgotten how the human body functioned.

Bobo did not call for his guards, for he wasn't afraid. Instead, he begged with his beautiful voice and cried with his beautiful eyes for mercy.

His voice did not work, for the woman was deaf.

His looks did not work, for the woman was blind

His tears did not work, for the woman was a witch.

The woman carried out her work, deforming his face with her thread and needle. She cut his tongue out with her scissors and pressed her boiling hot iron against his scalp to leave him permanently bald.

When morning came, his guards found a pool of blood, and the window open wide. Bobo had run away, from shame and horror at his new reflection

He wanders the forests now in his disfigured form, cursed by the witch to live forever hungry, his face so ugly it scares even the dogs away.

This isn't his end.

If you see his hunched figure and blackened face among the trees, approaching you, you must run.

For Bobo's magic still hasn't left him.

His blue eyes are still charmed. If you let him get close enough to you, you will look into his eyes and fall under his spell.

You'll reach your hand to him. He'll bow down and kiss it like you were royalty. And one by one, he'll eat the fingers off your hand.

For some reason, even when he can satisfy his hunger entirely, he never does. He'll just leave you handicapped for the rest of your life.

I think it's because, even in death, he wants to laugh at us.

THE BOY IN THE WHITE SUIT

A. E. STUEVE

It was late, it was Halloween, and it was storming, but none of that bothered Arty. She had taken the night off from work, school, and family and she was going dancing. The club, a large and noisy place that called itself Speakeasy without a hint of irony, which therefore was ironic, was new and she knew the bouncer.

"Getting in for free," she whispered as she parked her car and sat, telling herself she was allowing the rain to let up before she got out. She gripped the steering wheel, determined, for once, to have fun. Some pop hit from the nineties teased from the speakers, trying with all of its one-hit-wondrous might to force her to believe that tonight was "gonna be a good night." It helped her stay determined. Determined, for once, to force the worry for her little sisters and brothers from her mind. Determined, for once, to let the anger at her deadbeat dad and dead mom not stand at the forefront of her emotions. Determined, for once, to enjoy the night like every other twenty-two-year-old in Chicago on Halloween. "I deserve this," she added and stepped out of the car, suddenly unconcerned about the weather.

The rain was cool and it would have been pleasant if it wasn't coming down so hard that it felt like daggers against her bare shoulders. She ran with purpose, quickly grabbing the high heels from her feet and splashing through puddles toward the line of eager club goers shivering in the storm.

As she ran by, several people called out to her, letting her know where the back of the fucking line was, telling her she wasn't getting in, asking her if she thought she was so much better than them.

She ignored it. Or rather, she forced herself to ignore it, thinking only of the release of hours on the dance floor, her body moving with the music, her sweat creating a glow on her skin, and this tight dress making her feel so Goddamn beautiful she might just go home with someone and have a one night stand. Man, woman, it didn't matter as long as they treated her right and made her feel the way she thought she was supposed to feel: young, free, and in love with living.

The bouncer, Vince, grinned at her. She waved. He motioned for her to come closer.

Around her people booed and groaned their frustration. It was hard to take many of them seriously in their ridiculous costumes, slutty this and slutty that.

"What's she got that we don't?" Arty heard someone shout.

She turned and opened her mouth, ready to ask who said that. She'd show them what she had, two fists and a foot that had kicked more balls than were hanging in that line.

Vince's large hand squeezed her shoulder gently. His face now up against hers, his grey whiskers scratching her cheek, he whispered, "Around back, sweetheart. Through the kitchen. They know you're coming. I can't let you in this way for free. If Broom saw, I'd be out of a job."

She lowered her head. She understood. Eyes on the pavement, heels dangling from her pink nails, she walked past the line of laughter.

The kitchen was a mess of savory smells, sizzling meat, and bright halogen relief from the storm. Chefs, cooks, and servers smiled at Arty. She was Vince's girl, which to them meant she was family.

"But you get out 'efore Mr. Broom sees," said a middle-aged woman with a girth as wide as her smile. She held out a small sandwich to Arty. "Vince's favorite."

Having grown up learning to always accept free food, it was more of an instinct than anything that caused her to reach out and take the sandwich from the woman she'd never met. She tasted it and decided she'd marry this woman if she could make her this sandwich for every meal of everyday for the rest of her life.

Before she could propose, though, Mr. Broom entered the kitchen. A stocky man with a suit as black as his beady eyes and a gaudy Jack-O-Lantern themed tie, Mr. Broom was not to be trifled with. He shouted something in some Eastern European tongue Arty couldn't place and stomped toward the sandwich woman.

"Who is this?" Mr. Broom insisted, hands on his hips.

"New cook," the sandwich woman said. "Suiting up now."

Mr. Broom's eyes slimed their way over Arty like a pair of hungry leeches. A crooked grin slipped up the corner of his mouth. "Good," he said.

The sandwich woman's own eyes darkened and she offered a stifled tut of derision that Mr. Broom ignored.

"I take her," the sandwich woman said. "Vince's girl," she added and Arty could've sworn there was something akin to warning in her tone. "Forget him," the sandwich woman said, pulling Arty along. "He monster." She waved back at Mr. Broom and she moved Arty through a maze of ovens, cooks, dishes splashing into soapy water, and the manic shouts of a kitchen in the mix of a rush. Unable to keep track of all of the twists and turns in this place, Arty let herself fall in behind the sandwich woman, enjoying the sandwich that was disappearing in her mouth. When she had taken the last bite, they reached black flapping doors with round windows in their centers. "Here," the sandwich woman said, "is where you dance," and gently shoved her through.

And it was everything Arty had wanted and more. The music was loud, the lights were magical, and the bodies on the floor with her danced and danced and danced. She bought a few drinks, laughed with people she barely knew, and lost herself in the moment in a way she didn't think she ever had.

It was when she was fully immersed in the joy of unconcern that the boy in the white suit caught her eye. His hair was dark. His eyes were blue. He stood straight, back against the bar, looking like an angel. For a Halloween costume, it was nothing fancy, just some dress slacks and a matching jacket over a white t-shirt. His shoes, Chuck Taylors, were also white. The boy's skin was pale, almost deathly, but he smiled at Arty in a rare way that didn't speak of predation.

She smiled back.

He approached.

The dance floor seemed to melt away from him as he walked. Arty's focus couldn't be pulled from his thin face. She would've scoffed at her feelings had they not been her own. But she loved him. She didn't know how it was possible. She didn't know why. All she knew was that he brought with him a great and overpowering safety and joy she could not deny. She hadn't said a word to him, nor he to her. Yet she loved him.

And they danced. They danced fast. They danced slow. They danced together. Talking very little, the two of them had an understanding that defied expectations and possibilities. She was his and he was hers and together they could do anything. With her heart beating an echo in her ears, Arty held him close and decided she would never let him go.

But, as happens at all clubs the world over, the bar closed down, the lights came on, and the dancers went their separate ways. All of them save Arty and her boy in white, the boy whose name she never got, whose personality she never knew, and whose voice she hardly heard. They stayed together, holding hands while other dancers parted ways. Though his hand was cold, his eyes were warm and his grip simultaneously soft and firm.

"I love you," she said to him as the music faded to little more than a memory of sound in her ears.

He smiled in return. "I love you," he said.

"Hey!" Mr. Broom's shout broke through the fantasy. They both looked to the sound of his gravel road voice and shock rounded Arty's eyes. "You're a cook!" Mr. Broom added, accusation charging.

"Uh…" Arty said.

The boy in the white suit's hand tightened in Arty's, and without a word he pulled her away from the approaching man. The crowd of people coming and going as the club closed was sea enough for them to get lost in and the boy in the white suit seemed to make people part as they approached, speeding and winding their way toward an exit. Mr. Broom's shouts and curses grew faint as he struggled to keep up through the masses. Before Arty could register anything other than fright, they were running outside away from the club in the opposite direction of her car.

When they had run around the block once, Arty told him she had to stop. "There's no way he's going to chase us this far," she said.

"What about the bouncer?" he asked.

"He is my friend," Arty said, and winked.

He laughed at this, his eyes twinkling in the small sea of street light surrounding them.

She laughed too before pointing out that her car was in the opposite direction.

"Let's walk to it then," he suggested.

She nodded and pushed a few strands of hair behind her ears. They walked together in the cool autumn night. Wet leaves crawled across the street along with a handful of tired dancers full of drink, their costumes falling off shoulders, their makeup congealing in dried sweat. A light mist clouded the street lights casting a strange ghostly glow on everyone. Everything felt slow now, silent save for spare chatter and the ending laughter of a night well lived.

"What's your name?" Arty asked. His hand in hers still felt cold.

"Marius," he said softly, his eyes on the ground.

"Do you have a car?" she asked. There was so much more she wanted to ask, so much more she wanted to hear. With no way she knew to express these desires, she settled for this question.

"No," he said.

She eyed him, squeezing his hand. "Do you... do you need a ride?"

He sighed. "I do."

She led him to her car silently. She didn't remember parking so far away from the club, but she had been pretty keyed up earlier. Now she was still nervous. But it was different. It was new. She shivered, whether from the cold, damp air, or from the whirlpool of emotions inside her she couldn't be sure.

"We're here," she finally said after what felt like an epic journey in the misty early am hours.

"Thank you for the ride," Marius said as he slipped off his jacket. "You look cold," he added. "Take this."

With cheeks reddening, Arty took the jacket. Though it was cold, holding it made her feel warm. "Thanks," she said, wrapping it around her shoulders. "The heater in my car doesn't work, so this is great. Are you okay, though?"

"I'm used to the cold," he said.

She nodded, unsure how to respond. "Well, let's get in." She rummaged through her purse, found her keys, and unlocked the car. "Where do you live?" she asked as they climbed in.

"It's not that far," Marius said. "Take Archer Avenue south."

"Sounds good," Arty said as they pulled out of the parking lot.

Driving in silence, Arty let her mind wander into territory she dreaded. She dreamed of marriage, of babies, of a quiet family life somewhere far away from Chicago and her mad father and wild siblings. She dreamed of embracing the relaxing, ordinary life. Putting this strange man in her car went against everything she believed. It was foolish. It was dangerous. Yet she felt safe. The jacket resting on her shoulders felt natural. It felt like home. It felt like her future.

Lost in thought, she was jolted to the present when Marius said, his voice almost a whisper, "Please pull over here."

"What?" she asked. "We're by the cemetery. We can't—"

"Please," he said.

She nodded as she slowed the car to the curb and put it in park. More worried than afraid, she studied Marius. "What's going on?" she asked.

"Kiss me," he said and leaned forward.

When their lips met, the cold of his skin mixed with the warmth of hers and a jolt rushed through her.

It was perfect.

He pulled away after what Arty felt was far too short a period of time. "Goodbye," he said simply and stepped out of the car. "I'm sorry." He turned.

She saw him walk toward the great gate of Resurrection Cemetery and didn't want to believe it as he disappeared through the bars.

She jumped out of the car and raced after him. Afraid finally. But not for herself, for him, for Marius. The gate was ajar and she squeezed through, catching a glimpse of his almost ethereal whiteness yards ahead. He appeared to be floating. She kicked off her heels and ran through the soft, wet grass after him. The cemetery was a series of hills that she charged down and struggled up, keeping after him, screaming his name, crying.

Then he was gone. But she stumbled on, the flashlight on her phone sending a bright streak through the hazy air. When she was about to turn around, about to give this up and curse herself for a fool, her light fell upon a tombstone.

Marius Bregovy
1910-1934
Murdered on Halloween
Loving Husband to Artemis

Arty dropped her phone and crumbled to the ground.

The next morning a groundskeeper stumbled upon her sleeping on the grave of Marius Bregovy, wearing the whitest jacket he'd ever seen.

JENNY GREENTEETH

STEPH MINNS

The drifting snowflakes fascinated Alice. Beautiful and silent, they fell around her like magical feathers from a shaken pillow as she stood in the hotel car park. She opened her mouth, letting them melt on her tongue, drinking up their beauty. It was the first snow of the season.

A window opened above, disturbing her childlike reverie.

"If it gets any heavier, promise you'll turn back," Chris, her fiancé, called down.

"I promise. Got to get these shots though. I'll be back by two."

Climbing into her Corsa, she dumped the camera bag and safety hat on the passenger seat and headed out onto the main road, her destination the old abandoned steel plant on the outskirts of Bolton. This project should be a good earner, she reckoned, a photo documentary of the declining industry of Northern England for *Workplace* magazine. The site was a classic abandoned factory on the banks of the River Tonge, a jumble of stark brick buildings from the 1960s. It would be a perfect subject for a photoshoot. Alice followed the factory owner's suggestion and parked the car in a nearby lay-by, the entrance road to the site having been sealed off some time ago. It was a surprisingly rural location, and Alice had to walk across a field and through a small wood to reach the property. Climbing through the broken point in the chain-link fence that the owner had mentioned, she began sizing up the blank-eyed buildings. The two main blocks of the factory had precarious metal walkways which crisscrossed the structures, linking them together. Apparently, it had been extended at some point. Now it sat deserted and brooding in the way only empty buildings can. The swirling snow added to the bleak atmosphere and the sense of desolation. Buddleias growing through the buckled tarmac of the car park were now dusted with fresh snow.

Alice clamped on her safety hat and pulled out her camera to take the exterior shots. She was aware the buildings could be dangerous now but there was probably a perfect shot inside, some image that would perfectly sum up the stark sadness of the place as it fell into ruin. She decided to risk it and headed for the nearest door, which hung like a broken arm on its hinges. Picking her way carefully around dangling cables and broken concrete that littered the floor, she realized that she could hear rushing water and guessed that the river was actually surging along one side of the building. She spotted a metal stairway that led up to a doorway above. It looked fairly solid in the light that filtered through the broken windows so she climbed up it and stepped out onto the continuing metal walkway that ran around the outside of the building.

Alice peered down at the raging river below. Heavy rain, coming down from the hills, had caused recent flooding and the river was at its highest now. Brown, dirty-looking, rolling large tree branches and other debris along in its path: a wire shopping trolley, the frame of a children's bicycle. Craning her neck to look downstream, the river appeared to slow and bend out of sight into the woods. A murky green pool lay off to one side, covered with weed, which she assumed had once been used as part of a cooling process. She thought this was a good photo opportunity, capturing the run of the metal walkway along the side of the building. As Alice sized up her shot, movement in the water below caught her eye and she peered over the railing, curious. It appeared to be a naked woman swimming in the river but, she reasoned, why would a naked woman be swimming in the snow in a dirty river on an industrial park? The lady was quite a way down, thrusting against the flow of the water, her long, skinny, pale limbs moving powerfully, putty-colored buttocks breaking the surface. Long dark hair floated around her head, clinging to bare shoulders. She started to swim towards a small jetty underneath the walkway, obviously intent on climbing out.

Alice became uneasy, realizing she was about to be confronted by a naked woman behaving oddly in the middle of nowhere. Something about the gangly figure scrambling onto the platform disturbed her. Crouching, the woman swayed towards the bottom rungs of the metal staircase that led up to Alice's walkway, moving so fluidly that it seemed unnatural.

The snow was falling heavily now, swirling around the side of the building in eddies and that, combined with the oddness of the figure now approaching, prompted Alice to shoulder her camera ready to leave. As she was about to turn for the doorway, the odd woman let out a shrill cry and made a dash up the stairs. Alice was close enough now to see the eyes: glassy, like those of a dead fish, seemingly too large for the face. The woman's green-tinged lips pulled back to reveal long hooked teeth.

Alice shied backwards, slipping in her haste on the icy metal, before she scrambled upright again and bolted for the door. Behind her, she could hear the creature scuffling along the walkway. She plunged back inside the factory, looking desperately for somewhere to hide in the hope she could evade it somehow.

Squeezing into a large upright tool cabinet, she pulled the door shut behind her, praying it would not automatically lock. Through the keyhole she watched as the gangling figure stopped dead in a shaft of dull light directly opposite her hiding place. She could see it clearly now. It looked like an old woman, a hag, with shriveled breasts, drooping belly and hooked, webbed hands. The fish eyes seemed to glow a pale green. The dripping hair had the same greenish tone, like stagnant pond slime.

Terrified, Alice tried to stifle her gasping breath as she watched the creature peer about the building, obviously looking for her. *Please, please just go, go away,* she thought. She could hear it grinding its teeth, could smell a rancid mackerel smell mixed with what reminded her of river mud and engine oil.

Shaking, Alice cringed back into the tool cupboard and her camera flash suddenly went off, triggered by the pressing of her hip. The flash startled her, causing her to shriek and the light momentarily blinded her in the confined space. Blinking away stars, she peered frantically through the keyhole again to see that the creature had turned towards her hiding place and was crouched, scrawny legs tensed as though ready to make a run towards it.

Alice panicked, kicked open the door and fled towards the exit, a dull rectangle of light in the distance. *Please, please let me make it.* She heard the thing start after her, could hear it muttering under its breath, some alien guttural tongue. Staggering out into the car park and daylight, Alice's hopes sank as she realized she had yet to make it out through the wood and across the field to the sanctuary of her car.

The chain link fence tore at her hair and arms as she squeezed back through the gap, but then she was off and running, legs pumping. Twice she slipped on the snow but sheer terror got her back up instantly and running again.

When she realized the abomination wasn't following her, she slowed to catch her breath. The narrow path, worn by many dog walkers' feet over the years, took her through the strip of woodland where a deep, gushing stream, an offshoot from the river, had cut its way. Still pools of dank, weed-clogged water gathered in places. Alice had jumped over a narrow part of the stream on her way in, but now she couldn't find it.

Desperation drove her on, but eventually she had to stop alongside one of the pools, disoriented, her lungs burning from the effort of the run. The alarmed calls of a crow sliced the air and snowflakes melted on her flushed face. When a hard, spiny hand grabbed her ankle she let out a shriek of terror. Looking down, she saw a scrawny, unnaturally long arm reaching out from the pool beside her, clutching her in an iron grip. She kicked at the arm, tried to stamp on the wrist, panic rising, but nothing seemed to shake it. The head of the abomination slid out of the water now, mouth splitting open in a frightening leer that revealed hooked teeth the color of pond weed. Alice tried to kick at the huge glassy eyes, but she lost her footing on the muddy bank and went down hard on her backside. Her nails broke as she clawed frantically to pull herself free, but her captor reeled her in slowly, like a determined fisherman pulling in a catch, and she slid under the water, slime and weed quickly filling her nose and mouth. Alice struggled for her life, clawing at the hands that had slid now to her shoulders, twisting her round towards the creature. For a moment, they faced each other through a bubble curtain formed from Alice's last breaths. Then it gripped her head between its skinny frog-thighs and held her until she drowned in the green, icy water and clinging weed.

The creature pulled its prize into the deeper water of the pool to devour it. Small children were always the best, juicy and easy to digest. Easier to catch, too, but times had changed as centuries had come and gone, and she'd had to change with them, venturing closer to inhabited areas and taking an adult on occasion. This one tasted good and she chewed it down ravenously. Now she could go back to the river and rest in the deeper water, sprawled newt-like on the bottom in the current, until the next time hunger stirred her from her deep green reverie to feed once more.

Note: The legend of Jenny Greenteeth is known across the western counties of Lancashire, Cheshire and Shropshire (also known as Wicked Jenny and Peg Powler). As with any folklore and legend there are variations on the same theme, but the story is that Jenny is a terrible creature living beneath the surface of stagnant and weed-infested ponds, always on the lookout for the unwary who stray near the water's edge. Her favorite prey is children, whom she pulls beneath the surface and drowns.

The character is likely the creation of parents in centuries past, wanting to scare their children away from investigating dangerous ponds.

CARNIVALS WERE DIFFERENT IN 1934

RHONNIE FORDHAM

1934 was a different time. Not just in Savannah, Georgia, but in America. We didn't have many luxuries back then. Or much optimism, for that matter. Not when we were in the midst of The Great Depression.

I turned ten that year, a product of a particularly pessimistic era. At the time, I lived with my older sister Helen. She was a nurse down at Candler Hospital and a self-made woman through and through. Even with the age gap between us, she had no problem letting me stay with her after our parents passed. Like a guardian angel, Helen protected me from the *real* horrors out there. At least when I was with her, I never felt threatened by the rampant poverty or crime.

Of course, that didn't mean I had it easy. None of us did then. Even at the tender old age of ten, I was working as a newspaper boy. The pay was all right, and *The Savannah Morning News* let us paperboys work around our school schedule. Still, the job was tough. This was a far cry from the idyllic suburban stereotype of a young boy riding his bicycle and tossing headlines to smiling neighbors. No, I was stuck in a much rougher district: Harris Street. A working-class neighborhood full of rough men and immigrants who were new to the city.

My friends and I ran Harris. There was me, Colin, John, and Ricky. Colin was the youngest and a real wise guy. He had Irish blood like me, only Colin looked more the part, what with his red hair and scrawny build. Loud and obnoxious, John wore glasses and was our comedian. He was constantly cussing and getting in fights.

But Ricky was our undisputed leader. Our captain. Ricky was thirteen, so he was a little older than the rest of us. A little taller and a little cooler as well. He'd been in Savannah his whole life and knew the city better than our resident hobos. Ricky was a good-looking kid. Muscular and charismatic. With straight brown hair, he had an electric smile and a soulfulness to those dark eyes. But most importantly, he looked out for us like a supportive older brother. Or like the father we never had.

If it weren't for Colin, I would've been the runt of the team. I didn't have strength or a tough-guy attitude. Instead, I had to rely on my own ingenuity to stand up for myself. But I worked hard. And above all, I was just glad to fit in with the guys. Just glad to have friends during these rough years.

I was pretty clever, if not exactly a whiz kid. I guess I wasn't a bad-looking boy. I did my best to keep my thick black hair combed to the side, emulating the likes of Clark Gable and Gary Cooper, even if I was half their size. Helen always told me my blue eyes and dimples would make me a hit with the ladies someday. And I guess she was right when I married my wife Carolyn fifteen years later.

But in 1934, having friends meant the world to me. I just wanted their respect. Especially Ricky's. And so I worked hard out there on Harris Street. Regardless of how scrawny I was, I could bark out those headlines with the best of them. And I always kept my pocket knife on me. The sharp blade was good for cutting strings off the bundles or perfect for protection against some of the rival paperboys.

But through it all, I felt safe. Or at least, around my friends I did; we had a buddy system. We had to; it's not like the cops would've helped four working-class punks anyway. The police weren't friends for anyone on Harris.

As I said, this was 1934. It isn't that were we unaware of murderers, robbers, or child molesters, or all of these other dangers. It's just no one wanted to talk about it, nor could we afford to let paranoia keep us from making money. We didn't have the time or energy to worry over these horrors. It took everything we had just to survive.

However, the constant struggle didn't keep us from having fun. I still had a blast growing up. Especially with my gang.

Around October of that year, we got ready for our favorite event of the season: the fall carnival. Fresh off seeing *King Kong* the previous weekend (scared the Hell out of all of us!), our excitement only grew higher.

Saturday soon arrived. And like caged animals released into the wild, my friends and I raced down to Savannah's fairgrounds on 10th Street. The carnival our escape from school, the hard work, and the stifling pall of the Depression itself.

We entered the abandoned lot, marveling at its sprawling array of tents and small rides. Whatever corners the carnival's signs and lights couldn't illuminate were lit by the nearby streetlights. The cool weather was perfect, the atmosphere electric; the carnival's aura enchanted everyone. Live music surrounded us. The smell of fresh sweets soothed the soul, overpowering even the rough scents of cigarettes and cheap booze. I felt the communal bond, an organic joy missing from our everyday struggles.

My buddies and I rode the Ferris wheel and the wooden roller coaster. We even won a funnel cakes playing some of the games. As the night wandered past ten o' clock, the carnival's ambiance remained festive. Comforting even in the cold.

When Colin and John set off for the House of Mirrors, Ricky convinced me to stay behind. He had other plans... more adventurous plans. So the two of us walked off toward the back of the lot, Ricky in his patched-up gray jacket, I in my wrinkled red one.

Together, we made our way to the end of the fairgrounds. Far from the families. Far from the treats. The band music faded away, the closer we got to the final tent. A blue tent isolated on its own, dark woods crowded behind it.

Ricky and I stepped into this dangerous, darkly electric world of sleazy carnival barkers. Seedy jazz music greeted us. No longer were we around the pleasant locals. Instead, we were amongst the outcasts of Savannah, Georgia. The gangster types, the hobos on a diet of cigarettes, and a few couples too drunk to stand up straight, every one of them dressed in their Sunday clothes for these Saturday night sins.

Uneasy, I looked over at Ricky. "Are you sure we should be here?"

Ricky grabbed my arm. "Come on, chicken!" he teased in a Southern drawl.

I had no choice but to follow. But I trusted him. He was our leader. And above all, he was my best friend.

Nothing was around the big blue tent except dirt and a couple of exotic girls' tents off in the distance. The dim lighting further quashed the cheerful mood we'd enjoyed on the other side of the festival.

The two of us stood with this unsavory congregation at the front of the tent, right before a large podium. Looking around, I realized Ricky and I were the youngest ones here. Not to mention the only ones without cigarettes or alcohol in our hands.

Trying my best to be discreet, I leaned in toward Ricky's ear. "Is this the—"

"Freakshow," Ricky finished nonchalantly. Smiling, he squeezed my shoulder. "It's your turn to see it, Tommy."

A suffocating dread eviscerated me. I wanted to run. But to leave now meant having to run away in front of everybody… including Ricky. I couldn't afford to look chicken in front of him.

"It'll be fun," Ricky continued.

For once, I didn't say a word. Not because I didn't want to, but because I didn't want him to hear the tremble in my voice. I held my hands together in an effort to hide the shivers. This wasn't the movies where we could hide under the seats during the scary parts. I'd have to face whatever lived inside that tent. I had to confront the freakshow.

I noticed a small wooden sign hanging on the tent. Amidst splashes of many colors, its bold font stood out: *REVEREND ROB'S SHOCK MUSEUM.*

Soon, two men walked to the podium: one tall and slender, the other a stocky bald fellow with a wild beard.

The tall man was dressed in a black suit, the style of an undertaker coupled with the exuberant smile of a used car salesman. A long cane accentuated the outfit, and his black preacher hat lent him an authority that was anything but evangelical.

On the other hand, the man's friend was a complete slob. His hideous flannel shirt and coveralls drew disapproval even amid the poverty-stricken crowd.

"Step right up, ladies and gentlemen, for the wildest show you'll ever see!" the tall man barked.

A few of the other patrons whooped with glee. The smell of booze now joined the thickening cigarette smoke.

Restless, I kept stealing glances between the Shock Museum and conglomeration of rides, safety, and innocence shining from the other end of the grounds.

Ricky grabbed my hand. But not even his supportive smile could alleviate my unease.

Using his cane, the preacher man motioned toward the sign. "Tonight I, Reverend Rob, will show you the wonders of my journeys! The souls I've discovered from South America all the way to the Okefenokee!"

He leaned in closer, his baby blue eyes holding us captive to each and every word. "Come see the Shock Museum! Come see the strange beings only the good Lord Himself could've imagined!" With theatrical gusto, he pointed the cane toward the tent entrance. "Join me in this *experience*!"

Inside, the tent opened up into an arena of scary spectacles, each and every corner filled with Rob's exhibits. A few openings in the very back branched off to separated areas. I figured they were "rooms" for Reverend Rob's crazier discoveries.

The Shock Museum's dark confines cut us off the outside completely. Even the smoke and smells were gone. The vibrant jazz was now replaced by a tense silence. With just a few lamps scattered about, I felt like I was in a haunted castle or crypt rather than inside the Savannah city limits.

Confused, Ricky and I followed the crowd to the first exhibit. The spot looked filthy, with only sharp wires forming a makeshift barrier.

I turned to see the stocky farmer closing off the entrance. He glared back at me. A quick spit of tobacco from his lips the only hint I needed to stop looking at him.

Pulling me along, Ricky pushed through the crowd for a view.

Then a gurgled *caw* shattered my senses. Like the sound of a dying bird gasping for a desperate last breath.

Everyone jumped back in fright. Terrified, I jammed my hand into my pocket. Straight toward my trusted knife.

Ricky grabbed my arm. "It's okay," he said in a calm tone.

One look at him cooled my nerves; the older brother I'd never had had rescued me once more.

As excited murmurs replaced the cawing, I followed Ricky all the way to the very front of the crowd. And then I came to a second frightened stop. I let go of Ricky's hand and did my damnedest not to scream.

To my relief, I heard the other customers gasp. One man cried out like an Old Sparky victim.

This first exhibit was no mere warm-up. In fact, what I saw was grotesque, monstrous… disturbing.

There behind the chicken wire was a young woman. Or at least, what appeared to be a deformed woman. Her legs were skinnier than sticks and shorter than twigs. But the rest of her was normal sized... except for the feathers stuck to her pale skin.

The woman's face was squished together like melting human slime. Her mouth distorted, the lips protruding to form a vivid lipsticked beak. The woman's stringy hair stuck straight in the air to form a blonde 'comb.' With the speed of rolling marbles, her blue eyes scanned the crowd.

They latched right on to me. Leaning forward, the woman stretched those skinny pathetic arms out toward me. Her fingernails sharper than a bird's talons. And when she released another painful caw, I about collapsed in fright.

A fountain of saliva flowed from the lady's 'beak.' Her animalistic cries sounded like the howls of a lunatic trapped in an asylum, halfway between deranged woman and aggressive bird.

She clenched her fingers over and over as she glared and shrieked at me. Yet her body barely moved. All she could do was wobble back-and-forth like a broken jack-in-the-box.

Ricky pulled me back before my tears started falling. "It's all right," he reassured.

Even with the other customers watching me, all I could feel was the woman's glare; all I could hear was her continual cawing into the late autumn evening.

"That's enough!" A bark interrupted the woman's hollow, inhuman cries.

At Reverend Rob's command, the woman went silent. Her blue eyes looked over his stern face, and found no mercy there. Like a frightened child, the woman's tiny legs shook.

Everyone else fell silent. Rob had our undivided attention.

With a flourish, Rob pointed his cane at a small sign in the corner of the pen. *The Chicken Lady of Chattahoochee!* the sign proclaimed in painted letters.

"This here's my Chicken Lady, found in Florida!" Rob's tone was now boisterously cheerful; back to being a minister rather than a cold carny. "I rescued her down by the Chattahoochee River!"

Battling my inner dread, I looked behind me. I saw no sign of the fat man; the farmer was gone.

"Oh, yes, she likes it here." Rob flashed a smile at the woman. "Ain't that right, Judi?"

Like a deranged dog, saliva dripped down Judi's face. She kept her distance. Kept her silence.

"Just follow me, folks!" Rob bellowed. He led the crowd to the next exhibit. "The Shock Museum has no shortage of stunning sights!"

The Chattahoochee Chicken Lady's wounded gaze froze me in place. I could hear the crowd leaving Ricky and me behind. But I couldn't take my eyes off her. Off Judi.

"Tommy, come on," Ricky whispered.

Ignoring him, I kept my sights on Judi. Even from here, I could see her scrawny legs strain to stagger toward us. Her disjointed mouth struggled to move. The cawing only became more guttural. More desperate.

I reached out toward her. Vague hope flickered in Judi's wide ocean eyes.

"Shit!" I heard Ricky cry.

Judi's hope vanished. She stumbled back with pitiful speed, immense fear making her clumsy.

"C'mon, son!" The familiar voice hit me like a sucker punch. A tight grip ensnared my shoulder.

I whirled around, coming face-to-face with the good reverend.

"There's much more I want to show y'all." Rob's cheerful façade did little to hide his barely-suppressed anger.

"Yes, sir," I said meekly.

"We're sorry," Ricky told Rob. He wrapped his arm around me, taking up for me as he always did. "He just wanted a better look."

A wicked smirk crossed Rob's face. His grip loosened... but his glare never left my face. "Well. No need for that." He pointed toward Judi.

By now, she'd cowered back into a corner. Like a scared animal burying itself in the darkness. Only Judi had nowhere to hide.

"Judi's just fine," Rob said, his attempt at sympathy about as convincing as his purity. "She don't get lonely here, I promise."

I stole another look toward the pen. Judi kept staring at me. Her mouth quivered but couldn't utter a cry for help. Her thick feathers wouldn't even allow tears to stream.

From there, the show got even stranger. Fifteen minutes went by in a series of escalating chills and darkness.

Sure, there were your usual freakshow attractions. A hulking muscleman with arms bigger than anchors. An old woman billed as the Witch of Waycross who couldn't have been younger than 115, judging by the layers of wrinkly skin and patches of cobweb hair.

But the most frightening to me was another blue-eyed woman, a teenage girl Rob kept in a small pen. She yelled out over and over again through oversized teeth, her manic hands constantly at war with the dirt and her own skin. She was the Last of The Aztecs. The Pinhead of Panama City.

The woman had a pretty face and smooth skin, but her head was much smaller than the rest of her. As if a doll head had been placed on a full- grown human body. She was the inverse of the Chicken Lady. She had no hair, and she uttered growls and grunts from pale, chapped lips. Old blood stains and dirt marred her makeup, and the cheap costume jewelry she wore did nothing to hide a multitude of scars. She wore a tattered polka-dotted dress she'd long outgrown.

Like a confused puppy, Pinhead's baby blue eyes faced us. A long tongue dangled out her mouth, twitching in between bouts of her nonsensible vocabu- lary. A tongue of many bleeding cuts.

Rob kept her biography brief. And then, before she could come any closer, a quick whisk of his cane sent the Pinhead retreating to the back of her cage.

The crowd had no time to react. Rob was an expert at transitions and his next display was a doozy: naked Amazonians. Both men and women.

Excitement pulsed through the customers. Ricky's eyes shone like head- lights. For a preacher man, Rob sure knew how to capitalize on the sexual crav- ings of each gender.

Rob pointed toward the first room in the back. "Come witness their exotic beauty!" he shouted with enthusiasm to spare. "The beautiful models of the Amazon right here in Savannah, Georgia!"

Ricky and the others beelined toward the tantalizing spot. Begrudgingly, I followed.

Rob's swift hand pulled me back.

"No can do, son!" he said with subtle scorn.

"What...'" I replied in a trembling voice.

"You're too young, son."

Panicking, I looked around at the chuckling crowd. Even Ricky joined in on their laughter.

Rob motioned toward a sign by that first entrance. *Must Be Thirteen And Older To Enter The Amazon!*

"I'm afraid you'll have to wait here, boy," Rob continued.

"But I don't want to!"

Ignoring me, Rob led the customers inside the room. "Come on in, folks! Follow me into the Amazon!"

"No!" I shouted. Upset, I got ready to run right into that jungle.

Ricky grabbed my arm. "Hey, Tommy, relax."

"No! I want to go!" I said.

Ricky leaned down. "Look, we'll be right out." His relaxed demeanor somehow calmed me down. "I promise."

I looked over at the Amazon entrance. "You just wanna look at those girls."

Chuckling, Ricky gave me a playful hit on the nose. "Can you blame me?"

Even I cracked a smile.

"Look, I'll be right out." Ricky backed away toward the Amazon. "Just wait right here."

Folding my arms, I watched him scamper off toward the crowd.

"I'll bring you back when you're thirteen!" Ricky quipped. With that, he disappeared inside the room.

Immediately, loneliness descended like an early morning fog. My fear returned. Especially once I realized I wasn't alone. Far from it.

Manic mumbling pierced the silence. Alarm bells rang through my head.

Quivering, my eyes drifted back to Pinhead's cage.

There she was, an aberration, on all fours and leaning up against the wiring. Her tongue dangled out, an added taunt to go along with her assault of strange snarls and cries. Her blue eyes latched on to me.

I stood frozen in fear. Sure, I was sympathetic to her plight. But I still didn't trust her motivations… or her sanity, for that matter.

Then, in a sudden burst, she stuck her hand through the wire. A desperate, hungry reach for me, her snarling wilder and more frenetic.

I turned and ran toward the rooms behind me. All while, Pinhead's anguished growls followed me, reminiscent of a starved wolf on the prowl.

The unsettling noises stopped upon entering the third room. Here, everything was quieter and darker. This cramped space had a single lamp, my only guide in this wilderness of weirdness.

Aside from scattered crates and boxes, I saw a tall bookshelf standing to my left. Rows and rows of jars populated the shelves. Light glistened off the glass. The jars all held the same abstract figures.

Entranced by the sight, I staggered up to the shelf. And then I came to a frightened stop.

Now, I wasn't exactly sure what it was in those jars. I just knew they weren't animals, certainly not the small furry roadkill I would have expected as another Shock Museum novelty.

The figures were smooth. Their little arms and legs stuck out of folds of flesh, like antennae. Their angular heads and narrow eyes as underdeveloped as the rest of their bodies, malformed like so many of the people I'd seen in this museum.

Deep in my sickened gut, I knew what these beings were. Even in the gooey liquid, they had a clean radiance: bodies untouched by the sins of the world. Fetuses that hadn't been corrupted by the Great Depression... but had never survived to experience it either.

Dozens of the human fetuses stared back at me, preserved like exotic specimens. I realized this freakshow had taken a disturbing turn from the big top to the laboratory.

"Hey!" a high-pitched voice whispered to me.

Startled, I turned to see a little boy standing in the shadows.

"What's your name?" he asked kindly.

Fueled by curiosity, I approached the child. The closer I got, the further away from the lamp I went. I could tell the boy was close to my age. Scrawnier than me, he wore torn pants and a white undershirt. No shoes on those bony feet. Dirt covered his pale skin and decorated his dark hair. But the filth couldn't mask his vulnerable blue eyes. The combination of his mischievous smile and untidy appearance reminded me of a little boy right out of a Charles Dickens novel. Like the boy had been transported from a British orphanage to a Georgia carnival.

"Uh, Tommy," I stammered. As I approached, I was relieved to see no deformities or dry blood. He was normal enough, if pitifully malnourished.

"Tommy!" He beamed. "I'm Terry. Our names sound the same." His smile never wavered, and his bright blue eyes never dimmed.

"Yeah, that is funny," I said, too nervous to grin.

I looked over and saw a coffin positioned against the wall. The open lid revealed a male mummy, his arms crossed. Not a dusty crumbling corpse either, but well-preserved like those fetuses. The mummy's wrappings were a pristine white, his posture regal.

"Oh, wow!" I exclaimed.

Excited, Terry took a step toward me. "He's real, too! Daddy got him in Cairo, Georgia!"

The Shock Museum lived up to its name. Stunned, I faced the boy. "Your dad?"

The kid snagged my arm in a tight grip. "Yeah, he said I can pick anyone!" He leaned in closer, voice full of innocent exuberance. "I want you, Tommy!"

I struggled to pull away from him. The boy was stronger than I ever thought. Much stronger than me. "No! Let go of me!" I yelled.

Terry pulled me in closer. "Don't you wanna be my brother, Tommy?"

Horrified, I yanked my arm back. "No!"

The kid cornered me against the wall. Right next to the mummy.

"I already have a mama and a sister!" the boy gushed. "Mama's from Chatta-hoochee! She's *really* something!"

My body pressed into the tent's harsh fabric. "Leave me alone!"

"What'd you say?" a gruff voice barked.

A bright light blinded me as Reverend Rob swung his lamp through the dark-ness. He stopped beside Terry. Rob's glare contrasted by the child's wide grin. Their blue eyes formed an intimidating double-bit axe. And under the lighting, their resemblance was uncanny: The Shock Museum's resident father and son.

Like a cornered crook, I trembled beneath that spotlight of the lantern and jammed my trembling hands in my pockets.

"That's him, Daddy!" Terry yelled. "He's the one I want!"

Rob ruffled his hair. "We'll get him, son. Don't you worry."

"We'll be brothers!" he said to me with pride. Then he held up his shirt. A gaping crater of flesh covered his hip. The tapestry of dry blood, stitches, and exposed muscle ran all the way down to his ass. A streak of scarred skin ready for a teammate. "We'll be twins, Tommy!"

Rob cracked an evil smile. "The Siamese Twins of Savannah."

I couldn't even scream. All I could do was stare at their hungry blue eyes.

"I can already see it," the reverend continued with reverence. "Y'all will be the stars!"

Terry pulled on Rob's jacket. "Terry and Tommy, Daddy!"

"I told you I'd give you a brother, didn't I?" With a cold smirk, Rob turned to me. "And I always keep my promises."

Like a kid waving me outside to play, Terry beckoned. "Come on, Tommy!"

He grabbed the side of his chest, that vicious wound. "Now we'll be brothers forever!"

I fell further back against the fabric, further into the depths of dread. The cold air gave me a battalion of chills. And my hands dug even deeper in my pockets.

"You'll be fine boy," Rob said to me in a playful taunt. "You'll be a star like the rest of my family."

Panicking, I stumbled over into the mummy.

The mummy released a muffled yell! His arms flailed about in a stilted frenzy. Saliva soaked through the wraps ensnared around his mouth, muffling his cries. Yet another prisoner of Rob's museum.

He could barely move. His arms grasped for help in agonizing fashion.

"You little shit!" Rob yelled.

Lunging, he slammed the coffin lid shut. And just like that, the mummified man was silenced.

Then Rob reach toward me. Until my right hand felt a wooden handle. Old reliable was right at my fingertips.

"I got you, boy!" Rob shouted.

Terry jumped up and down, his energy uncontainable after all the years of Shock Museum loneliness. "Get him, Daddy!"

Rob snatched me up.

The pocketknife always made me tougher. And tonight was no different. Like I was back on Harris Street, I retrieved the blade and swung it at Rob.

I got him good. One hard lick across the face.

Rob cried out as a bloody line appeared on his cheek.

"No, Daddy!" Terry cried.

I shoved Rob away and bolted.

Terry's screams rang out like a young banshee. Waves of broken glass shattered, a backdrop for his tantrum.

I stopped near the opening and turned toward the scene.

Like a shattered aquarium, busted jars floated amongst the ocean of dark liquid. The small fetuses seemed nothing more than bobbing dead fish. A sterile smell wafted up, disgusting me.

Rob's furious eyes found me. "Come here, boy!"

Terry stood in a dark corner, his outburst now driven by rage rather than excitement. "He'll get you!" he screamed at me.

I looked on at the boy's blue eyes. Without the smile, they looked sharper than daggers.

"Just you wait!" Terry continued. "Daddy always gets them!"

Rob careened toward me, his steps heavy and ferocious. "Come here!"

Clinging to my beloved knife, I ran through that dark tent. Adrenaline warmed me from the cold but couldn't stop the constant shivers. I saw none of the other customers around. Not even Ricky.

As I ran, I wanted to close my eyes but couldn't. The Shock Museum sprawled out before me. There was Terry's Pinhead sister. The elderly witch. Rob's grotesque wife Judi. Their incessant screams swirled all around me, a haunting chorus like a prison of desperate animals crying into the night.

"Come back!" Rob's footsteps grew louder. Closer.

I couldn't slow down. I couldn't stop, even when I ran out into the cold late night.

It was much darker than it had been when Ricky and I first entered the Shock Museum. I stumbled through the ghost town of a carnival. There was no music. No crowd. No more agonizing screams. And no footsteps hunting me down.

"Ricky!" I yelled.

I saw him waiting for me just a few feet away from the big blue tent. Ricky recognized my panic and ran to me. I told him everything.

And he believed me once we saw the weird farmer emerge from the Shock Museum. He recognized us even through the darkness. His movements were swift and violent, as befitted a beast created by Reverend Frankenstein.

We saw a long machete dangling from the man's hand. The few lights around us glistened off its pristine blade.

I pushed Ricky back toward the carnival. "Run!"

I didn't need to tell him twice. We ran all the way, never stopping till we met John and Colin in town. Of course, they didn't believe us. But that still didn't stop Ricky and I from trying to talk to the police.

"Damn hooligans!" the officer scolded us. His dismissive irritation shot down any chance us working-class delinquents had with law enforcement. I guess I couldn't blame them. The Savannah police had their hands full at the time, and my story was so wild. I never got the chance to prove it either; by the following morning, the autumn festival was gone with the night.

Eventually, the Great Depression came to an end. But the nightmare was far from over; it had merely ceded to a greater horror: World War II.

I joined the service the moment I could. By then, I'd grown from a timid runt into a strong young man. But deep down, I'd never shaken that cold fall night in 1934.

I'd go on to see terrible things in the war, and more terrible things in life. But over eighty years later, those Shock Museum memories linger. The fear I felt that night remains. Especially when little Terry promised me that Daddy always got them.

THE RIVER BANDON

RAE MCKINLAY

It was the night of the year when the wheel turned towards November. November, the season of remembrance always seemed lonesome. My open crackling fire was ablaze, casting dark mischievous shadows onto the wall while the wind groaned and hammered on my windows. Restlessness was upon me; I had discovered an old Irish folk tale about the women who sang at the river long ago, back in the sixth century. It is reputed that if you have the gift of seeing beyond mortal sight, you can still hear their voices even now, when the nights draw in and the sun courses low.

Of course I didn't believe in myths, but for some reason this tale haunted me. I paced up and down, down and up, and in sheer frustration of not being able to sleep I pulled my coat from the wardrobe and took a walk by the River Bandon.

The moon peeked shyly over the sleepy landscape, casting dim light onto the cracked pavements. Everything was stony still. There is no such thing as total silence in nature, so if you come upon it, it should always act as a warning.

Against my better judgement, I put one foot in front of the other and strolled by the river. It was then I heard music, so beautiful that it would break your heart to hear it. And then my eyes were drawn to the old bridge where I saw an old woman with eyes dark-rimmed and sunken. Her body swayed and her eyes dazzled with wild abandonment. It was as if I was watching an old black and white scene from a movie. In any case, it was not a usual sight to see in Bandon.

Oddness aside, there was something appealing about her—something which drew me towards her.

As I approached her, she stopped dancing. She looked at me and said, "Look at my river. Look." She pointed towards the flood relief work. "Once my river was beautiful, but now she is broken by machines that rip out her heart."

Trying to soothe her fears, I told her, "The river is still beautiful. There's been so much suffering due to flooding. The river will be grand as ever once the flood defense work is completed."

She swiveled toward me, narrow sage-green eyes blazing. "Once upon a time this river was lined with trees. The trees kept the floodwaters at bay. Now, you inject my river with poison and smoke the sky so that we all choke, and when nature dances to this unnatural rhythm, you try to fix it."

Then I heard complete and utter silence. It was so uncomfortable that I brought my hands to my ears.

"This is a town of many silences," she said. "Many stories lie buried underneath the stones, waiting to be unearthed and told. Some people don't want the stories to surface. But they need to be heard, because there is power in the stories to heal. This town needs to heal. Do you know that this was a place where Holy Women dwelled? People came here requiring relief from all kind of ailments. When the wall was built around the town, their stories were crushed and silenced, and then the woman no longer sat by the river. Can you hear the sound of silence reverberating throughout the place? This will soon be the town of cracked silences."

The cold began to pierce me. A blush of irritation flashed on my face. I wanted to go home to my bed; tiredness had fallen upon me, and her words coasted over my head. I was too exhausted and too frightened to take it all in. So I moved to walk away from her. She placed her hand on my shoulder. Five twig-like fingers squeezed.

I turned around to look at her. She touched my face and with one finger, she circled my cheek. Her nail pressed into my skin, drawing a drop of blood.

I stood with my mouth wide open.

"You can't leave," she told me. "You have heard the music; you have now crossed The Threshold. Now you must stay." A cavalcade of phantom figures emerged from the river. They smiled at me. I heard the music once again, coming from all around me. I smiled with wonder.

But I looked around, taking in the moonlit scene, and observed a few Corby crows jigging on the ground. Realization struck me, cutting through my reverie; I had no option but to try and escape, or I would be stuck in this ethereal world forever.

The lights in the distance were fading, and I sensed I was being drawn deep into this other plane. I looked around again, and spied a sort of veil, beyond which I could see the city lights. As I watched, it drew downward, ever closer to the ground. Closing up.

I mustered all my strength and dashed towards the gap. Immediately I sensed the old woman behind me. I smelled her perfume, cheap and musty, as she lunged at me, grabbing my scarf and pulled it off. I ignored it, and with perhaps a second to spare I curled underneath the gap in the veil and sprinted to the safety of my home.

In the whisperings of twilight, I slumped into my bed wondering what she meant by my town being *the place of the cracked silences*. My head spun with suggestions. Perhaps she meant the multitude of contested historical stories, the sort of stories people kept quiet because they didn't want to open old wounds.

One thing I did know was that first thing in the morning, I would pay a visit to the library. I wanted to find out all I could about the Holy Women who once sat by the River Bandon, because after my experience, I can say I certainly believe in myths now.

AN OFFERING OF BLOOD AND BONE

B. R. GROVE

Lucien Deville scowled as his car passed the faded sign just outside of Deep Sleep. He'd hoped that when he left five years ago, it would be the last time he ever saw the place. Fate seemed to have other plans for him, however.

His sisters, Nathalie and Annette, had the common sense to leave their father, Ronan, well before Lucien. That was the curse of being the youngest child, he supposed: to be the only one left to put up with the fat bastard's mad ramblings. It was just his luck to be the only son as well. His father always harbored a misogynistic streak, and it showed itself completely in his will & testament, which stated that his house and business would only go to a male heir. Now that the old man was dead, it meant that Lucien had no choice but to come back to this wretched town. Curse him.

At last, the house appeared up ahead. It peeked out behind the seemingly endless trees that stretched on for miles, looking dark and desolate in the gloom of the grey, rain-swelled sky. Lucien pulled onto the gravel road leading up to the garage and parked in front of its giant aluminum door. He turned the car off and climbed out of the front seat. He stood there for a moment, his hand on the car door, staring up at his childhood home. It looked like the hollow head of a giant. The dark windows of the second floor peered down at him like eyes. He shuddered and went to gather his bags from the trunk. The porch was damp from the recent rainfall, and as he walked up the stairs, they creaked like the whole thing was about to give in any day now. Setting his bags down, he fumbled in his trousers pocket for the house key. Then he unlocked the door and pushed it open. It gave a loud creak as he stepped inside.

The small foyer was just like he'd remembered: the sea-green wallpaper covering the walls of the hallway, the matching mahogany coat hook and shoe holder off to the right, and the old light fixture that looked like a decorative bowl above him. None of it had the same welcoming warmth that it did in his memories.

He flicked on the light switch next to the door, and the light flickered on. It continued flickering. He sighed. Another thing to add to his list of adjustments. He took a deep breath and hoisted the suitcase up under his arm. Then he made his way up the winding staircase to his left, which led up to the second floor of the house. The upstairs hall was dark and all the doors were closed. He went for his old bedroom door and pushed it open.

It had been made into a room for storage. He cursed and continued walking down the hall. His parents' old room was at the far end. He went inside. All of the furniture was neat and tidy, and the drapes were closed. All around the queen-sized bed were cardboard boxes, some open with their contents still in piles next to them. Apparently, whoever came to collect the old man's will didn't bother cleaning up after themselves.

Lucien snarled and threw his bags down. After taking a moment to collect himself, he sighed. Then he shucked his peacoat, hung it on the doorknob, and started rolling up his sleeves. Cleaning was going to have to get done anyway, so he supposed he should get started.

He was exhausted and almost finished with the room when he came across it: a huge leather-bound book, wedged underneath his father's bedside table. He'd never seen such a book in his father's collection before, which was partially why it caught his eye. He knelt down and pulled it onto his lap. It was heavy, and as he opened it, he found that many of the pages were thin and brittle, as if they were hundreds of years old.

Its contents were confusing. The first few pages were written in French—a language he was as fluent in as he was with English—but much of it was archaic and incomprehensible. He flipped through the pages, noting how the handwriting changed the further he read, until he started to recognize his father's scrawl. As much as he tried to make sense of what was written—descriptions of their family home, and the woods that bordered it—he couldn't.

Then the drawings began. Captions underneath stated that they were supposed to be inhabitants of the woods, but they didn't look like any fauna that Lucien had *ever* seen. In fact, they were distinctly humanoid in appearance: bipedal, with spindly fingers and faces with two eyes and a mouth—at least from what he could see of their faces, many of which were shrouded in black.

There was one in particular which caught his attention. Its figure was feminine, with long taloned fingers. She wore a black shroud that covered her body and most of her face, save for a pair of full, black lips. The caption under the drawing read *La Veuve*: "The Widow" in French.

Lucien snorted. What was the significance of that name? What did it even mean? Farther down, still, was a phrase surrounded by a sketchy black circle. Translated as best as he could manage, it read:

> *"I speak these words to wake The Widow,*
> *Strong, Beautiful and Harsh is she.*
> *May she grant me my deepest hope,*
> *and give the results I wish to see.*
> *I swear to repay the debt I've carved,*
> *to keep this life I wish to own*
> *and satiate her hunger with*
> *an offering of blood and bone."*

He read the verses aloud to himself. They felt strange on his tongue, like the words were charged with electricity. Just then, the shutters blew open, overpowered by a sudden gale. He nearly had a heart attack before realizing what happened. Then he growled in frustration and slammed the book shut. He shoved it under his father's bed and stood up to close the window.

After a meager supper, comprised of whatever was available to him in the fridge, Lucien fell asleep in on the old velvet sofa in the living room. He awoke to eight chimes from the old grandfather clock beside the fireplace. He sat up, rubbing the sleep from his eyes, and looked out the bay window into the front yard. Darkness had already fallen, and he couldn't see much. As he sat there, staring and lost in thought, a sound caught his attention. It was a hiss of air, and it slithered through the cracks in the doors a and windows, ensnaring him and wrapping itself around his brain.

"*Come...*" It whispered.

He followed obediently, passing his shoes in the hall and walking outside barefoot. Something was calling him, he knew, and he intended to find out what it was. He followed the culling noise through the woods, the forest floor stabbing the soles of his feet the whole way there. He cringed inward, but didn't stop his stride.

The voice was a bit louder now, and he recognized it to be female. "*Come to me, le fils de ville...*" it cooed, as smooth as silk and inviting as the call of the void.

It felt like walking for hours, before he finally reached a clearing in the woods. The ground was soft here, save for a wide and dark pit in the center. A figure stood in the center, beckoning to him with a bony finger. He came closer, stomach sinking as he recognized what stood before him.

It was her: the female creature from his father's grimoire. The Widow.

She looked exactly like her drawing: body and eyes covered by a black shroud, black lips glistening like poison. The pale skin that was visible was rough and cracked, like the surface of the moon. Even through the shroud, he could feel her eyes burning into him, like a predator sizing up prey.

"Hello, Lucien," she purred in a voice dry as salted earth. "Son of Ronan, descendent of les sorcières Devilles."

"What do you want from me?" he asked.

"I would ask you the same thing," she replied. "You summoned me, did you not? I would not have entered this realm had my incantation not been spoken aloud."

The incantation? Lucien thought back to the verse he'd read in the book earlier and cursed himself for his stupidity. Of course it was an incantation! What else could it have been? And had he not felt the magic on his tongue as he spoke the words aloud?

"Mademoiselle..." he stammered, "I was not aware of what I was doing when I summoned you. If I knew that that was an incantation, I would not have spoken it. You can go back whence you came. I have no need for your service."

She let out a short laugh like the burn of hot metal on skin. "Well, isn't that a predicament," she sang mockingly. "Well, dear boy, your intent does not matter in this situation. You have woken me from my slumber, and a debt remains to be filled for that action alone."

A lump formed in his throat. He was such an idiot. He'd clearly cast powerful magic without meaning to, and now there were consequences. But of what kind? Did he even *want* to know? He swallowed before speaking again. "And what, if I may ask, does that debt entail?"

"The price you pay for my summoning is one of blood and bone. I need a life —yours or otherwise."

A life... So, a living creature. A blood sacrifice. He figured it made sense for a demon. "Done," he said. He'd been hunting before with his friends and their fathers. He could kill a woodland creature if he needed to.

"A *human* life," she added. "A life of sophisticated purpose."

It was like a stone dropped in his stomach. No... no, he couldn't. He wouldn't! A rabbit or a deer was one thing, but taking a human life?!

"That's... murder!" he exclaimed. "I can't do it! I won't do it! It's wrong! Vile, and cruel!"

"Your petty grievances mean nothing to me!" she snapped, her voice suddenly as harsh as a storming sea. Dark power surged through the night air, causing the black, arm-like branches growing from the pit to sway back and forth, like crowds of hands clawing their way back from Hell. Lucien shuddered and backed away, huddled into himself.

Then, as quickly as it happened, the Widow regained her composure and the wind stopped. She breathed in deeply and sighed. "I expect a single human life to be brought to me tonight. At the stroke of midnight, the debt will be paid, and I will not bother you henceforth, provided that you never call me here again."

He nodded, barely managing to speak. "Okay." Then he turned to leave.

"Lucien," she sang, coaxing him back. He was brought right up to the edge of her pit. She leaned in close, and he could smell her foul breath—rotten and stale like an ancient tomb. He gagged.

"Do not forget," she murmured, "that if you fail, it is *your* life that I will take."

Her grip on him vanished, and he ran, not stopping until he was out of the woods and running across his front lawn. He collapsed on the porch steps and cried like he'd just outrun the clutches of death. He supposed that he had, given the Widow's final warning.

If he didn't kill someone tonight, he was going to die.

He clung to the rickety wooden staircase like a lifeline, wanting to root himself in place so he could never leave or be taken away. It was foolish, so he sat up and buried his face in his hands. In a moment they fell to his sides in defeat, and he sighed deeply. He needed to get away from this place—to go for a walk. He couldn't stomach being around these wretched woods right now. Not until his debt had been paid.

So he stood and went inside to grab his shoes and his keys. Then he left the property. He walked down the empty dirt road, staying on the side with an empty field, rather than the woods.

As he went, he couldn't help but wonder about his family's history, and their relationship with magic. Ronan Deville never seemed the type to believe in occult things. How long had that spell book—that grimoire—been in his possession, anyway? It was so old that he wondered which of his ancestors had been the one to write on those first few pages. Were there other spells in there? Ones that *didn't* involve demons and murder?

Had anyone else in his family killed someone?

He shuddered. He might've had problems with his father, but never once did he think that he could be a murderer.

At last, he arrived at the edge of Deep Sleep's downtown. An empty gas station was on the opposite side of the road from him, and a small diner was on his side. He looked up at the neon red sign on the roof. It read 'Judy's.' He bit his lip. A cup of tea wouldn't fix anything, but maybe it would calm his nerves. He made his way to the double doors and went inside.

The diner was plain as plain could be. Rose-colored walls with framed paintings of faraway landscapes, black-and-white tiled floors, and eight booths all along the left side. Only the third one in from the door had guests—a rough-looking man in a cowboy hat and his balding friend sitting with his back turned. Lucien swallowed and went over to the bar. He sat in the nearest stool. He laid his head down on the cool, linoleum countertop and listened to the faint sound of Frank Sinatra playing through the jukebox in the corner.

"Can I get you something?"

He looked up and saw a pretty blonde waitress standing behind the counter. She wore a green dress with white trim, and the name tag on her matching apron read 'Marybeth,'

"Uh… tea. Earl Grey."

She nodded, her eyes narrowing. A sly smile slid onto her lips and a look of knowing filled her face. "Do I know you from somewhere?" she asked. "You look really familiar."

"I grew up here, but I moved away for a while. I just got back today," he replied. *And already he'd managed to royally fuck things up*, he thought bitterly.

"You kind of look like the guy who owned the pawn shop in town, Ronan's Antique*s*."

"Yeah, that was my father. Ronan Deville."

"Oh…" She patted her heart with one hand. "I'm so sorry for your loss."

He forced a smile for her. "It's all right, don't even worry." He held out his hand politely. "I'm Lucien."

She grinned and shook it. "I'm Marybeth. It's nice to meet you."

She brought him his tea, and they ended up talking for quite a while. He learned that she lived with her mother, that she was planning on studying nursing at the community college in Verne once she'd saved up enough money, and—judging by her body language alone—she was incredibly smitten with him. It would've been flattering, if he wasn't so put off by how trusting she was.

Too trusting.

A hideous thought blossomed in the back of his mind and pushed its way to the front. His stomach flipped.

This is it. She's the one.

He wanted to believe that it hadn't come from inside of him—that the Widow had planted the seeds of vileness inside of him somehow. He didn't want to think that he was capable of doing such a thing. But the primal need for survival is a powerful thing, and he knew deep down that he was determined to do whatever it took.

He hardened his heart for what came next. "Marybeth," he said, "I think you're a sweet girl. I was wondering if you would like to come to my house for a drink?"

She blushed. "Well…" she said, picking at the skin on her thumb as she fidgeted.

Say no, the little voice in the back of his mind pleaded. *Please say no.*

She giggled nervously before giving him a sunny grin. "Sure, why not?"

His stomach sank, and he grinned back at her.

After her shift ended, they left the diner together. She drove them back to his house in her car. His heart felt like an anvil in his chest, and nausea churned within him as he absentmindedly listened to her chatting.

At last, they parked in his driveway. They sat in silence for a moment, staring at the closed garage door in front of them. Then he turned to face her, and she took the opportunity to give him a kiss. Her lips were soft, and even though she smelled like the diner, he could detect a faint hint of lavender underneath.

She pulled away and looked into his eyes. "What did you have in mind for us tonight?" she asked.

He panicked for a split second, then answered: "How about a drink?"

She followed him into the house. He had her sit at the kitchen table while he took an unopened bottle of wine out of his father's cabinet on the right wall. It was all too easy, he thought, grasping the bottle tighter in his hands, trying to stop them from shaking.

"Are you okay?" she asked.

"Sorry," he said, setting the bottle on the table. "It's just that… this is my first time doing something like this."

She smiled sheepishly. "It is for me too," she admitted. "I don't really know what changed, but… there's something about you." She stood and meet his gaze. "It's in your eyes. I want to get to know you better."

She was only inches away from him. He jerked back, nearly tripping over one of the chairs. She blinked, looking hurt for a second.

"I think my father left the corkscrew in his study upstairs." Lucien let out a short laugh. "Damned drunk, he was. I'll be right back." He turned on his heel and rushed up the stairs.

Nausea rose from his stomach to his chest as he made it to the second level, and he found himself wandering into his old bedroom. Behind his father's large oak desk was the narrow closet he remembered from his youth. He pushed the desk aside and opened the door. Inside was a tower of boxes. Hanging from two rusty clothing hangers was his old baseball uniform from when he was a boy. The old man hadn't thrown all of his son's things away, after all.

Lucien looked down and saw the heavy, metal bat that he used to practice with, propped up against the back of the closet. He lifted it and held it in his hands. Envisioning what he was going to do with it caused him to sob, but an unnatural wave of calm overcame him and stifled the cry. Almost robotically, he turned and went back into the hall with his new weapon.

"Did you find it?" Marybeth asked when he went back downstairs. He gripped the bat's neck tighter as he stopped in the archway to the kitchen.

Marybeth stared at him from the table, confused. "Lucien? What's wrong?"

she asked as he stepped out of the shadows. He swallowed as he brandished the bat. She shoved herself away from the table then, her eyes wide with fear. "What are you doing?!"

He didn't respond. He couldn't, as he would lose his resolve. She turned to run for the door, but he lunged forward and grabbed her by the hair. She screamed as he wrestled her to the floor. He got on top of her and raised the bat over his head. She sobbed; pleaded; *screamed!*

In that moment, something inside of him shattered, and he brought the bat down with a sickening crunch.

She stopped moving. He brought it down a second time anyway, and then a third. Blood splattered across the floor along with parts of something dark and meaty. He wanted to vomit, but he wasn't sure if he could. He wasn't sure if he was in control of his actions anymore. He felt as if he were looking down on himself, as a spectator in his own body. He watched as, almost mechanically, he stood and went to the closet. He took his mother's old tattered coat off the hanger and wrapped Marybeth's head—or what was left of it—in it to avoid making any more of a mess. Then he went outside and got into her car.

He drove up ahead a few miles before deliberately swerving and hitting a tree on the left side. It wasn't hard enough to hurt him, but it was enough to dent the fender. He opened the door, turned off the ignition and left it as it was. With luck, the police would assume she'd wandered into the woods herself and disappeared. No one would be any the wiser.

He went back to the house. He scrubbed the floor as thoroughly as he could with cold water, not wanting the blood and brain to stain the hardwood, until everything looked as clean as it had before. He went out into the garage, where he found an old tarp from one of his father's old carpentry projects. Then he proceeded to drag the body out the door, and into the woods.

The Widow was waiting patiently as he pulled Marybeth's tarp-wrapped corpse over to her. A satisfied smirk rested on her lips.

"Here," he spat, shoving the body forward. It landed in front of the Widow with a thump. "Your payment. Never come back."

"That relies on you, my dear," she purred. She bent down to the body and unwrapped the tarp like a macabre Christmas present. "Such a pretty thing," she murmured, stroking what remained of Marybeth's hair amid the gore. Then she parted her lips, and her mouth opened wider than anything earthly was capable of. She descended on the corpse, swallowing it whole. Bones snapped and crunched like twigs. Lucien had to look away. He curled inwards on himself, arms wrapped tightly like a snake.

The vile noises continued and the ground started to shake. Then, all at once, everything went still and silent. He turned and saw that everything was gone. The Widow had disappeared and her pit closed up behind her.

Lucien left the woods. He started at a walk, which broke into a sprint halfway. The cold night air felt like the breath of some hideous creature on the back of his neck, and when he got to the house he burst inside and ran upstairs. He leapt under his father's covers and buried himself there until morning.

He listened to the birds wake and call to one another, before pushing the blankets off and walking to the window. He wanted to believe so badly that it had all been a cruel and twisted nightmare, but he knew that it wasn't. He knew what he'd done.

He looked down. A corner of his father's grimoire stuck out from under the bed. He pulled it out and sat down on the floor. He lifted it onto his lap once more and flipped through the pages until he reached the last one. It was Ronan's writing, and it said:

"Our family wanted to burn all of our grimoires, and forget that we'd ever been tied to the 'dark arts,' I kept this one and brought it with me to North America. Les sorcières Devilles will live on.

"I only hope is that when I am gone, our family's hidden legacy will find a new heir in my only son, Lucien."

Lucien buried the book outside at the forest's edge. He never wanted to see it again.

In the following days, the police came to his house to ask about Marybeth. Her mother had reported her missing, and they asked around until they found someone who last saw her leaving Judy's with him. He made up a story about her spending the night and then going home.

He was appalled at how easy it was to get them to believe him. They found her car where he left it, and drew the same conclusion he thought they would: that she'd gotten in an accident and wandered into the woods, or was abducted.

They never found her body, and only Lucien knew the truth: there was nothing left on this earth to find.

These days, Lucien rarely leaves his house. He's eighty-five now, and age has made it difficult for him to function like he used to. The young man he hired as the Ronan's Antiques store manager, Ryan, doubles as his caretaker. Every few days he comes by to check up on the old man, and brings him groceries every Friday. It's a kind gesture, one that Lucien feels that he doesn't deserve.

Ever since that horrendous night, sixty years ago, a tangible feeling of emptiness has burrowed deep in his heart. Some days he contemplates ending it all. Other days, he thinks about moving away: selling the house and business, and going to another city to start fresh, like he'd tried and failed to before.

He never has taken the plunge to do such a thing. In part because of the duty he feels to his family and this small sleepy town, but also due to something much darker.

Every night, in one form or another, Marybeth comes to him in his dreams. She appears as the sweet blonde he remembers, in her green waitressing uniform and with a sunny smile on her face. Then, as he's helpless to watch, cracks appear in her face and it shatters, and blood and brain matter ooze down her porcelain skin. She opens her mouth as wide as the Widow's pit and screams. It's an unholy noise, one which awakens him from his sleep in a cold sweat.

He is haunted by his actions, in the most literal sense of the word. And even if he were to pack up his belongings and go back to the big city, he fears that she will follow him, tormenting him with her memory and her presence.

He sits on the green velvet couch in the living room, staring into space. He begins to truly understand how his father must have felt at the end of his life: empty and bitter; sitting at home while others worked and toiled for him; waiting for the sweet release of death. Perhaps he *has* inherited his father's legacy after all, he thinks, and smirks in self-deprecation at the unfairness of it all. He closes his eyes and lays his head back against the couch, letting out his last breath.

As he slips away, he can only pray for forgiveness.

THE VEIL OPENS

GARY S. CRAWFORD

In a small house in a nice neighborhood in Lake Como, just a few blocks away from the oceanfront and boardwalk, two women, a grandmother and her mid-fortyish granddaughter, sat together as they held hands.

"You know, Susan, I do have to leave soon," the old woman said to her granddaughter. "I can't stay as long as I'd like to."

"I know, Grandma. I know. You said that before. The time sure did fly, didn't it? I can't believe it's… no… it can't be! It's almost five in the morning!"

"I know, dear. My visit was far too short, but I'll take what I can get."

"It sure was such a great surprise to see you! With Dan's and my schedules, and the kids and all the things they do, I just can't seem to find the time for myself anymore. But this was so nice. I don't care how late it is. I could talk with you for another twelve hours. I can't believe we've been gabbing this long. When can I see you again, Grandma? Soon, I hope?"

"I can't give you an exact time, but I'll be back before you know it."

"Oh, Grandma, you look so good! Just like I always remembered you, even when I was little. I guess my own age perception is catching up to me. I used to think you were so old."

"And I always thought of you as just a small child, Susan. You all grew up so fast, I could barely keep up with you. And now your children, my great-grandchildren, they're all grown up too, going to college, your oldest getting married soon. Where did the time go, Susan? Where did it go?"

"I wish I knew, Grandma. But all that matters to me is that you came by to see me. I have to admit, I was shocked when you rang the doorbell. I didn't expect you to come in the middle of all those Halloween trick-or-treaters. It's weird too, I was thinking about you while I was cooking dinner tonight—oh! I mean *last* night! I can't believe it's going to be light soon! We've been up all night yakking like teenagers!"

The old woman rose to her feet as she said, "Well, my ride will be here soon. We have to be going before sunrise. Those are the rules, and no one is allowed to be late! Give your old Grandma a hug and kiss before I go. They'll be here any minute to fetch me."

Susan hugged her grandmother tightly, her eyes wet, as the old woman stroked her hair. They didn't want to let go of each other as they heard people talking outside.

"See? Here they are, right on time. I don't want to leave, but I must."

"I understand, Grandma. You don't want to be late, so let's make sure you have everything."

"I only brought myself and my sweater here by the door, Susan. Here, I want you to have this. My old necklace that you always liked." She unhooked the clasp and the fine old silver chain slipped from her neck into her hand.

"Me? You want me to have this? I can't take it, Grandma. It's always been your favorite. I never saw you without it. I always thought it was so pretty."

"That's why I'm giving it to you, Susan. It was always your favorite, too."

"Are you sure?"

"Yes."

"I... I don't know how to thank you for this... I..."

"The look on your face is thanks enough for me. Think of me when you wear it. But I do have to leave now. One more hug and kiss, or I'll turn into a pumpkin. There we go. It feels so good, Susan. I love you so much."

"And I love you, Grandma. I can't wait to see you again."

"You will, dear. You will." She gave her granddaughter one more hug, draped her sweater over her arm and smiled as she turned for the door.

Susan walked onto the porch as the old woman walked toward the others waiting at the curb.

"Where's your ride, Grandma?" she said after her.

"Oh, just around the corner. Sort of in the middle for all of us. We can handle the walk. We're tough old birds, you know!"

"Bye, Grandma. I love you," she said, fighting back the tears.

Her grandmother smiled and blew a kiss, then turned and joined the others as the group walked toward the corner.

She saw them under the streetlight as they turned onto the next street and were soon out of sight. The early morning was chilly, so she wrapped her sweater tightly around herself as she went back into the house. She sneaked a peek at the corner before they went inside, but they were gone.

Just a few streets away, a man in his mid-fifties stood on his front porch shaking hands with his uncle, who was also ready to leave.

"Uncle Hal, it was so good to see you. So unexpected. You should've called first."

"Well, Tommy, there wasn't time to call. I was in the neighborhood, so I just stopped in to see you. I can't believe your kids are all grown with kids of their own. I should've stayed in touch with you."

"You're the only one who still calls me Tommy. Mom and Dad called me Thomas. Everyone else just called me Tom."

"My sister—your grandmother—called you Tommy. She always said that Thomas was too formal for a boy who was the perfect Tommy."

"I've missed her so much. So many years since we lost her. And you, Uncle Hal, the last of her generation."

"Yeah. I was the baby. Hard to believe an old codger like me was a baby, isn't it? Well, I have to get ready to go, Tommy. It's been so great to see you tonight."

"It was, Uncle Hal. Look, don't be a stranger, okay? Keep in touch. I want to see more of you. And the kids too. They need to know their family history, and you were there to see it. You can give them the real story, not the third-hand stuff I have for them."

"Oh, don't wait for me. I don't know when I'll be back. Your mother has all the family information. A good job for her to teach her grandchildren about who we are."

"I know you have to go. It was just so great to see you again. Come back when you can, okay?"

"I'll do that, Tommy. Give me a big ol' hug there, my boy. I have to go. Be well."

"Bye, Uncle Hal." He watched the old man walk briskly to the corner, where others waited for him. A tear formed in Tommy's eye as his great-uncle disappeared behind the hedges of the corner property.

The group walked slowly but steadily. No one said a word, but each wore a look of happiness. Three women in black hooded cloaks brought up the rear to keep the slower ones from straggling. Another group met them at the next street and joined in the procession. Three women in black cloaks followed them as well. No one spoke. They didn't have to.

Susan picked up the photo album she and her grandmother had been looking at and flipped through the pages.

"Yeah, I remember that, when Grandma took me on the pony rides that day. I was so little! And that one where she's pushing me on that old tire swing. And this one. She took this picture of me at my school play. I could find her in that dark auditorium because she had the biggest smile. Ha! And that one! I remember when those biker guys let Grandma and me sit on that big Harley! Grandma wearing that black leather jacket too! Oh, don't we look tough?"

She got up and took the teacups to the kitchen. As she washed the cups, she smiled so hard her cheeks hurt.

"All those memories. All the things Grandma and I did when I was little. I remember them all. Going out to dinner like I was a grownup, going to the beach, when she sat with me at the little table and we played tea party. When she took the training wheels off my bike and I learned how to ride a two-wheeler! When we'd take the bus from Belmar to Asbury Park to shop at Steinbach's department store. All those neat things we did together. I'll never forget them. I remember so many things we did. I remember when she…"

A teacup slipped from her fingers and crashed to the floor.

"… died. Oh no, I remember when you died, Grandma! No! When I was fifteen! But you were here! With me tonight! But you… died! Grandma! Grandma!"

She was sobbing as she ran out of the front door and up the street in the direction she saw them last.

"Grandma! Please! Come back, Grandma! Grandma! Please!" she wailed.

"Tom? Wake up. You fell asleep on the couch. Come to bed. It's almost dawn."

"Hmm? What? Oh, okay, Stephanie. I guess I did fall asleep. I was talking with my Uncle Hal and… wait a minute. How could I be talking to my uncle? He's been dead for almost twenty years. The last of my grandparents' generation. Maybe I dreamt it? No, it was real. He was here. I was talking to him. I showed him pictures of the kids, and their kids. We talked about all kinds of things. Family things. I couldn't have dreamt all that. No, he was here. He was really here."

"If you say so. Come to bed, Tommy."

"I didn't imagine this, Stephanie. I know I didn't. Wait, did you just call me Tommy?"

Groggy and half asleep, he followed his wife upstairs to their room.

The group of people walking grew steadily in size as the eastern sky turned from black to purple to dark blue. They soon gathered in a large field, almost two hundred of them. The women in the black hooded cloaks walked up a short rise as another woman, this one in a purple cloak, appeared before them from the crowd below.

"Are you all happy?" the woman in purple asked them.

The crowd murmured to the affirmative. Nods and smiles were everywhere.

"Were your family and friends happy to see you?"

Another murmur said yes.

"Then we have done our job tonight, ladies." She turned to the other cloaked women on the rise with her. "You have done well, my sisters."

"Ma'am?" a man in an older-style Army uniform asked. "What happened here tonight, if you don't mind my asking?"

She smiled and said, "For those who haven't met me yet, I am Diana. Some call me Lady Diana. I am in charge of what went on tonight."

"We really enjoyed what happened, but we don't exactly understand it, Lady Diana," an old man in a dark suit said.

"What happened to us tonight, Lady Diana?" another voice asked.

"Our time here is short, so I won't give a long explanation. What happened tonight is something that has happened every year, for a very long time," Diana explained, looking out over the two hundred assembled before her. "According to old Celtic tradition, and myth and legend, the night of Samhain, October thirty-first, what we now know as Halloween, is the time when the veil between the living and the dead is at its thinnest. You have been given the honor of passing through this veil tonight."

A murmur of approval—and confusion—rippled through the crowd.

"In our beliefs, the God passes over at Samhain and he leaves the veil open for others to enter—and also to leave—the realm of the dead. The Goddess mourns his passing and the days grow shorter and colder until the God is reborn at Yule on December twenty-first. The dead can visit the realm of the living while the veil is open. They are free to visit those they left behind, but for this night only. The dead who have come to this side must return before daybreak."

Many in the crowd nodded.

"The duty of the witch is to help you enter the realm of the living once again and to help you find your way to where you are going. It is also our duty to make sure you return before the sun rises. That is why Halloween is considered the witches' holiday. It is our most sacred time. We have done our job tonight, and soon you will be returned to where you belong."

"We all know about spirits visiting on Halloween, Lady Diana. I always thought it was just a fun thing for the kids," an old woman said.

"All the traditions of today's Halloween come from our ancient cultures. As you can see, they aren't myths at all." Diana smiled.

"What about the demons, or the ones who manage to escape?" another woman asked.

"They aren't demons, just mischievous spirits. Harmless, mostly, just a pain in the neck. We try to stop them, but a few always get past us. They don't have anyone to visit, but they knock on doors anyway. The people in the house know they aren't supposed to be there, so they bribe them with treats to keep them going on their way."

"So that's what trick-or-treating is all about!" someone laughed.

"You see," Diana went on. "In ancient times a candle was displayed in the window to welcome friendly spirits and to shoo away mischievous ones, and the occasional unfriendly ones who manage to get out. The Irish took this custom and placed the candle in a hollowed-out turnip, the jack-o-lantern, and then, in America, the custom was modified to include the pumpkin, much easier to carve than a tough old turnip. If the candle doesn't shoo away the unwelcome ones, then a bribe of cakes or candy would keep them moving."

"I always heard that witches were bad. I haven't seen anything bad from you witches tonight. Has anyone else seen the witches here do any bad things?" a man in a tan suit asked the crowd.

"No," was the unanimous answer.

"A short history lesson and then we have to move on." Diana smiled at several people before her. "In the old times, the witch was the Wise One of the village. Mostly women, but there were a few men. We were the teachers, the healers, midwives, pharmacists, counselors, crop experts. All over the world in every culture there was the witch, known by other names too, but always the same Wise Ones. But when the missionaries and the soldiers came to spread the new religion, we were seen as bad because we saw no need to change what had worked, and worked well, for thousands of years. They spread false rumors about us, and soon we were seen as consorting with the devil and killing crops and spoiling milk and making babies sick and other terrible lies. They hunted us and tortured us and killed us. They published manuals on the proper methods of torture to make us confess to things we were falsely accused of. We call this terrible period of history the Burning Times. But they couldn't get rid of us; the ones who survived went into hiding, and we exist to this day. And we still don't have anything to do with the devil."

Someone asked, "But doesn't the Bible say that witches…?"

"Exodus 22:18," Diana said seriously. "'Thou shalt not suffer a witch to live.' Yes it does. But when King James translated the Bible it had originally said, 'Thou shalt not suffer a poisoner to live,' He was terrified of witches, part of the hysteria of the day, and he changed the passage to mention 'witch,' The King James Version of the Bible isn't exactly the same Hebrew Bible he had translated and many people suffered for it. Who is a mortal man to change Holy Scripture?"

The silence from the people revealed they had understood.

"Now, my blessed ones, it is time for you to return. Please move toward your left and we will see that you make it safely back."

The black-cloaked witches moved to a place between two massive oak trees, the portal back to the realm from which the dead had come. The air between the trees shimmered as though heated. Six witches lined up at either side of the portal as the dead walked slowly into the shimmering air before them. Many stopped to touch the hand of a witch or to even place a quick kiss upon her cheek.

After a few minutes most of them had passed to the other side and looked back, each one smiling and content. A few stragglers talked briefly with the witches, and hugs and kisses were exchanged before they entered the open portal.

Diana had two people before her, a man and a woman, chatting briefly and then one more kiss before they passed through.

When everyone was on the other side, Diana raised her arms to the sky and shouted, "Blessed be those who are remembered! It is not goodbye; it is merely so long. May the Lord and the Lady keep watch over you. Blessed be!"

The shimmering air of the open veil began to spin, becoming a whirling mass of white energy until it slowly faded and disappeared. The veil had closed once more.

Diana sank slowly to her knees as she looked where the portal had been just a moment before.

A black-cloaked witch came up to her and put her hand on her shoulder. "Lady Diana, my blessed High Priestess, you have done well. Are you all right?"

Diana was crying softly, tears of happiness as she rose and hugged the woman. The others surrounded her, all smiling, reaching out to touch her purple cloak.

"Did you all get to see loved ones tonight?" she asked, sniffing back her tears.

They all nodded happily.

Just before she broke into sobs, Diana said, "I saw my mother and father tonight. I got to tell them things I wished I had long ago, before they passed over. We are truly blessed."

The full moon loomed low and bright in the western sky between the two oak trees as Diana slowly turned to face it, kissed the fingers of her right hand, and held her hand high toward the silver orb in the sky as she whispered, "thank you" in Irish Gaelic, "*go raibh maith agat.*"

The twelve other witches surrounded Diana in a circle, each facing the full moon, raising their open arms high as their hair began to blow softly, then whip about harder and harder until finally the long tresses of the thirteen women fell softly to their shoulders once again.

At the Mount Prospect Cemetery, Diana walked up the grassy hill to the graves of her parents. She carried a tray with some colorful flowers, a small garden shovel, a handheld grass clipper, and a small American flag. She clipped the shaggy grass around the headstone, dug shallow holes, and planted the small potted pansies her mother had always enjoyed.

She hummed quietly as she worked and was soon finished.

"I know you like the multicolored pansies, Mom, so I brought you some. They'll bloom until the first frost. And Daddy, you need a new flag. We can't have a veteran here without a flag, right?"

She pulled the bare stick from the American Legion flag holder and replaced it with the new American flag. Then she kissed her right hand, and touched the top of the family headstone, and smiled. Borrowing from Jewish tradition, Diana placed a small rock on the headstone to commemorate her visit. She took a strip of wood from her tray and leaned it against the base of the stone. It was a small hand-painted sign she had made that simply said, *It's nice to be remembered.*

THE MONSTER SHE FORGOT

G. R. DAUVOIS & R. C. BOWMAN

On the nights that trap us between the miserable wet of autumn and the unforgiving chill of winter—when icy rain drums upon the world, amplifying its somber cacophony as it slaps at turning leaves, then maddingly drip-drip-drips, when unsunned clouds have gathered so blackly as to hide themselves from our sight—you may see her.

She has no face of her own, yet too many faces to count. Sometimes, you see her them on the news, in the papers, plastered across billboards and flyers and webpages dedicated to the lost. Occasionally, you may see one of her faces glazed and frozen in a portrait, still cherished by elderly parents or aging siblings. But more often, we don't see her faces at all, because they belong to the abandoned: to the addicts, to the homeless, to the prostitutes, to the children nobody wanted.

To the ones we forgot.

Like most of the forgotten, she wanders.

On those wet, bitter nights, when the winter rain bores through to your bones and the wind whips you raw, she roams the icy highways, shivering in the downpour. Heavy drops splash up from the asphalt to drench her battered shoes and bleed into her socks. Her jacket clings to her like a second skin, glued by rain and sleet, leaving no room for warmth, nor even the memory of it.

As she wanders, she weeps. When she reaches up to wipe her tears, she feels only a gelid slick of rainwater over benumbed skin. She weeps and weeps, because she is sad—so sad. Her chest feels full to bursting from the weight of her grief, a metastasizing storm throbbing painfully against her ribs with every heartbeat. The sorrow drips like cold oil—soaking her muscles as the rainwater soaks her feet—drowning her from the inside out, squeezing her lungs, crushing her heart.

But *why*, she wonders? Why does she mourn? She doesn't know. She knows only sodden socks that flood her shoes with cold whenever she takes a step, sleeting rain, and dying leaves flashing pale whenever lightning leaks through the black belly of the storm. But she does not remember why she grieves, or what brought her to this road. She doesn't even remember her name.

But you might.

She has no name of her own, yet too many names to count. Sometimes you hear her names. Sometimes you hear them on the news, or the radio, or on shows dedicated to recovering the lost. Sometimes you hear her name rippling through a close-knit community, or whispered among schoolchildren, or written on websites dedicated to disappearances that will never be solved. But more often than not, her names are those no one remembers, or never knew at all.

She collects names and faces the way others might collect cards, marbles, rocks, and dolls. But unlike cards, marbles, rocks, and dolls, nobody wants these faces or names. No one wants to hear them or look at them, much less remember them. And yet, she only remembers the rain-slick highway, her sodden shoes, a rumble of thunder so powerful that the road reverberates under her feet.

How then does she collect these faces? Is she a killer? A demon? A forgotten monster, prowling the slums and backroads for prey?

She is not a killer, and too sad to be a demon. She was a girl once, perhaps ten years ago, or fifty, or a hundred, or a thousand—I do not know; and she does not remember. She recalls only the sleet, and the dark trees beside the road, so dense she could not slip her starving body between them if she tried. She remembers the road thrumming under her feet long after the thunder has faded. She remembers realizing that the road is rumbling not from the storm, but from a car, racing toward her from behind.

Terror overwhelms her. She looks to the trees, but they remain a dark, impenetrable hedge. She breaks into a run, but her old shoes slip on the asphalt and she nearly falls.

Then, clear as day, she hears a voice in her head, whispering: *This is the one. Be brave.*

The voice soothes her. For an instant, she feels a vague, comforting sense of *knowing*. Perhaps it is her mother. Perhaps a sister, or a friend, or a guardian long forgotten. Perhaps it is simply her stronger, unremembered self. But the moment passes, and once again she knows only that she is cold and wretched, and alone.

Because her mind is so full it bleeds, broken under the strain of too many names and too many faces; crushed by the weight of their memories and their pain. That is why she grieves: Though her mind is ruined, the suffering remains, with no memory to understand or mitigate it. Nothing alive or dead can endure such torment without a price. Her price is forgetting everything, again and again and again…

…except how it feels to jab her wrinkled thumb into the air as the car approaches. Everything except the profound relief that floods her when it slows down, headlights illuminating endless tunnels slashed by rain. She is so grateful that she cries—the tears, at least, are warm.

The car shudders to a stop beside her. It is old, and blue. The passenger door swings open. She stoops to look inside. In the driver seat is a man. Her stomach drops, though she doesn't know why. He looks nice. Broad-faced, honest-look-ing, with good, pleasant features and kind eyes. "Where you headed?" he asks.

She doesn't recall, so she shrugs as hot tears continue to stream down her face, thankfully hidden by the veiling rain. "Somewhere dry."

"Then come on in."

She slides into the seat. Warm air sweeps over her, deliciously suffocating. For the first time she can remember, she feels her storm-battered body—so tense, so numb, so tight and pained with cold—relax.

The man smiles. His teeth are nice, and his eyes are pretty. A clear, medium green, like seaglass. "How long you been out here?"

"I don't know."

"Storm can mess with your sense of time," he agrees. He puts the car in gear, and off they go, sailing through the storm, warm and dry within even as the pouring cold torments the night without.

The warmth, the dryness, the soothing rumble of tires over road, the steam curling off her sopping clothes… it is beautiful. Exquisite. Her eyes flutter closed, and she drifts.

. . .

She snaps awake when the car jolts.

The twin tunnels of the headlights still illuminate the rain, sheeting sideways and swirling with ice crystals. But the road before them is no longer the highway —it is not even paved—only a muddy, swampy curl of backroad.

She glances nervously at the man. The weight of her grief is tempered now, fading as fear begins to overtake it, punching through it like fresh growth through wet, rotting bracken.

"Almost there," he grunts.

Sure enough, the car inches through one last muddy dip, surges up a short slope, and halts. The headlights now shine upon a building. Not a house—more like a forgotten ranger station—small, with a peaked roof and peeling boards.

"Here we are!" he announces. "Good and dry, just like you asked. Now tell me, if you don't mind." He leans closer and gives her a smile. "What's your name?"

"I... I don't know."

He clucks sympathetically. Before she can move, he strikes forward and touches her hair. His deft fingers find a rain-flattened lock and twist it gently, almost lovingly. She watches, frozen, as raindrops bead together and slide along the curl. "You poor thing," he croons. "Don't worry. We'll get you warm." He observes her for a moment longer. His eyes don't seem pretty any more. They look flat. Lifeless. Almost unreal.

"Come on," he invites.

Then he retreats, slipping backward like a receding tide, and gets out of the car.

She sits there, staring out at the cabin. Her heart feels strange. Stringy, thrumming. She wants to run. She could run.

She *should* run.

He comes around and opens her door. She fumbles with her seatbelt, smiling nervously. When she manages to free herself, he takes her hand to help her out.

And she bolts.

She doesn't get far. He lunges after her, catching her around the waist. She twists and flails, and nearly slips free, until he drives his elbow into the back of her head. Stunned, she halts, then lurches in an attempt to twist out of his grasp, trying to run while reflexively trying to feel where he struck.

He drives his elbow into her head again, breaking her fingers. She falls into the mud. It's so cold it should be frozen, and sucks her down like quicksand.

"Where," the man asks breathlessly, "do you think *you're* going?"

"I don't know," she whimpers. "I don't know…" Black mud seeps into her mouth. The man laughs, then reaches down and pulls her up. The mire doesn't want to let her go. It grips as long as it can before releasing with a hollow, angry *pop*.

The man drags her toward the cabin. She wants to scream, but doesn't remember how.

Inside, the structure is cold and damp. Mildew blooms across the swollen floorboards, which creak under the man's weight.

He drops her, then squats down as if to gloat. His green eyes are flat, dead, lightless.

A sob works its way up her throat. She tries to stifle it, but fails. When it bubbles out of her mouth, making her face crumple, the man grins. His smile is flatter than his eyes, and mean, and so ugly.

Inhuman.

Only then does she understand: this is not a man. Not even a bad man. It is a monster.

He does things to her. Things only a monster could do. He maims her, mauls her, breaks her—pulls out her nails, cuts off her fingers one joint at a time, then her toes—yanks out locks of her hair and sucks at the bloody roots—hammers at her mouth with a lead pipe, shattering teeth; the cold air agonizing the exposed nerves as he forces her jaws open, and shoves the pipe down her throat: an obscene intubation that keeps her breathing through all else she is forced to endure.

Finally, there is nothing whole left in her. She can't shift her body an inch; she is too broken to do anything but cry. And cry she does. The tears fall and fall and fall. At least they are warm.

The man backs off with a sharp, excited intake of breath. Then he turns and busies himself in the corner.

She weeps again, but something is wrong. Tears fall from only one eye. She can't see out of the other, nor can she close it. She tries to touch it, but neither arm will obey. So her good eye spins in its socket, straining to see. But there is nothing past the line of her nose—only darkness where her left brow and cheek-bone belong.

The green-eyed man—the monster—turns. The floor creaks as he approaches with a big, dark blade in hand. *A machete*, she thinks dimly. How does she know that? How does she remember?

With a rapacious growl, he charges across the warped floor, and brings the flat of the blade down on her, again and again. He hits her head so hard her dead eye pops from its broken socket. Then he pulls her remaining hair taut, buries his face in it and inhales: rain, blood, gore and all.

Then, he asks with a broad leer, "Are you ready, my dear?"

She is unable to answer, to move, to think. She can't even cry anymore. The last of her tears are sticky and half-dried, already cold.

"Splendid!" He turns around and returns to the corner.

In a haze, she wonders what else he keeps back there. If this is his grand finale, it is sure to be worse than everything she's suffered already. She can't even imagine what it might be, or what he will do next.

Something surges up from the bottom of her chest, subsuming her fear. At first, she believes it to be heartbreak, a last mad rush of grief to drown her once and for all. But it is not—it is something overwhelming, something foreign, something powerful. Something she does not remember ever feeling before.

She watches the oblivious monsterman as energy pulses through her, galvanizing her ruined muscles, turning her broken bones into coals that grow hot, then hotter, scorching, volcanic—

In the searing eruption, her grief evaporates. Her heart grows light and strong, first drumming like rainfall on the cabin roof, then like thunder in the heavens above. Her split lip curls upward, baring her broken teeth. But *are* they broken? They no longer hurt, and her mouth... her mouth doesn't feel big enough for them anymore.

As if ejected by the upsurge of power, the pipe vomits from her gullet, and clangs to the floor.

Cursing at the interruption, the monster turns with a scowl... which grows abruptly slack, and his eyes as wide as saucers. The bloody machete glistens in his shaking hand, the hair trapped in the gore like spindly spiders in a glue trap.

Impossibly, his victim draws herself up—broken bones crack and grind, jolting her body with electric pain, which she rides like a wave to her feet. Her arms hang limply—joints he twisted and pulled from their sockets, muscles and tendons he ripped from their bones. From the cuts in her belly and those splitting her groin, from the stumps of her fingers and those of her toes, blood flows sluggishly over the floor; dark, and yet spangled with stars. She looks down at them,

frowning. Specks of reflected light, she thinks at first, but no—they are too...
alive for that, moving, growing...

The monster utters a bewildered sound. She looks up so quickly the cold air
whistles through her new profusion of teeth. From the corner of her good eye,
she notices her other eye bouncing, dangling from its socket by the optic nerve.

The monster's knees shake. He dips low, as though preparing to launch into
an absurd jig. Then his legs give out, and he falls as if prostrating himself. His
blood-caked machete clatters to the floor.

She lurches forward, trailing blood peppered with living stars. The monster
cannot look away from her. Tears gather in his flat green eyes, eyes so like
marbles. His mouth falls open, and his tongue works uselessly. Saliva dribbles
from his mouth, joining his tears as they spill down his face. Finally, he
manages: "P-p-p-please—"

Like lightning, she strikes and—slicing through his cheeks with newborn
claws—catches his tongue and rips it out. Blood cascades from his mouth to the
floor like so much rain. His eyes roll up into his head as if with rapture, and for a
moment he looks like the monster he is.

Floorboards creak behind her. She turns to see a terrible and awesome sight:
the living stars in her blood are blossoming, emerging from the tacky pools like
many-stemmed mushrooms, or alien blooms reaching for an incomprehensible
sun.

As the monsterman weeps, the quivering buds continue to grow... and
grow... and grow, sprouting arms and legs, hips and genitals, buttocks and
breasts, and finally: *faces*. So, so many faces.

With umbilical cords adangle, the starchildren come to her, one by one. Some
offer smiles. Some warm embraces. Some take her hand in love, some kiss her.
Some weep for what was and never will be.

Once all have paid their respects, they turn to converge on the monsterman.
Hunching up, he shrugs deep into his clothing like a turtle into its shell, covers
his face with his arms, but it does no good. His face—the face of the monster—
will be forgotten.

They do things to him that only monsters can do. They tear off and devour
his flesh—all of it, down to the last dangling, gristly scrap. They pull his carcass
apart like vultures ripping at carrion. They splinter and swallow the bones, the
guts, the hair, even the clothes. They lick his blood off the floor.

And then, curling together like a rout of sated wolves, they fall asleep.

As they sleep, they shrink. They become small, so small and light that they rise to glide upon the cold air like dust. They dance toward she who birthed them, flitting to and fro. She opens her mouth and they flow inside, past her teeth and down her restored throat.

When the last one drifts inside, she closes her mouth. She wonders why she had her mouth open in the first place. It is cold in here. The stench of mold pervades everything.

She looks around, nonplussed. For some reason, tears sting her eyes. Why is she crying? Because she's sad, of course; she can feel it in her soul. Heavy, hopeless, so overwhelming she feels as though she might drown in it.

She spies her coat in the corner—crumpled, cold, and stinking, but dry—and slips it over her shoulders. It's raining outside. Sleeting. It will be miserably cold. She should stay inside. But if she does, she knows somehow that she'll be sadder than ever. Too sad to breathe. Too sad to *be*.

She steps into the deluge. The door swings shut behind her. Gusting wind knifes through her coat and freezes the tears on her cheeks. She sees the highway in the distance, slick asphalt glistening through the dark, weeping trees.

Though it is cold, she goes. Though mud and rainwater suck at her shoes and soak her socks, she puts one foot in front of the other. Though she does not recall where she is going, nor why she so grieves, she returns to the road.

Because she is forgotten, she wanders.

She is lost. She has always been lost, and always will be. All of her names, all of her faces, all of their pain, are lost with her, as if they never were. They are abandoned. They are forgotten.

But never alone.

MORE FROM SOTEIRA PRESS

VISIT SOTEIRAPRESS.COM TO JOIN OUR MAILING LIST

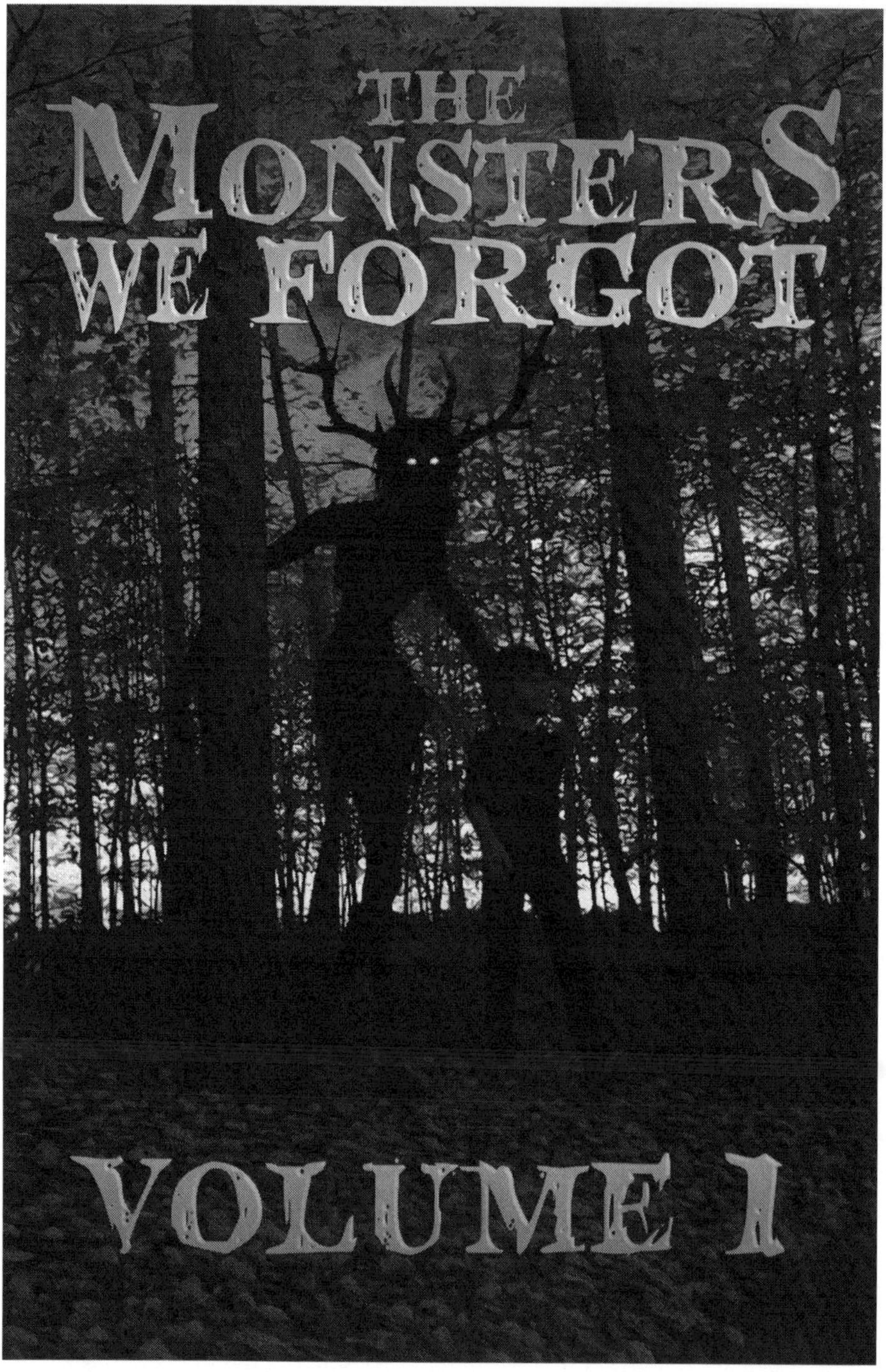
THE
MONSTERS
WE FORGOT
VOLUME 1

HORROR U S A

CALIFORNIA

AN ANTHOLOGY OF HORROR FROM THE GOLDEN STATE

The first in a series of terrifying anthologies showcasing horror in every state, "Horror USA: California" is all about the terrors, horrors, creeps, and shrieks unique to the Golden State.

HOARDER HOUSE

A NOVELLA BY R.C. BOWMAN

IN THE UNLIKELIEST OF PLACES, A HAZMAT CLEANER FINDS A HIDDEN WORLD. IT'S ETHEREAL, DREAMLIKE, EXQUISITELY BEAUTIFUL… AND FULL OF MONSTERS WHO WANT OUT. Originally posted to Reddit's Nosleep community where it met with immense success, this edition of R.C. Bowman's popular horror series is revised, edited, and best of all, features 10,000 words of new content!

FAIN HUNTER

HARDBLOOD Book I

G. R. DAUVOIS

Euthain Kürowin doesn't belong. A high-born elf of extraordinary beauty, he has every advantage in his Utopian enclave of gentle immortals; and yet, unlike his gentle kinfolk, Euthain constantly quells a storm of such violent impulses that even hunting—the most barbaric of sports in his peaceful society—barely satisfies him. Finally he accepts that the darkness in his heart is inescapable. He decides to exile himself in order to protect his deeply empathetic people from the rage within. But when a barbaric force invades the realm of the Wood Nymphs, Euthain seems to have found his place. In a terrible twist of fate, he must decide whether that place is fighting for his people... or serving at the side of their greatest enemy. FAIN HUNTER is the first book in the HARDBLOOD grimdark trilogy, which comprises the first part of the epic IMMEMORIAL saga spanning centuries and worlds.

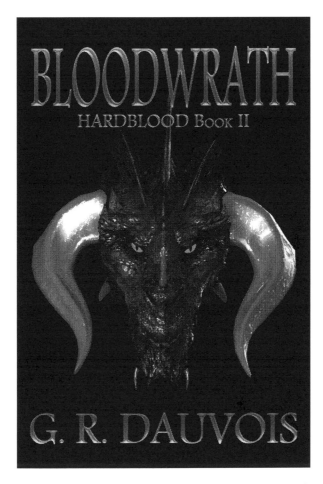

BLOODWRATH

HARDBLOOD Book II

G. R. DAUVOIS

Euthain Kürowin—pariah to his people, and lone champion of the gentle *Sylvain*—has traveled to the Black Mountain to confront the mysterious Molder whose monstrous minions have brought untold terror to the Nymphs of the Sylva. What he discovers within those caverns threatens to unravel all he has been led to believe about his people, and his place among them. Learning that he has been afflicted by the *Bloodwrath* —a soldier impulse that emerges whenever the Elvean race comes under cataclysmic threat—Euthain finds himself in greater conflict with his aberrant nature than ever before: Will he answer the call of his blood, and avenge the Molder's crimes, or will he surrender his outcast heart to the Molder's beautiful daughter Zhavelle, and thereby betray all he intended to defend? BLOODWRATH is the second book in the *HARDBLOOD* dark fantasy trilogy, which comprises the first part of the epic IMMEMORIAL saga.

Having set out in the company of the nymphet Kyji to
investigate rumors of a new threat to his home province of
Haven Dale, the outcast Euthain Kürowin finds himself in the
Gelid Plains, a vast desert of snow and ice. Starved for truth
and desperate to justify his many questionable actions so far,
he drives on despite the suspicion that the Molder has tricked
him into a fool's errand. When starving predators render his
dragon flightless, Euthain is forced to decide whether to push
on with his mission, or start the long trek home, if only to
ensure that the little Nymph in his company survives her
ordeal. Meanwhile, unbeknownst to them, an ancient menace
far greater than the one they have been hunting—a menace
that will decide the fate of not only the Elvean race, but the
entire world—is amassing its forces. Will Euthain's desire to
elevate himself from pariah to champion of the Elveni prove
meaningless in the face of such overwhelming odds, or will he
finally find redemption?

A new horror anthology from R. C. Bowman.

Slated for release in early 2020.

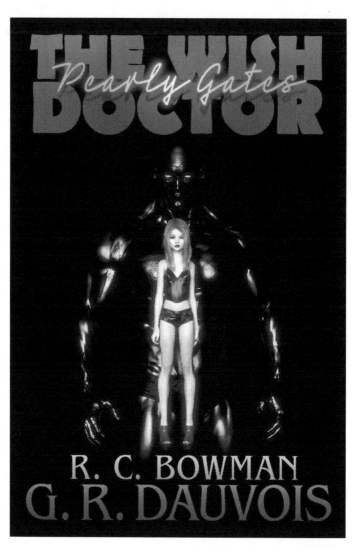

THE WISH DOCTOR

Pearly Gates

R. C. BOWMAN
G. R. DAUVOIS

Driven by the relentless impulse to grant intriguing wishes, an amoral killer suddenly finds himself trapped into playing guardian to a street child.

SLATED FOR RELEASE IN EARLY 2020.

Made in the USA
Middletown, DE
23 December 2019

81828206R00213